GARDEN OF THE PERVERSE ❧ Twisted Fairy Tales for Adults

Garden of the Perverse

TWISTED FAIRY TALES FOR ADULTS

Sage Vivant and M. Christian

THUNDER'S MOUTH PRESS *&* New York

GARDEN OF THE PERVERSE: FAIRY TALES FOR TWISTED ADULTS

Anthology Copyright © 2006 by Sage Vivant and M. Christian

Published by
Thunder's Mouth Press
An Imprint of Avalon Publishing Group, Inc.
245 West 17th Street, 11th floor
New York, NY 10011

AVALON
publishing group incorporated

First printing, April 2006

Page 353 represents an extension of the copyright page

Library of Congress Cataloging-in-Publication Data is available.

ISBN: 1-56025-754-7

9 8 7 6 5 4 3 2 1

Book design by Sara Stenem

Printed in the United States of America
Distributed by Publishers Group West

To our readers—real or imaginary.

TABLE OF CONTENTS

Contents

Contents

HOW TAIKI FOUND HIS WINGS *Hilary Jaye*

FROM THE SKY, the country was one vast expanse of greens and blues, a fanned-out display of peacock plumes. The rivers led to lush lakes dancing with fish, and along the lakeside rested a village called Yosei. It was a place of warm, toadstool-shaped huts, happy cows grown fat on the grass, and laughter rising up into the spring air. This was not a village anything like your village, however, for no one in your village, I am sure, can fly.

Now, in the village of Yosei lived a young man named Taiki. Taiki was unhappy. Although he had a strong name and good wings, soft to the touch and yet braced with sturdy feathers and sturdy bones, in spite of the fact that they spanned twice his height, in spite of the fact that they were as rich and shining in greens and blues as the valley in which he lived, Taiki was filled with sorrow because he could not fly.

Oh, he had tried. He had gone to the wood where the ground dropped away, running as fast as his feet could carry him to fling himself over the edge, whooping in elated terror. He had done this many times, but the best he had managed was a stiff-winged glide and a clumsy landing, for he lived in fear of the sky and his own wings. Time and again, Taiki had gone and yet failed, until his tries came fewer and further between and then, eventually, stopped altogether.

And so he sat on his branch, sad-eyed and alone, watching the village move below and above him, through the trees and above them. Even his home, high in an evergreen, was one he had to reach on foot and hand, climbing the ladder as he had always done since he had been a child.

"Why do you pout?" his father would tease him. "No one will love you if you never smile."

"No one will love me if I never fly," Taiki would sigh in return, and it was true: a flightless man was a loveless one.

So Taiki's days went. The young women who had spread their own wings passed by Taiki's branch, smiling and playing with the men who could fly. Taiki would sigh, watching them go, and his father would admonish him yet again to smile. But what was the good in smiling when his wings would not bear him? Off in none-too-distant skies, Taiki could hear the sweet sounds and ecstatic cries of mating flights, but they only pained him.

And then one day a woman passed under Taiki's evergreen, and while all the others who wandered by were too busy to bother to look into the eyes of the sad, flightless young man, Kiri did, settling to the ground to call up to him.

"Why are you pouting like that?" she called, smiling. "Come down from there and talk a while."

That startled Taiki. Did not everyone know of the one who could not fly? She is only humoring me, Taiki thought darkly, thinking he should tell her to go away. But he called back, "I will not come down. If you want me, you will have to come and get me."

"That sounds like a fine idea," Kiri laughed, and she hopped up, spread her wings, and flew to Taiki's branch. She was cheerful and pretty with bright, fire-colored wings, her skin tanned and smooth, her hair dark and windblown.

Taiki had not really expected the stranger to come to him at all, but it made him smile to have the attention of this beautiful woman who was so strong and lithe and who wore her leathers so well. Very well, then. Taiki felt himself growing as red as the woman's wing tips and smiled again.

"There," Kiri smiled a secret smile in return, "that's better than that moping. Why are you so sorrowful? Why do you sit here alone?" She put her long hand on Taiki's thigh and leaned close to look into his eyes, and that made him turn redder still as you can well imagine.

"I am flightless," Taiki sighed at her. "No matter how I try, I cannot make my wings catch the wind. I glide no better than a child's kite, and I land no better. There is no sadder life than mine."

"You have never had a need to fly, then," said Kiri wisely, nodding. "And if you think there is no sadder life, then think of all the creatures who have no wings."

But Kiri had not come to give advice to the flightless one, she had come to talk to a man, and talk she did: of inane, silly things, some things that made Taiki laugh and some things that made him turn red again, and just before she left Taiki, she cupped the young man's face in her hands and kissed him.

"Why did you do that?" Taiki gasped, his face flaming red once more.

"Because you needed it," Kiri laughed, and flew away.

The next day, Taiki sat on his branch again, but this time he moped just a bit less, and there before too long was Kiri, admonishing the young man to come down.

"If you want me," Taiki repeated with a bit of a smile, "you will have to come and get me."

So Kiri did. She hopped up, spread her wings, and landed on Taiki's branch. Then she put her arm around Taiki's shoulder and talked to him again, the same kind of meaningless chatter she'd shared the day before, about why the river was so blue and why the valley so green, how the air was so clear when one flew high in it. Taiki was entranced by her stories and her telling of them. He noticed a long time had gone by before Kiri cupped his face and kissed him again, and this time, Taiki held onto Kiri and kept her there a bit longer before letting her go.

"Why did you do that?" he asked her softly, noticing how dark her eyes were and how soft her skin.

"Because you needed it," Kiri smiled back, and flew away again.

So Taiki's days went. His father stopped telling him to smile, for the smile came more and more. Soon enough, it never seemed to go away. Kiri came up to Taiki's branch and talked to him and kissed him, and as the days passed there was more kissing and less talking. Day by day, by the time Kiri left, Taiki was breathless and hard and no longer bothering to turn red anymore. He looked every day for those crimson-gold wings and that dark, curling hair and the broad, strong curves of her body. He was never disappointed, for she always came back to him.

And then one day when Kiri had come and Taiki had all but fallen on her, Kiri laughed and said, "Today we are skipping the talking altogether, are we?"

"Yes," Taiki laughed. "You make me want more than kissing, too."

"Mmm. More than kissing sounds perfect." Kiri reached down into Taiki's leathers and stroked him, making Taiki stiffen all over and gasp, startled at how bold Kiri was.

"Why—why—?" was all he could find to say.

"Because I needed it," came Kiri's reply, even as her hand continued to pet and tease.

He thought he would die of it, it felt so perfect, hot and shivery all over him but especially wherever Kiri's beautiful hand landed. Taiki gasped and writhed and twisted, clinging to Kiri, until Kiri did the most unbelievable thing: she slipped out of Taiki's grasp and hopped up and flew into the air.

"What are you doing?" Taiki demanded, glowering and turning red. "Come back down here."

"If you want me," Kiri teased, "you will have to come and get me."

Taiki made a petulant noise. "You know I can't do that," he said quietly.

"That," Kiri said sadly, "is a shame. I suppose you still have no need to fly." And to Taiki's surprise, she flew away.

Taiki was afraid that day that he had offended Kiri, and that she would not want to come back to see a man both rude and branch-bound. But she did return the next day, and Taiki's irritation and worry only lasted until he saw Kiri's beautiful wide eyes and smile. Kiri hopped up and flew to Taiki's branch straightaway, and there was no teasing banter this time, only hungry kissing. Taiki was glad, and he was sure he would keep Kiri with him; he wrapped his arms and legs around Kiri's body and held her tightly.

But when Kiri's perfect hands wriggled their wicked way into Taiki's leggings again, Taiki forgot to hang on so tightly, and then he forgot to hang on at all. He cried out with the pleasure of Kiri stroking and petting him, teasing and playing, up and down the shaft, over the head, all around until Taiki was shudderingly close—and then she hopped up into the air again.

Taiki made a frustrated cry. "You are cruel!" he shouted. "Come back down here."

"If you want me," Kiri insisted, "you will have to come and get me."

"That is unfair," Taiki said. "You teased me."

"That I did." She shook her wings and beckoned to him.

Taiki could see what Kiri was doing, though, and he was proud and stubborn and would not go. Kiri flew away again.

So Taiki's days went. Kiri would come, and every day Taiki would kiss her and hope that she would not try to fly away again in that infuriating manner. But every day, Kiri would come and touch Taiki and drive him mad and then hop up into the air again.

And then one day when Kiri had come and Taiki had let himself be driven mad again, Kiri murmured, "I should drag you into the sky with me this time. You are stubborn, and I am hungry for you."

"You are just as stubborn," Taiki breathed with his lips against hers, "and you frustrate me when you fly away." So he thought he would frustrate her as well, and pushed his hand under her long tunic to touch her. She felt so beautiful, soft, wet, and swollen against his fingertips, he almost forgot how sweet her hands had felt on him, he was so lost in the taste of her mouth and skin and the lovely feel of her around his fingers. Her gasping moans told him that surely, surely this time, she would not fly away. Surely, she could not fly away.

But as she had always done, Kiri pulled back from him and smiled her secret smile, though this one was shaky and distracted. "When you said 'you will have to come and get me,' I came. Now it is your turn. If you do not come and get what you wish for, you will never have it." And she started to fly away.

This time, Taiki could see that Kiri was right. He reached for her and tried to keep her there, just to talk for a moment longer, but Kiri moved adamantly higher. Finally Taiki could take it no longer and he stood on his branch, wavering. He spread his wings, watching Kiri, wanting her. He hopped up and worked hard, staggering into the air, but only succeeded in getting halfway to Kiri before he had to glide to his clumsy, stumbling landing.

Kiri smiled down at him but then flew away, and Taiki climbed, lonely once more, back to his branch.

The next day, Kiri came back yet once more, and though Taiki knew she would only fly away again, this time he knew that he would go after her. She kissed, petted, and teased, and he

7

returned every stroke, kiss, and nip until they were mad for each other again. Finally, aching and panting, he stood on his branch and then hopped up into the air, flapping his virginal wings until he could do it no longer, and then fluttering down into a heap. Kiri made an unhappy noise, and her eyes were a little saddened, but she smiled her secret smile before she went away again.

So Taiki's days went. Soon, Kiri had but to show her pretty face, and Taiki was as hard as stone and as hungry as he could be. Soon, she had but to stand on his branch and make ready to fly before he was doing the same. He struggled and flapped and reached for her and then sank to the ground, but each day, his landing was a little less clumsy and his wings were a little less weak.

And then one day when Kiri had taken off and Taiki had followed, he did not fall. He stayed in the air, wings finally able to carry his desire where he wanted them to. Laughing, he flapped and fought his way to her, steering as best he could in the unfamiliar sky, until Kiri caught him up in her arms and kissed him.

They wrestled and played, and some say they saw Taiki performing the beginnings of his mating flight that day. But it was not long before his young wings tired again. Burning for her but unable to stay in the air, Taiki glided down to his branch, watching sadly as Kiri flew away yet once more.

Now, Taiki came to realize (as you have surely done by now) that if he did not stretch his wings more than just for Kiri, he would never reach into the sky long enough to stay with her. So even though he was tired, Taiki spent that evening and many more folding and unfolding his wings, shaking them, moving them. For now, he wanted Kiri with an almost painful hunger, but more than that, he began to realize that it was not only his body wanting her. His eyes lit up with he saw her beautiful eyes. His smile spread and grew when he thought of her lovely smile. It made his heart sing to hear and remember her beautiful voice. And so with the stretching, Taiki began to realize (as you have surely done as well) that he had fallen in love. He could feel it all over his body, in his skin and blood and bones, and most especially in his heart.

So one day, instead of waiting for Kiri to come to him, he hopped up and flew into the air to search for her. He flew a long time, but his wings did not grow tired this day, because this day he had not only the wind and strength and lust to pull him along until he spotted her in the sky.

"I see," said Kiri when she saw that he had found her, smiling her secret smile, "you have finally come to get me." But instead of going to Taiki, she shot herself straight up into the sky. Swift as an arrow she flew, gathering the wind under her feathers and then pushing it out again. Taiki followed; for now there was no place he would not go to catch her, especially not the sky.

Up and up they went, until at last he caught her, laughing. Taiki kissed her warmly and moaned at the feel of her soft lips. And murmuring in reply, Kiri held him tightly and folded up her wings.

Ah, she was so beautiful with her pretty neck arched back, her body supple and trusting. He held to her tightly as she reached between them, freeing his cock and raising her tunic, and as many times before as they had brought each other to aching need, now it was as though he had never felt it before, for now he felt it in flight. Every touch to his skin shot through him

9

like fire, and now, at last, his wings did not need to be told what to do. They stretched and curled around her shoulders just as her legs stretched and curled around his hips, and at once he sank into her and wrapped her up in him. The two lovers were one, and then they fell.

Her hair whipped about their faces as they cut through the wind, turning and rolling through the sky. The force of the air stole their moaning cries away, and even as they plummeted and spun toward the earth, the fire cut through them both. He thrust into Kiri and she pulled him further into her. She clung to him more tightly and Taiki's hands roamed her body, her face, her breasts. When he reached between them to pleasure her at last, rubbing his shaking fingers over her hard nub, she cried out sharply, her whole body tensing and shuddering against his. The solid heat of her, the fiery snug feel of her around him sent him tumbling after. Taiki loosed a hungry cry, his mating cry. As they fused themselves together in sex and wanting and finally having, his wings spread as if of their own volition and snatched them up from the ground that rushed to claim them.

How Taiki's heart pounded! But now, it was not out of fear of the sky or of his own flight. Now, it was all for the lovely Kiri, who clung to him tightly as he bore her back into the air.

"What magnificent wings you have, Taiki," Kiri smiled, petting his sand-colored hair, and Taiki beamed.

And as is the custom in the village of Yosei, Taiki replied, "You have my wings. They are yours."

So Taiki learned that day not that a flightless man makes a loveless one, but that a loveless man will ever be flightless no matter how good his wings, and that is truth.

BEAUTY THRASHER · *Jason Rubis*

THERE WAS A woman once who was neither old nor young, neither wise nor a fool, neither a beauty nor a slattern. Neither was she especially rich or poor. But as often happens in this sad world, she grew poorer rather than richer, and then poorer still, until one day she found herself walking a lonely road in old shoes, looking for work like any country maid.

We shall call this woman Rosalind, and as she has so little at this moment in her life, we will let her do without a surname as well.

As she walked, Rosalind glimpsed a small shape far away up the road. At first it was like a little black cinder stuck on the horizon, but it grew as she walked, until it became what looked like another woman making her way down the road toward her. This woman's gown was very fine, and there was a glinting and gleaming at her throat and fingers, as of many jewels. A rich woman, then. Rosalind was pleased to meet such a lady, because she thought she might ask for employment at her house. But as she drew even closer her pleasure turned to terror, because this was no human woman but an ogress.

Now an ogress is somewhat different in appearance and behavior from an ogre, being altogether more refined and less savage. This ogress was indeed well dressed, and well-coifed, and altogether well set-up. But sharp teeth are sharp teeth, and when the eyes of the person making toward you on a lonely road are like lumps of dirty ice in a drawn and paper-white face, you will take little comfort in their clothes and manners.

Yet our Rosalind knew better than to scream or to run, because she knew even the slowest of the ogre-kind can run like the wind. So instead she curtseyed and said, "Good morning, Madame. You are looking very well. Is there any way I can be of service to you?"

This is the way any sensible person addresses an ogress.

The ogress stared with her white and terrible eyes, and let her toothy jaws hang open in surprise. Then she shut her mouth, and dabbed delicately at the corners of it with a silk kerchief, and then let it open again, this time to laugh.

"You've pretty enough manners for a human woman, my beauty. Shall I eat you, or shall I take you for a servant?"

Not knowing what to say, Rosalind hung her head and said nothing.

"I've servant-girls a-plenty already, and expensive enough their keep is," the ogress mused. "But they're lazy sluts, and none have your manners. Well, come along, then, if you're coming."

The ogress led Rosalind off the road and through a marshy field to a dark forest. Into the forest they went, through miles of trees and dark, stony ground, until they came out onto a desolate plain. By then poor Rosalind's feet were aching, but she knew better than to complain.

In the midst of the plain was a single oak tree, standing barren and lonely. The ogress went to it and gave its trunk a sharp rap. The bark opened up onto a flight of stairs. The ogress nodded once to Rosalind over her shoulder, as if to say, "Follow me."

Rosalind's eyes widened as she descended the stairs after the ogress, and they did not stop widening, for where she had expected a filthy cave strewn with bones was a magnificent palace, glittering with gold and jewels and every kind of marvelous thing. Nor was it a cold and unfriendly place, as so many palaces are; it was made cheerful by many lovely serving-maids, who went about their tasks with song and gossip and chatter.

"Such a beautiful home you have, Madame," Rosalind gasped.

"A wretched hovel," the ogress grunted, scratching under her chin. "Now my cousin, the Ogre of the Southern Wastes, he has a home. He's the only one in the family who did well, as he wouldn't be shy to tell you."

She waved over a pretty maid and told her to get Rosalind a hot meal and an apron. And that was how her first day in the ogress' service began.

It was by no means a bad situation, for while the work was hard, the other maids were friendly, and the ogress proved, for all her grumbling and fierce looks, a good and patient mistress who loved to joke and talk. She seemed to enjoy the company of her maids a great deal and as for the girls, they were one and all devoted to her.

One day there was a great excitement among the maids. The ogress had, quite out of the blue, ordered them to make ready the largest and most luxurious bedroom in the palace. The girls made the bed and perfumed the sheets, lit candles, and set out trays of wine and sweetmeats. As they worked they all blushed and giggled and made certain impious remarks, until Rosalind asked what on earth was happening.

"Madame is taking a lover for the afternoon," one girl said, her eyes bright and mischievous.

"What sort of lover?" Rosalind asked, very cautiously. Fond as she was of the ogress, she couldn't quite see her with a lover. Certainly the images that came into her head then were nothing to provoke merriment.

"Oh, a handsome man, a great gallant!" the maid laughed. "Come, I'll show him to you!"

She set up a screen outside the bedroom door, and she and Rosalind hid behind it like a pair of naughty children. After a time a man entered the hall, flanked by two senior maids. He was quite a handsome man, young and tall with great muscles. He stood looking all about him, gawping like a monkey at the wonders of the ogress's palace.

Rosalind watched the maids lead him through another door. Just before the second girl closed the door behind them she took down something that was hanging among the many oddments and decorations on the wall. Rosalind had not noticed it before, and no wonder; it was simply a long piece of leather that looked rather like an old belt. It was a flail, such as farm-workers use to thrash grain.

Soon there came from behind the door a terrible noise, a slapping—soft at first, then louder and louder until it was like a rainstorm lashing an old roof. Then came an awful howling, like someone being beaten half to death. Rosalind clutched at her friend in terror, but the girl only laughed. There was a long silence then, and after that there came from behind the door a tender whispering and a gasping, and finally sounds of love being made. And from the sound, the folk making it were mightily enjoying themselves.

Rosalind was uncomfortable at first, because she didn't entirely like imagining what might be happening in the room. But as the noises became louder and more ardent, she felt herself grow excited in spite of herself. She could hear a woman's voice trilling with pleasure, but it was as sweet as birdsong, nothing like the ogress's raspy snarl. She heard a man's voice as well; a deep lusty growling that thrilled her to hear it.

The other maid seemed quite excited herself, and slid into Rosalind's arms, taking her hands and placing them over her breasts, as though asking by that sweet gesture to be held very tightly.

"Can you imagine?" she breathed, settling her head back on Rosalind's shoulder. "He's kissing her now, her mouth and her breasts, he's making her nipples like two little stones. And between her legs—he's kissing her there now, licking her place, finding her pearl. I play with mine every night, but oh, there's nothing like a man's tongue there, nothing in the world."

"Stop it now," Rosalind whispered, squeezing her until she

15

giggled and squeaked. "It's not right you should say such things. It's not respectful to Madame." But the little maid had become a lover in her own right, turning and kissing Rosalind's mouth, feeling her nipples through the stiff starched cloth of her uniform until they were also like two little stones.

Perhaps Rosalind might have resisted if it hadn't been for the lovers' music coming from behind the door, but those sighs and purrs and croonings made her case hopeless. She could not help but act as she felt. Soon she and the maid were gently grappling, each with a hand between the others' legs, each softly kissing each other's mouth, throat, and eyes. It was a playful loving that made a fire in Rosalind and when the maid's eager fingers quenched that fire it was like a swallow of a very fine, very sweet liqueur.

When the two of them emerged later from behind the screen, they found the bedroom door open and the other maids stripping the bed. They were chatting among themselves as though nothing whatever had happened, though they did give Rosalind and each other several long smiles. Of the ogress and her gallant there was no sign.

A few mornings afterward, the ogress took Rosalind aside and said, "Well, my beauty," (for she always called Rosalind "my beauty") "tell me now: will you take your wages and leave me, or will you suffer my whims and temper for another year?"

Rosalind was happy enough working in the palace and, as you might imagine, she had become rather curious about the ogress's love habits. So she said she would stay, and the ogress was pleased.

Another year passed, and Rosalind was promoted. As the year drew near its end, there was more giggling among the maids, and one day another man was brought in. This time, because of her new rank, Rosalind was given the task of helping prepare the ogress.

The two stood in the great bedroom once the bed had been made and the wine and sweets laid out. The ogress undressed in a quick, businesslike way, not shyly at all. Finally she stood naked—and she was a strange and awful sight in the midst of all the fine furniture and rich tapestries. Still, Rosalind was well used to her by now and even managed to smile. But when the ogress handed her the old leather flail, the smile vanished quite away.

"I can't beat you, Madame!" Rosalind cried, for the idea of hurting her mistress in any way really did horrify her.

"What's this?" the ogress snorted. "Fine time to grow a set of scruples! Pah! Give me a good whacking, my beauty, and put some muscle into it, if you please."

"But I'll hurt you!"

"Stuff and nonsense. Listen to me, my tender morsel. That scrap in your pretty hands is no common leather, but a magic flail. It thrashes all the ugliness out of a body and leaves nothing but whatever beauty that body might possess. So you've got a job ahead of you, you see, and I'd advise you to get to it. Otherwise this bloody man waiting outside, whom I've gone to so much trouble to procure for the afternoon will run screaming at the sight of me. He's a northerner, you know, and they're of a somewhat nervous temperament to begin with."

So Rosalind hit the ogress with the flail—very carefully at first, a little flick on the legs. The ogress cried out in disgust that she should strike harder, and harder still, until soon poor Rosalind was thrashing away with all the strength in her body.

17

The ogress's complaints turned into a bloodcurdling yowling that made the walls shake.

But as she yowled and Rosalind thrashed, an extraordinary thing was happening.

Every blow of the flail on the ogress's pasty and withered skin made it rosier and fleshier. Her crooked legs and humped back straightened. Her face grew rounder and far prettier, her eyes large and blue, her mouth full and wet. Her hair remained gray, but it brightened to a gleaming silver, and thickened until it hung around her shoulders and face like a lion's mane. The flail did not seem to hurt her at all—now she cried out in passion each time the leather struck her. Soon Rosalind had stopped lashing and stepped back in amazement, the flail dropping from her hands. Where the kind but ugly ogress had lately stood was now a mature but indisputably beautiful woman.

The woman smiled at Rosalind. "Well, my beauty," she said in a musical voice, standing on her toes and turning round several times. "What do you think of me now, eh?"

"You're the beauty!" Rosalind gasped. And indeed, the longer she stared at this lovely woman the more beautiful she found her, until she couldn't help but go to her and lay her head shyly on her breast.

"Here, what's all this now?" The ogress laughed, but her skin grew warm and she stroked Rosalind's hair with a tender hand. Rosalind considered her pink nipples, and then, like a lady allowing herself to eat a single piece of candy, sucked one into her mouth.

"Now, then!" the ogress cried, drawing hastily back. "A bit more observation of the proprieties, my beauty, if you don't mind! Don't do anything you'll regret later!"

Rosalind wasn't sure what had come over her. She began a pretty apology, but the ogress's new lover came in at that moment, and Rosalind forgot what she was saying. She could only stand there with an open mouth, for this man was even more handsome than the last.

Rosalind stood beside their bed, and watched their love-making with greedy eyes. It went on for quite some time, and got her so excited that she had to thrust a hand under her skirts in a way that was most undignified. Like most people, she had never actually watched a couple in the act of enjoying each others' bodies, and as most people do when they finally get the opportunity, she enjoyed it very much.

And more than that; as Rosalind watched the ogress lay with splayed legs on the magnificent bed, crying through pursed lips as her man's cock slid in and out of her, she conceived an idea.

The next morning the ogress once again asked if Rosalind would leave or stay. By now the flail's magic had quite worn off and she was as ugly and fearsome-looking as ever, yet Rosalind was almost glad of the reversion. In an odd way she had grown used to her mistress's fangs and claws and stony eyes.

Still, this time she answered differently. "I think, Madame, that I will take my wages and go."

"Ah," the ogress nodded, looking unhappy. "I'm sorry to hear it, for you're worth any dozen of these other little miseries flitting about here. Well in any event, I'll give you whatever you like for your wage, for I'm well pleased with your service. Name it and it's yours."

"I would like the flail, please. The magic one, that makes people beautiful."

"Ahh-hhh," the ogress said, her awful eyes narrowing. "My beauty's been paying attention. Well, listen to me, girl: that flail is no toy for human children. Take something else instead. I'll give you silver, enough to set you up with a good house and respectable business in any city you like. You'll do well enough with your brains."

"I would rather have the flail, Madame."

"Gold, then. I'll stuff your pockets with it; give you enough so you won't have to work at all. You can live like a queen in the world of men, all you have to do is give me the word."

"With respect, Madame, I would rather have the flail."

"Jewels! I have emeralds as green as grass, sapphires as blue as your eyes, and diamonds like fistfuls of stars. You can be an empress, a goddess! There won't be a woman in the world as rich as you!"

"I hate to be difficult, Madame . . ."

"But you want the flail," the ogress said wearily. "Fine, then. Excellent. I promised you whatever you like and I don't break my word."

She went and got the flail herself, and handed it to Rosalind. "But before you go," she said, leaning close until Rosalind could smell the carrion on her breath. "Take an old lady's advice. I don't grudge you this toy—I can make a hundred more without thinking of it. But just you be careful. Human children think they know what they want. They don't, that's my experience. They don't really."

Rosalind kissed her sallow cheek and the ogress waved her away with a clawed hand. "Go on, go," she snapped. "Before I pop you in the kettle, as I should have done the day I met you."

Rosalind kissed the other maids goodbye, and there were many tears before she left. But she did leave that marvelous palace, and went back to the human world. After long hours of walking, she came to a village, and it didn't take her long to find the best inn. It wasn't at all as fine as the ogress's palace, but it was a cheerful place all the same, with a good big fire blazing away on the hearth and plenty of food and drink for the guests. The innkeeper and his wife were as alike as two apples, both of them round and red-faced and always laughing.

"You seem happy enough with your husband," Rosalind observed, after she had been set before the fire with a glass and a plate.

"Well, and why shouldn't I be?" the wife laughed. "He's a good old soul, as much trouble as he gives me." And she gave the innkeeper's ruddy cheek a fond pinch.

"Some women would prefer a younger man," Rosalind pointed out. "Or one more handsome."

"What are you saying there, pet?" the innkeeper's wife demanded, looking rather offended.

"But no," Rosalind went on, as though she were thinking aloud. "You wouldn't trade him for a younger man, you love him too much. And he is a sweet man, and that's worth ten lovely bodies. But what if you could have both? Your husband's heart in a handsome young body? A body that could give you so much pleasure..."

The innkeeper's wife gave Rosalind an odd look. "I suppose..." she said doubtfully. "But no, it's ridiculous. You can't have both and there's an end to it..."

Rosalind drained her glass and said, "I can give you both. Come with me."

She took the couple upstairs to a vacant room, leading them as though it was her inn, not theirs. Soon the company in the public room were disturbed by a dreadful clamor from the upper floor, a loud thwacking and a screaming and crying fit to wake the dead. Not long after that came a very different kind of noise, a gasping and moaning and certain wet sounds that were as indescribable as they were easily identified. The pipe-smokers and gossips in the public room sat staring at the stairs with wide-open mouths, for this was a dull and respectable village and such noises were rarely heard outside the marriage bed.

In time a beautiful young couple descended the stairs, a gorgeous girl and her young man. They were very obviously the innkeeper and his wife, as those who had known them in their youth could affirm. But they were different now, both of them glowing with something strange and wonderful—yet the chief difference might have been that they were both somehow more themselves. Nobody could put their finger on it, but everyone was delighted.

That, then, was the beginning of Rosalind's new life. Every morning she woke to find lines of people outside the inn, waiting to hire her services. It bothered no one that the effects of the magic flail were only temporary. Perhaps they were secretly relieved to have their old imperfect bodies back the next day. In any case, they seemed quite happy to pay again a day or so later for another beauty-thrashing.

Rosalind became quite a rich woman in a matter of days, and a happy one, for she was a good woman. It pleased her to give people such joy, and she never overcharged or cheated her customers. Indeed, she used much of her fortune for good works.

"Even if the ogress had made me rich, as she offered," she said to herself, "I wouldn't be able to make folk so happy. I'm so glad I took the flail, sad as I was to leave the old darling."

But nothing in the world ever seems to go as it should, and soon people in the capital city were talking about the wonderful sorceress who could make people beautiful with a flick of her finger.

Now the queen of that country was a very beautiful woman indeed. She was tall and golden-haired and long-legged, and she was brilliant as well; she had studied warfare and history as well as dancing and poetry, and knew mathematics and the movements of the planets as well as she knew the shape of her own hand. She could ride a horse and fight with a sword as well as any man. Really, she was a far better ruler than her father had been, but still, she was not a good ruler. She was not often cruel, but she was never kind. She was very, very vain, especially as she began to near her middle years. She would spend entire mornings staring at her lovely face in a mirror, imagining she saw wrinkles where there was nothing but smooth skin.

So when this queen heard about Rosalind, you can imagine what her first thought was. And indeed, Rosalind was brought to the capital that very afternoon for a private interview. She was made to sit for hours in an unused room in the top floor of the royal palace, and long before the first hour had passed she had worked herself into a really terrible state of nervousness. When the queen finally appeared, Rosalind tried to stand up and curtsey and kiss her hand all at once. From the look the queen gave her, it seemed she had not made a very good impression.

"You're the woman who makes people young and beautiful," the queen said briskly, seating herself and crossing her legs.

"That's not quite right, Your Majesty," Rosalind said timidly.

The queen stared at her. "Not right? But that is what everyone tells me. This is the reputation you've garnered. Are you suggesting my educated and highly paid counselors have been telling me tales? For I may as well tell you that I mean to try your methods for myself. If you please me I'll give you a place at my court. If you displease me I'll be disappointed." The queen smiled nastily. "And I do so hate to be disappointed."

This was exactly what Rosalind had feared. "Perhaps you shouldn't, Your Majesty. Try my methods, I mean."

The queen raised a golden eyebrow. "What? Why ever not?"

"You see, it's the way I make people young and beautiful. I don't think you'd like it."

The queen frowned. "Mudpacks? Acid scrubbings? Corsets? Torturous exercise regimes? Don't gawk at me like a goose, tell me! Whatever it is, I've tried worse."

"It's this," Rosalind said wretchedly, holding out the ogress's flail.

"What, that old piece of leather you won't let go of? I had wondered about that. I thought it one of the eccentricities genius is prone to."

"It's a magic flail, Your Majesty. I got it from an ogress."

"An ogress, eh?" the queen said, stroking her chin thoughtfully. In those days the world was full of magical devices and beings, so she had no cause to doubt Rosalind's story. "And you do what exactly? Beat people with it? That's what makes them beautiful? Well, it does sound like something an ogre would think up." She sat staring at Rosalind for a long time more, until Rosalind squirmed and shifted in her seat like a maid who had been caught stealing silver. Finally the queen sighed and kicked off her slippers.

"All right, give us a tickle." She gave Rosalind a strange grin as she stood up and began undoing her robes. "Don't pretend you won't like it."

"Your majesty?" Rosalind quavered.

"Don't give me those sheep's eyes! Maybe your flail's magic will work, maybe it won't. If it doesn't, you'll find out what a real thrashing is. But I don't doubt you enjoy beating those fool bourgeois who've given you your reputation." The queen finished undressing and left her finery in a sweet-smelling pile at her feet. Naked, she was even more beautiful than she was clothed, a tall goddess whose skin and hair were alike golden. How on earth could the flail make such a lovely woman more beautiful? Rosalind's nervousness made her stand up a little too quickly.

"Ah, you see?" the queen purred, reaching out to toy with a lock of Rosalind's hair. "See how eager you are! I know something about your kind, you see. Can't wait to beat the mean old queen, can you?" The queen pouted her lips and spoke in a little childish voice that sounded very odd coming from someone so regal.

"Want to spank my bottom?" She turned and ran a hand over her ass, which was very round and silken and lovely. "Spank it 'cause I'm a bad girl?" she went on, pouting at Rosalind over her shoulder. "'Cause I tax the stinky old peasants? 'Cause I bring back beheadings and purge the aristocracy? Yes, you do. You wanna spank it make me cry!"

Rosalind didn't know quite what to think and she certainly didn't know what to say. "I . . . I don't want to beat you, Your . . ."

"Oh, of course you don't. Perish the thought. Don't doubt you for an instant. Well, you'll kiss it first. My ass. Go on! Kiss it. I want you to remember your place while you indulge yourself."

Rosalind had no choice but to go on her knees and press her lips against the queen's lovely buttocks. It was not entirely an unpleasant experience.

"Lick it."

Rosalind put her tongue out and, trembling with closed eyes, licked the queen's ass.

"And my feet. Might as well do this right."

Rosalind lowered herself down until her face was hovering over the queen's lovely bare feet, and kissed her toes. Without being told, she licked them. They tasted salty.

"Very nice. Now tell me: do you love me?"

"Yes, Your Majesty." And for most of that long, odd moment, Rosalind really did love her, as powerfully as she had ever loved anyone in her life. And she wanted to beat her. She wanted the weight of the flail in her hand and the slight pain in her arm as she swung and brought it down again and again on the queen's lovely nakedness. She wanted to see the queen red-faced and bawling as she hopped about rubbing her hurting ass. That particular thought made Rosalind feel rather feverish for some reason.

"Fine. Now we understand each other." The queen favored Rosalind with a demure little kiss on the cheek and then tickled her under her chin. "Now get to work."

Rosalind barely waited until the queen had turned again to let fly with the flail. As her arm came down the leather hit the queen's ass with a loud crack and the queen shrieked. Rosalind licked her lips and hit her again. Then again.

The queen was dancing like a randy tavern-girl, jumping on her bare feet and twisting about as though she couldn't make up her mind whether the beating she was getting was deliciously painful or painfully delicious. The noises she was making were somewhere between laughter and crying. Her face was something to see; her blue eyes seemed large as eggs and her red mouth hung open, showing her tongue and her teeth. Her hands leapt about her body, rubbing everywhere the flail hit her as though the welts itched rather than hurt. More and more, though, her hands found their way between her legs, until she was squatting and diddling herself like a madwoman, even as Rosalind beat her.

Rosalind took a step back, so excited that she could barely think, and as the queen squatted there moaning, gave her a very hard crack across the shoulder.

"I didn't think it would be like this," the queen gasped, just before the leather hit her.

And with that, she disappeared.

She truly did. One moment she was standing there naked, her pretty skin striped with red, her golden hair wild about her face. Then, just as the flail hit her, she disappeared as neatly as a bite of pie into a hungry man's mouth.

The queen was gone.

Rosalind, breathing hard and wiping sweat from her brow, looked all around her. She had a notion that the queen was hiding somewhere, but except for a few chairs the room was empty.

Then the door to the room opened and a stern-faced woman in a gray suit strode in.

"You've made the queen disappear," she growled.

"I'm sorry," Rosalind whimpered, for she certainly couldn't contradict the woman. "I didn't know the flail could do that..."

"Ignorance is hardly an excuse," the woman sniffed. "You've committed a very serious crime. Come with me, please." She led Rosalind down through the lower floors of the palace, past staring servants and whispering noblemen, out through a door to where a black coach stood waiting. Rosalind thought it rather odd that a coach in the royal service should be drawn by a pair of dragons, but she was far too afraid for her life to worry about that.

She sat quietly down, the flail still in her hands, and the woman sat down next to her. Within moments the coach started up and drove at breakneck speed out of the courtyard, through the streets of the capital city, and finally out into the green countryside.

Rosalind, utterly wretched, sat staring at her captor. "Please, ma'am," she whispered. "Where are you taking me?" The woman grinned at her in a strange way. The grin grew wider and wider, and toothier and toothier, until the woman looked oddly familiar.

"Madame!" Rosalind cried, throwing herself into the ogress's arms, for of course the woman in the gray uniform was no one but the ogress in a magical disguise.

"All right, all right," the ogress growled, stroking Rosalind's hair. "Enough of these histrionics, my beauty, we're both far too old for them. Just be glad I was keeping an eye on you."

"But I murdered the queen!" Rosalind howled.

"Murder? You did no such thing. Don't you remember what I told you about that wretched flail? It doesn't make people beautiful, as you persisted in thinking. It thrashes out their ugliness and leaves beauty." She shrugged. "That vain baggage back there was nothing but ugliness, pretty and clever as she was. Or perhaps whatever goodness she had was so faint and insubstantial as to make not much more than a wraith."

"Will she ever come back?"

"Naturally! By tomorrow morning her ugliness will have reassembled itself and she'll be kicking her hairdressers around just as usual. I have an idea she may have learned a lesson or two by then, though. Something about being discorporated tends to have an educational effect."

"It all came of wanting to help people," Rosalind sighed, staring down at the flail.

"No, my beauty. It came of misunderstanding, and that's a very different thing."

They rode on in silence for a long time.

"Well," the ogress said. "I can take you back to your lodgings, but I don't think that would be quite safe at the moment. Where would you like to go?"

More silence. The truth was that Rosalind had nowhere in the world to go, which is a terrible feeling. After a moment the ogress cleared her throat. "I could use a bit more help in the old hovel," she muttered, looking down at her claws. "If you're agreeable, that is."

Rosalind hugged her delightedly.

And so Rosalind passed the rest of her days—long and happy ones they were, too—in the ogress's service. The newer maids adored her. It's true there were some saucy girls among them, but they quickly learned not to presume too much upon her good nature. The ogress's chief maid, it seemed, had something of a taste for spankings.

THE SATYR ❧ *D. Antoni*

ALONE, SHE PICKED little purple flowers on the bare hilltop. Her mare nibbled at the same purple flowers, occasionally dipping its muzzle into the stream that wound out of sight, to feed the well of Mykonos.

The heat in her belly and the dampness between her thighs were sensations she had felt before, but hardly so strong as today. She felt as if hands lightly tickled her breasts, her stomach, to make the flow between her legs. She could only wonder, what will it be like, if just the anticipation is so delicious? She thought to strum herself as she had taken to doing since her twelfth year, when first the downy hairs had sprung there, but she decided to wait instead for the Satyr.

The Satyr.

He was rapacious, she had heard, brutal. It was by no means love for the creature to take a woman. Still, no woman had died from his attack. Indeed, those who had met the Satyr seemed to come to terms with their ravishment far better than did their men, most of whom would take another wife, discarding the first to grow old with her own family. And to tell her tale to other women.

She bent again to pick a flower, and the brush of longish grass on her thighs and her buttocks tickled yet more wetness from her. Instantly, heat flushed from her melt to her breasts.

"Please," she begged the beast. Could it possibly please more than this?

She was now of marriage age, promised to a comely young man to whom she had barely spoken. What would she say? Girls were not schooled, as were boys. She sang, and played the psaltry, and poured wine with grace, skills she was taught by her mother and sisters. Those same women, after a day's toil and in their cups, would speak of other skills, The Art of the Bed, they called it. It was a sort of theater, they told her. A woman could master a man's mood, could choose how she wanted their coupling to be.

"A man is always heated," said her sister. "And sometimes, you will be as well."

The mare snorted and pricked its ears at the hoof beats that thudded on earth and clattered on stone in the wood below. The girl thought at first that she saw a horse and rider, but the man's bare chest and belly, slick with sweat, merged into a horse's hindquarters. It raised its head to sniff at the wind and snort, then bounded up the hillside toward her.

Her body twitched as if to turn and run, but she knew instinctually that she would wish she hadn't, and anyway, it was useless to run from so swift a creature. She had not thought the Satyr would be so—animal—with black hair unlike a man's, but much like the black hair of its equine tail. And Zeus! The pink and bevel-tipped thing that slapped between its sleek, furred flanks.

It trotted to a stop before her and cocked its head, regarding her with neither malice nor with a man's intelligence. Its expression, she had not seen on a man before. Had she known the word she might call it lust, but her body knew the meaning of the creature's regard, and her pips stiffened and strained at the linen of her shift.

At the sight of them, the man-beast seized her shift at the breasts and snatched it downward, and it tore at her shoulders. Why had she not anticipated that, how would she get home?

The beast dropped to his hands before her and pressed its nose to her dampness, and snorted with pleasure. He stood and grabbed her roughly about her hips and turned her about. The strength! He turned her about as if she were a puppy, lifted her so that her feet kicked in the air and her head hung downwards, and proffered her bare backside to him.

"Please," she begged for gentleness, but the pain of her shattered maidenhead made her squeal instead. "Slowly!" she cried, but she was moist already, and there was no halting the thrusts of his giant cock, and her blood and juices were all the moisture the Satyr needed. He snuffled as an excited horse does, pistoning positioning her body on his long penis, and her girlish breasts slapped against her ribs in rhythm with the slaps of his flanks against her thighs.

It was exquisite, like the sensations she'd felt as she waited, but surely too strong! Would her chest not burst?

Instead, she felt a burst that seemed centered around the Satyr's member, but reached her chest, her toes, made her blind for a moment. She sobbed without sorrow at first, then with sorrow as the feeling passed, and she fell limp. Only then did she drop the purple flowers she had gripped tightly.

The Satyr pulled her violently against his rough, furred loins and grunted. She felt his whip swell and bob even inside her tight sheath, and wet as she was, felt new wetness fill her. This was a surprise, but of course? If I become wet, she thought, then a man (or a beast) must make fluids of his own?

The beast withdrew. She braced herself for it to drop her and skitter off, but still he gripped her hips. His prick jabbed rudely against her fundament, and began to press against the tighter hole.

"No!" she squealed. Surely no one made love there! And this was beyond lustful, surely this was obscene, and besides he would rend her!

But the Satyr was not asking, and its slick shaft pushed past her tightened arsehole, until she was certain she would rip. The satyr grunted, and he bucked surprisingly slowly, rhythmically.

She surrendered, allowing her bottom to go slack, and in moments the pain became less and the pleasure grew. He pushed deeper with every tiny thrust, and she felt the pressure deep within as her body as it accepted the animal cock. Surely it was pushing her stomach, her heart perhaps? to one side. When she felt he could go no deeper, the creature grunted once again. She yelped as his cock swelled again, and felt the slippery warmth of his seed flood her bowels as it had her melt. And she too shook as another attack of sensation rippled from her cunny.

The satyr's shaft popped from her backside as he dropped her rudely on her stomach, among the purple flowers. She lay breathing frantically, too weak to roll herself over. Instinct told her to lie as if dead, lest it take her again.

No kiss, no endearment. No lying in the sun stroking one another as she'd imagined with a man. But that is what I wanted, no? she thought. And besides, she could not imagine looking into the eyes of a man who had forced himself into her backside.

She only opened her eyes at the mare's frantic whinny. This could not be! For the Satyr had seized the mare's haunches, and rutted her as roughly as he had the girl. The mare attempted a kick, but the Satyr dodged it nimbly. At last his obscene lips curled, and he forced himself deeply into the beast, as he had the girl, and let go the same grunt of release. His pleasure done, he pushed the mare roughly away and trotted down the hill to the wood, while the mare cantered off and out of sight.

The girl closed her eyes, numb to what she had seen, but hardly numb in her body. The breeze cooled her violated cunny and bottom, which were frothed and wet with the Satyr's spendings, and pink with the tinge of her blood. She could only mew at the soreness. It was some minutes before she found even the strength to open her eyes again.

Her hips throbbed where the creature's hands had bruised her, and her nipples ached from the tightness. Only after three tries could she stand. Even then, she could not imagine how her wobbling legs would carry her home, if the mare did not return. And what of her torn shift?

"A hound," she said aloud, and grinned foolishly. She climbed a tree to escape, she would tell her father, which would explain away the scratches on her thighs. That would do.

She lurched to the stream, cupped water in her hand, and rubbed away the pink foam of blood and seed that covered her, from her puss and bottom to her knees. At last, she lowered herself into the stream, which would normally be too cool, but which soothed her ravished holes. She sat for several minutes, her eyes closed, her head resting on a pillow of moss. At last she ventured a hand fearfully to her cunny, but found it as tight as it had been the day before, though the maidenhead no longer obstructed her fingers. She felt more timidly at her rear, but found her bottom hole tight as well, though sore to the touch.

She would tell no one of the Satyr, not even the other women. That would ruin her for marriage. As for her maidenhead? She knew already what she would do—between a drunken groom, a play-acting shriek on her part, and he would never know.

Only she would know. Knowledge that would not belong to her husband first, something not even the women could tell her.

She alone would know.

THE WOMAN WHO MARRIED A WOLF ⟨℘⟩ *Cynthia Ward*

Once upon a time, there lived a king whom no one had ever seen, for his castle stood deep in the woods. But it came to pass that he sent a summons to the city and every hamlet of his kingdom, summoning all eligible young ladies to a ball at his castle, for he wished to choose a bride.

Now in the city there lived a young woman so beautiful that the sun, who has seen every thing, burned with a furious ardor whenever she stepped out-of-doors. But the young woman, whose name was Clarissa, rarely ventured from the mean hovel where she lived with her stepmother, for she was shy as a turtle-dove when the hawk is abroad. So Clarissa, though she burned with an unquenched ardor of her own, had no thought of seeking the king's attention, nor even of attending the king's ball.

Then her stepmother said, "Clarissa, I've made you a gown for the king's ball."

"Mother!" cried Clarissa. Her stepmother was a seamstress of great skill, but she had never made any clothes for Clarissa, because she resented her stepdaughter's youth and beauty. "Mother, I cannot attend the ball!"

"Will not, rather," said her stepmother. "You're meeker than a church-mouse. But you will go to the ball, and you will win the king's love and rescue me from this wretched hovel."

For Clarissa's stepmother was nobly born, and not content at living in the poorest quarter of the city. Clarissa's stepmother had wed a baron's widowed younger son, against her parents' will, and been disowned. Then her husband had run away with another woman, and left his new wife with his little daughter, Clarissa. Clarissa's mother had died when she was born, and her stepmother resented raising another woman's child by her faithless husband; so she beat the child. And when she saw that the child grew more beautiful with every passing day, she hid her good glass mirror from Clarissa, and dressed her in the ragged castoffs of the neighbor children.

So Clarissa did not know she was beautiful; nor that she was as kind as she was beautiful. "Mother," she said, "you cannot afford to waste your time on me—ow!"

Her stepmother lowered her fist. "Do not speak as if I never gave you care. Now, stand still while I prepare you for the king's ball."

Then she helped Clarissa into the gown. It was a beautiful, intricate construction of great beauty: a confection of satin white as snow, and velvet green as new cedar leaf, or Clarissa's eyes, and lace white as seafoam. Clarissa ran her fingertips over the fine materials that were sleek, or plush, or surprisingly stiff, for she had never worn their like.

Though her arm still stung where her stepmother had punched her, Clarissa could not help speaking. "Mother, you cannot afford to give me this—"

"Hush," her stepmother said, and slapped her, but lightly, to leave no mark on this night of nights. "The gown is no more than we deserve, Clarissa. And I will be able to afford a thousand such gowns, once the king sees you."

"How?" said Clarissa. She thought she had no chance to win the king, no matter how much her stepmother spent. She knew that every unmarried girl in the city, and the kingdom, would be traveling tonight to the castle in the woods. "Mother," she said, casting about for any reason not to attend the ball, "this dress is too modest—"

"The other girls," said her stepmother, "will seek to attract his attention with extravagant décolletage. They will be interchangeable and uninteresting as marble women. You alone will stand out, a living, breathing woman among statues. You will win him."

"But, Mother, we know nothing about the king save that he is king, and rich! He is a stranger to the kingdom, like his father, and his father before him, and I have no wish to marry a stranger. No one knows what he's like—"

"I know what he's like," said her stepmother. "He's a beast."

Now Clarissa's eyes widened, and she began to shiver so strongly that she feared she would snap her stepmother's stout stitches. "How do you know he's a beast?" she cried.

"All men are beasts," said her stepmother. "But women cannot live without them. So a girl should set her sights on the highest heights."

Then a coach-and-four fit for a king carried them away. The coach bounced and splashed over the stinking mud ruts of the paupers' quarter; then it rolled onto cobblestone, and into another world. Clarissa stared as the coach passed great fine houses, and the grandest house in all the city: the duke's palace, where dwelt her stepmother's parents.

"My birthright," said her stepmother.

Clarissa had never set foot in the duke's palace, and knew she never would. Her stepmother had lived in the duke's palace until she married. Why, then, did she say a woman needed a man to live, when the man she married had condemned her to the cold and hungry hovel in the poorest quarter of the city?

"Mother," said Clarissa, "let's turn around. Don't spend more of your coin on a coach far too fine for me—"

"Clarissa, would you walk to meet the man you're going to marry?" Her stepmother patted her knee, awkwardly, unaccustomed to offering reassurance. "Do not worry, Clarissa. This is your night. You shall win him. I spare no expense to secure your success, because afterward I need worry no more."

But her words only made Clarissa more uneasy. But the young woman settled back as if comforted, sinking into the luxurious brown leather with its intoxicating scent. And she breathed the scent deeply, and prayed it would relax her.

Then the coach was hemmed close suddenly by walls of forest; by fir and pine as thick as a wolf's winter pelt.

"Clarissa," said her stepmother, "why do you shake so?"

"Mother, there are wolves in the forest!"

"There is no reason to fear, Clarissa, with the coachman and footman both well armed," said her stepmother.

But Clarissa continued to shiver as the coach sped through the dark wood, and her shivers only grew worse when the forest opened abruptly and she saw, in the distance, a magnificent, castle of fitted and ivied gray stone, rearing in high battlements and turrets.

And Clarissa grew only more discomfited as a flourish of trumpets announced their arrival, and silent servants in gray livery led her and her stepmother past grand rooms, the smallest of which would swallow their poor hovel. Her breaths grew short, and her stepmother's painful grip on her arm only increased her trepidation. For they did not know their host; no one in the city or across the kingdom knew their host, king Richard Wilding, whom they had never seen.

Then a joyous music of viols, hautboys, and kettledrums resounded, and Clarissa and her stepmother found themselves in a ballroom even more grand and spacious than Clarissa had imagined, and more splendid than the heart of a diamond, facets ablaze with the silken colors of the dancing women. And Clarissa compared herself to those graceful, beautiful women; and because she never saw her own likeness, she thought that her fairness was unhealthy pallor, her golden hair straw, her glorious gown the faded rags of a poor little girl pretending to refinement and wealth. That her stepmother had once been a wealthy noblewoman meant nothing here. Clarissa knew she would never win the king, nor even attract the attention of the highborn men attending the ball.

This was the unspoken expectation of her stepmother, Clarissa decided: not that she would win the king, but that she would attract one of the noblemen or wealthy merchants at the ball.

But the ball had an open invitation; and any one who wished to, might attend. Who among the elegantly garbed men were noblemen or wealthy merchants, Clarissa wondered, and who were as counterfeit as she? Clarissa could not tell—she knew nothing of noblemen or merchants, save what her stepmother told her; and her stepmother never had any thing good to say about men. Indeed, Clarissa knew nothing of men, rich or poor. Her father had fled when she was too little to remember, eighteen years ago. She had no friends whose fathers she might know. And, though they fevered her dreams and fantasies, she was too shy even to think of approaching the poor, rude boys she glimpsed through her stepmother's shuttered windows. Clarissa knew only what her stepmother told her, that men were beasts.

And men were all around her now, and some women, too, who leered at her like hungry beasts. For they all saw what Clarissa did not, that she was more beautiful than any woman under the sun; and they burned like the sun at his greatest ardor, desiring only to cast Clarissa upon the ballroom floor and wrench off her gown, and put rod or tongue or finger inside her.

Now a frightful dizziness came over Clarissa, for never had she been the center of others' regard; and despite her stepmother's tight grip, she pulled her arm free and ran.

But there was nowhere to go. Clarissa found every door closed, and watched by swordsmen in bright armor, who stood motionless and vigilant, though their eyes blazed like the sun and their members strained against their gray breeches when they saw Clarissa. Onward she ran, seeking escape, until she found herself trapped in the farthest corner of the ballroom.

Near to swooning, Clarissa pressed against the wall, as if it must have a secret door that would swing open at her touch. But the wall was as obdurate as the swordsmen's faces.

Then a hand closed upon Clarissa's elbow. She nearly screamed; and she trembled, and dared not look up. The broad hand, thatched in black and gray hairs, closed its long, strong fingers firmly on her delicate chin; and the fingers raised her head easily, though she struggled not to look up. She saw polished black boots, then black hose, then black velvet trunk-hose with a codpiece flap that was strangely and enormously distorted. Clarissa went rigid as she realized what she looked upon.

But still the hand forced her head up, away from the frightening, fascinating evidence of desire, until she looked into a man's face. The face was like a marble carving in its paleness and virile beauty, but not in its expression of concern. The eyebrows were a black bar beneath the thick, black, short hair; and the eyes were, luminous as the moon in mist, compelling.

Now the man's thin lips parted, showing strong white teeth, and his low, deep voice came to her, clear as a bell-note as it cut through the laughter and music and shrill talk. "Lady, are you unwell?"

"I'm fine," said Clarissa, praying that this impossibly handsome man would ask her to dance, and terrified that he would.

"You hate this crush of bodies, do not deny it," said he in cultured tones. "I recognize your discomfort because I share it." As he spoke, his exhalation flared his nostrils like a wolf's, and his indrawn breath strained the black velvet of his elegant doublet. The heavy cloth could not hide the power of his body, nor lessen his great height. He said, "Let us retire to my study, my green-eyed lady, and share a glass of wine."

Then Clarissa realized that this handsome, courtly man dressed all in costly black was the king. She tried to disguise her astonishment, but he saw, and smiled, the faintest of smiles.

And he led her to his library, a vast room filled with books and scented with leather, beeswax, and the sharp smell of lemon polish, which Clarissa did not know, but breathed with delight. Here great flames leaped in a stone hearth larger than her stepmother's hovel; and they cast a blood-hued light over the king as he poured blood-red wine from a cut-crystal decanter into matching goblets. Then he placed one goblet in Clarissa's hand, a heavy, sharp weight, and the coal-black and iron-gray hairs seemed to bristle on the back of his hand as his fingers brushed hers. His fingers were as heated iron against the ice of the crystal, and the ice of her hand; and Clarissa shivered.

"It is a pleasure to meet a girl who does not chase me through my own house, giggling where there is no jest," said King Richard Wilding in his low voice, dark as smoke in an autumn forest. His eyes were silver as the moon in midwinter. "You are different, my lady, and more beautiful than all of them together."

At his words, Clarissa opened her mouth to deny her beauty, and the king kissed her. Then the goblet slipped from her fingers and shattered, bleeding wine, as she melted against the heat of him, and with the sudden heat that rose in herself. She had felt desire for many of the rough, poor boys of the paupers' quarter. But she had never felt like this.

Then the king spoke hoarsely, and said, "I want you."

Now, Clarissa wanted him more than she had ever wanted any thing or any one, and she could hardly think for the images that filled her mind, of herself and the king naked. But she hesitated to answer, for she was afraid to deny the king, and yet did not want to break God's law concerning the proper behavior of maidens. And she knew too that if she gave up her virtue, she would never be able to marry well, and raise her stepmother and herself from poverty.

Then the king said, "I must have you now, my lady, and for all your life. You must marry me!"

So the king offered Clarissa what she never dared to hope for, holding it out to her like the goblet.

And so she whispered, "Your Highness, I will be your wife."

And she thought, if men were beasts, surely she had found the best of them.

At her declaration, the king shouted wordlessly with exultation; and he swept her up in his arms and strode from the library. As he moved with great loping steps through a dimly lit corridor, the king lowered his head, and his long gray-black hair fell over Clarissa's face, and she felt something like ice appear in the fire the blazed deep in her belly. For she did not understand how a handsome king could smell like an old dog.

Then Clarissa stiffened in his arms, and parted her lips to object, for the king was biting her breast. But then a shiver shook her, from the top of her head, to the tip of her toes in the fine dancing slippers that her stepmother had made for her to wear with the gown; and her plaint turned to a startled gasp. And as his teeth scraped her nipple through the heavy velvet, she moaned.

He must own a dog, she thought distractedly. For the king was rich, and lived deep in the woods, and so surely must keep a great pack of hunting dogs. He smelled like dogs because they must all sleep on his bed—

At the thought of King Richard Wilding in his bed, Clarissa forgot all about dogs and dog smells. For she was back to seeing herself and the king in bed together, naked—his body a little blurry, but moving on top of hers—and she groaned, "Hurry!"

Without raising his head from her large breasts, the king carried Clarissa up a narrow staircase, and down another corridor dimly lit by wide-spaced tapers. He was running now, and they were traveling a great distance, yet he neither slowed nor faltered, and his arms never sank with the weight of Clarissa's squirming body. And as he ran, he bit her nipple harder and harder, and it hurt, and she knew it should douse her ardor; yet it only increased the heat of her desire. She thrust her breasts into his face and tried to pull her gown below her breasts. But the bodice was laced too tightly, and she cried aloud with frustration.

Then the king carried her across the threshold of a great bedchamber, bright with white votives more numerous than the ones that burned in church every Sunday. And at the sight of the votives, Clarissa saw herself at the altar in a white gown and veil. The light of candle and hearth caused the heavy red drapes around the bed to glow like the wine they had not drunk. And the furs spread over the bed were all fire-reddened white, and they were piled deep as midwinter snow; and already Clarissa seemed to feel their rich soft caress of her naked skin.

But despite her fevered thoughts, she knew that it was not

yet time for her to be in the King's bedchamber, and she said, "My lord, we cannot—"

Then she fell silent, as three men stepped out of the shadows. Two were stone-faced servants in wolf-gray livery; the third, a grim priest in crow-black vestments, bore a Bible and ring case. And, though he still held Clarissa, King Richard Wilding extended a huge hand and snatched the case from the priest. One-handed, he opened the case and removed a great gold band, set with diamonds. The case fell to the floor, clattering on stone as the king, still holding Clarissa in his arms, seized her left hand and thrust the band with painful haste onto her finger, as he said, "With this ring, I thee wed."

The priest said, "I pronounce you man and wife."

Clarissa's eyes widened, and she said, "But I've not said my vow—"

"There's no need," her new husband said roughly, and he looked upon the priest and his servants, and in a voice like a growl, he said, "Go!"

And the servants and priest bowed themselves backward, the priest bearing the Bible, quill, and marriage contract.

Then the king slammed the door and shoved the bar across the door; and he turned and threw his bride upon his broad bed. And the impact knocked the breath out of her, though the furs yielded as softly beneath her as powdery snow. Then her husband looked down upon her, and she shrank back against the furs, for his face was twisted and fierce. And the tears started down her lovely face, for she was wed to a great and handsome king, and should be happy; yet she could not believe the strange and secret haste in which she had been married.

"It is my time," said her husband harshly. "It is my season!"

Then he seized the skirt of her gown and the linen petti-coats beneath, and the muscles bunched in his shoulders and along his arms as he tore the heavy velvet and stout linen from hem to hips. And Clarissa thought of her stepmother's hours and days of work, all undone by the king's great hands. Then the cool air touched her legs and she knew that she was half-nude, and her husband was pulling off her embroidered slippers, and gazing upon her naked legs.

Now his hot gaze kindled the flame in her belly to new heights, and the flame flared lower, as well, to her most intimate self; and the heat increased the dampness that did not quench the fire, but only fueled it to burn hotter. And the fire rose so high, it inflamed her mind, so that her thoughts about the king became even more indecent.

Whenever a patron came to hire her stepmother, or to carry away the finished garment, her stepmother made Clarissa hide, for she wanted no one to learn of Clarissa's beauty. And while Clarissa hid from sight under a pile of clothes in a dark corner, she sometimes heard young men talking in the little alley behind her stepmother's hovel. Always they talked of intimacies, but crudely, and always in the same way. They spoke of whether they might get their cod in a woman's nether mouth, which they called by vulgar names that made Clarissa flush where she hid, or else they boasted of a woman who had let one of them stick it in her, and might let the other men stick her too.

But Clarissa did not imagine the king sticking it inside her; or, rather, did not imagine only that. She imagined that the king kissed her bare breasts, and licked and bit them, and that he brought his lips and teeth ever closer to her nipples, which stood high and hard, as they did when she woke from a sinful dream. She imagined him suckling her nipples, and his teeth dangerously yet wondrously scraping and biting them, as his fingers caressed her belly, moving ever closer to where the heat was most fierce. So fervid were her thoughts that she very nearly felt his fingers sliding down her belly, over the bone, and into her slippery fire; and very nearly felt his fingers plunging into her, and out, and in, faster and faster; and very nearly felt them twisting her secret bump harder and faster. And she fancied that she felt him kissing and biting the tender insides of her thighs, and even daring to kiss her nether lips.

And she even imagined, most shockingly and excitingly, that he left the votives alight and the bed-curtains drawn, so that she might see her husband's body, and see what he was doing to her, and she to him. And she knew her lascivious thoughts were of such a wanton and shameful lewdness that not even a married woman should have them. But still she wanted these lewd acts visited upon her body, and wanted to suck and taste and bite her husband's body and manhood in similar fashion ere he thrust his member into her.

Then the king was shredding his own shirt, and she knew that the ferocity of his eagerness matched hers. And she marveled at the length of his fingernails and his eyeteeth, and wondered why she had not noticed before, that they were so long and pointed. Then her husband was naked to the belt, and she was distracted by his powerful muscles and the thick gray-black hair that nearly hid them. She had seen men with beards and mustaches, but had not realized that men could grow hair on their chests and stomachs and shoulders.

Then the king swept his fierce-nailed hands down, and his belt parted and cloth tore as easily as butter parted under a heated knife. And King Richard Wilding stood naked to his boots, terrifying, gorgeous, hairy, lean-muscled, and enormously potent. And Clarissa was afraid, and reaching for him.

Now the king reached for her with one arm, and he raised her head, cupping it like a goblet in his huge hand, as he said, "It may hurt, my virgin lady."

He pressed her face to his chest, vast and solid as a shield; and the hair of it brushed her brow and cheeks and lips. The hair was thick and rough, and the dog smell came to her. He pressed her lips to his nipple; and the heat grew wetter between her legs as she eagerly opened her mouth and sucked.

"It may very well hurt when I take you," the king said, "and so you must hurt me."

Then Clarissa tried to speak, to deny that she would hurt her king and husband, and that he would hurt her; but he held her face against his breast with such force that she could not utter a sound; and he tore off the scrap of linen that had preserved her modesty, and slipped between her legs. And it did hurt, so terribly that she feared she would split in two, and unwittingly she bit deep into his muscle, making bloody half-moons around his areola; and she nearly tore his nipple away.

And at that moment he howled like a beast, and fell off Clarissa. She looked upon her husband lying with shut eyes at her side, and the tears started from her eyes and his blood tricked from her mouth as she apologized many times for hurting him; but the king seemed not to hear. He lay on his back, silver eyes closed, the shield-plates of his chest rising as if to block quick sword-blows, as he breathed in great gasps.

Then Clarissa sat up suddenly, possessed by a forlorn thought. "My mother doesn't know where I am!"

"She knows," said King Richard Wilding. His voice was enervated, his eyes lambent slits. "One of my servants is speaking to her. Do not fear. Your mother will never again know want."

Then his eyes closed, and immediately his breathing slid into the deep regularity of heavy slumber. And Clarissa felt an aching disappointment, until her exhaustion overcame her, and she joined her husband in sleep.

She dreamed then, of swelling; of her breasts growing greater than suns, and her belly growing greater than the full moon. And then she dreamed of pain and darkness and blood, of gray-furred arms that pressed upon her swollen belly, until she birthed two tiny, blood-dark forms. Then she won to wakefulness at last, and with a cry she opened her eyes to morning light from the windows, and tearing agony between her legs.

Her husband the king was already awake. He sprawled against his great headboard with the animal indolence of tremendous vitality. And Clarissa wondered to see that his breast muscles were swollen, so they no longer resembled the hard flat plates of a shield, but rather the breasts of a woman. Then she saw that the king had each of his hands raised to his chest, and each hand cupped a tiny shape. In one hand was a tiny black-haired babe, and in his other hand was a tiny black-furred wolf cub, and they both nursed at his breasts.

Clarissa screamed.

"Behold our sons, my love," said King Richard Wilding through blood-smeared lips. "Are they not beautiful? Are they not marvelous?"

"Impossible!" Clarissa could hardly speak, for shock, for horror, for the pain of her scream-stripped throat.

"They are my children, born of your body. In a night they are born, in a day they will be raised. Because they grow so swiftly, we both must nurse them."

Clarissa cried, "How can you nurse?"

"Three things stimulate me to lactation," said the king. "The pain of your bite, the pleasure of my climax, and the eating of the afterbirth."

At the last of the king's words, a burning fluid washed up suddenly from Clarissa's belly, and choked her.

Then the king gestured, and Clarissa, looking where he indicated, felt only more ill to see a table spread with a feast of hacked beef, several roast fowl, a great cheese wheel with missing wedge, high-piled loaves of bread, platters of eggs and bacon and ham, a pyramid of red apples, pails of milk, and bottles of wine.

"You must eat, my wife," said the king. "You must maintain your strength to nurse our growing sons."

Then Clarissa looked once more upon the babe and the wolf cub, and saw that they had already grown too large to fit in their father's hands. She remembered how she had expected to live always in the squalor of the pauper's quarter and the poverty of her mother's disinheritance. She had feared that her children would grow up as hungry and desperate as she. She touched her wedding band; and old cares disappeared like a rabbit's winter fur with the spring.

Then Clarissa reached out, to the wolf cub as well as the baby, for both were her children.

And the king smiled, and placed his sons in their mother's arms, and she embraced them so tightly that they squirmed. She shivered as their teeth grazed her nipples, and she vowed she would keep her sons safe. She would never hit them, as her step-mother hit her. She would never feel them shivering in the winter cold. She would never need to wipe away their tears because she had no coppers for food.

Then suddenly she became aware of the aching fullness of her breasts, as her children's lips closed on her nipples and they began to suck. And she was startled by the painful pleasure that shot through her body like an arrow to her groin.

Then King Richard Wilding held food to her mouth, and a cup of milk. She drank and ate, voracious, her morning hunger a void dreadfully deepened by the suckling infant and cub. Their weight grew, and grew. Her husband raised her failing arms with pillows, giving support. And still the infant and cub grew.

And the king said, "They burn up every trace of nourishment in their growth." She felt a fang graze her nipple and shuddered. "I must leave you a while, my wife. I am king, and have business that cannot wait." He kissed her lips and arose from the bed. "I must make plans, for one or the other of my heirs may be my successor tonight."

"I don't understand," said Clarissa.

"When they are grown," said their father, "they will fight and one will succeed, and that one will fight me for my kingdom, which is greater than you can imagine. I have always been the

53

survivor, and trust I shall be again, but still I must make sure the inheritance is in order."

Clarissa cried, "You're going to kill your sons! How can you?" Then the full import of his words filled her, as chill as a corrosive ice, and she shouted, "How often have you done this?"

"In my memory, since the beginning of the world," he strangely replied. "I will kill him, or he will kill me—I know it, and they know it. They have all my memories, up to the moment I spent my seed in you, and they have the memories of my forefathers. They know I have lived a thousand years and killed ten sons. And these eleventh sons know the survivor of their battle is not likely to survive me."

Now the heads turned away from Clarissa's breasts, as the sons regarded their father. They were grown large enough now to stand on the bed, relieving their mother of their weight.

"Our sons have your green eyes, my love!" said their father. "But they are mine in every other way. I see it in the lines of their bodies and the resolve in their faces." He placed a slice of apple between Clarissa's slack lips, and said, "I must go. But I will soon return, so see that you stay in my bed, wife, and my sons with you."

Then King Richard Wilding was gone, and the door closed behind him.

And Clarissa spoke fiercely to her sons, saying, "I won't let him kill you!"

"Mother, he will not," said the boy, the black-haired green-eyed boy standing on the bed. Now he looked almost two years old, and he was seizing meat and bread off the table; and the black-furred green-eyed wolf-cub was bigger, too, and sinking his fangs into the roast beef and tearing away great chunks. The boy spoke again, saying, "Mother, he shall not."

"Already you can talk!" cried their astonished mother, once she had regained her voice. "Oh, you will not fight each other, my sons, and your father will not kill you, I swear it!"

Then, though she had not forgotten her husband the king's warning, Clarissa wrapped herself in the rags of her dress, and put her sons into slings made from her and her husband's discarded clothes. She wrapped food in white furs from the bed; then she turned to the windows, and knew that they were too narrow to slip through. She peered through one of the slits, and remembered that she was upon the second story of the castle in the woods.

Then she saw the king riding forth, upon a steed that screamed with terror and tried without success to cast its rider from its back. He spurred the horse along the road that led from the castle through a great garden of late-blooming roses, more brightly colored than the autumn-fired leaves of the wood. Then horse and rider disappeared into the forest; and Clarissa turned away from the window and, bowed under the growing weight of her sons, she slipped out of the bedchamber. As she neared the stairs, she put her sons down; and they descended the stairs on their own legs, with the wolf running before her, and the boy running behind, in a white fur that draped him like a cloak. As they descended, she saw neither servant nor swordsman, and asked herself, did they know; did they realize? Then she realized they must; and she knew she would find no help here.

Then as they neared a great door that opened unto the rose-garden, and the wood beyond, a man appeared suddenly before them, a swart southerner in a green tunic and hose, with great leather boots that rose above his knees. He was the king's gardener, trained in the art in a far, hot clime where roses bloomed in abundance. He had only one arm, for before he trained as a rose-gardener, he had been a warrior, who lost his right arm in battle against the Mohammedan infidels; yet he wore a sword on his belt. For he had trained himself to use his sword in his left hand, and had regained the swordsman's balance lost with his right arm; and he wore his sword always, for he had heard that the forest of this far northern kingdom, whence he'd come to tend a king's roses, was full of wolves, and he had heard the song of wolves on many of his nights in the castle in the forest.

And when the gardener saw a woman running toward him, he knew that she must be the king's wife, for there was no other woman, nor any girl, in the king's castle. And he realized that the king's wife must be fleeing the king, for she bore a great bundled trove of foodstuffs; and he cried in his strange accent, "Halt!" And as she looked upon him with a blanched and terrified face, he wondered whether she feared because she had been caught, or because he had only one arm. And he said, "Would you steal from our king? Lady, your puppy will not help you."

Then Clarissa stood straight and said, "That is no dog, but a wolf, and the king's son as surely as this boy. Both were born of my body in the night."

At her words, the gardener fixed his eyes upon the dog, and was amazed to see that it was no lowly mongrel, but a proud wolf. And the boy stepped out from behind Clarissa, his eyes fierce, and the gardener's eyes fixed upon him. Then the gardener looked upon Clarissa with pity, for he thought she must be mad, to dress in immodest scraps of cloth, and think that a boy of three years and a part-grown wolf had been born of her body in a night.

Then the boy said, "My mother speaks truth. Look upon my brother's eyes, and upon mine."

Then the gardener saw that the wolf had green eyes with white around them, like a man's eyes, and he saw that those eyes were entirely like the boy's eyes, and entirely like the woman's; and he saw too that the boy and wolf had grown larger than when he first looked upon them. And he took a step back, in fear.

And the boy said, "We mean you no harm, faithful king's man. But we must warn you that our father the king is other than he seems."

And Clarissa said, "My husband the king means to kill his sons. I pray you, dear gardener, do not take our lives or bar our way; and we will go away with my mother."

Then the gardener said, "Your mother returned to the city last night."

Now tears sprang into Clariss's eyes, in amazement that her stepmother had left her, and fear at finding herself alone in her merciless husband's castle; and she fell half-swooning to her knees. Then she clasped her hands before her milk-swollen breasts, which heaved with the tumult of her emotions, and cried, "If you would only take us into the wild wood, kind gardener, we will never come here again."

And the gardener saw that she was as young and beautiful as the morning that spring turns into summer, and he saw the bare white flesh of her limbs and belly, and the swell of her hips and breasts against the satin and velvet rags that barely preserved her modesty. Now, the gardener had been without a woman for many months, since he had come to this distant northern kingdom with its ugly, pallid, yellow-haired women, who looked as icy as the olive-skinned, black-tressed southern women were passionate. But as he looked upon the young woman, whose face was burning and breasts were rising with strong sentiment, the gardener understood at last how the northern men might feel desire for their pale northern women. And Clarissa kindled in the gardener's heart and loins an ardor greater than any he had ever known before, an ardor even as great as the sun's when he looked upon Clarissa. And as she was so beautiful, the gardener took pity on her, and said, "I will take you and your sons into the wood, where the king will not find you."

And he took Clarissa and her sons through his own private postern, so that none might seem them slipping away, and thence into the rose-garden, and the wood. And he led them with many glances at the boy and wolf, who seemed to grow larger with every glance; and with every glance, he thought of drawing his sword. But then he would glance at the beautiful young woman, who also walked behind him, and keep his hand from the hilt. And every time he glanced at Clarissa, his second sword strove to slice through his hose, and ached with the excruciating desire to sheathe itself in her most intimate flesh. But, though he had been living for many months as chastely as a monk should, and was no noble-born knight, nor even a gentleman, he would never dishonor a Christian woman's virtue.

And at length he said to the woman and her uncanny sons, "Away with you then, poor children;" for they were deep in the wood, and he thought that the king would never know where they had gone, nor that he had helped them to flee. And he thought too that the wild animals would surely devour the woman, and her witchy children, and spare the king this witchy wife who must be in league with the devil, to birth an animal and half-grown child in a night. And too the gardener feared that, if he continued onward with Clarissa, he would shame himself by acting like a virgin shaveling at sight of his first naked woman, and spill his seed. And so he turned and strode swiftly away, and left them alone in the wood.

Now, when the poor young woman found herself alone save for her strange sons in the wild wood, she felt full of terror, even of the very leaves on the trees; for Clarissa had but rarely ventured from her mother's hovel, and never gone near to the forest. So she began to run over the sharp stones and matted leaves, and through the thorn bushes; and her sons ran faithfully behind. In her fear, she knew not where she went; and she left the game trail that the gardener had led them upon. And the wood was tangled, so that wild roses snared her ankles and slashed her limbs, and branches whipped her face. Blood jeweled her white skin like ruby bracelets and necklaces; and the ancient, close-set trees made her shiver with the feeling a man has who is locked into a dungeon cell for all his life. And on Clarissa ran, for as long as her bare little feet would carry her; then she fell half-fainting from hunger, and lost.

But she had not run very far, for her sons' suckling had drained her strength. And her sons fell beside her, boy and wolf, for they had not eaten in many moments, yet had never ceased to grow, and were weak and failing.

Seeing them fall, Clarissa half-raised herself and opened

the white furs she carried, and thrust pieces of meat or cheese or apple into her sons' mouths. With her hands she raised water from a murmuring brook to her man-child's mouth and her wolf-child's muzzle. And her sons grew larger, and fed themselves, and gave food and water to their mother. Now she staggered up onto her bleeding feet, ignoring the pain, and beckoned her sons to follow; and so they did. She knew that she must soon come to the city wall, or a road, or at least to the edge of the wood.

But she remained trapped in gloom. Now she began to fear that she ran in circles, or that the forest was enchanted; and she would never escape.

Then she tripped over a tree root, and collapsed in dead leaf. She looked up to find red autumn apples, and open space, and sunlight; and hope flared bright as the sun above, which had flared with ardor at the sight of her, and she rejoiced at reaching the end of the wild wood. Then she realized that she had come only to the edge of a clearing, and cried aloud in dismay.

"Mother, you must rest!" her man-child insisted, taking her hand with the hand of a fourteen year old, though a fourteen year old with unnatural strength. His wolf-brother looked more than half grown; and he placed a heavy paw on his mother's chest. She struggled, but could not rise.

Then the wolf gulped meat, and the boy fed himself and his mother. When the food was almost gone, the wolf ran away.

"Where is he going?" Clarissa cried. "It's not safe—!"

The boy said, "My brother is safe. It is not yet time to fight our father. And my brother is stronger than any wolf."

In shame, Clarissa said, "I haven't even named my sons."

The boy said, "Who survives our fight chooses our name."

Then Clarissa realized that her husband the king had never asked her name. And she remembered what he had told her about their sons, and she cried, "You cannot kill your own brother!"

Her man-child said, "One of us must die, Mother, or we shall never be whole. And then we will be nothing more than easy prey for our father."

Clarissa cried, "I won't allow it!"

Then the underbrush rustled, and the wolf emerged, with a kill; he was dragging a hart with antlers that branched like an oak. And he tore open the hide with his frightful wolf-teeth, and he and his man-brother ate. The boy held out a piece of red-dripping flesh to his mother; but she shook her head, shuddering.

The boy said, "I can make a fire."

"I have already eaten my fill," said Clarissa, untruthfully.

Then the boy and the wolf ate until nothing was left of the hart but fur and entrails and bone. Now the boy reached up, and his mother saw that he was taller still, nearly a man's height. And he seized a great apple-laden bough and bent it down, and his wolf-brother seized the bough in the fangs of his long muzzle; and the brothers pulled as the muscles rose in bands and knots under the wolf's fur and along the boy's shoulders and arms and chest. Then the heavy bough snapped, near to the trunk, and the boy and wolf dragged the bough to their mother.

And the boy plucked an apple and held it out to her, saying, "Eat, Mother, for you are so pale, I fear you will perish."

Then Clarissa took the apple from her man-child and began to eat, and so great was her hunger that the apple's sharp, sweet taste filled her mouth with a painful flood of saliva. And the boy, looking now fifteen, buried the waste from the wolf's kill, and the wolf went forth again. Soon the wolf returned, dragging a great boar, and Clarissa's sons ate, and she refused the raw meat they offered her. Then her man-child insisted that she eat more of the apples that he plucked from the broken branch, and the wolf disappeared again, to hunt.

Now Clarissa felt stronger, and when her man-child held out another apple, she did not take it, but touched the boy's face. And her finger traced sharp cheekbone, and followed the hard line of his jaw. A soft sparse beard brushed her fingertip, and she saw that matching hairs grew like black down on his chest and belly, and made a line that disappeared into the white fur he now wore wrapped about his loins. And she perceived that he looked eighteen years old, which was her age. And he looked a tall, robust, masculine eighteen.

And she whispered, "You look human."

The boy said, "I am not," and pushed strands of fair hair from her brow. "How unlike my memories you are!" His voice was tender; yet it was deep now, a man's voice. "There are no dams of my kind; so we are borne by human women. And all the women who birthed my ancestors either went mad at the knowledge of what they had borne, or else tried to abandon their sons."

At his words, Clarissa shook her head, slowly, as if in a fever dream. "I feel mad."

Then the wolf returned with a deer, as the sun sank out of sight behind the trees. And as the brothers ate flesh and Clarissa ate apples, the woods-gloom deepened; and grew deeper, and cooler, as the ardent sun dropped reluctantly below the trees to the west.

Now the moon rose, full and silver as the king's lambent eyes. And in the distance, a wolf howled.

Then the man rose on his two feet and the wolf rose on his four paws. And the huge young man told the huge young wolf, "Father is coming, my wolf-brother. It is time."

Now brother fought brother, and red blood and black fur and hairs flew in the silver light. Clarissa shivered in terror at the clash, and she screamed at her sons to stop; but they did not stop.

Then in despair she cried, "You need not fight! Do not believe your father's words!"

"We don't—fight to—please—Father," said the man as he struggled to close his hand upon the wrist of his other arm, which he held like a bar across his writhing wolf-brother's throat. "We fight—because—we—must!"

Then he screamed as his wolf-brother sank fangs into his arm; and they were tumbling erratically into the clearing, a great spinning ball of black and white and red.

"That isn't true!" cried Clarissa, as she fought her terror at the sight of her sons' red-smeared teeth, and trembled at the verge of the wood. "Cease your brawling now!"

But they did not cease, and the flying droplets of blood became fat drops and globes as they tumbled and screamed and howled and fought under the full moon. And though Clarissa cried, "Stop!" as often as her speeding breath permitted, her sons did not stop fighting; and she saw no way to stop the fight.

Then the tumbling paused, and the wolf pressed forward

against the bare arm that held him back. And as the wolf-claws sank ever deeper into the other arm, and the wolf-jaws pressed ever closer to the bare white neck that strained away from the dripping fangs, the wolf-tail rose up in counterbalance.

And Clarissa's fear for her children overpowered the terror that held her back from them, and she ran into the clearing. There she seized the wolf-tail, tangling her delicate fingers in its thick black fur and clenching her hands upon its length. And in the extremity of her fear, she grew strong with the God-sent strength of a mother who fears her children's deaths are near; and she pulled her sons apart.

Now the wolf, distracted by the grip upon his tail that dragged him back from his man-brother, glanced at his mother. And his man-brother seized his wolf's head and jerked it around. Clarissa screamed. The wolf screamed. And an answering howl, distant and terrible, shook the leaves of the apple and of all the trees of the wood. It was an eerie, melancholy cry, that seemed to voice the grief in Clarissa's heart, as the man twisted the wolf's head all the way around, with a terrible cracking of bone, and tore the head off.

Then Clarissa wept, for she loved her wolf-child full as well as her man-child. And the man knelt, weeping, beside his wolf-brother's body, and seized the black-furred hide along his brother's ribs. Then he pinched the hide away from the flesh, and wrenched his arms apart, and tore open the hide. And then he sank his teeth into the bared flesh on his brother's bones.

Now horror and revulsion shook Clarissa as much as grief, and she cried, "How can you eat your own brother's flesh?"

Then her man-child looked up from his brother's torn

flesh, and with his brother's blood on his lips he said, "Mother, I must, or I am surely dead."

"This is surely a lie of your father's!" said Clarissa.

But her son said, "I am only half of what I must be, 'til I eat my other half; and half a man-wolf cannot kill Father."

At these strange, devilish words, Clarissa rose to flee; and then she sank down again. For she had lost one son, and could not abandon the son who still lived.

Then the man ate all his brother's flesh from his brother's bones, until they were bare and silver-white beneath the full moon. And the man tilted up his blood-smeared face and howled like a wolf. And as his wolf-howl rose to the moon, he fell forward; and as he fell, his face elongated, his fingers shrank, his feet stretched, his teeth protracted, and his white skin sprouted black fur. And he was a wolf.

And a gray wolf appeared, leaping from black shadow. And Clarissa realized suddenly that she had left a trail of scent and blood as obvious to animal senses as a high road wide enough for four coaches abreast.

And the gray wolf stood motionless, and opened wide its muzzle and spoke, in the voice of King Richard Wilding: "It is time."

Before he fell silent, his son was upon him.

His son's jaws fastened in his throat, but his body shifted, and with human hands he pried his son's jaws open. His hands were human, his shape was human; but he was covered with fur.

"You sought the element of surprise," said Richard Wilding, opening his son's wolf-jaws wider, wider. Blood dripped from his tooth-sawn fingers. Blood shone on his gray-furred neck. "You hoped that youth gave you superior speed, though you knew better."

Even as he spoke, his son altered, the muzzle flattening into a human face, slipping from his father's deadly grip. Then they rolled upon the grass and leaf-mold, spraying blood; and they changed shape fluidly, wolf and man and man-wolf, as they fought. And Clarissa watched, trembling, and dared not interfere, for her interference had already doomed one son.

Now her surviving son was a man, embracing his father, seeking to snap his father's back. But his father was not so easily defeated; he stood unbowed and naked, a man whose back might have been made of finest sword-steel. And he tightened his hands on his son's throat, and sank his thumbs into the soft flesh under his son's jaw, forcing the head ever upward and backward. And as he pushed his son's neck near to the snapping point, the king raised his head in a triumphant laugh.

The laughter was as a fire kindled in Clarissa's heart; and she rose up and struck her husband's head with the thick end of the broken apple-branch, and said, "I will not lose both my sons!"

At her blow, her husband staggered; and she struck again, with all her might; and she was as strong as she had been when she seized her wolf-son's tail. And she struck yet again, even as her son's legs altered, rising off the ground. Then Richard Wilding screamed, and took his hands from his son's neck to seize his stomach, which gaped suddenly red, from rending wolf-claws.

Then, silently, he fell. The king was dead.

The new king arose, wholly a man in body, and clothed only in blood. And Clarissa screamed.

"Do not fear, Mother," said the new king. "I am not badly hurt." His eyes glowed green in the darkness, eerily lambent as his father's silver eyes had been. "That has never happened before," he said softly, "a mother helping her son."

"I could not let him kill my only child," Clarissa said, and embraced him.

The news spread through the city and the kingdom, that the castle in the woods held a new king, Roy Wilding, an unknown heir come to power at the sudden death of his father. No one knew who his mother had been, but rumor said that the old king had been married before, in a far country, and had his son raised there in secrecy. The new king lived in the castle in the woods, with his newly-married, newly-widowed stepmother, a young woman from the city—or so said an aging seamstress, who claimed to be of noble birth, and mother to King Richard Wilding's widow. But when the seamstress traveled to the castle in the woods with great pomp, she was turned away by the king's men, with never a glimpse of her stepdaughter, who wanted nothing to do with the stepmother who had beat her and then abandoned her. And the stepmother returned in ignominy to the city, and the people decided that she was a liar; and she lost all her custom, and then her rented hovel, and went raving through the streets, ignored and growing ever madder, until she died in a filthy alley.

No one in the city or the hamlets knew that the king was a man-wolf, or that he was also king of the pack which protected him as men by day, and ran with him as wolves by night. But rumors spread that the old king's young widow had a lover, a swarthy southern man who had been a crusader against the

Muhammedan infidels until he lost an arm, and who had been badly scarred in trying to save the old king from wolves; but most in the city and the kingdom thought these rumors naught but wild tales.

But everyone knew that Roy Wilding, the new king, was a rich and handsome young man, unmarried and of marriageable age. And the young women of the city dreamed of dancing at a great ball at the king's castle in the woods, and of finding their destiny in the king's arms.

THE SNAKE WOMAN'S LOVER ~ *Catherine Lundoff*

MY FLESH BECOMES scales, my feet a serpent's tail. My belly slides over the icy flagstones of my own castle, slithering forward alone. Always alone. She is never by my side in these dreams and I wake, sweating to the dawn.

They lived happily ever after: this is the way the story ends. So we learn when we are but babes at our nurse's knee. Always it begins with 'once upon a time,' with no knowing what is to come. And had I known then what I know now, I should have never left my father's keep. But I was young and foolishly brave and I would not heed warnings or advice. Instead, I went to court to serve my king, dreaming then only of honor, love, and adventure. There I met a lady, the like I had never seen.

This then, is what went before I came to the pass I now find myself in. I heard the talk from the courtiers long ere I beheld her. They whispered that the king himself sought to bring her to his bed but I heard no word of his success. Beautiful and terrible they said she was, like a dragon or a tiger, not the way women's beauty is praised. My curiosity, my obsession grew with each passing day until I had to see her, had to speak with her. When that moment finally came, I saw no dragons but knew her only as the fulfillment of my heart's desire.

What she felt when she first saw me, I know not, though I was held a handsome youth and a brave knight, broad of shoulder and strong of arm like warriors of old. I wore the Holy Cross on my shield with pride through battle and tourney and many ladies longed for me to pay my court to them. But there were none like her and I saw them not. I pursued her as I would a hart or stag and she smiled upon me. So certain I was that I saw love in her face that I never thought to ask what she saw in mine.

I remember the feel of icy stones on cold scales, my way lit by the last of the night's torches. I remember the strange wildness I saw gazing out of her green, green eyes and wonder how my own eyes appear in these dreams. If there were any to see them.

Then I saw only the looks that followed her at court. How they lingered, almost like a timid caress, yet turning abashed and afeared to other views when she returned their regard. But not I, for I had never known fear or doubt before. I desired her as I had desired no other woman, not merely for her beauty but because I wanted to conquer what others dreaded. Then, too, I wanted the sons she would bear, sturdy heirs of my body from those wide hips, and the daughters as beautiful as she. Their faces looked out at me from her eyes.

THE SNAKE WOMAN'S LOVER

There were other things that I saw as well, and things I heard when first I spoke of her to my companions. Witch they said she was and Fay, and in my heart I knew it was so. Certain there were those among my former friends who say now that I should have listened and watched more closely. I hang my head for the shame of neglecting their counsel but in those days, I was a man in love. I fought with some and turned others from my door to haunt only hers.

There I remained for several moons before I asked her leave to address her father as I would have asked no other woman. She looked upon me kindly and did not say me nay. I went then to her father, a knight from distant lands who had come to pay allegiance to the king. Swiftly, too swiftly, did he grant me her hand and her dower. Yet I did not mark it then, not even when he left after our wedding in the manner of one who parts with tainted goods he never thought to sell. Not a thought did I give to this then but today I believe I would give him his daughter and the dower thrice over to be whole once more. But perhaps I will feel different on the morrow.

Then I loved her and ruled my lands with her at my side. The first year of our bond, she bore me a son, and a daughter the second. More children followed, just as I had dreamed when I first looked on her. And such children they were! Beautiful and perfect, but for my eldest son. He had eyes slitted like a cat's and was quick and sly and cruel. Still, I tried to love him for her sake for she loved him best of all. I even made him my steward on his seventeenth birthday so that he might learn to rule after me for her sake. I did it despite my fears that he hoped his wait would be but a short one.

71

At night my sleep was often unquiet, my dreams full of monsters unseen but always nearby, watching me. I woke shaking, fearing the feel of their claws in my flesh. Trembling lest they lie in wait for me in the dawn's light, their fangs ready to feast on me, to consume me until I became one of their number. Always too I felt desire, moving hand in hand with repulsion and I tried my hardest to forget this. Always I awoke shivering next to my bride, her warm flesh comforting my night terrors until I could forget my fears, my unnatural longings.

That I shall never forget nor cease to love at least a little. Her beauty calls me even now in my waking dreams. I want her as she appeared to me then, as I want nothing else, not even my peace and happiness. I want until my flesh burns with it and as long as I live, I shall want no other.

Yet all was not well between me and my lady wife, despite the comforts she brought me. Each Sabbath eve of our wedded life, she kept to her chambers while I watched the candles burn down and yearned for her. In my waking dreams, she lay in her bath, her round, full ripeness glowing golden against the marble sides. Red lips and black hair framed the green eyes that spoke at once of spring glades and of wild forests. My flesh hardened at the memory of her soft glory and in the rage at her absence that I could not bear to confess to myself.

It was on one such Sabbath eve that I sat and watched the flames, thinking of her walking in the gardens in moonlight, her lips parted in song, and the vines lengthening as they followed her slow stride. The very flowers blossomed at her call as I had myself. For she had chosen me of all the lords at court, all those who craved the feel of her breasts in their hands, the soft wonder of her thighs but dared them not. I laughed to think on it and remembered on, my eyes lost in the tapestry before my chair, one truth ringing loudly above all others: mine, she was mine.

The sun had not set when my son, the steward of my lands, came into the room as soft as if on a cat's paws and my thoughts scattered like birds before... but no, I banished all thoughts of slitted green or yellow eyes. These were the stuff of nightmares and left for sleep alone, not to be seen when I was awake, the ruler of my lands and family. None should know that my nights were haunted.

He paid no heed to my distraction, asking instead those questions that he had asked on the dozens of Sabbath eves that had gone before. Did the Countess—his mother—keep to her chambers this day? Would she do so after the king arrived? Always he spoke this way though I suspected that he knew the answers and asked only to torment me.

Each day for three years, he had spoken to me thus: first, of harvests and kingdom, and last and oh so softly! of my lady wife, his mother. Naught but praise had he for her wisdom, her goodness, but some emotion that I could not fathom hung on his every word. Why did his mother keep to her chamber each sennight? Surely she had told me, and he as my son had the right to know. But perhaps I could not tell him. Then he would begin again on another line of questioning.

He spoke, his words hissing from his lips like a serpent's. "How well my father bears with his wife's absence! How patient you are with her woman's moods. But surely my Lord, my father, you know what she does in those apartments whence even her maids and the children are barred? It cannot be forbidden to you." And again. "She will not keep to her chamber thus when the king is here, depriving him of her beauty and wise counsel, no, surely not. My Lord will need her by his side."

His words broke against the wall of my thoughts, just as his hatred roiled beneath their waves, though I failed to hear it at first. For I loved him not and had but little faith in him, however I tried to conceal it. That day in my folly, I heard only one word of what he spoke: forbidden.

The fury of a fool swirled within me as I remembered what she had told me when we wed twenty years ago. Each sennight she was to keep to her chambers and I might not see her until Sabbath morn. Forbidden. That was the word she used, my Countess, my own. True, there were softer words around it, set to lull and soothe but there it remained, cold and hard in the midst of them all. Was I not Raymond de Colombiers, master of these estates and vassals, and indeed, of she who shared my bed? How could my wife's bath be forbidden me, I who loved her more than gold, than kin, than life itself?

I tired quickly of my son's presence and tried to let my anger leave me for these were not thoughts that I might share. Moreover, what use had I for kings when I had such a one as she who laid in a dark green pool some corridors away? My skin still bore the marks of her pleasure from this very morning and my fingers found them while I thought only of her as a man enchanted. My steward spoke on though it was clear that his father's mind was elsewhere until I could bear it no longer. My hand waved him hence though neither king nor pastures would wait upon my pleasure.

My ring I gave him to place my seal on such judgments as he

needed to make. I gave it away as if it meant nothing, as if I could not see the hunger for power shining in his eyes like the gold he craved. He cast me one look over his shoulder as he went, a glance filled with scorn. But I watched him leave and cared not.

True, after he departed I thought more on the coming of the king, as he had surely intended. Here was my lord come to see his demesne for the first time since my father's death. Surely he would be pleased. The people prospered, the merchants were rich, and the land flowered. They said it was due more to my lady wife than to me but what cared I for that? They whispered too that she was an enchantress who held me in thrall and right they were.

Right I was also to be held for I was determined to be happy thus. I had even removed the old priest when the simpleton began to speak of dark powers yet drew up short of the word "witch." The new priest understood his place better, speaking well of both lord and lady. I would let nothing come between us, neither God nor king nor man.

But that day doubts assailed me anew and I wondered if I was as sure of my lady's heart as I believed. What of the king? What power had I to prevent him from conquering hearts where he chose and commanding what I might prize most? Would the king be forbidden my wife's chambers as I was this day or would she welcome him with parted thighs and soft gasps? If it were so, would he take her with him when he rode away? My heart screamed with rage.

These visions of the fool I was danced before my eyes and I forgot that she loved none but me. I remembered only that I owned, that she was mine and no other's. My steward, for I will not name him my son, not now, yet his words had burned in my mind even when I thought I paid him no heed. They planted my fears one on top of the other and lit the tinder beneath. Still I cannot blame him for all of it: my jealousy rose from myself alone and I can blame no other for the results.

On that day of happily ever afters that might have been, my thoughts turned unceasingly on the king and my lady wife. My jealousy knew no truth. Why should I be barred from what the king, if he so commanded, might enjoy? Why should I not go to my wife, my Melusine, and feel her beneath me, floating in fire-warmed waters? I must know that she loved no one but me. I had conquered where others feared to go and that victory must remain mine and mine alone.

At this thought, I rose in anger with the word "forbidden" ringing in my ears. It sped my steps through the corridors to her chamber door. The stone halls echoed behind with my passage and the guards stood straighter and taller when I passed. But they were as nothing to me.

A turn, a stair, a few strides more and I stood still before the oaken boards. From within I fancied I heard the water slide caressingly over her limbs and the gentle sound of her breath. I rested my head a moment against the solid beams of the door, weighed down by a sudden fever that made my hands tremble.

Then I thought I heard another sound, one I dared not speak of aloud. My loins burned with fire, until I trembled against the wood of the chamber door. My breath rose and my heart ran like a deer pursued by the dogs. I entered my dreams even as I stood there, awake in my own hall and I felt the scales of creatures unseen slide past my own flesh. I felt their forked tongues and fangs taste of me while I gave them all that I had, surrendering even as I took them in unholy union.

Forbidden she had said it was and forbidden it should be that a common man should lie with such as she. But I had known her touch both waking and sleeping and I was no common man. This I knew even as my knees trembled beneath me. I would know all the king might know, all the secrets that my beloved held. Like an idiot, I thought, too, that I would love her still, that I would desire whatever I found on the other side of the door, no matter what that was.

With that, I threw it open and went in to greet my beloved, my Melusine. There I found the substance of my dreams, and my downfall. Even so, had it not been for the tip of her tail draped over the side of the bath, I might have denied the monster she was. As it was her slitted eyes met my own and she hissed a single word through transformed lips and tongue, "Husband?"

I will never know if there was love in those eyes; I only know that in my rage and my desire, God help me, I took her. I embraced her in her other form as I would the creatures from my dreams, though my soul cried out against it.

When I woke on the Sabbath, I looked upon she who lay beside me and I ordered the executioner to my steward, her son's door. There would be no more words, no more cunning. I thought then to erase what had come before, to return only to the sweet days we had known when we were first wed. I knew the crime I had committed after the words were spoken, after it was too late, and my son lay dead in the grave. I knew that I had killed him with my fears, my jealousy, as surely as if I had swung the blade myself.

But even this was for nothing. Now each night I go and lie beside her to stare open-eyed at the ceiling above our bed so that none will know me for a coward. When I sleep at last, I know only the hard cobbles beneath my scales and the ache of being absolutely alone.

Each morning I beg her to enchant me again, to make me forget what I know and each day she says only one thing to me, "There are many kinds of monsters here." Then she turns away, hatred in her eyes and leaves me to sit and watch the candles burn before the tapestries. Here I remain, unable to go or stay, knowing that my beloved remains at my side only to send me the dreams that fill my mind with horrors. Such is my punishment. For this, too, is how the story ends: with an open door and a man gazing at the unclean depths of his soul.

AMETHYST'S FEATHER *Michael Michele*

ONCE UPON A TIME, in a land not so very far away, there was a fairytale princess of a girl named Amethyst. She was fair of face and form and so, had many admirers.

Odes were written about her beauty—hundreds just about her eyes, which were described as aqua, ocean, and lapis. Whatever their color, often dependent upon her mood, everyone agreed: to look into them was to fall in love.

Some of her love-struck swains would wait until she rose from a chair, only to sit upon it and bask in her fading warmth. They would look for single, precious strands of her hair and keep them like treasures.

Grown men lay in beds next to willing wives and refused to touch them. They preferred to close their eyes and dream of the way Amethyst would respond, if only a man might be lucky enough to touch her vanilla-scented skin. The deviant among them spun feverish fantasies where she knelt at their feet, doing things unholy at their whim.

Many wore bruised knees from fervent prayers for even a smile from her rosebud lips. Some struck bargains with the devil (who profited greatly from her refusal to bestow even the slightest hope upon anyone).

Amethyst did not know any of these things and, had she known, she'd not have cared; though she moved, sat, spoke, and sometimes even looked her suitors in the eyes, her mind was elsewhere, along with her heart.

The jealous said she was stuck-up. The spiteful said she was too stupid to know of the stir she caused all around her. The envious said people were only attracted to her because she was so detached from all of them; her beauty overshadowed by her coldness.

None of these things were true.

AMETHYST WAS LOST in daydreams of a time when she'd been a chubby-cheeked child, just beginning to bloom into a woman. She'd climbed over a towering wall and run away—her spirit of adventure taking over her good sense, her mother said later.

She'd gotten lost in the primordial forest surrounding her home, wandering for a day and a night in the cold unknown.

She stopped when she could go no further, one of her dainty, bejeweled shoes gone astray. Her feet were cut and blistered, her dress torn and dirty. The long, red hair boys would someday write poems about was a cloak of ratted tangles she wrapped around herself for warmth.

When the moon rose high in the sky on the second night she huddled in the hollow of a welcoming tree, making a pillow from fallen leaves. She cried pitiful tears until she fell into a fitful, exhausted slumber.

When she woke it was darker than dark, and colder than cold, but it was far from quiet. She heard many noises—the skitter of tiny toenails on bark, wind whispering through trees, owls hooting. But the noise that alarmed her—made her sit up straight, ears tuned—was the sound of heavy footsteps coming closer and closer, until finally they stopped, right by her shallow hiding place.

Amethyst whimpered and squeezed her eyes closed, sinking as far as she could into the sheltering tree. She prayed in this moment of terror, not to any god but to her mother.

When she dared peek to see what had come for her, she saw a man. Crouched, peering into the tree, he was illuminated by moonlight. His face was handsome, his expression calm, but he was a stranger.

She looked at him, a fat tear rolling down her cheek. The man reached into the darkness and captured it on the tip of his finger. It shimmered there like a jewel, bewitching Amethyst and drawing her cautiously from her hiding place.

She allowed herself to be soothed and gathered into his arms. He lifted her atop his fine horse, a wildly beautiful creature. There was no saddle yet, when they settled upon its back, she found the seat most comfortable; she lay perfectly nestled within the man's arms, her bottom snug against his thighs.

He was slender, his age hard to tell. He looked young in some ways, wise and old in others. He was tall. His hair was very long, very dark. His eyes were hauntingly beautiful. His touch was gentle.

Amethyst decided to trust him and relaxed her body against his as they made their way through the forest, and over the fields of heather surrounding her home.

It was only later she realized she'd not told him where she lived or spoken a single word to him, not even a "thank you."

As they rode he talked to her, his breath warm on her flushed cheeks. He told her stories of far-off places and magical things. He wove tales of a life that might be had one day for a fairytale princess of a girl, and a man with no home. He spoke of love, passion, and happily-ever-after. He hinted at grownup things they might do together or, even with others. He said no matter what, he'd always belong to her, and she to him.

She listened, turning her face into his chest. No one had ever spoken to her of such things. Her mother had only talked of the love between a husband and his proper wife, and of the necessary coupling that would result in children.

Amethyst listened to the man speak of other things and imagined each and every one in vivid detail. She'd thought she was all alone in her secret desires, a very bad girl for dreaming and longing for such wickedness, but he made her feel safe, understood. He made her feel as though anything were possible.

By the time the strange man rode away, leaving Amethyst at her garden gate, she was in love. Spellbound and overwhelmed by emotion, she was never able to think of much else as she grew up.

She never cared about the boys and girls who looked at her with such want, was never moved by the songs sung to her beauty, and never dreamed of another. She just waited, dreaming of his return; she knew he would come for her someday—he had promised. He'd whispered his name into her ear before he left, like a secret, and tucked a raven feather into her hand.

She never told anyone what happened while she'd been lost; they had no idea the incident had forever changed her. No one pushed her to speak of it, and soon everyone forgot the adventure that haunted her.

WHEN SHE WAS a grown woman her father decided it was long past time for her to marry. As was the custom, he picked her husband—not worrying at all over what she might feel about his selection. He chose a man who had a fine reputation, and lands benefiting him in their joining with his own.

When Amethyst was told her father's plan, she wept for days. She cried so many tears the creek twining through her garden became a river of salted water that did not evaporate until she was long dead. Every bloom in her garden withered to dust, except for the lilacs; these flowers bloomed more lushly than ever before.

She dared not tell her father of her daydreams or of the girlish crush she still carried within her heart, but she held the raven feather like a talisman, and prayed day and night.

On her wedding day, she was a vision in virgin white. Her skin was winter-pale, all color gone from her cheeks; the blood in her had rushed to her heart, which seemed to cry out with every beat for her man with no home.

As her father led her down the aisle to her husband, each step she took was heavy. Halfway there, she looked up into the eyes of the man chosen for her. He smiled, a handsome smile. He looked happy.

She knew he had a good soul. He'd spoken to Amethyst during their "courtship"—of his hopes and dreams, of the children they would raise, the contented life they would lead. He was a nice man, a kind man—a man very much like her father. Everyone agreed they were perfectly matched.

Amethyst slowed. Her father frowned, tightening his grip on her arm. She looked back, over her shoulder, just as a raven flew into the church, pushed by a howling wind that opened the heavy doors with a bang. The bird shrieked, a haunting cry that pierced the serene harp music, its breast tinted violet by a stained-glass window that cast a shard of splintered light upon its heart.

Amethyst stopped, looking up at her startled father. She kissed his cheek and whispered, "Forgive me," before picking up her skirts and running as fast as she could out of the church.

No one chased her, not at first, so shocked were they. So, she was quite alone when she finally slowed, as lost as she had been when she was a child, deep within the great woods.

Her cheeks were stained with tears and she was blind to the path she left behind her; bits of wedding dress littered the forest floor, lace and finery, something old, something new, something borrowed, and something blue, titian strands of hair dotted with seed pearls. Her veil fluttered like a flag in the treetops until the wind blew it far, far away.

She wondered if she could find the hollowed out tree, the very one in which she had hidden as a child. If she succeeded, would he come for her then? Would he find her there?

She searched all through the day and into the night, stopping only when she could not take another step. She fell to her knees, in a meadow dotted with lavender, and made the grass there her bed, the purple wildflowers her pillow. She drifted into a deep, deep sleep.

When she woke, it was darker than dark and colder than cold, but it was far from quiet. She heard the sounds of night—the whir of Night Herons, the stirring of leaves moved by breeze, and finally, faint footfalls.

When she opened her eyes she knew she was being watched; the tiny hairs on the back of her neck stood at tingled attention. She held her breath, cautious, flattening herself upon the ground. Her weak night-vision saw nothing, until a wolf stepped into the clearing and was illuminated by moonlight.

He was raven black and, even from where she sat, she could see his eyes were hauntingly beautiful; they reflected the moonlight, glowing silver. They seemed to lure her, those eyes, to draw her in, and so she rose, walking to him as if in a trance.

He waited until she'd almost reached him, then he turned away. Amethyst followed, without thought or fear, through the maze of trees to an even deeper, darker part of the forest.

Try as she might, she could never quite catch up with the wolf though her fingers ached to touch his fur, and she wanted just one more glimpse of his eyes. She had to hurry at times to stay with him, pushing away the branches that reached for her like fingers, like lovers.

He led her to a perfectly rounded clearing in the thick forest. Surrounded by large, purposefully placed stones, the place reminded her of something; the memory tugged at her. The wolf rounded a tree set in the middle of the circle, an ancient, craggy, twisted thing. She followed him through a maze of gnarled, half-dead branches. In some places she had to crawl, for the limbs dipped so low they almost touched the ground.

"Stop," she called to the black wolf, wanting to rest, to cling to him, to somehow make him explain what was going on. She followed him one last time around the enormous trunk of the old tree and, when she came to the other side, he was gone as if he'd never been there at all.

Amethyst began to cry, slumping against the rough bark. Her anguished tears wet the mossy, verdant ground at her feet. Rooted tendrils sprang from the earth, winding around her ankles. Whip-thin sucker branches slid around her, circling her waist and wrists. Before she could so much as move a muscle, she was bound tight to the tree trunk, her hands lifted high, her feet spread wide. She was unable to do more than wiggle and scream, her loud cries scaring the bird from the trees; their black silhouettes drowned out the moon's light.

This time, in her moment of utter terror, she didn't pray to god or her mother; she prayed to her love, and this time he came.

He walked to her, laying a finger on her tear-streaked cheek. He slid his hand into the bodice of her gown, his fingers curling over her heart's racing beat as if to soothe it. He cupped her breast, brushing his thumb over her nipple.

She stilled, so many questions falling away—swallowed in the storm his touch on her body stirred. She only wanted more, more of whatever he would give her. She was afraid if she gave into the need raging inside for answers, he would leave, so when he drew a knife and cut her tattered wedding dress away, she did nothing more than shudder against the cold blade.

He smiled at her for the first time, and it was like watching the sun come up after a long, dark night; his face lit with it, became boyish. She wondered how old he was. He'd not changed at all from her memory of him. That was odd, wasn't it? She felt drugged, the time before and the time now somehow melting together until all she knew was this moment, bound to this tree, naked—just a fairytale princess of a girl offering herself to this strange man she loved with all of her soul.

"Please," she finally said, the word coming from her before she could stop it, a plea for something she didn't understand, and couldn't name.

He didn't ask what she begged for. She understood this was not because he didn't care, but because he knew. He laid his body full upon hers, covering her with his warmth. He smoothed her hair, freeing each tangle as his mouth found hers and suckled a path to the pulse on her throat. He reached between her legs to cup the downy soft red fur there, tugging until the mound beneath his palm plumped, swelling. His fingers dipped inside, finding the petals of her sex slick and wet.

She moaned, arching into him, wanting this, wanting him, saying again, "Please."

He spoke to her softly in the husky voice she remembered so well; he told her how he had waited for her to seek him out, how he had needed to be invited, needed to be asked here. He said her wishes were made sacred by her tears. He told her of his loneliness.

His touch became more insistent. Something hard pressed to

her stomach and two of his fingers slid up inside her. She felt a clench of dull pain, a flow of virgin blood and pangs of fear—darkly exciting.

She writhed against him. He stilled her, his sharp teeth piercing the skin of her breast, making the tiniest of marks near her heart. He lapped at the droplet of blood that welled, laving her nipples with his tongue and nibbling on them when they rose, as if in offering to him.

She liked it, this back and forth between want and fear, pleasure and pain, but as he worked his fingers into her—even as the desire in her blossomed into a live thing that gripped her belly and made her insides shake—her mind screamed as if trying to wake her from a nightmare.

"No," she said, the word bubbling up with a will of its own. She heard her mother's voice and the echoes of all the girls she'd grown up with. Surely none of them would feel as she did, surely they wouldn't want the things she craved. They'd be afraid. They'd be modest. They'd be . . . good.

"No," he repeated, as if the word were foreign. He parted her lips with his, sharing his breath with her, drinking from her mouth until Amethyst was light-headed, grateful for the bindings that held her fast.

He grasped the hard thing pressing into her belly, sliding it between her thighs. With his other hand he lifted her bottom, tilting her hips. His turgid, hot flesh nudged her sex. "But, you invited me, Beloved. You belong to me; there is no going back," he said, kissing her again, his mouth lush on hers.

She reveled in his touch and drowned in the moonlit gleam of his eyes. She felt the brush of his long, dark hair caressing her breasts like silken butterflies as he leaned into her, and she knew he was right, no matter what anyone else might think.

She moaned as he pressed against her. She opened herself to him and the roots that bound her fell away. Clinging to him, winding her hands in his hair and her legs around his waist, the whole world faded away and everything came down to just the two of them, flesh to flesh.

A loud gunshot rang out in the forest, reality slamming through Amethyst's sensual haze. She slumped against her strange lover, and fell to the forest floor, in a dead faint.

The last thing she heard was the sound of his anguished cry as he crashed through the brush, running away. The last thing she felt was the wetness of her lust, slipping down her inner-thigh, like a kiss.

WHEN SHE WOKE, she looked up into a kind face. She recognized him, the man who was to have been her husband. She found she could not meet his gaze. She cried, closing her eyes, letting him lift her into his arms, letting him take her home.

Everything now seemed so clear. She felt like a true fairy-tale princess awakened after one hundred years of sleep to find everything changed.

Her betrothed told her he loved her and would wait for her to be well; he said everything was going to be all right. He handed her over to her mother, who enfolded her in caring arms, bathed her, and left her tucked safely in her bed, alone with her memories and thoughts.

It was only later Amethyst realized she'd not said a single word to her rescuer, not even a "thank you."

She thought of her husband-to-be, of the promise in eyes, the sincerity of his love offering. She wondered if she had a future with him, and envisioned a life much like the one she had always known, like the one her parents shared, like the one all the girls she knew wanted so badly.

She thought of the years she'd spent dreaming of that day so long ago, when she'd been lost in the forest. She thought of the wolf, of the tree, of the things she'd felt there. She remembered the pain and the secret pleasure, the shame, the desire, and the love.

She imagined what everyone else would think, but most of all, she contemplated what she thought, and before the night was dawn, Amethyst knew what she had to do.

She gathered her most precious things—the raven feather, a tiny glass sailboat, and a necklace with a heart strung from it.

She left behind a note for her parents, telling them she loved them, that she'd be back someday if they could accept her into their hearts, no matter what paths she walked.

This time she didn't climb the great wall and sneak away; she walked right through the garden, past the fragrant lilacs and over the river of salted tears, out the gate.

Amethyst wandered into the night, knowing she might never find the hollowed out tree, the meadow where she'd slept, or the ancient oak surrounded by magical stones.

There was much she didn't understand, but she knew her lover would find her, wherever she was—she belonged to him as surely as the stars belonged to the night.

SAPPHENSCHWESTER ❧ *Sharon Wachsler*

ONCE THERE WAS a beautiful young woman named Sapphen-schwester. She had creamy skin and a voluptuous, curvy figure. She was a feminist, so she didn't usually wear a bra, but her breasts were deliciously perky because she was only eighteen years old.

Sapphenschwester was also very bright. In fact, she attended a prestigious university in a New England city sur-rounded by many other fine universities. This meant that there were always lively fraternity parties with earsplitting music and sticky floors to visit; and fine cuisine to sample, with her choice of mushroom or pepperoni on top; and stimulating classes to attend on the postmodern deconstructionist textual analysis of pre-machine-age archetypes.

Although Sapphenschwester appeared happy, she had a hidden life that caused her both anxiety and pleasure. For, in an Internet chat room one night, Sapphenschwester met Eldendyke, with whom she shared many interests: her love of cats, science fiction, the Indigo Girls, and the WNBA. Every day Sapphenschwester and Eldendyke emailed each other, and every night they IMed. Sapphenschwester learned that Eldendyke was a very accomplished lesbian, who had been bedded by many women, and who had seduced even more. Once they had seen each other's JPEGs, they knew they shared true love.

Thus they decided that during Sapphenschwester's Winter Break, which was just one week away, Eldendyke would fly out from San Francisco, where she was a tattoo artist, to meet her paramour. Sapphenschwester was overjoyed at the prospect of spending her break with Eldendyke, but she was also overcome with worry, for her secret—which she had kept even from here beloved—was this: Sapphenschwester had never made love. She was riddled with fear that once Eldendyke discovered that she did not know how to be a true lesbian, she would find her lovemaking lacking, and leave her.

But it was not for nothing that Sapphenschwester attended an ivy-covered college. On Friday evening, she put her brain to work, and by bedtime Sunday she had devised a plan.

On Monday, after her classes were finished, she showered and dressed. She let her long, dark hair—which she usually pulled back with a scrunchy—fall in loose ringlets down her back. She put on a tight, black, low-cut midriff shirt that exposed her darling round belly and ample cleavage. She hung gold and purple earrings from her lobes that matched her low-rider purple and gold silk pants (which made her ass look great). She zipped on a pair of black platform boots and finished her toilet by applying a layer of plum-colored lipstick. On her way out, Sapphenschwester's roommate told her she looked, "Totally fuckin' hot," so she knew that the first part of her plan had succeeded.

With these encouraging words, Sapphenschwester set out for the Women's Collective house, where it was rumored that many women-loving-women resided. However, when she walked in, she discovered that there was a meeting in progress in the common room. Sapphenschwester's cheeks turned rosy as all the women turned to look at her.

"Oh, I'm so sorry!" she exclaimed, "I didn't know you were holding a meeting!"

"That's OK," said an upperclasswoman with an extremely friendly smile. She had a buzz cut and a steel bar through her eyebrow. "Make yourself at home," she patted the cushion next to her.

Sapphenschwester made her way to the appealing butch. As the women around her debated heatedly how to prevent dishes from piling up in the sink and whose fault it was that this kept happening, Sapphenschwester mulled over exactly what she would say. She also marveled at her good fortune in having this rare chance to speak to the whole house at once. (Sapphenschwester didn't know that the Women's Collective held meetings like this at least once a day.)

After the dish debate was tabled, a woman with an orange mohawk and a "Fuck Bush! I do!" T-shirt proclaimed, "The floor is open!" Sapphenschwester tentatively raised her hand.

93

"Go on, grrrl," the eyebrow-bar woman growled.

Twisting her hands in her lap, Sapphenschwester began, "I'm a Freshman here—" but faltered because an irritated buzzing had broken out.

"'First-year student,'" a lithe girl with a sheath of long, blond hair corrected.

"Oh, I'm sorry. Yes, I'm a first-year student and I've met another girl online—" Again, murmurs raced around the room, stopping Sapphenschwester short.

"Is this 'girl' older than eighteen?" asked the blond.

"Oh yes!" exclaimed Sapphenschwester. "She's twenty-four!"

"Then she's a woman, not a girl," stated the stately young woman, twirling a strand of golden hair.

Sapphenschwester felt a little annoyed at the interruptions. But she also realized how much she still had to learn and was increasingly certain that she'd made the right decision in seeking out the Women's Collective to help her.

"Anyway, Eldendyke is flying across the country to meet me this Saturday. She is an accomplished lesbian, but I am still a virgin." Many of those assembled exchanged glances at the word "virgin." The woman next to Sapphenschwester licked her lips. "I am afraid that if she discovers how inexperienced I am, she will find me a terrible lover and leave. So I've come to ask you to teach me the way to love a woman correctly. Will you help?"

"We will have to discuss it and come to consensus on it," declared the orange-mohawk woman. "Come back tomorrow night at this time. We will give you our decision."

Sapphenschwester took her leave, thanking the co-op for considering her proposal. She made her way home, excited and nervous. To calm herself, she ate a pint of Ben & Jerry's New York Super-Fudge Chunk and watched *Alias*.

Sapphenschwester fidgeted all the way through Tuesday classes, particularly a boring rendition of Schneewittchen in German class. That evening, she donned a flowing dress of silver rayon and pulled her shiny hair into an elegant knot, secured with sparkling hair sticks. She slid silver bracelets onto her wrists and silver hoops through her earlobes, then headed once more to the Women's Collective.

When she entered, the group was in a meeting. "It's the responsibility of the woman who brings the guests to make sure they've washed their plates!" a tiny woman with flashing eyes was shouting. "It's not fair to the women who cooked that night to have to wash extra dishes!" Sapphenschwester looked around. Some of the women were crying. Others looked angry. One sat knitting in the corner, a faraway look in her eyes. The buzz-cut woman was playing cards with a stringy woman with dreadlocks and taffy-colored skin.

"Oh dear," murmured Sapphenschwester, "I didn't realize your meeting was still in progress. You probably haven't gotten around to talking about me."

"Oh no," laughed the dreadlocked woman (after putting down her cards and mumbling, "Gin"). "We came to consensus on you first thing. Fastest decision we ever made." Then she gave the comely first-year-student a grin that left Sapphenschwester in no doubt as to what that decision had been.

"What say we adjourn to attend to our sister in need?" asked the girl with the long gold hair. There were murmurs of assent. "We made up a duty roster," the blond explained to

Sapphenschwester. "Every evening you'll come here and a different woman will have you as her pupil. We hope that meets with your approval. We've never had so many volunteers for educational programming before. If this goes well, we're thinking about doing an outreach project."

Then the pale coed let a dreamy smile spread across her face. "As it happens, you're with me tonight. My name is Crystal." She held out her slender hand, which had long, opalescent nails and rings with pale stones on many of her fine fingers. Sapphenschwester shyly put her hand in Crystal's, and a tingly warmth stole up her fingers. As if she were filled with bubbles, she floated in Crystal's sweet-smelling wake through a door with a Rhiannon poster on it and into a small dorm single with a thin bed on a metal frame.

However, it was not for nothing that this Women's Collective member was named Crystal, for all around the room scarves and crystals hung, each of a different pale hue, reflecting the glowing beauty of the room's inhabitant. The lamps wore shades of pastel pink, yellow, and blue and the windows held emeralds and sapphires that set prisms dancing on the walls.

Crystal wore a batik peasant skirt and blouse that matched her topaz-blue eyes. Her willowy arms and legs were dusted with the same silken hair that fell from the crown of her head to her waist. Sitting on her bedspread, Crystal tucked her feet beneath her and beckoned Sapphenschwester.

Sapphenschwester stepped tentatively toward the narrow cot. "Should I take my clothes off?" she asked.

Crystal let out a gentle laugh that sounded like wind chimes on a spring day. "No, darling. Tonight I will teach you to kiss."

"Just kissing?"

"Don't wrinkle your lovely brow," Crystal's silvery giggle sent a shiver down Sapphenschwester's back. "I promise you, you'll never think of it as 'just' kissing again."

Sapphenschwester felt dubious, but crossed to the bed, turned her face to Crystal's, leaned in, shut her eyes, parted her lips, and waited to be kissed. Instead of feeling Crystal's lips, she heard Crystal's melodic laugh again. Sapphenschwester opened her eyes. Crystal looked bemused. "My darling Sapphen-schwester, this is why kissing—good kissing—is never 'just kiss-ing.' It is the beginning, middle, and end of a process of lovemaking with the mouth. But even before this, we must learn each other through touch—through the hands."

Sapphenschwester had heard that lesbians just lay in bed, holding hands, and that sometimes a curse called "lesbian bed death" struck. But she had assumed these were myths. Now, she wasn't sure. Crystal put Sapphenschwester's hands, palms up, in her lap. Then she lightly ran a finger up Sapphenschwester's arm. Sapphenschwester felt her skin grown warm under Crystal's touch. Crystal began to caress Sapphenschwester's arms, sometimes scratching gently with her smooth, polished nails, sometimes making spirals on Sapphenschwester's palms or in the inner crook of her arm.

Sapphenschwester felt like a tuning fork resonating to Crystal's touch. They were close together, their legs entangled. As if tipsy from champagne, Sapphenschwester slowly rubbed Crystal's palm with her thumbs. Meanwhile, Crystal used her other hand to tickle the back of Sapphenschwester's neck with her exquisite nails. They were both breathing hard as Sapphenschwester once again leaned forward, mouth open, for her first kiss. Instead, she felt Crystal's fingers trace her lips.

"I want to discover your lips with my fingers, first," the lithe woman whispered, "and you can do the same." Crystal took Sapphenschwester's hand and brought it to her downy cheek. Sapphenschwester marveled at its softness. She thrilled as her finger traced the peaks and valleys of Crystal's seashell-pink lips. Even more tantalizing were Crystal's fingers circling her own lips. She wanted to taste and devour them. On this impulse, Sapphenschwester ran her tongue around Crystal's fingertip. Crystal let out a soft "Oh," as Sapphenschwester began to suck on her finger—sliding it in and out, running her lips up and down, and sometimes sucking it very fast and hard, so that Crystal's knuckles met her teeth.

"That's divine. I've never had anyone do that before," gasped Crystal.

"Really?" Sapphenschwester mumbled around Crystal's finger, so that it sounded like "Wehwee?" She was surprised. It seemed so natural.

"Where did you learn to deep throat? You don't have a gag reflex! Have you been with men?" Crystal accused.

"No!" Sapphenschwester cried, aghast. "When I said I was a virgin, I meant it in every sense." She thought for a moment. "I got strep throat a lot as a child. I had so many throat cultures I guess I just learned not to choke when something was deep inside my mouth."

"That may come in handy in future lessons," Crystal muttered.

"What?" Sapphenschwester asked.

"Nothing. Now, when you start a kiss, you want it to be gentle and soft, with your lips closed. Don't dive in like you're fishing for my tonsils."

Sapphenschwester flushed. "But, we get to open our mouths and use our tongues eventually, don't we?"

"Oh, yes," Crystal smiled. "My, you are eager! You also want to have good lip tension and moisture—not sloppy and loose, but not tight and hard, either."

"Oh dear!" wailed Sapphenschwester. "I had no idea it was this complicated!"

"Relax," Crystal reassured. "Just follow my lead and the rest will come naturally."

Crystal pressed her sweet, glossy lips against Sapphenschwester's. It felt marvelous: the connection, the softness, the smell of Crystal's skin. Soon Crystal parted her lips, and Sapphenschwester followed suit. They nibbled lips. They ran their tongues along each other's teeth and explored each other's rich recesses. As their passion grew, Sapphenschwester lost track of time and place. She didn't know how Crystal came to be lying on her or when they had started grinding their hips against each other. She only knew it must never end.

Then Sapphenschwester felt an overwhelming urge to have her fingers in Crystal's mouth. With their arms and legs still entwined and their tongues dancing with each other's, Sapphenschwester freed one arm to trace the edges of Crystal's lips. Then, quick as a flash, she slipped her finger into Crystal's warm wetness. When Sapphenschwester's exquisitely sensitive fingers felt Crystal's teeth gliding thrillingly against the whorls of her skin, she understood why it was so enjoyable to be serviced in this way.

Sapphenschwester alternated between feeding Crystal her tongue and her finger, driving the blond wild—never knowing which delicious organ she would suckle next. Sapphenschwester was damp all over. She reached down to slip her free hand under Crystal's blouse.

"Ah, ah, ah...." Crystal shook her head, panting as she pulled away. "This is where we stop for the night."

"But!—" Sapphenschwester protested.

"No, we have a duty roster; the Collective felt you must study kissing first. And you have. In fact, I plan to add your finger sucking technique to my repertoire. You will become a great lesbian—of this, I am sure."

Sapphenschwester felt proud—and horny—as she walked back to her room. In bed, she tossed restlessly until she finally gave in and masturbated furiously to fantasies of going much further along the path of sapphism with Crystal than they had that night. Sapphenschwester came in a rush, then fell asleep.

Sapphenschwester arose in a jittery mood. At breakfast she spilled yogurt on her blouse. She returned to her dorm to change. Hoping to entice her next instructor, Sapphenschwester slipped on a lacy black push-up bra—the clasp in front—and matching panties. Then she donned denim Daisy Dukes and see-through black chenille blouse. During Women's Studies, Sapphenschwester daydreamed, rubbing the seam of her shorts against her chair and sending her musky scent into the air—causing those seated around her to pay no attention to the professor. However, she did catch a bit of the discussion about monogamy being a tool of the patriarchy.

When Sapphenschwester arrived at the co-op, several women were in the common room, talking, studying, and eating. "Hi, cutie," called the dreadlocked woman who'd been playing gin at the house meeting. "You're mine today."

Sapphenschwester blushed. Her new mentor was tall and lanky. Her black plastic-frame glasses gave her a studious expression that was belied by the twinkle in her hazelnut eyes. Her locks were secured with a rubber band and she wore faded blue jeans and a sleeveless black T-shirt that showed off a boyish figure—except for the small, pert breasts whose nipples scraped against the cotton fabric.

"Crystal has good things to say about you," the stranger said as she crossed the room. She stuck out a tan hand to shake Sapphenschwester's pale one.

"Oh, well, I—" Sapphenschwester stammered, her heart racing as their hands touched.

"No need to be embarrassed. It's college. We're all here to gain knowledge through study and life experience, right?" Again, her words seemed serious, but her tone was jovial. "I'm Kendra. Follow me to my looove nest," she jiggled her eyebrows. "It's on the third floor." As they climbed, Sapphenschwester couldn't help staring at Kendra's round, firm ass in front of her. Was it OK to check out another woman like this, or did such behavior objectify Kendra? Whenever Sapphenschwester sped up to try to walk beside her new teacher, Kendra's long strides moved her ahead again. Could it be that she wants me to appreciate her glorious butt? Sapphenschwester pondered.

"It ain't much, but it's home," announced Kendra,

swinging open a door. The room held no prisms or scarves, but many posters of musicians. Sapphenschwester picked out Melissa Etheridge, Tracy Chapman, and Queen Latifah, but there were others she didn't recognize. In the corner, an electric-blue guitar stood on a stand.

"Oh, marvelous," Sapphenschwester breathed. "Do you play?"

"Well, I play at playing," Kendra said ruefully. "I'm not very good."

"Oh no," Sapphenschwester protested, "I bet you're wonderful!"

"Well, then, you lose that bet. But don't worry," she cut off further protests, "I'm good at other things. Let's focus on those, all right?"

Sapphenschwester was chagrined: Kendra was taking time from her schoolwork and music to teach her, and she was repaying her by making her feel bad about her lack of musical ability. Sapphenschwester vowed to set things aright. "I'm eager to learn from and appreciate any skills that you are so generous as to share with me."

"Then come over here," Kendra patted her comfortably rumpled and soft blankets. "Let's start with a review."

Yes, thought Sapphenschwester, this one doesn't waste time, as she practically landed in Kendra's lap. The two women kissed passionately while exploring the contours of each other's faces, hands, and arms. They ran fingers through each other's hair, bit each other's necks. Sapphenschwester took Kendra's smooth cafe-au-lait hand, with its blunt, strong fingers, and pressed it to her face. Then, as she had done with Crystal,

Sapphenschwester sucked on the other girl's full, firm lips and fingers in turn. Soon she was alternating between index finger and tongue, drawing in each as far as it would go. "Good Lord!" Kendra exclaimed, "This must be what Crystal was talking about. Thank the Goddess for strep throat!"

Sapphenschwester looked with confusion into Kendra's chestnut eyes. "You're very good at that, is what I'm saying," Kendra grinned. "But, let's move on. Lie back."

Her mentor began tracing lazy circles around her breasts through the gauzy blouse. Sapphenschwester grew aroused and leaned forward in delighted anticipation of Kendra's hands and mouth against her bare nipples. But Kendra's hands stayed over the tissue-thin cloth. Sapphenschwester moaned and whimpered. She tried to grab the teasing hands and put them under her shirt. She attempted to take off her shirt and bra, but Kendra swatted the tortured girl's hands away.

"Listen, lovely: in sex you can only go forward, not backward," whispered Kendra, as she continued her teasing. "In a relationship, once you cross the border into sex, it is almost impossible to return to the place in your relationship before you had sex. The same is true of the body; if I were to play with your clitoris and make you come and then return to your breasts, you would not experience the ultimate enjoyment your breasts have to offer."

"Does that mean you're going to play with my clitoris and make me come?" Sapphenschwester held her breath.

"No, honey, that was my point. We chose this method of helping you master one step at a time to give you the best possible education—and enjoyment—of the process. If you'd consulted the duty roster on the bulletin board, you'd have seen that tonight's lesson is 'Breasts.' Ah, but don't look so crestfallen," Kendra purred, "breasts are wondrous gifts from the Goddess. Lie back. You'll see."

Sapphenschwester stretched out on the cushy quilt. Slowly and deliberately, Kendra unbuttoned Sapphenschwester's blouse. When the filmy fabric fell away to reveal Sapphenschwester's lustrous orbs thrust forward by the lace push-up bra, the dreadlocked woman adjusted her sturdy glasses to take in the enticing view.

"Do you like what you see?" asked Sapphenschwester, nervous at the hush in the room.

"Oh yes. These are beautiful gifts, and finely wrapped, too."

Sapphenschwester glowed with pride, and a less familiar sensation that was radiating out from her maidenhead. Kendra planted light kisses on Sapphenschwester's belly and chest. Whenever Kendra came into contact with the girl's bosom, she wriggled and whimpered, thrusting out her chest for firmer, longer-lasting contact—which did not come.

"Ah, lay still, little sister. Remember what I said and enjoy this first time, because you can only ever have one." With these words, she touched Sapphenschwester's breasts through the black lace. She swirled her fingers around each mound, always stopping short of the aureole. Sapphenschwester gave herself over to moaning, then held her breath as Kendra slipped a finger under the edge of the bra. But the experienced lover-of-women only ran her index finger along the top inner edge of lace. Sapphenschwester squirmed, feeling the moisture pool inside her virginal home. When the pretty coed could stand the teasing

no longer Kendra unhooked the brassiere and Sapphenschwester's breasts fell open in front of her.

Kendra smiled delightedly at the first-year-student on her
back, mouth, and legs open beseechingly, her body covered in the
dew of desire. Kendra ran her fingers up and down Sapphenschwester's torso, careful not to touch her nipples. However,
each time Kendra's nimble fingers approached her nipples,
Sapphenschwester shifted, trying to elicit this most precious
sensation.

But it was not for nothing that Kendra had studied the guitar, for she played the girl laid out in front of her like a beautiful
instrument. As if she were sliding her hands up and down a
finely crafted bridge, she strummed and plucked, eliciting such
melodic sighs and whispers from the dark-haired lass that
Sapphenschwester herself started to feel like she was vibrating
with rapturous music.

Finally, Kendra moved her agile hands to Sapphenschwester's nipples. She danced circles around their edges, causing them to pucker and stiffen. She rolled her hands across their
tops, touching all of Sapphenschwester's ample bosom. The virgin felt as if a glorious wave of warm honey was spreading
throughout her body. Kendra sucked gently first on one, then
the other, claret nipple. Sapphenschwester gasped and writhed,
wondering if this was acceptable behavior for a virginal lesbian,
and then decided she didn't care. Her lace panties were soaked
and she was wild for Kendra to explore the treasures inside these
undergarments. Sapphenschwester didn't think Kendra could
possibly make her feel more horny than she already was, but this
was further proof that Sapphenschwester still had much to

learn, for while Kendra sucked one rosy bud, she simultaneously took Sapphenschwester's other nipple between her fingers, rolling and pinching it.

Sapphenschwester was flooded with urgent need and called Kendra's name, digging her nails into her back. If Kendra continued, Sapphenschwester believed she might very well be carried to orgasm. As if her dexterous partner read her thoughts, she suddenly pulled away from the rapt girl and said, "That is what I have to teach you about the joys of breasts. I wish that we could go farther, but I mustn't be greedy. I must allow my other sisters their chance to take you under their, uh, wings," she winked.

Sapphenschwester was astounded. "We're finished? What about my turn to practice on your breasts? Surely it is equally important—if not more so—to learn to give as well as receive?"

"You are very bright, and it's commendable that you do not wish to become a pillow princess. But, sadly, I am not endowed with sensitivity in my breasts. I was happy to titillate you, but you would waste your efforts should you try to thrill me likewise."

Sapphenschwester was dumbfounded. From the first moment she saw Kendra's compact breasts pressed against her T-shirt, Sapphenschwester had wanted to touch them. "Surely there can be no harm in trying? I mean, it does not hurt you to have them touched, does it?" she inquired with concern.

"Oh no," Kendra laughed. "I don't mind it. I'm not stone or anything."

"Stone?"

"Never mind—that's another lesson. You go ahead and play, if you like."

They exchanged positions and Sapphenschwester did to Kendra what had been done to her. To Sapphenschwester's disappointment, Kendra was as good as her word: though the dreadlocked girl was relaxed—her eyes shut and a smile on her face—she was not aroused.

But it was not for nothing that Sapphenschwester had gone through a highly competitive college application process. She believed in "stick-to-itiveness" and following her instincts. And right now her deepest desire was to take one of Kendra's yummy breasts—as delicious-looking as a little scoop of butterscotch pudding—full into her mouth. First she licked and sucked at the glorious nipple. Then she opened her mouth wide to embrace Kendra's large cinnamon areola. She alternated the pressure with which she sucked, from feather-light to insistent. Kendra shifted below her and let out an almost inaudible moan. Sapphenschwester allowed the hinge of her jaw relax completely and thus was able to take in the entire breast. Kendra arched her back, pressing Sapphenschwester more tightly against her chest, which was now rising and falling rapidly as she reveled in Sapphenschwester's skills.

The girl continued to experiment. She rolled her tongue across Kendra's nipple, lapped at it, bit it gently, bit it harder. All the while she sucked, sometimes lightly, sometimes forcefully. She was careful that with each new trick, Kendra's breast was always entirely covered by her mouth. Soon Kendra was writhing and Sapphenschwester had to work to stay with her. Meanwhile, Sapphenschwester's own excitement mounted at the response she was eliciting. She switched her ministrations to Kendra's other breast, marveling at the

transformation her mouth had wrought: the aureole had contracted like a closed flower around the beautiful pulsing bur-
gundy nipple.

She sucked and bit the second breast while continuing to
play with the first with her fingers. It was now exquisitely sensitive—even gentle caresses caused eruptions. "Oh! Oh baby, oh
baby," crooned Kendra, running her fingers through Sapphenschwester's locks and wrapping her blue-jean clad legs around
the intrepid student. "I—I don't think I can take much more."

Sapphenschwester reluctantly relinquished her spot. They
sat together, hugging fiercely, their faces in each other's hair.
"What a splendid learning experience this has been," intoned
Sapphenschwester. "Thank you so much for your kind tutelage."

"I must echo your words," Kendra adjusted her glasses. "I,
too, have been enriched by our session. You will become a great
lesbian—of this, I am sure."

On her way out, Sapphenschwester paused to check the
duty roster. It said:

SAPPHENSCHWESTER' EDUCATION
TUES: Crys, kissing
WED: Ken, breasts
THURS: Z, C&C
FRI: WC, ATG

Why switch to initials for her last two teachers? Were their
identities secret? And what did "C&C" and "ATG" mean?
Sapphenschwester lay awake that night, her body humming like
the strings on Kendra's guitar. She imagined Crystal and Kendra

kissing and rubbing each other's nipples. She fantasized that the three of them were harmonizing to one another's sexual longings. With this film playing behind her eyes, she touched herself until she was satisfied, then fell asleep.

During her Psychology 101 exam the next day she struggled to answer the essay question about the central role of penis envy in normal female development. In biology lab, she set her Bunsen burner flame too high and almost blew up her test tube.

Fleeing to her dorm, she showered then donned a short, eggplant-hued suede skirt and a white blouse with a sweetheart collar. She braided her hair into an elegant French braid and put on her purple suede boots.

Raucous laughter emanated from the Collective's lounge. There, several women sprawled around a table covered in bottles and large plastic cups. Crystal and Kendra waved. "We're playing 'I Never,'" called Crystal. Sapphenschwester was about to ask how the game was played when she noticed Kendra nudge the buzz-cut woman next to her. The stranger grinned wolfishly at Sapphenschwester and galloped over.

"Alright!" cried Sapphenschwester's new teacher, grabbing her in an exuberant hug. She was a short woman with freckled skin and a dark brown flattop so rigid that Sapphenschwester guessed she could balance a coffee cup on it. "I'm Zee," the new woman announced. "We're gonna have a great time, right?"

"Yes, I hope so. I mean, I'm sure we will," Sapphenschwester faltered, thrown off balance by Zee's ebullience. Sapphenschwester studied Zee and liked what she saw: a stocky woman clad only in boxers and a ribbed white tank top, with thick hair covering her arms and legs. In addition to her eyebrow piercing,

Zee had a tattoo of a leopard on one arm and a Dalmatian on the other. "I like your tattoos," Sapphenschwester said.

"Thanks. I like them, too."

"Do they have any special meaning?"

"Yes. It's like cats and dogs can live in the same space, in the same person, like yin and yang, you know?" Zee gesticulated wildly. "Domesticated and wild. And when they come together, they might attack, or they might sleep together, and you think they can't change their spots, but actually neither of them are born with those spots, they have to grow into them, see?"

Sapphenschwester didn't see, but she nodded anyway.

"Enough talk. Let's get down to it," Zee pushed her against the wall and had her mouth against the girl's before Sapphenschwester had time to react. Her first thought was to push Zee away. Then she felt a shudder go through her body as Zee's fantastic—and revelatory—kissing technique took over. No introductory, closed-mouth, gentle kisses here: Zee snaked her tongue in and out, ran it along Sapphenschwester's upper palate, and behind her teeth. When Sapphenschwester leaned into her kiss, Zee suddenly jerked back and left Sapphenschwester gasping. In the next second, Zee plunging back in, biting Sapphenschwester's luscious lower lip.

Sapphenschwester's mind, usually so clear, had evaporated and left in its place a whirl of desire that raged as fiercely as Zee's leopard; she bit and snarled and wrapped herself tight around Zee. The applause, whistling, and catcalls brought her out of her haze as she realized she was still in the lounge. Their audience watched hungrily, grinning hugely. Sapphenschwester blushed from her scalp to her toes as she slid from Zee's grasp.

Zee laughed and bowed to the crowd, encouraging them to dig into their pockets and throw spare change at her feet. With a jolt, Sapphenschwester realized that Zee had gotten a thrill from undoing the virgin so completely in front of her housemates. This ticked Sapphenschwester off. It also made her wet.

"Come on," she whispered, uncharacteristically gruff, "Aren't you supposed to take me to your room?"

"I'm not 'supposed' to do anything except teach you certain ABCs—especially Cs—of lesbionic love," she smirked. "How I do it is entirely up to me. I could throw you down on that table and you'd get your lesson here, in front of all these dykes."

"No, you couldn't, because I'd leave!" snapped Sapphenschwester, who throbbed at the image of all those eyes on her—splayed on the table while Zee brought her to a fever pitch of excitement.

"Oh, you would?" Zee leaned against the wall.

"Yes, I would," rejoined Sapphenschwester, who knew her face must be tomato-red, and who was beginning to wish that Zee would make good on her threat.

Zee burst out laughing, grabbing Sapphenschwester around her plump waist. "You're adorable. Don't worry, you hot little thing, we're going to my room."

Sapphenschwester had learned in her Women's Studies class that being called a "thing" was objectifying and that diminutives such as "adorable" and "little" made women appear childlike and powerless. Nonetheless, she believed nothing could be quite so gratifying as to have Zee squeeze her and call her a "cute, adorable, hot little thing" all night. In a bit of a daze, the voluptuous beauty followed her new educator to her second-floor room.

If Kendra's room had been a bit untidy, Zee's was complete chaos; clothing, books, papers, and CDs seemed to have been flung in every direction. On the rumpled bed, the mattress showed bare at one corner where the sheet had skidded off.

Zee kicked a few things out of her way as she strode toward the bed, bounded onto it, and turned, apparently expecting Sapphenschwester to do the same. However, Sapphenschwester trod carefully, partly because her suede miniskirt wouldn't allow the sort of leaping about that seemed to be Zee's habit, and partly because she was worried about stepping on, and breaking, something of Zee's. "C'mon!" barked Zee, "I won't hurt you! Unless you want me to," she laughed.

"No, it's just that I—" Before Sapphenschwester could finish, Zee bounced off the bed, swept her trainee into her arms, and threw her onto the mattress. "Oh my God!" ejaculated Sapphenschwester. "Are you crazy? You could have hur—" Once more Zee was on her, pressing her mouth and body against Sapphenschwester's. Again, Sapphenschwester melted into Zee's strength, only marveling that she had not noticed earlier that Zee's tongue was pierced. She enjoyed rolling her lips and tongue over the stud and gently tugging it with her teeth. However, just as Sapphenschwester was settling into the kissing, Zee sat up. Astride Sapphenschwester's hips, she commanded, "Take off your shirt."

Sapphenschwester's confusion showed on her pretty face. "But aren't we supposed to go slowly, because the first time is always special and—"

"You seem like a quick learner to me," Zee interrupted.

"And I already know Crystal did her job—you kiss great—so let's see if Kendra pulled her weight."

"OK," blushed Sapphenschwester, unbuttoning her blouse. She was carefully folding it when Zee ripped it from her hands and flung it on the floor. Again, Sapphenschwester had the curious sensation that what should be making her burn with anger was fanning a very different fire. Then, without even waiting for Sapphenschwester to unhook it, Zee yanked Sapphenschwester's bra up so that her tender spheres fell free. "Show me what Kendra taught you."

Sapphenschwester raised her hands to Zee's breasts, but the tattooed teacher lowered them. "No," she smiled, "do it to yourself."

This intriguing idea had never occurred to Sapphenschwester. Realizing this, she wondered why Kendra had not included it in her lesson. She felt a twinge of guilt—hadn't the guitarist taught her a great deal and given her much pleasure? The Collective had come to consensus on the one correct way to teach sapphic enchantment. Thus, Kendra and Crystal had surely lead her down the right path.

Sapphenschwester was frowning in contemplation when Zee tentatively cut in, "You don't have to do it if you don't want to, of course." She rubbed her palms down her shorts.

"Oh no, it's not that!" Sapphenschwester's cheeks blazed with nervousness and exhilaration at the thought of touching herself for Zee. "I was just thinking. It's not important."

"Good"—the cocky attitude returned—"then show me what you can do with those gorgeous tits."

Sapphenschwester bit her lip, trying to remember exactly what Kendra had done. Zee leaned forward, "Just close your eyes and go to town," she whispered. As Sapphenschwester shut her lids and moved her hands over her skin, Kendra's heavenly caresses came back to her. She circled her breasts with her fingertips; she teased and twisted her nipples; she brought her nipple to her mouth and sucked. As she pleasured herself, her breathing quickened and so did Zee's. They rocked against each other, Sapphenschwester still pinned under her pedagogue.

Then Zee grabbed Sapphenschwester's hands and pressed them over her head, stretching out on top of her. "Yes," she purred, biting Sapphenschwester's neck, "I see you know your way around a pair of knockers."

"Yes! Now I'll touch yours."

"No, I'm not into that."

"Oh, but Kendra thought hers weren't sensitive either, and—"

"This is different." She began expertly fondling Sapphenschwester's breasts. "I don't like to have mine touched. I like to do the touching."

"Does it have something to do with stones?" Sapphenschwester asked.

"Uh, partly. Sort of."

Sapphenschwester was about to speak again. But it was not for nothing that Zee had a leopard on her biceps. She pounced on her prey: lip-to-lip, they kissed, they pawed at each other, they rolled over and over, making animal noises. Zee thrust her leg between Sapphenschwester's thighs and pressed hard. The girl gasped, trying to wriggle out of her skirt for greater contact. She felt such a fire where Zee's leg rubbed, she cried out with longing.

Her guide knew her need. Kissing Sapphenschwester's neck and chest, she slipped her hands under the innocent's skirt. Zee pressed her palm against Sapphenschwester's lilac panties, then brought her hand to her face, inhaling its rich aroma. "What does 'C & C' stand for?" panted Sapphenschwester. It had finally dawned on her to ask.

Zee barked with laughter. "Clit and cunt, of course!"

Sapphenschwester's hand flew to her mouth. "You used the 'C-word'! That's an offensive term!"

Zee roared again. "No, it's a beautiful word, for a beautiful place. I'll show you." Zee gently pushed Sapphenschwester back onto the mattress, and again slid her hands under the skirt. She stroked Sapphenschwester's thighs until the girl strained against the restrictive suede, trying to allow the teasing fingers nearer her melting center. Sapphenschwester reached for her zipper, but Zee caught her hand. "No," she shook her head. Instead of giving in to the girl's obvious desire, she slowed her pace, like a cat delighting in playing with what it's caught. She inched her eager charge's skirt higher in miniscule increments.

When the skirt was bunched around the girl's waist, the studded woman slipped a finger inside Sapphenschwester's panties, now limp with her virginal juices. Sapphenschwester mewed and trembled as Zee's hand brushed the triangle where her hair grew thick.

With her plaything's mewls reaching new heights, Zee finally pulled the soggy panties down to Sapphenschwester's ankles. "Now we start with the first 'C'— the clit," breathed Zee as she stroked Sapphenschwester's pearl ever so lightly.

The dark-haired beauty was transported into a fog of delight. Under the experienced woman's touch, her clit became deeply colored and engorged, sending excitement through her body. Her eyes sparkled, her cheeks glowed, and her limbs tingled. Yet, some aspect of fulfillment eluded her.

As if reading her mind, the buzz-cut woman grazed her fingertips across Sapphenschwester's creamy, delicate folds. With finesse, she fluttered her digits a centimeter at a time into Sapphenschwester's pristine depths, until she reached her maidenhead. Sapphenschwester writhed, begging to be taken.

"This might hurt a bit," Zee cautioned, but Sapphenschwester screed, "More, more!" and scraped her nails down Zee's back. As the talented butch burst her dam and plowed in, Sapphenschwester yowled her approval. She bucked and shook against Zee's hand, which bore the bloodstain of Sapphenschwester's transformation.

Zee had to struggle to stay with the wildling. But it was not for nothing that Zee had a dog emblazoned on her skin, for she desired only to please—with loyalty, patience, and devotion. Moving her fingers inside of Sapphenschwester, she simultaneously lapped at her clit, the smooth metal stud adding additional sensation.

Carried by a tide of rapture, the young woman jerked against Zee's mouth. With an almighty howl, Sapphenschwester came, spasming around her lover's fingers.

When she was done, the two embraced and kissed.

Sapphenschwester tasted her own tangy juices on the other's lips. "See?" chided Zee. "How could 'cunt' be a dirty word when it brings such joy?"

Sapphenschwester nodded. "From now on, I will say the word with affection and pride." Then she turned and announced, "Now it is my turn to practice on you!"

"Ah, well, I don't actually like the same things as you."

"How can that be? It felt so wonderful!"

"What we did together felt wonderful for me, too," Zee smiled. "So, let's leave it at that." She hugged the exuberant girl.

"But I want to use my mouth and hands on your clit and cunt to satiate you."

Zee took Sapphenschwester's plump hands in hers. "There is something you can do to bring me pleasure, but it involves a different 'C' word."

"Anything!"

"OK. Shut your eyes," Zee commanded.

Sapphenschwester complied. She heard some fumbling near the bed, a couple of clinking sounds, then, "Open up."

Sapphenschwester gasped. Jutting out of the fly in Zee's boxers and into Sapphenschwester's face was a purple silicone phallus.

"'C' also stands for 'cock,'" the wearer of the device stroked its length.

"B-b-but," Sapphenschwester stammered, "You can't feel—, I mean, it can't feel—it's not the same." She looked quite desperate with confusion.

"Don't worry, gorgeous. You don't have to do anything you

don't want to," Zee's face took on the hue of her adopted member. "I just thought it might be fun.... You said you wanted to pleasure me with your mouth—"

Sapphenschwester rallied. "I do! I was just taken by surprise. But," she added shyly, "you must tell me what to do."

Zee's smile was expansive. "Just do to me what Crystal and Kendra report you do so well with fingers."

The girl-turned-woman wrapped her warm fingers around the base of her tutor's member, eliciting an "Mmm...." Encouraged, she ran her hands over Zee's ass, thighs, and magenta appendage. "Do you want me?" she heard from above. "Do you want my cock?"

"Er, yes, um, I do."

"Say it. Say you want my cock," Zee emphasized the last word.

"I want your uh—your cock." As she said it, it became true. "I want your cock, Zee. I want to swallow you, to suck on your big, beautiful cock."

"Oh wow," Zee wobbled, "I wish I could come in your mouth. I wish I could shoot all over your face."

Sapphenschwester pondered this request as she moved her fingers up and down Zee's shaft, feeling its rubbery ridges and bumps, swirling her fingers around the head. She pressed the base against Zee's clit and licked the head with her warm, wet tongue. Then she swept her tongue down the "vein" on the underside. Zee's groaned and swayed her hips. Sapphenschwester took the dick into her mouth, moving it in and out, first just the head, then deeper and deeper. Zee gave a guttural growl that reminded Sapphenschwester about the flattop's tattoos—about yin and yang residing in the same person. She suddenly realized how to satisfy Zee's ultimate desire.

"Take off your shorts," she ordered.

Stumbling, the butch complied, revealing a black leather harness over a tangle of dark, wiry hair. Still sitting on the edge of the bed, Sapphenschwester wrapped her left arm around Zee's upper thighs, pulling her in tight. She licked and sucked, taking the cock further and further in, to the back of her throat. The packing woman's eyes widened, "Oh God." She threw back her head and closed her lids. "Thank God for strep throat."

As Sapphenschwester continued the blowjob, she used her free hand to seek the home of Zee's pungent, spicy odor. Under the harness, Zee's slit was wet and open. Sapphenschwester's finger slid in easily, but Zee cried out with apprehension.

"Don't be alarmed, my darling," Sapphenschwester reassured. "I only want to fulfill your wish. Please trust me." Looking into Sapphenschwester's eyes, Zee saw her sincerity and relinquished her fears.

While Sapphenschwester continued her rhythmic sucking, she slipped a second finger into Zee's open cunt, searching for the spongy upper portion of the vaginal wall about which she'd learned in high school AP Biology. Miss Grimm (her favorite teacher and the field hockey coach) had informed the class that this tissue was the inner extension of the clitoris, known colloquially as the "g-spot." When massaged correctly, it caused an ejaculatory orgasm.

Thus Sapphenschwester continued to fervently suck cock as she caressed Zee's g-spot. When Zee's groans became louder and her muscles began to tighten, Sapphenschwester knew she was on the right path. Fluttering her fingertips coaxingly against the inner nubs, Sapphenschwester felt the first clenching wave. With a roar, Zee let go, spurting her glorious jism into Sapphenschwester's face and hair. Then she collapsed onto the bed, kissing the talented beauty and crying. Sapphenschwester understood that these were tears neither of sadness nor of joy, but of some combination—a deep release that could not be put into words.

When both were calm and still, Zee sighed, "Ah, Sapphenschwester, I am sad to let you go, but you will become a great lesbian—of this, I am sure." So the young woman made her way to her dormitory and fell deeply asleep.

On Friday, Sapphenschwester breezed through her classes, took an afternoon nap, showered, and changed into a Lilith Fair T-shirt, artfully ripped jeans, and well-worn Doc Martens. She strode to the co-op for her final class.

As usual, the lounge was a hub of activity. What was unusual was the room's setup: the curtains were drawn, the floor was covered with futons, and the chairs had been pushed to the sides of the room, as had the table, which now held a pile of towels and various bottles, packets, and accouterments. "Hi," Sapphenschwester said and waited for WC to step forward. None of the dozen coeds made a move. Sapphenschwester raised her voice with new confidence. "So, who am I with tonight?"

"Me," Crystal lifted a glimmering hand.

Sapphenschwester was wrong-footed. Hadn't she been told it would be someone new each night?

"And me," Kendra sang out.

"Me, too," growled Zee.

"And me," piped up the snippet of a woman who had led the last dish discussion.

"And me," intoned a woman built like a linebacker.

"Yours truly," waved an Asian-American dyke with streaked-blond hair.

"Wait a minute, wait a minute!" Sapphenschwester interrupted. "'WC' stands for?..."

"'Women's Collective,' that's right," nodded one with a Texas drawl.

"And 'ATG'?" Sapphenschwester asked weakly.

"Anything goes!" all assembled chorused in unison.

Sapphenschwester swooned onto an armchair behind her.

"That's right," the Texan grinned. "We've decided that tonight you're just going to watch. That's very educational."

Sapphenschwester gasped, but the other women paid her no attention as the Texan expertly roped Sapphenschwester's ankles and wrists to her chair. Instead, around the room, pairs, threesomes, and groups formed and began to strip. As she took in the scene of sapphic bacchanalia, Sapphenschwester was electrified with curiosity—and mounting frustration.

The extremely large woman was on her hands and knees getting vigorously fucked from behind by the petite woman, who sported a pink dildo in a fuchsia harness. Every few thrusts she'd spank the Amazon, shrieking, "Do you always wash your guests' dishes?" However, since her mouth was full of Zee's magenta wonder (which Sapphenschwester remembered with longing), the big woman's assurances were indecipherable—providing more fodder for her spanker's zeal. All wore expressions of bliss.

121

Sapphenschwester's attention was then caught by the mention of her name. "Let me show you what Sapphenschwester taught me," Crystal was saying to the woman with the drawl. Crystal took the Texan's fingers, sensuously licking, then deep-throating them. "Mmm, that's nice," the Texan murmured, as Crystal slid her hands under her shirt.

"Oh yeah, oh yeah!" Sapphenschwester recognized Kendra's voice. She and a woman who shined like ebony had their mouths glued to each other's breasts. From their euphonious utterances, the pair were clearly enjoying themselves immensely, and Sapphenschwester felt her own nipples harden at the memory of her time with Kendra.

"This is a little trick that Zee passed on," an auburn-haired beauty was telling the woman sporting the mohawk. Sapphenschwester saw the punk seated on the edge of an armchair, while the natural redhead kneeled in front. "I'm gonna play with your g-spot while I lick your clit," she explained. "Then you can spurt all over my face." Sapphenschwester's own face turned hot as the redhead buried her face into the other's snatch.

Sapphenschwester was squirming in her seat, rubbing her thighs together, her panties wet. After each Collective member attained orgasm and cleaned up, they gathered around Sapphenschwester. The Texan undid the bindings.

"It's your turn now," the Asian-American student said with a wicked grin. "You're the guest of honor."

"But she told me—"

"No, we wanted you to enjoy the show and get nice and turned on."

"Let's get going!" Kendra rubbed her hands together as she

gestured to a futon. The rest followed. They started undressing her—so many hands at once—hands lifting her shirt, untying her laces, lifting her legs to pull off jeans, socks, underwear— that Sapphenschwester barely knew it had started before it was done and she was lying naked on her back. They converged on her. Kendra played with her right breast, the redhead with her left. Crystal sucked some of her fingers; Zee pushed her tongue into Sapphenschwester's yielding mouth, and two sets of mouths—she couldn't see whose—were sucking her toes, a most curious, yet lovely sensation. Hands massaged her arms, legs, belly. A finger lightly stroked her clit. Every nerve in her body was firing, with all sparks blazing toward her cunt, which ached for attention. Then a finger entered her, then two, sliding smoothly in and out.

"Now, turn over," someone whispered, as the fingers withdrew from Sapphenschwester's pussy. She whimpered in protest, which elicited chuckles. "Why? Wha?..." she managed. Two strangers propped her up. "I'm Julie," said the Asian-American woman, "and this is a bloop stick." She held up an aqua creation that resembled a small, slender dildo with three progressively larger bumps. "And this is a flogger," she brandished a braided leather handle with many leather strips hanging from it. "I know it looks scary, but I think you'll find it feels really good. But if you ever want me, or any of us, to stop, just say the word, OK?" Lightheaded from being roused from her excited state, Sapphenschwester could only nod as she gazed at the towels, condoms, gloves, and bottle of lube arrayed next to her ass.

Many hands flipped Sapphenschwester spread-eagle on her belly. Again, she was lost in a sea of sensation—fingers ran through her hair, nails tickled her neck and back, mouths teased her fingers and toes, palms kneaded her calves and thighs. Then a fantastic new sensation arose—hands making sweeping circles on each butt cheek, sending hot chills into her cunt. One hand moved ever closer to her asshole.

Sapphenschwester would have thought that a lubed finger swirling on her asshole would feel unpleasant, but it was quite the opposite. To her amazement, when the digit entered, it made her clit tingle and her face flush. The finger fucked her slowly, and Sapphenschwester found herself pushing to meet it. She heard those around her breathing heavier; their touches becoming more insistent.

A bigger finger entered her and she rose to it. But as her hungry ass opened, the digit became smaller and then larger, and she realized it wasn't a finger, but the bloop stick. Before Sapphenschwester had a moment to panic she was swept away in the sensation of the second "bloop" entering her: a moment of pressure, then a dreamy wonderment. When the final bloop slid in, it sent her into the clouds.

As the flogger's first thuds began to redden her cheeks, Sapphenschwester realized that Julie had been right—it didn't hurt. It magnified Sapphenschwester's awareness of how full her ass was and made her feel unbelievably sexy. As the thuds landed harder, they sent vibrations to the silicone toy, which sent shivers straight to her clit. She rocked and moaned as each shudder of her flesh lapped at her clit and cunt.

Sapphenschwester felt endlessly powerful, yet totally relaxed. The only thing missing to complete her ecstasy was for her clit to be touched and her cunt to be filled. "Oh yeah, oh yeah, touch me, touch me!" she called out. Never mind that many people were already touching her, that she was covered in hands. Her sisters knew what she meant, and with some light pressure on her clit and two fingers curled into her cunt, she came. Screaming, clenching down on the butt plug and the fingers, she squirted her woman juice onto the Collective's much-used futon. She burrowed into the mass of bodies, endearments whispered among them like leaves rustling among forest trees.

After thanking the co-op for its many kindnesses, Sapphenschwester glided home to sleep. Eldendyke arrived the next morning. She and Sapphenschwester spent a delightful month together, coming to know each other deeply. They committed to being each other's primary partner within a non-monogamous relationship. With a heavy heart, Sapphenschwester saw Eldendyke onto the plane back to California.

During the spring semester, Sapphenschwester tried to distract herself from her longing by losing herself in her studies or with periodic trips to the Women's Collective, where she was always treated warmly.

A week before Spring Break she took the subway to a nearby college and found her way to their Women's Studies House. A meeting was in progress. When the floor was open, Sapphenschwester announced, "I'm a first-year student and I've met a woman online. She's driving up from New York next weekend to meet me. She's an accomplished lesbian, but I'm still a virgin. I'm afraid that if she discovers how inexperienced I am, she'll find me a terrible lover and lose interest in me. I've come to ask you to teach me how to be a lesbian. Will you help?"

JADED *Mackenzie Cross*

THE WIND HELD its breath as ten million snowflakes dipped and turned, captive partners in gravity's dance. Each crystal's flight following a poetry of motion as unique as its shape. Yet each shared a common structure and would suffer a common fate, destined to add their small value in creating a mantle for his home. There was a time when this paradox would have interested him, a puzzle to be solved. Now he barely noticed the snowfall's silent pageantry.

Jaded turned from the window, his long, handsome face showing no emotion, for he had none to offer. The window at his back was one of many that ran the length of the long gallery, each rising from the floor to the lofty ceiling above. The gallery was baroque in style, with an excessive amount of gold leaf on the moldings and intricate pattern work on the tiling of the floor. Set high above the ground, it offered a variety of views of his magnificent gardens and estates.

Without a backward glance he entered one of the long corridors running perpendicular to the gallery. He had promised his brother and sister he would take them on a tour today. The corridors of his home were not always what they seemed. Things often changed, so even though they had seen his house many times, it was not unusual for them to explore it anew. Since they were his guests, he let them choose where they wished to begin. Not surprisingly, they had chosen their favorite hallway. Like all the corridors in his lavish home it had a name, Passion's Path.

Under his breath he exhaled a sigh. In truth, he had little interest in this walk, and, in particular, this hallway. Still, there was always a glimmer of hope he might find something of interest, though he doubted it. It was a long corridor with doors spaced evenly apart along both sides. Each was the same; cheap wooden things washed with a simple white primer. Inscribed on every door was the same message in dark red letters, written lazily in his own handwriting, "You've been here before."

In the shadows of his steps, pacing in perfect synchronization, were his siblings, Cynic and Sarcasm. They laughed and joked, as was their way, about the length and character of the hallway. They enjoyed taunting him, endlessly trying to evoke a response.

"Your home is so different, so unusual, brother. How did you come up with such a unique hallway? You must give me the name of your interior designer," quipped Sarcasm, her dark eyes flashing in sharp merriment.

Cynic laughed as he joined in, his voice pitched slightly too high betraying his excitement, "He dare not. He's much too proud to share."

Jaded did not bother to turn around as he made his reply, his words soft and dry as the falling snow outside his home, "I remind you, it was your suggestion to walk Passion's Path with me today. As I recall. you said it would help 'cheer me up'."

"All these years and you still never suspect me of an ulterior motive? Shame on you brother," Cynic said.

Jaded had neither the energy nor motivation to respond. He paused for a moment and glanced over his shoulder, his lips compressed into a dour expression. Their grins were sardonic and wide. Both were dressed in their preferred fashion. Cynic's clothing was always extravagant and flamboyant, an assault to the senses. Today, he wore a cape with a swirling pattern of bright greens, reds, and for good measure, violet. Jaded refused to speculate on what might lie underneath. As usual, he wore a pointed cap on his bald head.

Sarcasm preferred more muted garb, but always in at least two distinct tones. Today she wore fabrics of cream and aubergine and dressed in layers, allowing the colors to overlap, so it was difficult to tell where one ended and the other began. Unlike Cynic, she radiated power and confidence in her every movement. She had a keen eye and a sharp tongue, as Jaded had learned on more than one occasion.

Jaded was dressed all in black, the same color as his hair and his eyes. There had been a time when he enjoyed wearing colors, but that, too, was a long time ago.

Turning slowly, he continued his journey. The corridor now appeared endless in both directions. Its floors were bare wood, stained and dented, the product of too many footsteps pacing the same route for too many years. His footsteps.

He stopped in front of a door. There was nothing to distinguish it from the rest. All suffered from flaking white paint over cracked wood, and the cheap plated doorknob had seen much use. As he opened the door, the rusty hinges squeaked in protest. It had been some time since his last visit.

An avalanche of music blasted from the room. Mostly a funky bass more felt than heard. Over it, a slinky blues line from a wailing guitar.. The door opened into a dark space, illuminated by a single overhead spotlight, tinted crimson. Captured in its circle of light was a woman, well-curved; a generous amount of flesh without being excessive. She wore veils of red silk tied cunningly to her body. Long and flowing hair cascaded in all directions as she moved in time to the music.

Her body undulated within the confines of the light's sharply defined space. The pieces of silk were slowly removed. Her flesh was perfect, without blemish, without a scar. Her lips were slightly parted, an exquisitely subtle expression of desire.

Jaded closed the door and opened it again. Same room, same music, but a different girl appeared. This time she was long and slender, with thick, red hair and sea-green eyes. He performed the same routine and found another, this one a black-haired gypsy beauty. And yet they all moved in the same way, for they were all aspects of the same female. She had many faces, many guises, but her name was always the same. She was Seduction, and few could resist her charms.

There was a time when Jaded would have entered the room and watched the dance to completion allowing the girl to weave her magic upon him. Each body type was another territory to be examined. But when all had been explored, what was there left to discover? Now, he felt no reaction, no budding curiosity to see what lay behind the final wisps of silk. He turned and slowly continued his journey.

"Hold a moment brother, why are you so quick to depart this innocent scene?" asked Sarcasm.

"He feels if he does not look, he will be able to resist her charms, isn't that right, Jaded?" answered Cynic tossing his cape back from his shoulders. Beneath, his clothing was a riot of yellow and purple. Jaded winced at the sight.

Jaded's mood was barely touched by their teasing. "Would you enter then, Cynic? You are welcome to stay and watch the show while Sarcasm and I continue." As he expected, his brother shook his head back and forth in a series quick jerky movements. Cynic would not be content with merely watching.

"Come on then, you asked to walk with me today. Let us continue on our way. There is nothing for us here." His words pulled them away from the door where Seduction continued to dance, the music spilling into the hallway. Although there was a fair amount of sighing and teeth gnashing from Cynic, Sarcasm only smirked as they took up their positions, flanking Jaded to either side.

The music faded as they walked. Soon, there was only the sound of their footsteps. Jaded came to another door and stopped. He contemplated the closed portal for a long moment before deciding to open it.

The door revealed a room of a character and shape familiar to anyone who has ever stayed in a hotel. Non descript and common, it contained a table, a desk, and a poorly done print hanging from a frame bolted to the wall. A large bed with many pillows and bolsters, covered in a dark mauve duvet, was the room's primary feature. It could have been any of a thousand rooms, interchangeable and without lasting memory. It was a room forgotten as soon as it was left.

On the bed was a female, naked and bound. The binding was a simple thing, an *X* created with cheap nylon rope attached at her ankles and wrists. Her arms and legs were stretched out on the diagonal, pulled tightly allowing little movement. A pillow had been placed under her ass, so her shaved cunt would be easily accessible. The aroma of sex was pervasive, filling the space like a stuffed suitcase. Her hips rose and fell with a thrusting motion, an expression of need. As the door opened she turned her head to face him. He could see the wildness in her eyes. "Take me, Master! Use me! I am your fuck thing!" Jaded knew her well, for he had visited with her on many occasions. She was called Slut.

He closed the door and opened it again, and again, and again. Same room, different women, but each and every one of them was Slut, all eager to serve as a vehicle for his lust. But what was the point? He had fucked them all, more than once. Many, many times in fact. Too many times perhaps.

He stood examining her objectively. Noting how her hands clenched at the ropes binding her, and how the lips of her cunt throbbed in the same rhythm. Once upon a time, his cock would have hardened at even the thought of visiting her, using her completely, having her orgasm over and over then leaving her a whimpering, crying thing. Once he longed to conquer her, and make her his possession. Now he had no reaction, felt no arousal, no interest. He couldn't even be bothered to close the door as he turned away. Behind his back Cynic snickered.

"Jaded," Cynic drawled, his words dripping with false sincerity, "as long as you're not going to use her, do you mind if I have a go?"

Jaded was not surprised at his brother's request. When it came to sex, Cynic was predictable. He turned and waved his hand saying, "With my compliments, brother." There was a noticeable lack of enthusiasm in his voice.

Cynic wasted no time entering the room. Not bothering to remove his clothing he unzipped his pants and pulled out his cock as he climbed onto the bed. Straddling the girl's shoulders he stuffed his tool down her throat. Jaded could hear a deep primitive hum of satisfaction coming from Slut's throat as she applied herself to the task. This was her sole purpose.

Jaded remained at the door with his sister watching the brief performance, hoping he would get some small vicarious thrill from the role of voyeur.

"He certainly is . . . endowed, isn't he?" said Sarcasm quietly. She was careful not to do anything that would distract her brother's rutting. It would put Cynic into a bad mood, which would be no fun at all.

Jaded knew Cynic's overly small appendage was an ongoing source of irritation. That Cynic should sport such equipment was indeed an irony. There was a time when this thought would have caused him to chuckle. But he had not laughed in a long time.

"How gracious you are to offer him your leftovers," his sister suggested, "our parents would be pleased to see how you take care of him."

Jaded enjoyed his sister's company. At least when she spoke the words sounded pleasant, even if the meaning was not. Still one does not get to pick one's family.

While he was the eldest, all three of them were the bastard offspring of Truth and his occasional coupling with their mother, Futility. There were other siblings, but they rarely saw each other. Their family gatherings were not happy affairs. Truth did not care to be reminded of their existence, and so he had commissioned the noble architect Care to build each of them a dwelling place, far from his own palace. Each house had its own name. Jaded's home was called The Balances. Care, it appeared, had a sense of humor.

In the room, Cynic had become hard enough to fuck the girl. Slipping down her body he entered her and began a frantic humping. Leaning forward he grabbed onto her breasts savagely twisting her nipples. From past experience Jaded knew it would not be long until his brother was ready to climax.

"You bitch! You love it, don't you? Tell me you love it, you whore." His words were gasps, punctuated by his thrusting.

"Yes, Master. I love it. I really do."

"I knew it, you cunt. You're all the same. Tell me you want to drink my come. Tell me you want to drink it all." Cynic couldn't keep the venom from his voice.

"Oh yes, Master. Let me drink it. I love drinking come!" Slut knew how to appear sincere.

As he reached his climax he pulled out and tried to get his cock into her mouth. He had waited too long, it seemed, for he ended up splattering her face instead as he came in long gasps. He used his fingers to wipe the stuff up and had her lick them clean. There was a big smile on her face.

When he was done, he got off the bed and headed to the door.

"Don't go, Master! Please fuck me again!" She thrust her cunt up as far as she could, straining against her bonds.

"You really are a slut, girl," said Cynic closing the door behind him.

"Yes, Master. Thank you, Master. Please come back, Master!"

Rearranging his clothing, Cynic rejoined his brother and sister.

"What did I tell you, eh? They're all the same."

For the first time, a ghost of a smile lit Jaded's eyes. Cynic always said the same thing after his visits with Slut. He seemed to never tire of making the same observation. Then the smile faded. Jaded realized Cynic was completely right and that was why he no longer visited Slut himself. No matter how many ways he used her, she was always the same. And, knowing that, she lost her appeal.

His somber mood reasserted, Jaded turned and continued down Passion's Path. Slut's pleadings faded as they walked away.

After a time he stopped again. Sarcasm would be miffed if he didn't find something for her amusement. He opened another door with a tired, practiced ease to find a room with yet another girl.

Sarcasm peered over his shoulder. "Well, here's a pretty sight to make the fit of your trousers uncomfortable, brother!" she said, her eyes quickly filling with interest.

The floor was a gray slab of concrete. The walls were once

finished but now revealed bare studs, with only small spots of drywall still clinging here and there. The air was damp, redolent with the scent of mildew. Thick wooden joists ran the length of the room, running parallel until they disappeared into the darkness at the other end. Three white candles formed a triangle around the girl. She hung from chains, arms stretched above her head, wrists locked into leather cuffs. In her teeth she held a whip; a black thing with tight braids and a vicious thong at its end. Her body was a map of welts and bruises from previous beatings. It was evident she had been well punished.

She saw him and opened her mouth letting the whip drop to the floor. Her eyes were filled with defiance. She would not be conquered, she would not be controlled. She spoke just a single word, "More!" It was a challenge.

But Jaded was unmoved. Neither the whip, nor the body could capture his interest.

"Used to be a time when even the thought of a whip would arouse you, Jaded," remarked Cynic taking a quick glimpse. "It's so very, very sad when the thrill is gone, eh?"

Sarcasm didn't wait for permission or invitation. She knew he had picked this room for her. Walking into the room, she bent down and picked up the whip. Then she began to walk slowly around the girl.

"I think you and I are going to be friends, my dear. There are lessons for you to learn, and I will offer you some gentle help in learning them. Shall we begin?" Sarcasm's words were languid, overlaid with sensuality. The bound girl took a deep breath and closed her eyes. She said nothing.

"Give it to her, Sis! You know she wants it." While he did-n't like being interrupted, Cynic had no problem being a pest to others.

As the whip fell and the screaming began, Jaded turned away and continued his walk. The girl would keep his brother and sister occupied for some time, but he knew how the scene would end. The same way it always did. Her name was Submission. At some point the cries would turn to pleading and then to begging. She would end up on her knees weeping her need to serve. Sarcasm would take it, satiated and fulfilled. And Cynic, as always, would enjoy the show.

Jaded walked alone for a long time. Sometimes he would pause in front of a door, but never for very long. He knew every door and the contents of each room. They ranged from the inno-cent to the perverse. They covered the full gambit of desire, from sweet young virgins to orgies of man and beast. Passion's Path had it all. And Jaded had sampled every pleasure, every desire; he knew them all. There was nothing left to try, nothing left to amuse him. He felt a certain quiet despair as he contemplated an eternity lacking in excitement and desire.

Lost in his funk, he was unaware he had reached the end of the hallway. Facing him, blocking his path, was a new door. A door that did not hold the message, "You've been here before."

For the first time he was surprised. He had always thought the corridor had no end; that it continued forever. Intrigued, he opened the door.

Inside was a simple, comfortable room. Rich wood flooring covered carelessly with Persian carpets. The walls were also wood paneled and had the rich sheen of decades of careful waxing. The furniture was heavy-set and covered in leather. On one side of the room, embers smoldered in a fireplace. The scent of pine filled the air.

In the middle of the room, next to a small table, there was a girl. She knelt on the carpeted floor, her head bowed, wrists crossed behind her back and thighs wide open. She was not a pretty girl. He could see her weight was perhaps too high, her skin stretched in places, and somehow he knew if he lifted her chin and examined her face there would be lines that Age had inscribed, as she does to all mortals.

Other than the dark red glow from the fireplace, the room's only illumination was from a peach candle sitting on the table next to the girl. Jaded found it strange the candle should be peach. For some reason the color made him smile. Only a small smile, but even so it was a wonder to his heart. It had been a very long time since he had smiled.

Jaded walked through the quiet and sat in a chair beside the girl. She flowed from her position and prostrated herself at his feet, her cheek resting on his shoe. Her movements were a joy to watch.

"Who are you, Girl?" He felt no urgency to hear her answer. He wished to draw out the experience for as long as possible.

"Whoever you want, my Lord," her voice was a whisper, a breath of sensuality with a hint of desire. Her voice was a cleansing balm; it asked for nothing and offered everything.

"What do you want, Girl?"

"Only to please you, my Lord."

"Why? Why would you wish to please me?"

"It is who I am, Lord. It is my nature and my destiny."

138

"And if it pleases me to leave you, and never return?"

"I cannot lie, Lord, I would be saddened beyond all measure. But I would be contented knowing you would be pleased. For that is my entire wish, Lord, your pleasure."

Jaded made a small movement with his foot. She understood, for she had been well trained. She slid her head up his leg and rested it in his lap. He reached out and stroked her blond hair. Her sigh was one of complete satisfaction.

"And if it pleases me to rape your ass until it bleeds?"

"I would beg you for it, Lord, and I would thank you for the privilege of being your pleasure thing."

"And if it pleased me to whip you, covering your body in bruises?"

"I would only be grateful to be an instrument for the release of your passion, Lord."

"Even if I took your life, Girl?"

For the first time she raised her head and their eyes met. His so dark, hers the palest of blue, almost glowing. She spoke in a measured tone, "My life has always been yours, Lord. It always will be yours."

In a quiet room, at the very end of the corridor known as Passion's Path, in a house called The Balances, Jaded sat with a girl. Her name was Surrender and she was his slave. They spoke in quiet tones, of matters both trivial and weighty as the snow gently fell outside.

And perhaps, what he lost in passion, he gained in contentment. For all Truth's children, even the bastards, are allowed moments of rest from time to time.

THE REAL STORY OF STRONG JOHN AND PRETTY SUE

Bryn Haniver

"YOU LOOK A little nervous, child."

I was surprised to see Grandma in the doorway. She hadn't been by in years, I could barely remember what she looked like. Still, she had grandma clothes on—a drab, baggy cloak topped by a large hood. I could just make out her eyes glinting in the dim light of my room.

"Hi Grandma," I said, motioning her in. I didn't have the energy to get up—for some reason I'd been feeling weak and helpless as of late.

Grandma shuffled up to the bed and said "I heard you were out of sorts, dear. It often happens before a wedding."

I nodded. "Did Ma send you in to cheer me up?"

Grandma's big blue eyes flickered towards the door. "Something like that," she replied. "Perhaps a story would help."

I doubted it. Still, what could it hurt? I was nineteen, about to be married to a very handsome newcomer to our town, a boy who was strong and kind and said he loved me. So why did I feel so—blah? I was getting married before the stigma of being unwed at twenty. Why couldn't I be excited and happy, like I was supposed to be?

Grandma sat in the chair near the bed. "Well, this tale starts with a handsome young man who's name was...." She paused, her hood turning towards me.

I rolled my eyes, and said "Strong John."

"That's right dear. Strong John. And everybody knows Strong John was..."

"Tall, handsome, and honest," I chimed in.

"Indeed," she nodded. "And soon after Strong John was old enough to make his way in the world, he traveled to a nearby village and met a beautiful girl."

I sighed. "Pretty Sue."

"Precisely," Grandma said. "Pretty Sue. The most beautiful girl in the village. And when Strong John and Pretty Sue saw each other they immediately fell in love. And their parents, indeed everyone in each of their villages, couldn't have been happier, they were such a beautiful young couple."

I sighed again. This wasn't helping. Grandma's tired old voice didn't exactly make the tired old story any more exciting.

Grandma raised an eyebrow at my sigh, but continued. "And then they got married in a Big, Wonderful Wedding, and the two of them lived happily." She paused and looked at me more intently. "Ever," she continued as her eyes, burning from the dark hood, locked onto mine. "After."

My skin prickled. I didn't remember Grandma's eyes being so large, blue, and intense. I wondered if her face was all wrinkly underneath that hood. Still, this was silly.

"Grandma I know that story. Everybody knows that story. You didn't even tell it that well. You left out the details of the Wonderful Wedding, you left out their First Sweet Kiss..."

Grandma leaned back and shrugged. "Pish posh," she said. "You've heard all that before. Hell, you're about to live it, for better or for worse." She stood up. "The Story of Strong John and Pretty Sue. Everybody tells it. Sometimes it's even true."

Suddenly she leaned in close to me, her cloaked head all I could see. "But most times," she whispered, "the Shades are part of the story. Even if the village elders don't want them to be. Even if they forbid talking about them. Have you heard of the Shades, child?"

Transfixed by her sibilant whisper and an earthy, sensual, decidedly ungrandma like smell, I could barely shake my head.

She stood up. "Well perhaps you should," she said, her voice softer, lower, more firm than before. "You're a smart girl. You show some promise," she continued, more to herself than me. She moved towards the door, not shuffling this time, much more graceful. She glanced out into the hallway. She closed the door. She locked it.

I sat up straight in bed. "Uh, Grandma?" Somewhere in that dark hood I could see teeth gleaming in a smile.

"You look a little nervous, child."

I nodded as she moved towards the bed. She cinched her waist strap a bit, making her robe less cumbersome. It allowed her to move more easily, and set off some decidedly ungrandma-like curves. This time she sat on the bed.

"Much to the dismay of Righteous Villagers Societies every-where," Grandma said, "Strong John and Pretty Sue don't always meet up right after he makes his way in the world. Sometimes, perhaps in the forest between villages, or along a lonely stretch of ocean cliffs, Strong John encounters one of the Shades."

I shivered, and Grandma affectionately tucked the com-forter up to my neck. "Would you like to hear such a story, child? A real story?"

I nodded.

"Wonderful. This is the story of Strong John and Pliant Shade."

TWO DAYS AFTER Strong John set out to make his way in the world, he was walking along a lonely stretch of coastline when he came across a small cottage. The humble building was set at the very edge of the cliffs, and John could hear the surf thundering below. As he was hungry and tired, John decided to knock and see if the owner would let him rest for the night.

He gave the heavy oak door a firm, confident knock, and it soon opened to reveal a beautiful young woman. "Good evening, kind woman," said Strong John. "My name is John and I'd sorely appreciate a place to shelter tonight. Where is your husband?"

She looked at him with large, misty green eyes. "I have no husband," she replied. "I live here in my humble cottage, alone. My name is Pliant Shade."

John didn't know quite what to make of it. In his village, young women did not live alone. They didn't go out alone, and they rarely even stayed in alone. Young women pretty much always had a husband or chaperone with them. Pliant Shade was very beautiful, a petite lass with a generous tangle of curly red hair that framed her pale, near perfect features. Beautiful, and clearly old enough to be married.

"Well, I, g-guess, uh..." John stammered, suddenly out of his element, for once unsure of what to say or do. How could he ask to stay overnight at the cottage now?

"But do come in, Sir," Pliant said, "for it is starting to rain." She took his large, strong hand with her own, tiny, pale one, and in he went.

"BUT GRANDMA," I INTERRUPTED, slightly confused. "In addition to being tall, handsome, and honest, Strong John always knows what to do. I've never heard a story where he stammered!"

Grandma raised an eyebrow at me, or at least I think she did—I still couldn't really see much of her face in that hood. It was cool in the room, but I really didn't think she needed to leave it on.

"You'll find, dear child, that the standard story of Strong John and Pretty Sue doesn't entirely prepare you for what you might encounter when you make your own way in the world. Many a Strong John finds himself at a loss after leaving the familiar surroundings of his village. Now keep quiet and listen."

INSIDE THE COTTAGE, Pliant was a very gracious hostess. She removed John's damp cloak, she got him seated in a large, somewhat stiff-backed chair, and she put on some tea. As she was leaning forward to hand him the tea, John couldn't help but notice how tight her bodice was, and how the creamy globes beneath seemed to surge upwards out of it.

As he took the tea from her hand, the splendid sight made him surge upwards. His hand twitched and a bit of tea spilled onto his leg. Strong John began turning a pink color, but was saved from further embarrassment when Pliant Shade gushed apologies and quickly walked towards the back of the house.

She emerged shortly after wearing only the bodice. Her legs were bare. Her smooth, round ass was bare. Her stomach and navel were bare, with the white bodice still laced tight across her chest. Strong John, too amazed to speak, finally noticed that the area between her legs was also bare, or rather covered only by a red patch of hair. It was the first time our hero had ever seen...

"GRANDMA! WHAT KIND of story is this?" I pulled the blanket down a bit, warmer now. But Grandma, whose storytelling voice had become silky smooth, just gave me a shut up and listen glare. So I did...

JOHN WAS GLUED to the chair, the tea forgotten. Pliant walked across the room, knelt in front of him, and then lay across his knees. Her breasts were mashed against his left thigh, and her bare ass was upturned over his right.

"Spank me," she whispered. "I shouldn't have spilled the tea."

Although out of his element now by a long ways, Strong John hesitated only for a second before bringing his large hand down. The smack was loud and left a red mark on her bare skin. The cry she made, which was not a cry of pain, not at all, made John throb.

"More. Please," Pliant whispered. So Strong John kept spanking her upturned ass, and she kept squirming against his legs. After a while she began to cry out and shudder and reach for him, freeing him from his strained britches, jerking him as she came. Strong John shot his tremendously large going-out-into-the-world load all over her back, the both of them grunting and gasping like animals.

Shortly thereafter, she took him down into her basement. As the humble cottage was set high up on a cliff, there was plenty of space for a basement and Pliant Shade had made good use of it. The earthy rooms below contained a lot of leather, numerous shackles, and a remarkable assortment of ways to tie up a beautiful young woman. Strong John did not continue making his way into the rest of the world for quite some time.

I NOTICED, NOW that the story was over, that I was no longer feeling blah. Nor was I happy—this was something different, something like the feeling I'd get when I looked down the path that meandered away from our village. I'd never taken more than three steps down that path.

"Well dear? Did you like the story?"

"Yes Grandma. But I feel a bit strange."

"Good," she replied. "You know, it isn't always Strong John that gets distracted by the world's complexities. Pretty Sue doesn't always wait patiently in her house. Sometimes she wanders the world a bit, and sometimes she comes across a Shade." Grandma smiled. "Would you like to hear such a story, child?"

I nodded. Eagerly.

"Wonderful. This is the story of Pretty Sue and Peg Shade."

*

ONE DAY IN the village, Pretty Sue, who had been old enough to make her way in the world for a couple years, got a bit bored with waiting for her Strong John to arrive and sweep her off her feet. So against the advice of her family and friends, she ventured out into the forest.

"What's the harm, really?" she said as she skipped along a path, her lovely white dress trailing behind her. The trees had no immediate answer, but Pretty Sue stopped abruptly at the sound of hoof beats.

A rider astride an imposing horse came to a halt on the trail ahead of her. "What ho," said a delightful voice. "What's a lovely maiden such as yourself doing alone in the woods? Are you lost?"

Pretty Sue looked up at the most beautiful man she had ever seen. Long blond hair framed features so fine they were almost delicate, and his eyelashes were thick enough to set any woman's heart aflutter.

"N-no, I'm not quite lost," she replied. "I'm just out for a walk. My name is Pretty Sue."

With a smile that took her breath away, he replied "And pretty you are indeed, my Lady." He dismounted with a graceful flourish, and was suddenly right in front of her. Pretty Sue melted into his large, soft eyes.

"My name is Peg Shade," he said, which jolted her out of her reverie.

"Peg? That's an odd name for a gentleman," she replied.

He kissed her. Right on the mouth, with lips as full and soft as her own. Before she could melt daintily against his chest he had her dress down to her waist and was licking her nipples.

Pretty Sue, unused to such attentions to say the least, began moaning with pleasure and pulling at his tunic. In what seemed like mere seconds they were both completely naked in a small clearing next to the trail. Sue found herself lying on her back in the soft grass while this strange but beautiful man's tongue worked wonders between her open legs.

"Please," he said, rising up. "Would you kneel for me?" Pretty Sue could clearly see his throbbing manhood, and had a pretty good idea what he'd do with it were she to kneel in front of him. Nonetheless, she got onto her hands and knees in the soft grass, letting out a cry as he slid into her from behind. Gentle at first with her delicate maidenhood, his thrusts soon became deep and true. Bucking back against his lean body, Pretty Sue's first orgasm filled the clearing with her sweet cries and musky fragrance.

After taking a moment to catch her breath, she said "Truly that was the most wonderful feeling in the entire world. At last, I have met my Strong John. Er, Strong Peg I mean."

"Well..." said Peg.

Aghast, Pretty Sue turned to look at her new lover. "Well? What do you mean well? What's the matter?" She couldn't help but notice he was still rigid. Hadn't he come at all?

Instead of replying, he stood and walked over to his horse, which had been munching grass contentedly in a corner of the meadow while the two of them were frolicking. Still completely naked and breathtakingly beautiful, Peg dug into a saddlebag and came back with something that looked like a small harness, and another item that looked like... good gracious, thought Pretty Sue, it looks just like his erect penis!

"WHOOA, GRANDMA." I was a bit confused, and if the truth was to be told, a little overheated. As this story had progressed my body had warmed considerably, and I'd pulled the covers down to my waist. Finally I kicked them off completely, not caring that my underclothes were thin silk and now a bit damp and clingy. I couldn't help but think what it would be like to kneel naked in a meadow and let a handsome stranger thrust into me from behind...

"Yes dear?" Grandma asked. "You look a bit flushed." As she said it those gleaming blue eyes roamed down my mostly exposed body.

"Well, how could a man be carrying his own penis?" My face felt red.

"It's a facsimile dear—aren't you just so delightfully naïve?" She continued to talk as she rummaged in her cloak. "You see some people make artificial phalluses out of wood, or other materials. Some of them are very realistic, some stylized— it's something of an art form, really. Though they do have their practical uses as well."

Then she handed me something. I gasped as my fingers closed around it—Grandma wasn't kidding. The wood was smooth, dark, perfectly polished. Though the lines were styl- ized, there was no mistaking the shape, which of course I'd seen in village animals and two mostly inadvertent glimpses of naked men.

"What's it—for?" I whispered.

Grandma winked. "There are a surprising number of creative uses child, but why don't you just hang onto it for now while I finish the story?"

Running my fingers along the smooth sides, I mumbled "Yes Grandma."

"BUT WHAT ONE earth are we going to do with that?" Pretty Sue asked.

Instead of answering, Peg Shade asked her "Did you like being on your hands and knees?" Pretty Sue nodded. "And did you like the way it felt when slid this," he motioned down to his still erect penis, "deep into you?"

Sue nodded again, as just the thought of it was making her feel juicy.

"Well," said Peg, with a sly grin. "I like that too."

Pretty Sue didn't get it. He handed her the phallus and she held it, caressed it, but still she didn't get it. Peg took her hand and lifted her to her feet, his body lithe but strong. He knelt in front of her and attached the harness, which fit snug around her hips and ass. And then to her amazement, he attached the wooden phallus to a specially constructed ring on the front of the harness.

Staring down at herself, her wood pointing straight forward, she finally got it when Peg took the phallus into his mouth. The sight of his full lips leaving slippery trails while his large eyelashes flickered up at her was somewhat overwhelming for poor Sue. Soaked, she reached down, grabbed the phallus by the shaft and rubbed the wide base against herself.

When it was completely covered in his saliva and her juices,

Peg turned and got down on his hands and knees in front of her. When he looked back over his shoulder, his eyes seemed so eager there was no way Sue could resist. She knelt behind him, grabbing his firm buttocks to steady herself. There was only one place for her wood to go, and his hand came around to guide it in. At first, she was too overwhelmed to even push, but the grunt of lust he made as the polished and slick phallus sunk into him made her legs quiver.

Pretty Sue grabbed Peg Shade's long blond hair and proceeded to fuck him. She was gentle at first, but her thrusts soon became deep and true. The dominant position she was in made her wild—soon she was squeezing his hips and pounding into him with adrenalin-fueled lust. Finally, she reached around to pump his twitching manhood, never stopping her frantic thrusting until he spurted all over the meadow and collapsed on the grass beneath her. Pulling herself out, she screamed her new-found passion and power into the clear blue sky above.

"DO YOU NEED some help with that, dear?" Grandma asked. Caught up in the heat of the story, I had barely noticed her slide the sweaty silk off my breasts and begin pinching my throbbing nipples. The phallus was between my legs and I was rubbing it against myself as if I had the worst itch in the world.

"You're not really my Grandma, are you?" I whispered.

The smile in that cloak was huge and her eyes sparkled as she shook her head.

"So why did you tell me those stories?"

Her fingers stopped, making my nipples ache for them. "Most folks think the Shades are evil," she said, her voice harder now. "That's why the village elders won't let anyone tell any stories but Strong John meeting Pretty Sue. Over and over, the same story. So young men and women like you dodge the Shades by marrying too young or remaining overprotected. But often, instead of living happily ever after, Shades come to haunt your hasty marriages..."

The itch between my legs was becoming unbearable. "Who are you, really?" I asked.

She pulled the hood back, revealing a woman of striking beauty, perhaps ten or twenty years older than me. Those intense blue eyes and gleaming white teeth were framed by a lovely, mischievous face. Then she opened her cloak, and I gasped.

Her body was strong; well tanned with firm breasts and not so subtle muscles under her smooth skin. She looked nothing like any of the village women I'd ever seen—we were rarely allowed outside, and pale and soft as a result. I'd always been taught that paler and softer meant more beautiful, but this woman took my breath away.

"I'm Saffa Shade," she whispered, taking the phallus from my fingers. "And I can help you with that itch you're feeling."

And so begins the story of Pretty Jen and Saffa Shade, which involves young Jen's first, second, and third orgasms as well as some surprisingly athletic activities on the bedside chair. But let's leave that one for another time, shall we? After all, there's a Big, Wonderful Wedding to prepare for tomorrow.

Isn't there?

THE PIPE OF THORNS ⦾ *Remittance Girl*

ONCE UPON A TIME there was a young man who was handsome and charming and engaged the imagination of all those around him. Like many young men, he was also fickle and faithless and bestowed his attentions too liberally. He would regularly tempt young ladies of quality into indiscretions, always whispering promises of undying devotion as he relieved them of their clothes, their shame, and then their virtue.

In truth, no one blamed Gerald, for it is the nature of youth to spread its seed as far and wide as the landscape will allow. He was young and rich, with a golden-tipped tongue. Even the young women who fell beneath his spell and were left adrift and weeping in his wake could not really stay angry at him for long. For must be admitted, he gave as much pleasure as he took.

Although his mother berated him with accusations of heartless-
ness and threatened him with the specter of social scandal, his
father winked at his lusty son and daydreamed nostalgically of
his own fancy-free youth.

As the years went by and Gerald grew older, many women
attempted to ensnare him; ladies feigned that they were with
child, or truly believed themselves to be. Others cried that their
health could not bear the strain of his departure. Still others
thought themselves driven mad for want of his affections.

Through those years, Gerald did indeed become fond of
some of the women he dallied with. There was Lucretia, with
her fine black hair and laughing eyes, who rode him for sport
like a stallion. Bettina, rounded and luxurious, whose gorgeous
mouth felt at once like a deep feather bed and a hot pool of
molten rock. There were many, many whom he cared for. And as
he matured, he began to feel the burden of the call that pulled
him from one pair of arms and into the embrace of another.

One day, while taking his morning ride in the park, Gerald
fell into conversation with Bertram, a friend with whom he
sometimes played at cards. Now Bertram was himself something
of a self-confessed philander, and the two had enjoyed many
evenings out on the town, wooing ladies of stature at supper parties or descending into the darker, more forbidden places, where
women were to be had for two shillings an hour.

"Gerald, old chap, if your evening is free, why don't you
come along with me to Limehouse? I've heard there are places
there were a man can lose more than just his money," Bertram
said with a nefarious grin.

"I don't know," Gerald sighed, "those poor Chinese women look so glum and bedraggled. And they have lice! No, I think perhaps I'll give it a miss, old chum."

"You mistake my meaning, dear boy! We won't be going for the women. It's the opium that is the true entertainment."

Gerald had heard about opium, the blood of the weeping poppy said to bring marvelous dreams and visions as a man lay smoking. This, far more than the brothels, piqued his interest and he agreed to meet Bertram at eight-thirty.

The evening was cold and foggy. Gerald met Bertram and they proceeded eastward by hackney cab. After a lengthy drive, the carriage drew up in front of an old church. Across the street stood a decrepit warehouse. The stench of the river was almost insufferable and gaslight bathed the filthy street and turned the fog luminous in the most sinister of ways. Gerald shivered and pulled his collar up around his neck, but Bertram tipped his hat and set upon the door of the building, hammering at it with the head of his walking stick. At first there was no sign of life inside, and two slatterns ambled by offering their wares and giggling.

The eldest and the uglier of the two spoke. "Ya won't be wantin' whot they've got on offer there, gentlemen. That stuff'll make you useless to any woman. It's the bane of our trade, that filthy stuff is!"

But before either Gerald or Bertram could respond, the door of the warehouse creaked open. Heavy smoke, sickly sweet and acrid, billowed out to join the fog in the street and through it stepped a small, meaty-looking Chinese, who glanced nervously up and down the street and then gestured for them to enter inside.

What seemed at first to be a warehouse was instead a doss house. Row upon row of wooden bunks held the dark nestled lumps of human forms. As they followed the doorkeeper down a mazelike path, here and there a prone shape would groan or cough or rise from it's pallet like some dead creature coming back to life. If the smell on the street had been foul, it was beyond description in the overcrowded press of the room. They were led through a door and Gerald was shocked to find he had stepped not as he expected, into some lower level of hell, but into the confines of a very pleasantly appointed salon.

A well-dressed woman of some thirty years rose from her place by a cozy fire and approached them graciously. She was the most exotic looking creature Gerald had ever seen. Coils of coal-black hair were intricately looped and draped about her head and cascaded down a creamy neck, settling pretty on a generous and smooth-skinned bosom. Her eyes were oriental, but the color was astonishing. Irises like cornflowers and the largest, blackest pupils he'd ever seen.

"Welcome gentlemen! Such an unpleasant night to be out and about. I hope that we can afford you some amusement here, and make your journey worthwhile."

The delicate hand that Gerald took and held as he spoke felt like something made of fine, unglazed porcelain. He asked her name.

"We have no names here, Sir, for the adventures we begin from here might take us anywhere, and make us anyone, but for the sake of expediency, you may call me Mai."

"You are most charming, Mai. I do hope you will be patient with us." Gerald smiled his most seductive smile at the stunning woman before him. "We are uninitiated to adventures you refer to."

Mai returned his smile. "I see. Well, Gentlemen. If you would follow me I shall act as your guide, if you will allow me, on this first journey.""

She led them through a set of carved doors and into a dimly lit room beyond. This room was far more Eastern in decoration. Low, velvet couches lined walls hung with silk tapestries. Upon them scenes of craggy mountain peaks and rampant dragons, mists and lonely trees, long Lisas gathered beneath peaked gables, all the images set tinder to Gerald's imagination. Above them hung lanterns with painted glass windows, splaying soft and varicolored lights about the room.

Mai clapped her hands softly and, from behind a tapestry on the far wall, two silk-sheathed eastern nymphs minced forth on tiny feet and led each man to his own couch, urging them to lie upon them.

"Li and Ping, prepare the pipes, please."

Gerald stretched out on the divan, feeling awkward to be recumbent in the presence of a lady standing. For, although their hostess was certainly no gentleman's daughter, still he felt himself to be in the presence of someone who deserved his politeness and respect.

Mai stepped delicately to a low table supporting two bronze lions in the Chinese style and put the flame from a small oil burner to three slender sticks of incense. Then, when the sticks were sending up hair-like tendrils of sweet-smelling smoke, she took up a small metal rod and struck it against the body of one of the lions. It chimed sweetly. Mai began to chant something in a language Gerald didn't recognize. He watched all this with fascination and, when the woman fell silent, he asked her what she had been doing.

"I'm begging the Gods to bless you with a good journey," she said solemnly.

He was beginning to think that this was by far the most amusing evening he and Bertram had ever shared. He noticed his friend was distracted watching the two imps in the corner as they gathered sundry objects onto raised trays and came back bearing them with grace.

"If you please, Sir, I would ask you to allow Ping and Li to prepare your pipe for you and attend to your needs," Mai said to Bertram, who was trailing an idle finger down Ping's silken thigh.

Gerald could tell from his friend''s visage that the proposal pleased him very much indeed. Even more gratifying still, he understood that this meant he would have Mai's attentions all to himself. He watched Mai bend to pick up the second tray and bring it over to him. He could not see the feet beneath her evening dress and it seemed to him that she did not walk, but floated towards him instead.

Before his divan, she lowered herself onto a rich oriental rug and set the implements beside her kneeling form. Now he had occasion to look at the objects on the tray, the most remarkable of which was a long, slender bamboo pipe with a round, covered bowl at one end. Beside it was a shallow black dish containing what looked like black marbles, a tiny, lit burner, and a thin metal needle of some length.

"Now Sir, shall I amuse you by telling you your future

while I prepare your pipe?" she asked. She took the needle and pierced one of the black spheres and began to play it back and forth over the open flame of the burner.

"Oh, by all means," replied Gerald, amused.

"You will take a long journey..."

A thick pungent smoke began to rise from the skewered sphere. Mai transferred it to the pipe and held it out for Gerald to take. He made to rise from his recumbent position to receive it, but she indicated that he should remain lying down. He guided the pipe's mouthpiece to his lips.

"And you will meet a mysterious raven-haired woman..."

She held the end of the long pipe so that it sat above the flame of the burner and inhaled deeply, her breasts rising most attractively in her elegant bodice, encouraging him to follow her example. He drew hard on the pipe.

"And your life will be changed forever."

A thick, choking smoke billowed into the depths of his lungs causing him to pull the pipe from his lips and expel it in a fit of coughing.

"Yes, the first inhalation is something of a shock. The next will be easier to take. Pull the smoke down into your chest and hold it inside for as long as you can." She smiled, assuring him. Her eyes fluttered and slid half-shut. "Be assured, once you have the knack of it, you will not remember how you ever found it unpleasant."

Gerald nodded and took another deep pull. She was not lying; this time the smoke slid velvet-like to the bottom of his lungs and, although he had the desire to cough again, he fought it and held the vapor in. It seemed the smoke lay coiled in his chest for a while and then floated upwards inside his body until it filled his eyes with tears. He expelled it in a sinuous stream.

"Again..." Mai urged. And again he drew the poppy vapors. A feeling of utter warmth and peace drew itself up his body like the softest coverlet. He gazed, heavy-lidded at the woman in front of him as she turned the pipe around and puffed on it herself. After several bowls of opium, Gerald closed his eyes.

He felt time drift sideways like a heavy-laden vessel floating downstream. The sound of his own breathing; the hissing of the opium resin as it bubbled, viscose in the pipe, a slow, low drum beating inexorably in his ears, everything was before him; everything was within his grasp. All the joys and travails of the world seemed as nothing to Gerald now, mere inconsequences in the landscape of his existence.

Images, memories, songs came whirling up, lending each other meaning. The faces of women he'd been with, the taste of them, the timbre of voices raised in laughter or hoarse with ecstasy, the warm wealth of their bodies and the redolent scents of their pleasure. The memories of each of them filled him with pathos. The arch of one's back, the tender shudder of another's coming, and hunger.... what boundless hunger for something more than what they had made together. Slowly the hunger became a dragon, flying through dark skies, sweeping down to devour naked women as they lay, unaccountably, on beds in the middle of a huge poppy field. He was the dragon and his hunger knew no bounds.

In the midst of these dreams, Gerald felt warmth against his cheek and grudgingly opened his eyes. Mai's face rested near his, perched beautifully upon a white arm. Gerald perceived a distinct glow about her head, deep gold like a halo. He reached out lazily and pulled her head close to his, until their lips met, and he felt a molten river flow between them where their skin touched.

Her eyelids fluttered half-open and he felt her smile against him. Without breaking contact, she moved onto the divan beside him and stretched out along his body. At every point they touched, even through the damnable layers of her gown, Gerald felt a storm of passion, every inch of his skin had an appetite of its own. It was a strange hunger that built, a lazy dragon's hunger, as he kissed her lips somnolently, tasting the bitter taint of opium on them and idly he regretted that, between his legs, his cock had not stirred at all.

Gerald tasted every part of her face, her neck, the broad expanse of her chest. He longed to taste the rest of her, but somehow, he could not summon the energy to undress her. And she responded in a similar fashion, plucking motes of his skin between her lips, nuzzling his cheek and neck, threading and rethreading her fingers through his hair.

Then, by stages, oblivion.

When he awoke, only Li and Ping were there. They offered him tea and informed him that Miss Mai had retired, and his friend had left.

GERALD RETURNED AGAIN and again to the opium den in Limehouse. Each time, Mai was gracious and each time she saw to his pipe personally. But every time he awoke, she was gone. One night, just as he was about to smoke the pipe, he changed his mind and refused it.

"I want to make love to you. Awake. Without the opium," he said.

Mai settled the rejected pipe back onto the tray and looked at him impassively.

"Please," Gerald pleaded. "I will pay you…whatever you ask."

She cocked her head and smiled. "I am not a prostitute."

"I must have you, all of you, just for one night."

It seemed to Gerald that Mai considered his request for a moment. Finally she rose and held out her hand. "Very well, if it means so much to you," she said laughingly, as if he was asking for something of far lesser value than what she had already given him.

Never had a woman agreed to his attentions so lightly. It shocked him, and yet it stopped him not a moment. He rose from the divan and, taking her hand, allowed her to lead him past the tapestry that covered a passageway at the end of the room.

What she led him to was a plain, clean room with a bed, a wash basin and an oil lamp that gave off a soft glow. She bade him sit on the bed and stood before him undressing. The layers of clothing fell away into multicolored puddles at her feet. He watched entranced and mute as she disposed of her dress, her petticoats, her corset, and beneath it, a thin cotton shift that she pulled over her head.

There was no shame in her and no guile either. She allowed him to take in all the lines of her nakedness, from the plump globes of her breasts, the dusty nipples, the long slender line of her belly to the dark nest of hair at the top of her thighs. Then slowly she turned, and he sighed at the glorious bow of her back. At the base of her spine, just above her buttocks, Gerald saw a dark stain like a birthmark. He reached out to touch it and heard her laugh. She stepped backward, toward him and into the light. It was a black dragon, a tattoo.

Gerald slid his hands over the softness of her bottom, pulling her closer to him by the hips. He lowered his head and pressed his lips to the dark, tangled picture etched into her skin. She moaned then and arched her back, and was in motion.

Mai turned to face him, pushing him backward onto the bed. She crawled over him like a child, tugging off his jacket, fumbling with the buttons on his vest. Clawing and ripping at his shirt and his trousers, she was frenzied in her movements.

She was like no other woman he had ever been with; she didn't simper or giggle or blush. And, although he would have liked to believe it was he who had seduced her, it would have been untrue. Her desire matched his in every way. Once he was fully unclothed she set upon him like a beast. He reached out for handfuls of her as she moved over him, kissing him here and there and everywhere. When she reached his cock, blood-engorged and pointing towards the heavens, she took it into her mouth, laving it with her tongue, sucking.

Gerald thought he'd died. For a moment he lay upon his back, paralyzed with the pleasures offered by her attentions. Then, hungrily, he pulled her body around until she loomed above him, the wet hairs of her cunt glinting in the lamplight. At first he planted delicate kisses upwards, hesitant to offend her. Few women, in his experience, were amenable to this sort of activity. Mai was different. His first hesitant forays were superceded as she lowered herself onto his mouth, shuddering as he stroked her inner lips with his tongue.

Taking hold of her hips, he pulled her down onto him

firmly and pressed his tongue up into her passage. She stopped her energetic attentions to his cock and groaned. Her hips rolled, her thighs shivered and, after her initial pause, she again took his cock deep into her mouth and fed. Several minutes later, she rose up off him and held herself stiff for a moment before letting out a plaintive cry and collapsing onto him in a series of beautiful convulsions. Her liquids spilled out of her, covering his face. She tasted like opium . . . sweet and dark.

Now Gerald could no longer hold himself back. He turned her onto her stomach, and lifted her hips to meet his throbbing, weeping cock. Entering her was exquisite, her passage fiery hot around him as he forged into her. It was then she turned her head to look back at him. Her lips parted, wet and red, her eyes cerulean and dilated, and what hunger . . . what hunger.

She met him thrust for thrust as he fucked her, spreading her legs wide to take him in as deep as he would go. Gerald slowed his pace, to bring her again before he finished, and she made a low, rumbling noise that came from deep in her throat. She was his animal or perhaps he was hers. For within a few strokes, she wriggled away from him and turned around, pressing him back onto the mattress and climbing astride his hips.

As she lowered herself to engulf him, Gerald realized that he had dreamed this many times while drifting on clouds of opium: the vision of her taking him in like this, impaling herself upon his cock over and over, the sweetest of self-made wounds. He pushed his hips up to meet her, and each time, it set her breasts trembling. He reached to touch them as she rode him. He squeezed and rolled them, finally taking her nipples between his fingers and pinching them hard. She whimpered and rode him harder still. Finally, he could not wait any longer, he sat up, buried his head between her breasts and grabbed her hips, goring into the depths of her body as he erupted. Mai wailed and wrapped her arms about his head; the hot flush of his come had brought her to her own little death.

For a long while afterward, she did not move and did not release him, as if she could not bear to feel herself emptied. Then they lay side by side and, as drowsy as Gerald was, he could not stop touching her in all the places he'd dreamed so long of touching.

Suddenly a terrifying thought came over him. He could not imagine himself with anyone but her, he didn't want to be without her, and yet he knew himself too well. His own hunger would lie dormant for perhaps a week or two and begin to gnaw at him. He would proclaim his love to her and, at that moment, he would mean it with all his heart. But slowly the bit would chafe, and as much as he cared for her, he'd be off looking for someone new. Not this time. Not this time, he swore to himself. His muscles seized with his own resolve.

"What is it that worries you?" Mai asked.

Gerald considered lying as he always had, but this time it would be different, he insisted to himself. He stiffened his resolve and began to tell her everything. His faithlessness, his inability to be happy with one woman, his insatiable drive to delve into new flesh, and just the telling of it made him miserable.

"I don't want to be like that anymore," he said. "I don't want to be with another woman, ever again and yet I don't know how to stop myself." As he said the words, he was struck by how deeply he meant them. The knot in his throat grew, making his voice tremble. Tears pricked at the corner of his eyes. "I never want to do this, ever again, with anyone else," he sobbed. "Only you. Only you, Mai."

He reached for her and pulled her snug against him and buried his face in her silken black hair. Then he cried like a baby. For shame, for want, for all the things he could not have.

"Is this truly what you want?" She pulled her face towards his and looked at him with great concern. "Truly? Will it make you happy?"

"Yes. It's truly what I want. The only thing I desire."

Gerald fell asleep, Mai's head on his chest, with his arms around her warm form.

When he awoke, it was to the sound of a door creaking open. He looked up drowsily and saw Mai, clutching a robe around her body. She smiled and walked towards him. It was only then that he saw she was not alone. The short, stocky coolie followed her into the room and stood at the foot of the bed. Gerald had never noticed before how old the man was. His thick, solid body belied his age, but looking into his face by the light of the lamp, Gerald could see that he was quite ancient. In his hands he carried a covered cup.

"Gerald," said Mai, sitting on the bed next to his prone body. "Are absolutely sure that what you told me is what you really desire?"

Gerald sat up and took her hand in his. "Of course it's what I want. More than anything."

She looked at him again, her eyes demanding the truth. "You are absolutely certain?"

"Completely."

Mai turned and took the little covered cup from the old coolie. She spoke to him in a respectful tone and he answered her, not as a servant, but with authority. Gerald could not understand what was said. They were speaking in what he assumed was Chinese.

She turned back to Gerald and offered him the cup. "Then drink this and you will have what you want."

For a moment, he hesitated and wondered if this wasn't some kind of foreign poison. Lifting the little lid, he inhaled the steam rising from the liquid in the cup. It smelled sweet and green like flowers.

"What is it?"

Mai smiled at him and his heart flushed with emotion. "It's tea, an ancient recipe."

"What is it made of?" asked Gerald.

"Roses. A rare and special rose."

Gerald raised the cup to his lips and let a little of the warm liquid trickle over his tongue. Rose-that was exactly what it tasted like, rose petals . . . and something else. He tilted the cup and drank the tea down in one draft and waited to see if he felt anything—any dizziness or unsettledness—but he felt nothing at all, only sleepy and warm.

Mai returned the empty cup to the coolie and accompanied him to the door, listening and nodding to the old man's foreign words. Then she closed the door, and came back to the bed, allowing the silk robe to slide off her bare skin. She climbed into bed, nestling against him. Gerald sighed contentedly and slipped into a deep and dreamless sleep.

In the morning, he awoke to her movement in the bed next

to him. He smiled to himself and pulled her tight against him. Gerald felt the first stirrings of lust as he pressed against the warmth of her bare skin. Brushing her hair off her sleeping face, he kissed her cheek, and then her nose, and then her lips. They moved into a smile and she returned his affection. His fingers traced a line along her body, from her smooth shoulder to the concave sweep of her waist and the peak of her hip. She stirred and mewed drowsily, pressing back against his cupped body. Gerald gazed a path to the silken triangle between her legs and gently eased his fingers through the curls, feeling the wonderful promise of her moistness as he parted her nether lips. Mai moaned, and opened her thighs to his touch. He obliged her by sliding his fingers into her cleft. She was so wet...so utterly ready for him.

Between his own legs, he felt his cock become turgid against his thigh and, for a few moments, he applied himself to stroking the wet folds of her cunt. But soon he began to feel a distinct itching in his own groin and the itching became quite maddening. He left off his attentions to Mai and pushed his hand between his own legs, intent on quieting the discomfort he felt there.

As his hand encircled his cock, he felt a cruel, sharp pain in the palm of his hand, as if he'd been cut or bitten. Immediately he pulled his hand from beneath the covers and looked. There was a small, deep cut in the center of his palm. Droplets of blood welled and ran down the lines of his hand and onto his wrist. Fear seized him and frantically he pushed back the bedclothes and surveyed his own naked form.

Nestled between his thighs lay his softening manhood,

studded with sharp, dark barbs. At first he thought he had been pieced by them and gingerly he explored each node. But the spines weren't angled inward, they weren't piercing his skin; all along the shaft of his penis, they grew outwards like thorns on the thick stem of a rose.

Mai stretched and rolled over to look at him. "Let's smoke," she whispered.

FENCES

or The Story Of Prince Rupert The Not-Particularly-Handsome   *Kate Dominic*

ONCE UPON A TIME in a land over the hill and far away, there lived a not-particularly-handsome prince named Rupert Fencer (pronounced Fon-SAY"). Fencer was his mother's family name rather than his father's (for reasons I will tell you later). Suffice it for now to say that Prince Rupert's parents both loved him dearly and were proud and honored that he was their only child and heir and would someday be the king.

Prince Rupert was tall and strong with a ready grin and twinkling brown eyes that sometimes disguised his exceptionally quick mind. He had long, straight red hair that was so thick and glossy it could be styled into nothing less drastic than a ponytail held back with a tough leather thong. His face was dusted with freckles and his nose burned easily in the sun. He also had an exceptionally long tongue, which he'd used when he was younger to clean his face up to his cheekbones when he'd been eating his favorite dish of barbequed spare ribs and corn on the cob. (This was a habit that gave his parents and tutors and even the king's royal advisors the vapors. They were all quite grateful when he started using his napkin, which was, as everyone knows, what all mannerly people should do, at least in public.)

As Prince Rupert grew older and his tastes expanded, his face was still sometimes covered. But now the covering was reddish gold stubble that grew thick and bushy on the rare days when Prince Rupert could get away with excusing the royal barber (at which times he always respected the polite requests by his beloved royal parents to not make public appearances when he looked so pronouncedly not regal).

Prince Rupert rarely excused the barber, however, because Prince Rupert rarely took days off. He was the crown prince after all, and although he was already twenty, he felt he still had much to learn before he would be ready to succeed his father as ruler of the kingdom of Aze. The people of Aze were mostly farmers and artisans and merchants who took their work seriously. By and large, they insisted on entering only trades they enjoyed and in which they felt fulfilled. But they worked long and hard to make the kingdom beautiful and comfortable—and to create sufficient inventory for the lucrative markets at home and abroad that sold the handcrafts for which the kingdom of Aze was famous.

There was little time for vacation, and Prince Rupert was rarely ill. Although many in the fabulously wealthy family from which his beautiful queenly mother came were prone to the vapors (the vapors being a very common affliction back then),

Prince Rupert was healthy as a horse and possessed of muscles usually found only on blacksmiths or those in the king's royal infantry after an exceptionally long campaign march. This was a good thing, because when his royal tasks were done, Prince Rupert was fond of training and especially wrestling with the members of the king's royal infantry—and the king's royal guards and the king's royal horse trainers and pretty much everyone from the king's royal food tasters to the king's royal seamstresses. His strong shoulders, easy laugh, and propensity not to gloat when he won at gambling (which he almost always did) endeared him to his compatriots and in general to the ordinary people of the kingdom of Aze as well.

He was also much loved by his friends for his penchant to masturbate often and loudly with them. This was an acceptable social practice for adults in the kingdom of Aze, though of course people were expected to discreetly retreat to private quarters to so indulge. What gave Prince Rupert's tutors the vapors was that Prince Rupert considered the rooms in which he and his friends took their instruction to be private quarters. Whenever the lessons strayed from accounting and history, those being Prince Rupert's favorite subjects, the bored young prince would lean back in his chair, close his eyes, and slide his hand down the front of his pants. As the tutor droned on about protocol and precedent and tradition, Prince Rupert would sit there with a satisfied smile on his flushed face and stroke his princely penis until he jerked and grunted and princely semen covered his princely hand and the front of his princely pants. This always brought the tutor (and the lesson) to an abrupt halt, not that any of the rest of his compatriots were listening anyway by then, because when the prince was masturbating, his friends (and sometimes, even his tutors) felt it only polite to join him.

The fact that Prince Rupert masturbated with commoners horrified the king's royal advisors, who routinely succumbed to exceptionally dramatic attacks of the vapors when they were informed of the latest exploits of the one they called That Upstart, Crown Prince Rupert the Not-Particularly-Handsome. The king's royal advisors took their jobs very seriously. In fact, they took their jobs so seriously that over time, they became convinced that their advice was much better for the country than the king's own decisions—not that any of them were brave (or foolish) enough to announce that conclusion to the king, of course.

The king's royal advisors soon came to see Prince Rupert's activities as an affront to the kingdom itself because nothing so frivolous as enjoying an orgasm could be good for the kingdom unless the royal advisors themselves declared such to be. The royal advisors drew good salaries and lived in comfortable homes and wore stylish garb. They usually had reasonably attractive, or at least sensible, ordinary spouses, who by and large would have been quite happy to share orgasms with them. People in the kingdom of Aze always loved their spouses and enjoyed having sex with them. After all, the story of Prince Rupert the Not-Particularly-Handsome is a fairy tale, and true love is important in fairy tales.

However, the royal advisors had come to spend so much time arguing and, well, advising rather than actually doing anything productive (even masturbating), they now looked down their noses at those who did lowly things like the handwork for which the kingdom of Aze was so famous. While the royal advisors' spouses occasionally complained and fumed, more than one assistant to the royal advisors muttered under his (or her) breath that a long masturbatory session was exactly what the king's royal advisors needed—especially if a lot of anal stimulation were involved. The assistants, however, kept their mouths shut because they didn't want to be fired. So, the king's royal advisors went on about their business with their noses in the air (and their spouses disgruntled), certain in the belief that because they were the king's royal advisors, they were the ones who should control the kingdom's treasury and command the kingdom's people and especially decide who had orgasms and when and for what purpose—all for the good of the kingdom, of course, because after all, they were the king's prestigious royal advisors.

The royal advisors researched and reinterpreted and revised everything from ancient scrolls to the latest tax ledgers until they gained sufficient "irrefutable" evidence to prove their philosophical assertions. Then the royal advisors drafted a new royal document declaring that the royal advisors and not the king should henceforth rule the kingdom of Aze—for the good of the kingdom, of course. The only problem with their plan was that pretty much everyone in the kingdom of Aze (including most of the tutors) wanted the king and queen to continue ruling the kingdom, and they wanted Crown Prince Rupert to rule after them, even though he was not particularly handsome. If the royal advisors wanted to retain their heads, they had to find a way to convince the people of Aze that they, the royal advisors, were the only ones fit to rule.

Then one day, the royal vizier, who was the head of the royal advisors, came into their secret meeting room, chortling with sinister glee and waving a handful of very old scrolls. The royal vizier had discovered that many years ago, the family of Crown Prince Rupert's mother (the queen) had actually been fence makers, hence their name, "Fencer." The family now pronounced it "Fon-SAY," which sounded much more royal and prestigious than Fencer. The Fencers would have changed the name officially long ago, but no one in Aze, not even the current king, had enough money to pay the layers upon layers of estate taxes, much less the legal fees for revising the centuries of documentation associated with such a monumental change. So the family simply changed the pronunciation, which didn't cost a single copper and mostly kept everybody happy.

Over time, the Fencer family had stopped making fences and gone into the much more lucrative marriage business instead. Fences were sturdy and sound and everyone needed one, even if it were only inexpensive and wood-hewn. The income was steady and sound and although the Fencers were not rich, they were quite comfortable.

Some of the Fencers, however, wanted bigger, fancier gowns and robes and carriages and homes—and they wanted them right then. It was about that time they realized that in addition to fences, the Fencers had also become known throughout the land for their beautiful daughters and sons. The Fencers called a family meeting and after a short but fractious discussion and a not-so-close vote, the family stored their tools in the barn that was soon to become a carriage house and started declaiming far and wide about their delicate, musically-inclined women with exquisitely fine faces, large breasts, and well-curved hips, and their deep-voiced, chisel-jawed men with smooth hairless backs and chests, long silky foreskins, and thick, heavy cocks that stayed hard for hours.

The more the family proclaimed, the more the rest of the kingdom and, indeed even those in the lands beyond, noticed that Fencer women and men did indeed sing and dance (and fuck) with the utmost grace and talent, to the delight of all around them. The Fencers wore the latest styles and most ornate jewelry artisans could design. Their children were always beautiful and every one grew up to have the Fencer family traits. So, of course, it wasn't long before the Fencers commanded the highest dowry fees in all the land—and in all the lands beyond. Across hills and dales and lush green valleys, there was no greater distinction than to be able to say, "My bride (or groom) is a Fencer." Men's dicks got hard and women's panties wet just watching a Fencer stroll through a garden on the way to join a spouse for an afternoon rendezvous. Even the term "Fencer," especially when written on an official schedule, came to mean the time specifically set aside at an event for the guests and participants and even the hosts to discreetly retire to their quarters to dream of the Fencer loveliness and masturbate to a satisfying orgasm.

Eventually, the king took a Fencer wife, as did his successor, and the successor after him. The next king was so pleased he decreed that from then on, all royal heirs, whether male and female, would always take a Fencer spouse upon ascending the throne. And their heir would carry the prestigious family name of "Fencer" until he or she ascended the throne, at which time he or she would follow the time-honored kingdom tradition of simply using the title "king" or "queen" and his or her given name.

This pleased the Fencers no end. By then, the extended Fencer family had grown to include roughly ten percent of the population in one form or another. Fencers lived in all parts of the country, with particularly large branches at the main family estate near the royal city as well as in the Southeast, the Most Western Peninsula, and the Far Northlands. The family kept the geographical distinctions well in place to avoid accidental inter-marrying, especially when negotiating spouses with the royal family. This kept the Fencer bloodline strong and their most-envied traits always bred true.

The Fencer wealth and power grew until it almost rivaled the king's, which made more than one of the king's royal advis-ers more than a little bit nervous. The king's royal advisors were all not-Fencers. While it was generally agreed that, by and large, Fencers would have done as well advising the king as any others in the kingdom, the Fencers in general (except for the current queen and Prince Rupert) were much too busy with physical delights to be bothered with things like advising.

The Fencers had always been interested only in their own pleasures and pursuits. They had no intention of displacing the royal family. But as time went on and petty jealousies grew, some of the not-Fencers in the kingdom, especially those who were royal advisors, came to believe that some day, the Fencers just might take control of the kingdom, especially the treasury—at which time, the not-so-beautiful, not-so-wealthy, not-so-well-endowed, and perhaps not-even-so-sexually-inclined members of the not-Fencer populace would be left out in the cold because they were, well, "not-Fencers." After all, while there had never been a paucity of farmers or artisans or merchants or other working people in the kingdom of Aze, there were no guarantees that there never would be. If it came down to the populace supporting either the pleasure-loving Fencers or the not-Fencer king's royal advisors, the king's royal advisors did not intend to have to start working with their hands themselves!

When Prince Rupert was born, that he was not particularly handsome was immediately apparent to one and all. His parents loved him just the way he was and showered him with attention and unconditional affection, which is, of course, what all children deserve. By and large, the general populace didn't care what Price Rupert looked like so long as he, like everyone else in the kingdom, did his job—which is, of course, the way the populace of any land should treat each other. As Prince Rupert's personality became more evident, most of the people of the kingdom loved him even more, which pleased the king and queen no end. (It even pleased most of Prince Rupert's tutors.) The Fencer family, however, especially those still residing on the large, fabulously wealthy main family estate kept a politely aloof distance, holding their collective breath that on Prince Rupert's twenty-first birthday coming-of-age medical exam, his mere looks would turn out to be just an unfortunate fluke while the rest of the family traits bred true.

After the royal vizier's announcement, the royal advisors held their collective breath as well, but for a very different reason. They were hoping Prince Rupert would prove to be what the royal advisors came to call "a throwback" to the original Fencers—one who was a mere fence maker and thus unfit to rule the kingdom of Aze. So, the royal advisors watched like vultures, chortling as they gathered "evidence" to support their claims.

The older Prince Rupert got, the more they chortled, for there did, indeed, seem to be some evidence.

Prince Rupert the Not-Particularly-Handsome, like all Fencer men, was prone to tearing his clothing. His muscular shoulders had split more than one royal shirt when he wrestled with his companions. However, Prince Rupert eschewed the crotch-hugging hose the rest of the Fencers wore in favor of more serviceable blousy trousers. This, indeed, the royal advisors considered to be telling, because when Prince Rupert's exuberance got out of hand when he was wrestling, his pants just tore at the knee or up the back, rather than in front where his cock and balls would fall out—a rather frequent occurrence for all other Fencer men, who, of course, could not help it, being endowed the way true Fencer men were.

There had even been horrified whispers one time when Prince Rupert's pants had split, when he was rolling across the courtyard in a mock battle testing two of the best of the king's royal bodyguards. A valet told everyone he had seen a thick dusting of red hair on Prince Rupert's ass. The Fencers, as one, shuddered and refused to believe such a thing could have happened to one of their own! So while the king's royal advisors waited with bated breath, the Fencers crossed their fingers and knocked on wood and rubbed their cocks and clits for luck and waited for the royal physician's report.

The physician had barely finished speaking when breathless messengers dove for their horses. Although Prince Rupert was still not-particularly handsome, he was astoundingly healthy. From the top of his head to the tips of his toes and everywhere between, both inside and out, he was sturdy and strong and well formed. His back and chest were also befurred with thick red hair—which the physician referred to as lush and silky, though the Fencer's could fathom nothing beyond the word "hair." Worst of all, the princely penis was a mere 5 inches when it was flaccid—only 6.2 inches when the prince was thoroughly aroused, with a foreskin so short the head of his penis was always exposed. (The physician included a discreet footnote that Prince Rupert could, however, pull his foreskin forward enough to just barely rub it all the way over the head when he was masturbating—an activity at which he was extremely adept.) Most shocking of all, Prince Rupert ejaculated after mere minutes of sexual stimulation—and afterward, he required a full two hours and oral stimulation (the physician wouldn't say by whom) to become erect again.

The king and queen beamed with pride in their son, and Prince Rupert's friends hustled him off to the pub to try to pry out the name (and barring that, a detailed description) of the assistant who had provided the oral stimulation. In the marketplace and meeting rooms, however, the king's royal advisors whispered and schemed and voiced their concerns to all who would listen (and quite a few who didn't really want to, but felt they should because it sounded like this was going to be big news). By day's end, dowry prices for Fencer fiancées had plummeted. People whispered that if an anomaly like Prince Rupert— a throwback!—could happen once, it could happen again! The marriage brokers wanted guarantees, and barring that (because of course, no one could guarantee what kind of child would be born), a reduced price on every contract.

Clothing designers and jewelers and restauranteurs suddenly

no longer offered lines of credit to those who looked even mar-
ginally attractive (in case they were soon-to-be-poor Fencers in
disguise). Horse traders and the purveyors of fine carriages
quickly followed suit. Even those who styled hair and did bikini
waxes had no openings available in the foreseeable future—
unless, of course, one was paying cash. The beautiful men and
women gathered at the Fencer family estate for an emergency
family meeting wept and wailed that they were ruined—
RUINED—and all because of that horrible not-particularly-
handsome Prince Rupert with the too small, too quick dick.

While the Fencers and the general populace of the kingdom
discussed the rampant rumors and the potential economic
impacts for each of them personally, the kingdom advisors met
again, this time to finalize their plans. Their rhetoric was more
virulent now, because they were sure that now the time was ripe
to overthrow the king. The kingdom advisors declared that the
Fencer influence had outlived its usefulness—if, indeed, Fencer
influence had ever been useful at all. The advisors declared they
were tired of looking at beautiful faces in places of power and
wealth. They declared they were fed up with public admiration
of large-breasted, curvaceous women and men with long foreskins and thick, hard cocks. While the advisors reserved the right
to take Fencer spouses for themselves—after all, the advisors
would know how to properly control the Fencer assets—the
advisors declared they most adamantly did not want the Fencers
deciding who got to partake of the Fencer beauty and sexual
proclivities. The Fencers were fence makers—not "advisors"!

The advisors especially didn't want the Fencers, or the general populace, for that matter, to stop work and masturbate or

have any other kind of sex whenever the urge came upon them. The advisors declared that decisions about when and where and how often and especially with whom the populace should masturbate or marry or reproduce should only be made by objective, serious, and properly qualified people like the advisors themselves—not by people distracted by their own excessive beauty or sexual attributes or barely-controlled urges. Licenses would be available presently for all controlled activities—for an appropriate fee, of course. In addition, only dispassionate specialists, namely the advisors themselves, were to decide matters related to the treasury—all for the good of the kingdom, of course. This especially included rationing which of the kingdom's famous handwork would be used within the kingdom and which would be created only as the fabulous marketable goods for which the people of Aze were known throughout all the lands near and far.

When the advisors' tirades had died down and after several days of intense discussion (while Prince Rupert and his companions were cavorting and spending their money with wild abandon in the marketplace and especially in several of their favorite pubs, because after all, it was Prince Rupert's twenty-first birthday coming-of-age celebration), the advisors finally came to the consensus that it was time to act. They drew up a fine, gold-gilt scroll stating that Crown Prince Rupert the Not-Particularly-Handsome was obviously a throwback to the fence makers of old and completely unfit to rule; it was time to give full power in the kingdom to the kingdom advisors.

The king took one look at the proposed laws and declared them a load of hogwash. He called for a chamber pot, ceremoniously dropped the scroll he'd been handed in, and closed the lid with a thump. Then he reminded his advisors that they were "the king's" royal advisors, and if they didn't have enough to do in their well-paid time, he'd be glad to have Prince Rupert put them to work in the stables while their replacements settled in. The king then issued a royal proclamation decreeing that he was well pleased with his son—as pleased as a king could be with his crown prince. And to show his faith in his son, the king announced he and his queen would be going on an extensive holiday starting the next week. Prince Rupert would stand in the king's own stead for the duration of the trip. So the king's royal advisors had damn well better get used to answering to a not-particularly-handsome crown prince, because it wouldn't be all that long before he was their not-particularly-handsome king!

With the naïveté of good people who underestimate the evil of which greedy, frightened, power-hungry people are capable, the king and queen loaded their traveling finery in the fanciest carriage in all the land and set off for the kingdom next door. They'd barely cleared the border when the advisors clapped Prince Rupert in irons, threw him in the dungeon, and announced to the populace that their king and queen had betrayed them to the neighbors and Prince Rupert was at death's door with a highly contagious plague. They sealed the borders and took control of the treasury—for the good of the kingdom in this time of social and economic crisis.

Then, as the thoroughly stunned populace watched in growing horror, the advisors announced that as of that moment, all Fencer engagements were suspended pending a full investigation into the reproductive qualifications of the affianced Fencer. Since the advisors had irrefutable proof that the uncontrolled

Fencer tainting of the kingdom's most noble bloodlines had led to the current crises, only designated, specially-vetted noble people, like the advisors and their peers, would be allowed to reproduce with Fencer spouses—providing the physician's reports concurred, which not surprisingly, they all did. In addition, already-married Fencers were to clothe themselves in peasant clothing and cover their faces so as not to unduly influence the sexual urges of those around them and thus undermine the workings of the kingdom. There especially were to be no "Fencer" interludes in any public—or private—schedules in the kingdom! Anyone who disagreed with the new laws would be promptly escorted to the dungeons—for the good of the kingdom.

The advisors, now calling themselves The Advisors for the Good of the Kingdom, said they would be sure to notify the populace when Prince Rupert died. Then they upped the quotas for production, doubled taxes, canceled all holidays and weekends (and insurance for physicians), and told the people to get back to work.

When Prince Rupert's guard told him what was going on, the prince was enraged. Not only had the advisors thrown him into jail with a horrible hangover and torn pants (this time there was a hole in the knee as well as a split down the back), they'd done so just before he was to enjoy a Fencer with a cadre of guards from the prison (both men and women) with whom he frequently went drinking. After eight hours of uninterrupted sleep and two mugs of willow bark tea, Prince Rupert lay on the floor of his cell on his guard's cloak. The guard's pants and loin wrap formed a comfortable pillow and the guard was squatting over Prince Rupert's face. With his wriggling tongue seated deeply in the trembling guard's ass, Prince Rupert (and his companions) set about plotting to retake the kingdom.

Prince Rupert's strong forearms were braced on the floor, his elbows bent so his cupped palms formed a comfortable chair for the guardsman seated above him—a well-spread chair that let Prince Rupert lick and lave and root his exceptionally long and exceptionally talented tongue deeply up the hot, sensitive anus quivering above him. With each deep, lingering tongue fuck, the guardsman moaned and jerked his cock. The second guardsman, the woman sucking Rupert's cock, took that as her cue to swallow Rupert's cock deep into her throat, which made Rupert thrust his hips and tongue even harder, which made the second guardsman thrust her naked pussy up for the attentions of the third guardsman who was busily fingering both the second guardsman's pussy and her own.

Prince Rupert was a firm believer in the physical, emotional, and intellectual benefits of a good, thorough Fencer in the middle of each day—especially when one needed to think clearly. Experience had also taught him (long before the fateful physician's report) that both stress (and an untended erection) were distractions that could, and indeed should, be removed by a refreshing Fencer. A few minutes later, Prince Rupert's cock was spurting into the second guardsman's mouth, the first guardsman's asshole was spasming over Prince Rupert's deep-thrust tongue while semen landed in large splotches on the cloak, and both the second and third guardsmen were writhing through their orgasms. After a few minutes more of contented cuddling on the cloak in a pile of naked arms and legs, they began to make their plans.

The first guardsman announced that according to his lover (a talented equestrian messenger who was entering his second year of employment with the Fencers), the Fencers had done an abrupt about face and decided that despite Prince Rupert's not-particularly-handsome face, he was indeed strong and industrious. He was also now the best asset of all branches of his Fencer family—indeed, of all the kingdom of Aze!

Prince Rupert wasn't particularly concerned with what the Fencers thought of him. He never had been. He was, however, determined to clap the advisors (by whatever name they called themselves) into irons and, if they'd harmed so much as one member of the populace, to throw the advisors into the deepest, darkest dungeon in the castle. Borrowing a spare pair of the pants from the captain of the king's royal guard (whom Rupert had defeated in two out of three well-fought wrestling takedowns the day before his birthday), Prince Rupert led the members of the king's royal infantry and the rest of the king's royal guards—and the king's royal horse trainers and pretty much everyone from the king's royal food tasters to the king's royal seamstresses and even some of the Fencers who had decided it was high time they got involved in what was going on around them—up the stairs to the armory to draw weapons.

As the rest of good people of Aze stood by cheering, Prince Rupert and his followers marched clanking and clanging through the marketplace and through the poorer and then the wealthier parts of town and finally up to the fine mansion the Advisors for the Good of the Kingdom had commandeered for their meetings. When the vizier threw the doors open to see what all the ruckus was about, Prince Rupert put his sword to the vizier's throat and backed him into the exceptionally well-appointed conference room. Prince Rupert's followers marched in behind him and, with all the exits blocked from the outside, the prince asked which of the former advisors to the kingdom wanted to come quietly to the dungeon, and which wanted to be run through on the spot.

Not surprisingly, all of the advisors decided to go quietly to the dungeon. Many of them looked truly shocked when they were pelted with rotten vegetables and horse dung as they were marched through the streets.

"But we were acting for the good of the kingdom!" one distraught former advisor wailed. "Why aren't they thanking us?"

"Because you weren't acting for their good, and you know it," said Prince Rupert in a disgusted voice the likes of which his friends had rarely heard him use before. "You've stripped the people of their freedom and their sexuality, things which people will never allow in the long run, no matter how much you tell them it's for their own good." Prince Rupert was so mad he turned his sword on its side and smacked the man squarely across the butt. "Think about it, you idiot! Our entire economy is based on the creation and export of handcrafted sex toys! If you destroy people's sexuality—if you destroy the Fencer!—we'll all starve! Now keep walking. If you've harmed either one of my parents, I'll personally run you through with my sword."

Fortunately for all concerned, the king and queen (and the rest of the populace) were fine. The minute the king and queen walked back in the door of the castle, they hugged their son ferociously and personally thanked each and every one of the royal entourage who had supported Prince Rupert. And when they were finished, the king took off his belt and the queen picked up her hairbrush, and they marched down to the deepest, darkest dungeons, where they had a long, private, and very loud conversation with each and every one of the former advisors. By the time the discussions were over, each and every teary-eyed former advisor had expressed true remorse and sworn undying allegiance to both the current king and queen and their heir. And they'd all agreed to write a personal letter of apology to Prince Rupert before their spouses would be allowed to post bail.

Now, in an old fashioned fairy tale, the former advisors would have been executed, Prince Rupert would have claimed a princess from among his followers (or from a carriage from the Fencer family estate), and everyone would have lived happily ever after. However, this isn't an old-fashioned fairy tale. It's a new-fashioned one.

Since no one had been irreparably harmed, neither the king nor the queen nor Prince Rupert really wanted to execute any of their populace, not even the disreputable former advisors. They did, however, agree that something had to be done to keep the former advisors from ever again becoming a threat to the people and prosperity of the kingdom of Aze. After long discussions with the former advisors' disgruntled spouses, Prince Rupert discovered that the advisors had forgotten the benefits of both polite discourse and a daily (at a minimum) Fencer. So, the prince transferred the former advisors' personal wealth to their spouses, along with the irons into which he'd originally intended to clap the miscreants, and directed the spouses to keep the former advisors out of polite company and, indeed, under lock and key until such time as polite discourse and the proper appreciation of a good Fencer had been well and permanently learned. He told the spouses they would be held accountable along with their former-advisor spouses if a problem should ever arise again.

As far as a princess was concerned (Fencer or otherwise), Prince Rupert still hadn't decided if he wanted a princess or a prince for a consort—or even if he really wanted just one consort at all. At the moment, he preferred to spend his non-working hours (and his Fencers) in the amenable company of the members of the king's royal infantry and the king's royal guards and the king's royal horse trainers and everyone from the king's royal food tasters to the king's royal seamstresses. So, he agreed to father an heir, one way or the other, and the king and queen told him to keep his door closed during his daily Fencers, because while it was one thing to know theoretically what their son was doing, it was quite another to know he was doing it right now.

So, the king and queen each got a mug of willow bark tea for their sore shoulders from the captain of the king's royal guard and told him to start selecting recruits (including a few Fencers) for the new king's royal advisors. Then the king and queen clasped hands and walked upstairs for their own private welcome-home Fencer. They studiously avoided so much as looking in the grand hall where Prince Rupert and his followers and every Fencer within riding distance was holding a celebratory orgy. And when the king and queen got to their room, the queen looked out the window into the courtyard below and saw that the townspeople had arrived to join their son as well. So, she smiled and closed the curtain, and started pulling the pins from her hair. Her husband opened his traveling chest and took out a jar of the new personal lubricant for which he'd negotiated a most-favored-kingdom agreement with the neighbors they'd been visiting. As his wife let her velvet dress drop to the floor and stepped towards him wearing just her queenly stockings, he set the jar on the table next to the bed and tore open the front of his ready-to-split pants. He'd never been a Fencer himself, but he knew how to appreciate one.

And they all lived blissfully ever after.

CAT'S EYE *Lisabet Sarai*

GENERALLY, THE VILLAGE people avoided Nimon. When he was a child, they used to call their own children inside, if he happened down their street. They would peer from behind half-closed doors and whisper among themselves. Now that he was a young man, they greeted him politely, but without warmth. They bought the marvelously clever carvings he hawked from door to door, utensils and ornaments, but no one invited him in to sit by the hearth and share a glass of cider.

With his tawny skin, jet hair, and lithe body, he was a handsome man, and prosperous, too, by village standards. Nevertheless the village beauties never assailed him with flirtatious banter, the way that they did the other youths. They stood awkward and quiet, with eyes downcast, until he passed. No father had approached Grandma Moira, with whom he made his home, with offers of a dowry.

Simple people fear what they do not understand, and no one understood Nimon. The rumors had been repeated and embellished in the nineteen years since his birth. His mother Leileah, a fair virgin of good family, suddenly and inexplicably grew heavy with child. Disobeying her parents for the first time in her life, she refused to reveal the father. And when her time grew near, she shunned the attentions of the midwives, fleeing on her own to the forested hills. A week later she returned with her ebony-haired, green-eyed son.

The village folk, including Nimon's mother, all had hair the color of straw, eyes the color of sky. The babe was strange in other ways, too. He would stare at you for the longest time without blinking, his oval pupils huge and midnight black. His pudgy fingers were tipped with nails much longer and sharper than a normal baby's. He never cried.

After his birth, Leileah became as silent as her child. Her lovely flaxen hair grew long, tangled, and unkempt. Her cornflower eyes sparked with madness. Within a month, she left her parents' home, moving into Grandma Moira's big, ramshackle house at the edge of the hills.

Her family pleaded for her to stay. Secretly, though, they were relieved to have their stranger of a daughter out from under their roof. It seemed natural for her to go to Moira, strange drawn to strange. No one saw much of Leileah or Nimon after that. The people normally didn't tend to bother Moira, unless they needed a healing draught for their cows, or a love potion.

When Nimon was two, the wasting sickness came to the village. Nimon's mother died early; her parents followed a few weeks later. Some folk said that Leileah was punished for taking a stranger to her bed, and her parents for rejecting her afterwards. But people always like to talk. In truth, many in the village died; were all of them transgressors?

Still, tales of Nimon's mysterious parentage were always popular around the winter hearth. The father was an Arab prince, some claimed, who had galloped by the village on his white stallion and ravished Leileah as she was working in the fields. Others said that he was the Lord of the Underworld, well known for ruining innocent virgins and carrying them back to his subterranean kingdom. A forest demon, still others claimed. Hadn't Leileah fled to woods to give birth? Didn't the child have animal eyes and claws? Then someone would laugh, and change the subject.

So Nimon grew to manhood; orphaned, raised by a wise woman whom most people called crazy, and shunned by the village. For the most part, he didn't care what the people thought of him. He roamed the forest, slinking along trails that only he could see, bringing colored stones or wild herbs back to his adoptive mother. He ran through the fields, naked and glorying in his strength, laughing when the girls busy with the planting or the harvest blushed and looked away.

Some nights, though, as he lay on the ground staring up at a ripe moon, he felt a kind of emptiness come upon him. He didn't recall his mother's face, but he remembered her smell, the warm, musky smell of unwashed female skin. It seemed to engulf him on these nights, drowning out the fragrance of honeysuckle and fresh-cut hay. These nights his penis swelled up hard as the oak logs he used for his carving. Touching himself was simultaneously pain and pleasure. He grasped his erection with both hands, squeezing and pummeling his flesh, desperate to release the demons that seemed to be warring inside him.

He remembered the women in the fields, with their skirts tucked up above their knees and their bodices damp with sweat. He tried to imagine them without clothes. But the images of rounded limbs and rosy breasts kept slipping away. Instead he saw only a whirlwind, swirling shards of darkness that circled faster the closer he came to the climax.

When he finally exploded, raining sticky seed all over his thighs and belly, the dark ebbed away. He still felt empty, but the ache was less. His body was light as the dried husk of a leaf. If he didn't hold to the earth, the wind would simply take him.

It was midsummer in Nimon's nineteenth year when the cattle began to die. Nearly every day, the villagers would find a bloodied carcass, some yards away from the bulk of the herd. Deep wounds scourged the poor cow's hide, marks of some powerful beast's claws. Whole chunks of flesh were torn away, leaving gory holes that soon swarmed with flies.

The headman of the village ordered sentries posted to watch over the herd as it grazed, but this did no good. Somehow the watchers always seemed to become sleepy, or distracted. They were roused only by the buzzing of the flies upon remains of the latest victim.

"Magic," the villagers muttered among themselves. "Witchcraft." Some even wondered if the mysterious Nimon might be responsible, but didn't dare voice that thought. Besides, several times he had been seen selling his wares in the market at the same time that the alarm was raised out in the pastures.

The fencing the village raised around the grazing ground did not stop the predation. If anything, the carnage increased, two calves slaughtered in a single afternoon. Finally, the headman had no choice. Carrying his best hat, he walked out to Moira's rambling homestead at the edge of the hills.

The withered old lady met him at the gate with a smile that seemed polite and sincere. "Well met, Yarnor. It has been many months since I have seen you. What brings you to my door?"

Was there irony in her voice? Yarnor couldn't afford to worry. "Well met, Grandmother Moira. I come seeking your help."

"The cattle." She didn't really need to ask.

"Yes, Grandmother. We've tried everything, but we haven't managed to glimpse the predator, let alone catch it. We fear that there's some enchantment here, that this beast is something unnatural."

Nimon, perched on the porch carving, looked up.

"Do you have any idea what kind of beast it is?"

"None, only that it is cruel and gluttonous and can wrap itself in some kind of glamour to prevent us from seeing it."

"So? Why do you come to me?" Moira did not completely hide her amusement. Yarnor swallowed his annoyance and discomfort.

"Lady, we know you are wise and have some knowledge of things unseen. We hoped that you might give us some clue as to how to catch the beast."

Moira laughed. "Me? I am a healer. You need a warrior." A

sly smile twitched at her lips. "But perhaps Nimon can assist you. He is tall and strong. And he also has some acquaintance with the invisible world."

"Nimon," she called over her shoulder, "would you attend us, please?"

The young man unfolded his limbs and stretched, then glided over to the gate. His movements had an almost unearthly grace. He stared at Yagnor for a long time with those dark, wide-pupiled eyes before he spoke.

"Good afternoon, Headman. So you need my help to protect your assets?"

"Goodman Nimon, it is said that you know the ways of the wild things, that you are familiar with the forest and the hills. Perhaps you can find out this creature's secrets, track it to its lair, and dispatch it. If you can help us, we would be very grateful."

Nimon could see how much it cost the headman to ask for the assistance of an outcast like himself. He found the man's unease oddly satisfying. He waited for a while before responding, just to watch Yagnor's discomfort intensify.

"Goodman Yagnor, I do not know if I can catch your cattle-killer. But if I do, what will be my reward?"

Yagnor was already prepared for this question. "Each family in the village will give you one of its cows. You will end up a wealthy man."

"Cows!" Nimon snorted. "What would I do with cows? I am, as you have said, a man of the forest and the hills, not some cowherd to haunt the pastures. And I already have enough wealth, and more, from my craft, to keep Mother Moira and myself in bread and beer."

Yagnor looked desperate. "Please, then, Nimon, do it for the good of the village that you belong to." The plea sounded hollow. Both men knew that under other circumstances the village would never claim him as its own.

Nimon turned the possibilities over in his mind. Perhaps if he succeeded, the villagers would be more willing to acknowledge him and include him in their society. But was that what he wanted?

Yagnor feared that the long silence meant that Nimon was about to refuse. He was well aware that even as he parleyed here on the outskirts of the village, the beast was probably enjoying another bloody meal.

"Nimon," he blurted out finally. "If you can catch and kill this thing, I will give you my daughter Freyda to wife."

Now there was an offer! Nimon knew Freyda by sight, though they had never spoken. She was rosy-cheeked and merry, one of the most boisterous of the maidens when teasing the other young men. When he passed her, though, admiring the ripe flesh hidden under her bodice, she blushed silently.

Nimon gazed into Yagnor's eyes and saw fear, fear that Nimon would accept, and fear that he would refuse.

"Very well, I will make an attempt. Tomorrow afternoon I will hide myself and try to discover what manner of creature is wreaking havoc with your herds. When I know this, I will know how to attack it."

"Thank you, Goodman Nimon. We are all grateful."

Nimon laughed. "Wait to be grateful until after you have seen what I can do."

He stood with his adopted mother, watching the headman

hurry back to the village. Moira laughed and ruffled Nimon's hair. "Well, son, fate seems to be playing on your side."

"Are you so confident that I can succeed in this task?"

Moira smiled affectionately. "You were born for it. Come inside. I have something for you."

The crone led the way into her dim workshop, where the mingled fragrance of herbs hung sharply in the air. She swung open the lid of a dark wood chest and rummaged among the contents. "I know that it's here... Aha!" She emerged holding what appeared to be the tooth of a large animal. It had been pierced at one end, and a thong of leather threaded through the hole.

She laid the pendant in Nimon's palm. "I have been keeping this for you. It is a token from your father."

Nimon grew pale. "My father? My father is alive?"

"Alas, no. When your mother returned to his cave, ready to give birth, she found his life bleeding away, taken by hunters. She stroked his jet fur gently until the last light left his eyes. Then, brave woman that she was, she took her knife and hacked off this tooth, just before his body crumbled to ash and blew away. The birth pangs struck her immediately after."

"Fur?" Nimon gazed at the tooth in wonder. "Who was my father? What was he?"

"He was a man, and not a man. He could walk upon two legs, but his natural form was a great black panther, lithe and full of power."

"You saw him?"

"Once, from a distance. I came upon the two of them on one of my herb walks, entwined in an intimate embrace. They were beautiful together. I kept my distance, not wanting to disturb their tryst, but he caught my scent. Before I could call out reassurances, he had changed to his four-legged shape and bounded away."

"And my mother?"

"She was in some kind of dream. Her eyes were closed but she was smiling, ecstatic. I left her there in the forest. I knew that she would be safe with him watching over her.'

"But he was not safe himself," said Nimon in wonder.

"None of us really are, are we?" Moira took the talisman and hung it around his neck. "Here. This should help you on your quest."

Something shifted inside Nimon as the ivory fragment came to rest against the bare skin of his chest. His sight became more acute; the workroom no longer seemed dim but as bright as the day outside. He sniffed and could distinguish all the separate fragrances that swirled in the dusty air: the moldy sweetness of rosemary, the piercingly bitter pennyroyal, the grassy scent of sage, the pungency of garlic, all mixed with smoky paraffin and stale beer and new-mown hay and rat excrement.

"Go out to the pastures, Nimon. Don't wait until tomorrow. Go discover the nature of this marauder who has so unsettled our poor village."

Nimon was suddenly moved to kneel before her. "Bless me, Mother. Give me your benediction and protection."

The woman's gnarled hand rested lightly on his head for a moment. "My son, you already have my blessing. You have always had it. Go now, and find your destiny."

Nimon moved swiftly, loping through fields and along the dirt roads to the common pasture, which lay on the other side of the village. It was nearly sunset when he finally arrived at the rolling acres of green. All seemed peaceful. The cattle meandered through the long grass, unhurried and undisturbed. Their scent of dung and milk was strong in his nostrils.

Nimon climbed a tree, hiding among the foliage, and waited. He was more alert than he had ever been. He could hear the crickets in the sod, the beetles gnawing in the tree bark, the tinkle of the lead cow's bell, a faint gale of laughter from the village more than a league away. He grasped the panther tooth hanging around his necked and tried to quiet his breathing. He had to be patient.

He began to fantasize about Freyda, imagining her unclothed, her arms wide to welcome him. His penis throbbed pleasantly at the image. Then his thoughts slid away to his mother and her lover. What would it be like, to couple with a wild thing such as his father had been? Ecstasy, Moira had said. Certainly, it would have to be extraordinary…

A harsh shriek brought him back to the present. He realized that he had been drifting, lost in his daydreams, and cursed his lack of discipline. But it was not too late. Gazing through the leaves, he saw shapes moving in the dusk, far across the pasture. The cry came again, unearthly and haunting, mixed with the pained moans of a wounded animal.

He vaulted from his perch and raced across the field. As he came closer, he saw an enormous white bird, some giant eagle or falcon, hovering over a blood-soaked calf. The bird was as tall as a man.

Scaly black talons were buried in the cow's body. A hooked, razor-sharp beak tore away huge chunks of flesh, which disappeared into the thing's dark craw. Nimon watched, fascinated, as the creature ripped at the calf until its bones began to show.

The eagle's silvery feathers were streaked with gore. It looked up from its meal, fixing its golden eyes on Nimon and shrieking again, as if angry to be disturbed.

A thrill ran through Nimon's body. There was intelligence in those eyes, awareness. This was not some mindless predator driven by blind hunger. Drawn, he edged closer to the creature.

All at once he was buffeted by a mighty wind. Grasping the half-consumed calf in its claws, the eagle beat its wings and climbed into the air above him, deafening him with another raucous cry.

Caught in the whirlwind, Nimon flung his arms over his head to protect himself. The eagle did not attack him, however. It flew off toward the western mountains, rising so high and so fast that he lost sight of it in a few moments. Even with his enhanced vision, he could not follow its path. He cursed and stamped the ground in frustration.

How could he hunt a thing with such wings? His body surged with new power, but he was still a creature of the earth. He had only the vaguest idea where the bird had gone.

Still, he had promised to track and destroy the thing, and that thought gave him an odd pleasure. He headed in the direction of the mountains, ragged silhouettes against the lingering glow of sunset. He sniffed, trying to catch some scent of the creature on the evening breeze. There was an iron-tinged hint of blood, but nothing else.

All at once he noticed something gleaming in the grass, pale in the twilight. He bent to pick up the feather, which was as long as his forearm and had a distinct metallic cast. Thoughtfully, he thrust it into his belt and walked on. He encountered another silvery pinion, at the edge of the woods that cloaked the foothills. Nimon smiled to himself, remembering the light that danced in the bird's eyes. Perhaps, after all, the creature wanted to be found.

Nimon slipped into the forest and began to climb. Whenever he was unsure of the way, he found another feather that pointed out the true path. He moved steadily, deliberately, pausing often to sniff the air. Hour after hour, he trudged on. The trail became steep and rock-strewn. The trees thinned. The full moon shone down through the gaps in the foliage, painting the trail a cold silver. In the distance, Nimon could see the peaks he sought. They seemed far away as ever.

He sank down onto a fallen tree by the side of the path. He was hungry and thirsty, and close to exhaustion. How could he climb any further? Yet how could he give up? His destiny, Moira had called this quest, and he knew in his heart that she spoke the truth.

He clasped the talisman hanging around his neck. "Please, Father," he whispered. "Please, help your poor human son." He closed his eyes and imagined the magical beast that Moira said had begotten him, sleek and strong, bounding up the mountain to the summit.

A sudden dizziness swept over him. Earth and sky reversed as he fell, helpless, to his hands and knees. The stars became streaks of light; the moon swelled until he feared its brightness would blind him. An earthquake, Nimon thought, as the ground trembled beneath him.

Then all was quiet. And all was different. Nimon began to move, and discovered the delightful stability and power of having four legs and a counter-balancing tail. I've changed, he thought. Like my father, I have taken on my beast shape. Energy surged through his limbs. His exhaustion had vanished. He could see, it seemed, for miles. Scanning the mountains blocking the horizon, he caught a flash of silver, halfway up the highest peak. Yes. There.

The tangy scent of his prey rose around him, emanating from the salvaged feathers that now lay scattered on the ground. He picked up one in his jaws and loped off into the night, toward his distant goal.

Nimon ran, gracefully, effortlessly, always upward. He sprang from boulder to boulder, leaped over treacherous ravines, sent sprays of scree tumbling behind him as he raced across bare stretches of gravel.

Time flowed strangely. The shiny spot grew larger and glittered in the moonlight. Soon Nimon was close enough to see that it was a small mountain lake, round as the moon itself, nestled at the base of a sheer cliff.

Nimon slowed his pace to a walk. He heard a noise, a faint splashing in the water. The astringent odor of the eagle hung in the air around him, tickling his nostrils. Now was the time for stealth. There was little cover, but he managed to crouch behind a pile of broken rock on the shore.

He turned his attention to the water. At first he saw nothing. Then, as his eyes adjusted to the reflected brilliance of the moon, he caught a glimpse or two: pale skin, slender limbs, a single graceful human hand.

She rose from the water, shaking moon-silvered drops from her naked form as she strode toward the cliff. She was nothing like the village women. There was nothing soft about her. Her breasts were palm-sized mounds that hardly shook as she walked. The full bosoms of the villagers bounced and wiggled with very step. Her thighs were sleek and muscled. Her hips and buttocks curved gently away from her waist, unlike the lush, fleshy bottoms of the women he knew. Nimon felt his unfamiliar male part growing hard. He growled softly.

A mane of hair so white that it was nearly transparent cascaded down her back. Though she had been submerged in the lake, her platinum locks appeared to be dry.

Nimon was transfixed by her unearthly beauty. He lay, motionless and hidden, as she crouched by the edge of the lake. There were shadows behind her, perhaps the mouth of a cave. Who was she? And where was the great, fierce eagle who had led him to this lair? Was she the bird's keeper?

There was something on the ground in front of her, crumpled and shapeless. As Nimon watched, the woman picked up a bone from the pile and began to nibble on the shreds of flesh that still clung to it.

Horror and desire surged in Nimon's breast as he suddenly understood. His roar echoed through the canyons. He gathered his strength, his tail twitching, then sprang, clearing the lake and landing next to the beautiful, unnatural creature. He roared again, baring his fangs. He could smell her blood now, mingled with the blood of the calf and the bird-stink.

The woman screamed, her voice rising into the piercing shriek Nimon had heard in the pasture. She rose from her haunches, the transformation already beginning. The quicksilver hair streaming over her shoulders reshaped itself into great wings covered with shimmering feathers. Her bare legs blackened and shrank; her feet grew vicious talons six inches long. Her face molded itself into the proud visage of a bird of prey, hooked beak designed for tearing flesh.

Only her eyes, golden and ageless, did not change.

Nimon wanted her. The passion had no name and no object; it was pure lust raging through his animal body. He leapt at her, burying his teeth in her neck, humping his hind quarters against her bristly feathers. The eagle shook itself, trying to dislodge him. He held on tighter, the metallic taste of her blood an aphrodisiac.

With a shriek, she rose into the air, taking him with her. She flew straight up the cliff face. The wind whistled around them. The sky reeled as they continued their vertiginous ascent. Then he was caught in the whirlwind, darkness swirling around them, invisible wings beating against his face, desire welling up in him and threatening to burst.

Nimon recognized the vision. Almost lost in his lust and confusion, still he laughed.

The wind died away. The eagle-woman came to rest on the summit. She shook herself and Nimon tumbled off onto the bare rock. The dizziness of transformation overwhelmed him briefly. Then he was conscious of rough, cold granite against his naked skin.

He opened his eyes. They met the golden gaze of the bird-woman. "You are the one," she said, or perhaps her words were only in his mind. "You are the one I have been waiting for." She reached for his penis, swollen and aching and hard as the rock on which he lay. Straddling him, she buried the organ in the slick, hot depths of her body.

Nimon gasped as she clutched him with her inner muscles, forcing him deeper. A fire seemed to rage inside her. In his mind he saw pictures of mountains exploding, molten rock seething and tumbling down the slopes. He felt that himself, felt himself melting and flowing, setting the forests ablaze, burying the world that was.

Her fire met and mingled with his. They rose together. Nimon briefly wondered if she had reassumed her winged form. He found himself in the whirlwind again, but now the darkness swirled with bright sparks the color of her eyes. Chaos streamed around him, and Nimon welcomed it at last.

He woke to her smile. She was dressing his wounds with some soothing poultice, the marks she had left on him during their coupling. She pointed to the crusted blood on her shoulder, where his teeth had pierced her skin. We need to be more careful in the future, he thought to say, then realized that they really had no need to speak.

"Iriea," she told him, in response to his unasked question. "My name is Ireia."

Three weeks later, Nimon showed up at Yagnor's door. The headman was visibly shaken to see him.

"Nimon...we thought...we worried...The lightening, the forest fire, it was the same day you disappeared, so we assumed..."

"Have there been any more killings of cattle?" Nimon asked with a half smile.

"No, that ended the night you left as well. We thought that perhaps you and the beast had both been consumed."

"Very nearly," Nimon said. He pulled out a silver feather eight inches long. "I have conquered the predator, or at least assured that it will trouble you no longer. Here is a token of my success."

Yagnor gazed at the magical object for a long time. Then he searched Nimon's eyes. Finally he sighed. "Well, then, I suppose you must have your reward."

He turned to call into the house. "Freyda? Come outside, daughter." The house was dim, but Nimon could see Freyda's plump form, along with her mother, cowering by the hearth. She didn't move.

"Daughter, do not disobey me." Yagnor tried to hold on to his dignity. "Come here at once."

Nimon laughed. "Never mind, Yagnor. I don't want your daughter. I already have a bride." Iriea stepped from the shadows and took her place at Nimon's side, her paleness a dramatic contrast to Nimon's dusky skin, both sharply different from the headman's ruddy complexion.

Yagnor gasped at Iriea's unworldly beauty. "Well..." he began.

"Marry us, Headman. Marry us now. I don't want my child to be an illegitimate outcast the way I was."

Yagnor's face brightened. "Of course. Just let me go get the record books." He gave Iriea a look of frank appraisal. "Welcome to the village, Lady. I hope that you will be happy here."

"Oh, don't worry, Yagnor. We won't be staying here. We know very well that this is not where we belong. Everyone has always made that clear. Now I understand why."

To Yagnor's credit, he blushed with embarrassment as he went to fetch the official register. He knew that he was in Nimon's debt, several times over.

Nimon turned to his bride and kissed her, inhaling her faint avian tang. Her eyes glowed, wild and full of love. "Don't worry, Iriea. This won't take long. We'll be back home soon."

SHE COMES STARS *Kathleen Bradean*

I WANT TO worship at the feet of a Goddess.

The ad I posted was that direct.

Her reply was also to the point: "You may bow to me."

She stoops to conquer. To her, I'm not subhuman; I'm human. That's low enough.

She's divine.

The metal, spiked heel of her boot presses against my taint. My hard-on is pinned painfully in my tight jeans.

Her unlikely throne is a white plastic chair on the covered patio of Pinks, the Los Angeles hotdog stand to the stars. The fatty, spicy scent of the grilling sausages is torture. I haven't eaten in God knows how long.

Goddess, she corrects my thoughts as she presses that dagger-heel deeper into my groin.

My mouth waters for the thick hunk of fudgy chocolate cake in the case near the register.

Irritated by my divided attention, she makes me see myself through her eyes. It always takes a moment for my brain to adjust to her expanded sight. It's like suddenly having the vision of a bumblebee. I can't begin to explain the dimensions she sees in, much less understand them. There are nameless colors that exist beyond human vision. Textures sing.

Humbled and awed, I kiss her offered foot.

She presses it back into my groin, grinding the sole of her boot against my balls as if she's squashing a bug.

Smoke from her cigarette drifts to the electric pink bougainvillea overhead. White lattice encloses the patio but the blue dumpsters in the alleyway are still in sight. Beneath our feet, shocking green lawn carpet refuses to lie flat. Wrinkles and valleys interrupt the surface like waves on the ocean.

Autographed photos of celebrities who've eaten here hang from the top of the wall. There are two limos in the narrow parking lot beside the stand. Stargazing isn't allowed though, so I don't know if the person at the next table is famous. My Goddess must always have my complete adoration and attention.

Small brown birds claim crumbs on the ground. They chirp constantly. The sound gives us both a headache, or she shares hers with me. Either way, I wish the high-pitched noise would stop. I'm hung-over on sex.

To my eternal damnation, I've learned that the catch when it comes to a Goddess is that she is absolutely inhuman, meaning that she is not human and she doesn't give a damn if I am. So what if it makes me catatonic to leapfrog through human history in search of abasement? If I curl up in a fetal position after she sells my body to the Marquis de Sade, does she care? Oh no. She revives me, pokes me, prods me. She demands, as her green convertible Jaguar roars down the wrong side of the autobahn at three hundred miles per hour, "Just what the fuck is your problem anyway?"

You wanted this.

Sure. I wanted this, but I wanted it different, somehow. I wanted to be in control of my domination. I wanted it to be like my jerk-off fantasies. This...This constantly defies my desires, and yet, reveals them in stunning clarity. My Goddess cuts to the heart of my libido, guts it, tacks it up for everyone to see, dissects it, splices, and wallows in it.

Back when I was merely obsessed with the idea of a Mistress, I could only imagine the high of being bent over a café table in Paris, pants torn away, ass cheeks receiving blow after blow of punishment for breaking her arbitrary rules.

I may be the only person ever sodomized in the Tokyo subway at rush hour, shafted in the midst of the Boston Marathon, and buggered on the plaza at Saint Paul's. I've left enough DNA samples around the world to thwart a million forensics experts. My spit lubricated the tip of the Great Pyramid at Giza before she ordered me to squat down on it. My seed splashed over David's perfect marble buttocks. My blood splattered on the stone lions guarding the New York Public Library.

She brings my thoughts back to Pinks, and her, with a hard slap across my face. Jaded Angelenos merely glance at us, and then away. My humiliation is never complete, so she twists her foot until I yelp.

Perched on her shoulder, watching me, is—I'll say a raven because it is vaguely bird-like and it's black, but the creature is something out of an unknown mythology. Its wings are like black crepe and muslin. For a bird, it has a remarkably saturnine expression. She calls it Chaos.

Chaos and my Goddess exchange a look of pure devilment. They turn to look at me. My balls try to retreat into my body, but she has them tightly bound by a leather strap so that they can't escape her. They strain at the skin of my sac, ready to burst.

I writhe, my hard-on excruciating. I'm going to come blood, I think.

She taunts me with false pity when I whimper. Chaos cackles. In our little universe, my Goddess is the center, and I'm less than space dust, but there is no question that she deserves my adoration.

I could ejaculate sonnets to her thighs; plump, white, voluptuous. One day I hope to delve into the cleft between those legs and taste her honeyed nectar.

Her skin is pale, as luminescent as the daytime moon. She wears sunglasses so inescapably dark that light doesn't reflect off their surface. Instead, it is absorbed, as if she wears black holes before her eyes. If I look close enough, I swear I can see time and matter bend around her face.

She wears her hair in a geometric bob. It is thick, black, mathematical perfection.

Shall I compare the brilliant coloration of her lips to pomegranates? They are satiny red. True red, infrared, but oh, she is ultra-cool.

Her jacket is classic black leather, cut to fit. The matching skirt hugs those thighs and caresses the lush expanse of her bottom. Her ass is a plum I'd love to sink my teeth into. I suspect that inside her boots she is *sur les pointes* like a ballerina, so extreme is the curve of the arch and the height of the heels.

Jacket black, hand white, nails freshly dipped in the viscera of a kill.

IMMUNE TO NO SMOKING ordinances and hostile, politically correct glares, the Goddess smokes.

No. It's so much more than that.

Perched between her middle and index fingers is a slim white cigarette. Her middle finger extends just so, flipping off the world, while the index finger crooks around the contraband.

She lifts it to her cupid-bow lips. They part. First, her tongue snakes out to wet the stage. Then the cigarette touches that silken red platform.

Across the patio, a man's shaky sigh announces his orgasm as she inhales. My Goddess has that effect on a lot of people. She exhales. The lesbian with a french fry in her mouth climaxes.

Chaos cackles at their embarrassment.

I often wonder what other people see when they look at my Goddess. Is she a frosty blonde in flannel for the lesbian? A Hollywood bimbette for the man? The other way around?

Her languid hand brings the cigarette to her mouth again. She exhales two columns of smoke that curl towards her nose from her bottom lip like the smoldering fires of Hades.

We ordered food. At least I think we did. Small details about real life don't stick in my mind anymore. I tear my gaze from my Goddess to see if food is coming.

She bounces her foot until I turn back to her. Those vulpine lips curve into a cruel smile.

"Oh Goddess," I moan.

Her eyebrow cocks up over the top rim of her sunglasses.

I want to come, but if I admit it, she'll never allow me to. Petulant with need, I finally snap, "You're not supposed to be smoking in here."

"No one minds."

"I do."

She holds my chin between her thumb and forefinger. "Always the good little boy. Kiss ass." She lets go with a jerk that sends my head spinning.

"Do you worship at my feet?" She has no reason to ask, but she often does.

Impaled, I lean forward. It hurts, man it hurts, but at least I have something to hurt. Verbal castration isn't thorough enough for her taste. At my first mistake, she shaved me and sent me back in time to fifteenthth or sixteenth century China as a eunuch in the Forbidden City. A lifetime I suffered with those dickless bastards; conspiring, vicious, sycophants, before she retrieved me.

No matter how much pain she inflicts on my balls, I'm eternally grateful that they're there.

"Do you worship at my feet?" She hates to repeat.

"I do." That isn't enough. I can see from the set of her mouth that I need to say more. "I worship you."

Her lips part.

"I love you."

Her bosom slowly rises and falls. Her thigh relaxes. I catch a glimpse of heaven in the dark space up her skirt. Her rich scent wafts to me.

"I adore you."

Her jaw is slack.

I lower my face to her crotch.

Chaos attacks me. He batters my head and screeches.

My Goddess snaps out of her reverie. The cigarette rises to her mouth again, but I notice a tremble in her hand. She slaps her thighs together.

"Naughty boy."

She relishes every syllable of those words. Because they taste so good, she rolls them around her tongue like a bonbon.

She looks to the ceiling. Her chin points up, exposing her alabaster neck.

I try not to groan as I force myself onto the spike, lower, lower, until I can press my lips to her jugular to suckle like an orphaned vampire.

She takes a drag on her cigarette. Her exhale is an extended sigh.

I'm grumpy because I haven't been allowed to come for three days. I think it's been three days. It might be three years. We jump across time and space as her whim carries us, and she is very whimsical. How can anyone track time that flows along a mobius strip? We go on tangential loops that are lifetimes long only to return to when and where we were before. Linearity holds no appeal for her.

"You really shouldn't smoke in here."

"Oh all right."

*

Rather than put out her cigarette, she moves us to a café in Amsterdam where she can smoke.

She knows that I hate Dutch food. I'm starving, and pissed off, but I don't dare risk complaining again.

In this city, they let the houseboats dump untreated human waste right into the canals. The reek wafting off the brown water makes me gag. I'm breathing like a carp. Instead of smelling the September scent of the canals, I can taste it. After scraping the flavor off my tongue with my teeth, I press my nose against her throat where she smells of myrrh.

Tears stream down my face as the heel of her boot slices through the fabric of my jeans and into my skin. I watch one tear lurch down into her cleavage. Lucky little bastard.

"You want a sausage, baby?" she croons to me.

Chaos cackles. I should know better than admit to any desire except her, but I nod. She unzips the front of her skirt and pulls out a sausage that looks suspiciously like my dick.

"On your knees."

I kneel before her. She slaps the sausage penis against my face.

"Deep throat it."

She pushes my head down onto it. The back of my tongue tastes wiener juice.

"Lick it."

I lap wide strokes over the length of it. I've learned not to mind sucking real cock, but fellating sausage is a new depravity for me.

As I service her meat, I feel a ghost sensation on my dick. I experiment with nibbling kisses. The nerves in my cockhead tingle. I work the tip of my tongue into the slit. The probing intrusion brings a moan from my throat. The more I throw myself into it, the more I feel.

I go to extremes to pleasure myself. With my lips in a tight ring, I slowly push down the shaft of sausage. It's like being in the tightest pussy ever. The mirror sensation feels so good on my dick that I grasp the base and stroke while I lap at the head.

The other diners protest. Even in Amsterdam it's déclassé to wave around an erection before the cocktail hour. Besides, we're not in the right part of town to stage a sex show.

Two American college boys at the next table suppress their lust with thoughts of violence.

"Are you a chick with a dick?" The blond one calls out as he kicks his chair back.

Foolish humans.

My Goddess turns her head at a glacial pace. Her lips purse into a kiss that she blows from her open palm. It flutters across the distance and lands on his erection. I see a shiny stain spread on the front of his grungy jeans. His friend jumps up, yelling, as he comes inside his pants too.

My Goddess leans forward to run her tongue up the side of my face. I hate it when she does that, but I enjoy seeing someone else on the whip end of her tongue.

"My boy knows better than to come without permission."

She unzips my fly and pulls out my dick. Her grasp is rough. "He's always hard for me. Aren't you, baby?" she coos while watching them.

My Goddess. My tormentor.

She leers at the boys and makes them come again. As she laughs, cruel and wicked, I tinge jealous.

I'm relieved when the fashionably grungy young men grab their backpacks and stride away. One turns back to flip her off.

"Fucking bitch! Freak!"

Distance emboldens cowards.

With a dismissive wave of her hand, they hurtle into the canal.

How I love her!

She slaps my cheeks with the sausage to get my attention. "You haven't earned your meal yet. Suck this like you mean it."

She pushes me down on the sausage. Her hips thrust up as she fucks my face. My throat rebels, but my dick loves it. Cock wins every time. I force my throat to relax and take it. My exposed dick feels the hot, wet embrace of tongue. I slurp around the head. Heaven. I give damn fine head.

She lets me feel every sensation as I kneel on the sizzling sidewalk. My lips clamp tight down the length of my shaft. Every broad-tongued lick I swirl over the head makes me shiver. My balls tighten. I can feel come ready to surge up my dick.

The question is always, "If you could give yourself head, would you?" Oh yes. But would you swallow?

She pulls the sausage out of my mouth. It's slick with my saliva. I'm panting. Is she going to make me beg for the dick? I will. I'll grovel. I want it bad.

"Go ahead and take a bite."

She can't be serious.

"Bite the sausage. Eat it."

She's an artist. Her medium is cruelty.

I gingerly close my jaw over the tip of the sausage. My balls, once again, try to retreat. She lets me feel my skin break under my teeth, but mercifully shuts off the psychic connection after that. Ravenous, I devour the sausage until my nose grinds against her *mons*.

Around us, diners burst into spontaneous coital combustion. Men curse in several languages. One woman silently slams her forearm onto the table as she rides it out. Her flowered summer skirt hikes up her thighs with each grunt and twist of her hips. The other women are more demure. There's no mistaking the rush of pink in their lips and the distinctive coloring across their cheeks though. The scent of twenty different women perfumes the air.

It's a garden. A garden of earthly delights.

I PITCH FORWARD, face down in a lawn. The blades of grass are as finely honed as daggers. We've moved to a tropical garden. Ah—the garden of earthly delights. It always takes a moment for my brain to catch up to my body when my Goddess shifts scenes on me.

Every color sparkles as if the plants, birds, and butterflies are newly minted. They are living jewels. Distinct scents perfume the air. Even the earth smells of clean minerals without the hint of decay. Water falling down a stream is so pure it almost hurts to look at it. Where can I be?

The beginning, she tells me. There is awe in her voice I've never heard before.

My hands are bound behind my back. From the strain on my elbows I know that leather gauntlets cover my forearms. They are laced together. My sphincter grasps the large plug shoved into it. Cruel metal rings press around my cock.

Bringing me to my knees, my Goddess bares her breast. Her skin is blue-veined marble, yet warm and soft. Her pale-blushed nipple teases my bottom lip.

"Wanna bite?"

Her offered breast is now candy apple red. Oh temptress! Snake!

Her tongue flickers between compressed lips so fast that I almost can't see the vibration. She lets me imagine that flickering over my tightly bound balls.

Her fig leaf is slightly askew. It almost falls and almost reveals in a tease what women who shed veils understand all too well. I want to burrow behind the leaf and plunge my tongue inside her.

Chaos rises to slap my face with his bedraggled wings.

"Forbidden thoughts will expel you from paradise," my Goddess warns.

True paradise is between her thighs. I can smell her brine. I want her, not the garden around us.

THE SCENERY CHANGES again. My stomach lurches. We're at sea. We're on a ship. I can hear the groan and creak of the wood as we ride up and down waves. Overhead, the sails crack in the wind gusts.

Her knees press into my stomach as I drape over her lap. My legs are spread wide so that I feel the breeze against my dangling balls. Salt spray cools my buttocks. I squint against the bright sunlight. Jolly Roger's gap-toothed smile leers at me from a big black banner.

I've fallen into the hands of pirates.

Onto the hand of a pirate, she corrects as I feel her fist in my rectum.

I get her little joke. I'm being rogered.

From the pirate flag, the skull above the crossed bones winks at me.

Her hand rotates carefully in my ass.

It isn't enough that she uses me. She has to make sure people witness my humiliation. I see the crew of the ship slowly converging. A woman on the ship! Orgasms explode like fireworks in her honor.

The rancid human reek of the crew overwhelms the scent of the ocean. I wonder if the worlds she takes me to are real. This one smells real enough. Every version of reality is as real as anything else, I decide. An avatar of an avatar. Then her hand pulses against my prostate and I thrash so hard that I can't think.

I realize that I'm babbling. Rock hard, I writhe against her plush thighs.

Oh Goddess! Let me make an offering across your altar.

I'm filled. My sphincter quivers and grasps at her frail wrist. I thrust my ass in the air as I beg her to fuck me harder.

I'm your goddess-damned hand puppet. Make me talk, mistress! Make prayers fall from my lips as you stroke my soul!

My balls are tight. "May I come?" I beg. I'm moaning and growling. I try to clamp my teeth shut but can't stop the animal sounds pouring out of my chest.

My fingers are digging into the deck. I brace and lift myself off her warm lap to try to see her arm entering me. Obligingly, a mirror appears behind us at a slight angle. She wears elbow-length black leather gloves.

Oh fuck. Is that ever hot.

Curious members of the crew creep forward. Some fondle their dicks.

Will she offer me to the pirates?

Sorry boys, I've been stretched. Your pricks won't even register after this reaming.

"May I come?" I beg again.

She seems transfixed by our reflection in the mirror. For once the cigarette is gone. The sunglasses disappear. Her satin red lips part as she draws in a breath. Those dark eyes reflect our reflection from the mirror. A thousand smaller pictures of us cascade into her dilated pupils until they are infinitesimally small.

"Please?" I whimper. "Please let me come, Goddess."

"Not yet," she says in a ghost of her voice.

"Fuck me," I beg as I rock onto her arm. I am so full.

She wriggles her fingers.

This is by far the most arousing thing she's ever done to me. I am abased. Love for her wells in my chest.

Her thighs part. She pants. I smell a deeply forbidden scent—earth and heaven, brimstone and brine.

The pirates watch her skirt ride up in rapt attention. They can smell her too.

I'm closer guys. I was here first.

Tremors run through my sphincter as I try to keep her in my ass. I grasp at her, clenching down hard enough to break a mortal's wrist. I don't want her to go. She fills me. She completes me.

"I love you," I confess.

I suspend myself on one tortured arm as I plunge my thumb to her clit. Her focus goes into another world and she withdraws her hand from my ass. She spreads for me.

"Don't do it," she mumbles. "Mistake."

Mistake? I am the King of Mistakes. I gave my soul to a Goddess.

No one can imagine what it's like to be so addicted to humiliation that I sob when she chooses to romance with coos and kisses instead of pain. I suffer horrible nagging doubts as her attention wanders away to the pretty boys dancing together in clubs. I have sweating nightmares about boring her. When I sulk, she doesn't bother to ask what's wrong, because she doesn't care. Or maybe it's just another of her exquisite cruelties. Fear and hope make for tortured nights. Then, as I'm sure it's over, and I'm hoping she'll allow me to go mad again rather than exist in sanity without her, she's inspired to create a fresh hell. She takes me lower, lower, but I'm so relieved that she still wants to test my limits that I kiss her feet and praise her name even when she brands me a heretic and hands me over to the Inquisition.

Don't tell me about mistakes.

Chaos squawks and beats my head. I send him crashing to the deck.

I plunge ahead. Ambrosia gushes from her sex. I sink on all fours before her and suckle on her clit. Nectar of the gods coats my tongue.

My hips thrust against air. Hard for so long, my dick aches. I'll go mad if I don't fuck something.

I fight to my feet.

Chaos rises again. His wings cut across my sight.

My Goddess spreads her legs. Wild on her scent, I plunge my dick into the beginning of time. I press her knees to her chest and big-bang slam her.

The sound of wet fucking is music. Growling, crying, she sings. It's a symphony of sex.

She tightens around me. If I try to pull away now I'll leave it all behind—cock, balls. She has them in a relentless grip that pulses like quasars.

Her fingernails dig into the flesh of my ass. It hurts like hell and turns me on. Her eyes half-close and her mouth hangs open. Her round ass rises from the deck to ride my cock.

If the pirates still watch, if they still exist, they stand in silent awe.

"Give me your cock," she growls in the voice of gods, angels, demons, a chorus of deities. Her thighs imprison me.

I have no desire to refuse her.

The slide in and out of her becomes my entire existence. I withdraw as far as she'll allow so that the plunge back in will be that much more intense. The only sound I hear is my blood surging through my veins.

How to praise her? "I worship you. I adore you."

Her sex throbs at my words.

Chaos is frantic. He appeals to her, but all reason is gone from her eyes. She's immersed in the rut. He attacks me, but I'm immune to pain.

"I pray to you, my Goddess."

She comes stars. Planets trickle down the inside of her thigh.

The ship is gone. The sky is gone. The sea is gone. There is only the void and her pussy.

"I love you."

She squeezes my balls. "Worship me."

I come like a fire hydrant spewing on a summer street. I think I will never stop. She milks my balls dry, suctioning out the last drops from the depths of my scrotum with her insatiable cunt.

My heart goes supernova, exploding into bits. She births a universe. I fall into the nothingness.

"Fucking Goddesses," Chaos complains. "I was growing fond of that last version of creation." He rises on wing into the new reality.

MIRROR, MIRROR ON THE WALL ⌕ *JJ Giles*

TORTURE. DOES ANYONE alive even know the meaning of the word? I sit here in my tower, a cylindrical edifice, fifty-three stories piercing the fabric of the heavens. It's little more than a rocket ship mired in the death and decay of fecund soil unable to blast me away from this place. When I designed it, I envisioned the ultimate phallic symbol standing straight and proud with the power of regeneration in its soul. The shrubbery at its base grows in pairs, monstrous orbs teeming with birds that feast on berries and then slip away, unnoticed. Its exterior windows remind of the hundred-headed hydra watching the busyness of ordinary life without becoming involved.

The lower levels of this superlative cock contain the offices of my architectural firm, spaces filled with creatures whose very lives depend on their willingness to destroy. Destroy they must:

231

the land, the trees, the seas, the habitats of all creatures to see their own visions take root and become real. For the upper stories, I had something more practical in mind. Those who slave must be housed.

The central shaft of this building is no less than fifty feet in diameter and stretches between heaven and hell. On the platform within that shaft is my bed. From there, I watch.

All of them, on some level, belong to me. Whether they merely work for me to create destruction unparalleled in the history of mankind, or simply shuffle papers matters not. I own a piece of all of them, an infinitely larger piece than those they're married to, those they're in love with, and those that have passed on whom they still hold dear. Foolish, all of them.

I've hired them all. Once even a particle of them belongs to me, it cannot be returned. Out of greed, out of lust, out of some errant sense of humanity they give themselves over to become puppets on strings, or shadows upon my walls. Shallow, feeble, mindless they are when they nod, or smile, or cringe in my presence. Little do they know they are but angels and demons, clothed in flesh, waging the eternal battle between good and evil, minions of the gods of both Dark and Light.

From the shaft in my tower, through two-way mirrors, I not only watch, I listen. I see pride. I feel desire. I feed on the humiliation they heap upon one another. I laugh at the praise they offer, not to bolster another's esteem, but only to be loved in kind. Those moments of stolen sexuality on the tops of desks and in cleaning closets entertain me. Like elementary school children, they exchange notes about me, converse in hushed tones, always asking, "Who is he?"

For that they'll never know the answer because they ask not the proper question.

Burned into my psyche as if by firebrand is the day she walked through my door. I call her she, for in my soul she remains nameless. Had I known she existed, I would have stolen her at birth, but such are my own limitations. Even I had to wait, wait for fate and my own temptation.

CAN EVIL BE tempted? Evil is temptation.

Three years ago, she arrived wearing the ultimate disguise. From a place as far-flung as Phoenix, she walked through my door at the appointed hour, her portfolio in hand. Strands of delicate gold and burnished bronze wrapped carefully around her head and twisted in back. She wore a gray business suit and a black camisole. I think it was the shoes, black leather with a delicate strap around her ankle that destroyed me. Those four-inch spikes called heels stabbed at my heart.

"Good morning, Ms. Gryffin," I said calmly.

With only a glance at my eyes, she murmured, "Mr. Cavanaugh. It's a pleasure to meet you."

Pleasure. Can a child of twenty-four begin to understand? At that moment, she was already mine, yet I allowed her to lay her designs out before me. I must admit, a few were outstanding because they became part of the landscape, rather than something that replaced it. Another of a fast food joint designed to fit an English garden was adequate. It pays the bills. We spoke briefly of her knowledge of explosives, and how to drop a building such as mine into the hole from which it arose.

Throughout that interview, she refused to be insolent, try as

I might to capture her gaze. She surrendered like a lamb laid upon the altar as a sacrifice. Though the azure hue of her eyes caused my heart to trip, the first emotional response I obtained came when I said, "You're hired." I saw a shiver. And then a smile.

"Thank you," she said warmly. "I hadn't believed it was possible."

"But that's what this world is about," I instructed. "Anything is possible. Do you have a place to live?"

"No. I have reservations to return today, but since I need to find a place, I will change them."

"Not to worry," I said. "If you're interested, the top third of this building is all apartments. I live in the penthouse. And we do have several vacancies just now."

"Really," she said excitedly.

"Would you prefer an ocean view or something that looks over the city?"

Maintaining control of her excitement, she said, "The ocean, Sir. Please, the ocean. But . . . can I afford this?"

"It's a company perk," I told her. "Twenty-two percent of your salary pays the rent and utilities. However, should you choose to work elsewhere, the cost rises to four thousand a month. Would you like to see it?"

I believe she was stunned. Yet she rose from the chair like a delicate vine in search of sunlight. "I would, yes. I hope I'm that valuable to you."

"Ms. Gryffin, please. Never have we had anyone come to us who knows so much about architecture and implosions. Your value is unquestioned."

"My father was a Navy SEAL. When he got out of the service,

he started his own business. I was maybe three when I'd sit on his lap and we'd look over the plans of a building for the best way to demolish it. I was ten when I went to work with him."

"Practical experience. Something I can appreciate."

I escorted her to the forty-ninth floor, the most spacious I have with an ocean view. I slipped the key card into the slot opening the door. Her complexion paled to see the Italian marble floor of the entry hall, the Waterford crystal sconces flickering with the amber hue of a single electric flame. Seduced by this everyday magic, she moved cautiously toward the stone fireplace and then perched on the built-in bench before the window.

"This is unbelievable."

I smiled. "Three bedrooms, three full baths. Kitchen, dining room, of course." I moved down the hallway toward the double doors of the Master suite. Dutifully, she followed.

With an explosion of breath that sounded something like "Oh God," she waltzed happily into the room. Heavily, she plopped onto the built-in platform designed as a king-size bed. "Just a mattress here," she noted. But it was on the mirrored wall her vision focused. "I'm not sure I can stand to look at myself that much."

I laughed a little. With a shrug, I offered, "Keep the draperies pulled."

"I can do that." Finally, her vision connected to mine, her stare unflinching. "Daddy thinks this building is a modern-day interpretation of the Tower of Pisa. I...think it's something more...interesting."

Unable to control my reaction, I burst into laughter. "You, Ms. Gryffin, would be correct."

235

FOR THREE MONTHS I watched her computer habits. The sites she visited. On the thirteenth of October, I responded to her ad seeking a Master. Through the pretense that I lived in a distant place and this would be a long-distance relationship, I gained her trust. Only rarely did she respond during working hours. Every evening was passed chatting with me. At the end of another three months, I received:

KITTEN: My Lord, Your screen name. What does it mean?
DREAMDESTROYER: Only that your dreams must be destroyed
    before you can envision Mine so that we can be together.
KITTEN: My Lord, I need you desperately.
DREAMDESTROYER: It is for Me you live, precious. Tomorrow by
    special courier a package will arrive at your office. After
    hours, return to your apartment and follow the instructions.
KITTEN: Anything You wish, my Lord.
DREAMDESTROYER: Correct

Though I invited her to join me for lunch in the executive dining room, she was beyond comprehension. The package I'd sent was placed on her desk, a seat of honor, yet she had refused to disobey and open it earlier than I'd instructed. She excused herself with a comment about a deadline for a design, yet I could scent the pheromones already seeping through her skin. Work was impossible for her. But I hadn't hired her as an architect.

At precisely five o'clock, the package was held in her clutch like a baby as she made her way to the elevator. I rode to the forty-ninth floor with her and bid her adieu. Quickly, I went to the penthouse and then opened the door on my shaft. Naked and nestled comfortably in the chair on the platform, I pushed the lever that lowered me to view her.

Already her hair had been released from its bondage and flowed around her shoulders like molten fire. With the package placed on the white down comforter of her bed, she bent over it, her nails slicing the tape holding it closed. With a hand clutched to her heart, she laid it open to remove the floral-scented tissue. Delicately, she grasped the single red rose and held the velvet of its petals to her lips. Again, she reached in, this time for the hand-written note.

My beautiful angel,
As we have already discovered, it is for Me alone that you live and breathe. Because you have begged so shamelessly to be permitted to offer a sign of your surrender to Me, I will now allow that. Before the mirror you've told Me about, I want you to kneel, the ass on the carpet, the knees spread wide.

Apparently, she'd read only that much before she tore the fabric from her body and placed the box on the floor. Unhesitant, she placed the stem of the rose between her teeth and settled beside the box. With the letter in one hand, she continued to read:

The rabbit fur mittens—gently on every square inch of skin.

The corner of her lip twisted over the stem of the rose as her hands slipped into the skins. As I'd taught her through instant messages and letters, she folded her legs underneath and sat back, the V created by her widely spread knees reminding me of a delta, fed by the mouth of a river. The strain on her inner thighs captured my attention, yet the ripple of the muscles of her abdomen pulled me upward as she arched back, the better to the thrust her breasts into her hands.

With the most symmetrical movements, as if solid bone had melted into waltzing ribbons, her arms stretched long. The mittens slid up her back and dallied over the protruding ribs. In soft delicate circles they stirred ever-widening tremors through her upper body, every nerve coming alive with indelicate flinches. As if to worship only Helios, she stretched long to the newfound heat, the mittens rising over her swelling chest, slowing only to leave tender kisses on the throat, before covering her face to reacquaint her with her desperation. The elbows held tightly to her breasts slowly parted like the petals of an exotic bloom, hidden to all creation other than the snakes that slither around the roots. The nipples burst forth, rigid, posed like pulsing orbs of red light warning of an imminent melt down.

Somehow my body moved in concert with hers, connected by a shared mentality, a common lust. I slid forward to the edge of the chair as if I could be closer to her, divided as we were by my looking glass. Vicariously, I felt the seduction of the fur.

Her body rolled forward again; her hands grasped at the note. A tremor of understanding flashed in her eyes. She slipped one hand out of the mitt to grasp the monstrous phallus inside. Unhesitant, her pelvis thrust toward me as she reached behind to slip the loops of the harness over her ankles.

Never have I seen one so controlled, so intent on upon savoring each enticing sensation, so willing to be carried to the next level, each circle descending to the pit. With her head thrown back, her hips hovered over the phallus as if it were an arrow ready to pierce her flesh and ultimately, her sanity. The muscles of her thighs strained to hold her in mid-air. They quivered uncontrollably as she lowered herself slowly.

At the touch of the phallus, her entire body shuddered and drew my attention away from her thighs. As if the first soft sweet inch of it had the power of unlocking her sexuality, a river of moisture slid down the shaft and soaked into the carpet beneath her. Her abdomen convulsed as might a boa constrictor's laboring with a meal twice its size. The first timid gasp from her chest escaped as if to expel all unnecessary volume and make space for me.

When most of them merely fall onto it, impaled as it were, she ingested it. By millimeters it disappeared, the nine-inch length of it completely gone from my sight as her ass once again caressed the carpet. What must that feel like, to be devoured so slowly? To know that the control I command has been wrenched from my grip? All I knew at that moment is that she was, and would forever be, the Temptress Extraordinaire.

Noticeably, her breasts swelled and her hands reached up to fondle them. So lost she was, not in the exhibition, but the sensations. Minutes divided those small stimulations she seemed to cherish, from the moment she picked up the note again. Anxiously, she thrust her hand into the box. Tears dripped from her eyes.

A flash of chrome bored through the mirror like a crack of lightening. I crouched low, the better to be closer to her. The naked hand opened a clover clamp as the furred hand raised a breast. Like a moth dancing around a flame, the soft rubber tips seemed compelled to bite into the rigid flesh of the nipple. Damnable women, she denied that piece of steel its pleasure as she merely dusted it around the nipple. When the decision was made or how, I still don't know. I've rerun the tape a thousand times to see the clamp jump out of her hand and latch onto its prey.

With a wounded yowling, she cried out. Engulfed in pain, her body stretched long and fell forward, yet her consciousness kept her securely planted on the phallus. Both hands locked onto the tortured breast and tried to pull it from her body, the suffering in it too great to retain it. As much as I would have liked to reach out and take it from her, the wall of glass forced her to enjoy my ministrations in solitude.

Tears washed down her cheeks as guttural emanations from her throat increased in intensity. I heard her garbled voice, unable to discern words, yet the rhythmic gyrations of her hips reminded of a dance propelled by a chant. As if she willed it, the other clamp bit down on its target. Without removing the rose from her teeth, the lips grasped the chain between the clamps.

I dropped to my knees; the better to press my own neglected agony to the cold glass. The first few drops of moisture burst forth, those two or three drops being the humiliation of a cloud burst in the face of a hurricane. A river of wanton lust poured forth from her body flowing over the shaft like the torrent of a waterfall. Mesmerized, I watched as her arms stretched long and her hips began to roll. The muscles of her abdomen ignited each other. The wave rolled up her body and shook the breasts.

The melody to which she danced remained fully enclosed in her mind. Yet the rhythm beat within me, as her hips swayed and occasionally cocked. In an opposite direction, her head rolled to pull the breasts away from her body, distorted to my utmost pleasure.

Out of my memory, I heard the sound of ancient lutes and foreign tongues. Could it be her, clothed in new flesh, come to haunt me, and torture me into my own nightmare...again? Because there was something so fresh about this one, nothing within so jaded that even the illusion of innocence had been destroyed, this new succubus I knew I could easily break. Like the sirens of old, clothed in silk veils, draped in precious gems, she danced before me. But this one rode the shaft, and tortured herself.

Her hips thrust now, as her body stretched long, the better to pound my implement of penetration. With her head thrown back, her breasts strained to caress her throat. The furred hand slid over her face to obliterate the last vestiges of the ego still lurking. The creature within roared to life and straightened her spine. A determined hand drove at the aching clit as the other grasped the chain from her mouth and pulled outward.

And then her vision locked on mine.

It thrust me backwards, the intensity driven at me with precision. I could feel the energy emanating like spikes of glowering red light capable of rearranging my sanity. It swelled within me and drove my cock into my hand. I felt a fuse ignited, saw a gauntlet thrown, and I laughed.

The creature within drove at her body while she hovered above, locked to me. Beautiful tears flushed from her eyes, she no more aware of her true self than she could comprehend the sensations delivered to the flesh. She'd given herself over to it completely; she'd given it to me. The evil inside was mine alone.

With violent contortions, her body shook with that first

orgasm. Deeply mired in an altered dimension, her lips closed on the stem of the rose. A drop of blood slid down her chin, yet I held her gaze somehow. Silently, I instructed: Just breathe, but don't leave me. I want you to fly...to come with me.

Though her body shook, she lifted her hips. The glass cock fell from her cunt. Easily, she swiveled forward and captured it behind. Maddened by lust, she thrust down hard.

At only the third circle, she weakened terribly. Blood spilt over her chin and dripped on her chest. She was on the verge of collapse when I stepped through the looking glass.

The hair on her head was as swollen as everything else about her. It flowed through my fingers like molten fire as I raised her. At the scent of her Master, the rose dropped from her teeth and her pierced lips locked onto my balls. Unhesitant, I wrenched her head back and thrust my cock into her mouth.

"Once again," I whispered solemnly as I pushed her onto the phallus to be broken a little more. The vibrations of orgasmic ecstasy in her throat felt like the wild rhythm of her chant. As though she'd never feasted, she swallowed every drop of my essence another two times. Only when she fell out of my clutch, unconscious, did I let her rest.

IS HER BEAUTY alone enough to drive me insane? Through the ages I've taken not only the most beautiful, but the most powerful. Agrippina the Younger, brood bitch for the Emperor Nero, threw herself to my bed when she realized her scion meant to murder her. I saved him the trouble, but left him the blame. And then Cleopatra, whose beauty was legendary rather than real, ruled half of the world, the better half indeed, when she chose

Caesar over me. Yet I was present when Death slithered to her throat and swallowed her whole.

The thief of my sanity requires more than mere beauty to tempt me. But what is it? It's not even her total surrender; a mind divided to both serve and exist. It's that she's so totally connected to me we rarely speak any longer. As carefully as I watch her, she studies me for silent commands and inaudible movements. With her vision ever connected to my feet, her eyes occasionally glance at my chest. By some eerie magic, she hears my inner voice.

Desire as I might to deny it, she has captured me.

In the years and tears of separation from my former self, she has yet to leave my side. Try as I might to find her edges, there seem none. What creature has the cosmos wrought in her, she who cannot be humiliated by the simplest of tasks? Of cleaning toilets? Who for hours on end is bound to an exhibition stand, spread open and used by my executives? Who can then be dressed and placed before those men, their combined fluids moist on her thighs, while she presents unheard of ideas? Who says things like, "Because the fabric of our lives woven in this modern age by technology changes so radically and dramatically, buildings must be disposable just as everything else is. Why not build the explosives that will take it down, into the pylons when you're putting it up? It would save millions."

How absurd! Yet... pragmatic. She leaves even me speechless. Her only quirk is that she carries the television remote with her as the ancients carried crosses. I can live with that.

Never have I found the key to her heart. Countless hours she's passed in unpleasant constriction forced to watch me with all others. She doesn't complain. Though I may leave her caged for days, she comes to me fresh and pure again. Loaned out to my executives for a week at a time, she returns with tears in her eyes, begging never to be parted again. An hour later, she's properly prepared to be presented to me. I take her in my arms and vow never to punish her for anything.

Yet, I do.

EVEN AS I sit here and write this, she's an enigma. I'll let her be for awhile; the flesh is exhausted again, but the soul inside still starves. Could anything sate it? Relentlessly, she watches silent video of implosions sent by her father. The purity of our sanctum is ruptured by the destruction on the screen, soundless carnage. Annihilation should sound like death and destruction. It should be filled with tortured screams and burning agony. But the kind she prefers, the thief in the night, is silent.

But why, always, does she have the TV remote? I wondered early on. She would press furiously on the keypad, and I'd watch with morbid curiosity, a lunatic feeding some illness. As time went on, it wasn't lunacy she displayed but some superior knowledge of languages. She was text messaging me in an ancient tongue. It showed up on my computer as slashes and loops, until finally I recognized it, and read the hymns she wrote to me, her god. Systematically, she destroyed my will to resist.

But the aggravations of daily life still churn. The short circuit in the fire alarm. That blaring horn has daily driven me out of my mind. Fuck it. It's a short circuit somewhere. For two weeks now, day and night, I've had to shut down the building while the fire department does a room-by-room search. Loss of industry. Loss of living space. It's costing a fortune.

And the electricians can't find it. Even now, the occupants of my structure are dawdling toward the stairwells to escape this nuisance, in the event it might be an actual fire.

But she who has captured me is smiling. The sirens have awakened her, and her beauty is restored. Her flesh retains the resilience of youth; her lips part to receive me. She stands before the mirror seeing only herself, but feeling me for she knows I am watching.

Her peacefulness brings such calm to my heart. Yet she's playful as she holds up the remote, her tongue washing her lips with the essence of lust. One of those devilish smiles strokes my own need as her thumb dashes over the keypad to send a message.

What is this? It takes time to translate.

"My Lord, my Love—now that you know you've been broken, I may reveal all. For your crimes against humanity, for your arduous love, for your greed, gluttony, wrath and lust, by God and all that is Holy, by Aphrodite, Cleopatra, Marie Antoinette, and Myself. By Alexander the Great and herdsman the world through, you stand convicted. Go ye back from whence ye came!"

The image of fire bursts on the screen; the screen blazes with preternatural fury. I hear the cackling flames and feel the heat pierce my body threatening to explode. It melts into ice, a brilliant flash of white replaces it. It's not text messager at all, but a remote. Detonation. Where am I going? I belong to no one!

"You whore..."

She laughs.

In the aftermath of The Cavanaugh Tower implosion, the death toll remains at one. The owner, Mr. Richard Cavanaugh, was found in the first day of the rescue effort. The building, due to malfunctioning wiring setting off the fire alarms was otherwise empty last Sunday, and thankfully a holiday weekend, the downtown area where the implosion occurred, empty. What was at first thought to be a terrorist attack, has the FBI wondering if it was a grandiose suicide instead.

The architectural firm of Cavanaugh, Cavanaugh and Associates, Inc., whose offices were destroyed, will maintain its operations from a remote location where all of its computer files are stored. A brother of the late Richard Cavanaugh, Daniel, is now CEO of the corporation, and promises to restore the area to even greater grandeur. A search warrant to examine Richard's personal files was issued yesterday.

In related news, the search for Richard Cavanaugh's personal assistant and known lover, Sheba Gryffin from Phoenix, has gone global. During the past three years of their relationship, in which they were known in the upper echelons of society as The Twins of Good and Evil for their eccentric flamboyance and unfailing generosity, they have never been seen apart. While the recovery effort at the implosion sight is yet to conclude and may yet reveal her remains, the FBI believes that she may still be alive. Because she may be able to answer their questions, the FBI requests that you report a sighting of her, but they ask that you do not approach her.

THE JEALOUS KING AND THE GENEROUS LOVER
Bryn Colvin

THERE WAS ONCE a great king who had spent his youth conquering his neighbours so that the whole of the island on which he lived was brought to peaceful life under his rule. He ruled well and wisely for many years, bringing justice and law to people who had lived with bitter violence for many generations. His subjects came to respect him, realising that under his direction they prospered, whereas before they had done nothing but fight and live from hand to mouth.

This king, however, was already past his prime, and he had no heir to follow after him. His two brothers had died in battle, without siring children of their own. The king and all his country knew that, without someone strong to follow after him, the land would fall back into chaos and war when he died. Although he was in his middle years and wore several scars from his warrior

247

days, the king was a strong and handsome man, and every maiden in the country hoped she might be chosen as his wife. Day after day, fair damsels were presented to him. Some could sing, and some could dance. Some came from old warrior families and offered alliances to strengthen the kingdom. Some had long legs and curving bottoms, others sported ample bosoms or slender necks. Each displayed her skills before the court, entertaining the assembly with song or poem, with gifts of finely woven clothes, displays of horse riding or other appealing qualities.

The king enjoyed these displays very much. He was still young enough to appreciate the turn of a shapely ankle or to find himself rising in admiration of swaying hips and rounded breasts. He never lacked for company in his bed. Lower ranking girls, who could not hope to be his wife aspired to be his mistress, were never in short supply. There was always some fair creature willing to wrap her legs around his back, or apply her dexterous tongue to the royal erection. While the king enjoyed such sports, he knew that he must have a legitimate heir by a wedded wife or all his work would be in vain and his country would fall when his life ended. The king knew that his wife must not merely be beautiful; she must also be clever and loyal. She must help secure the kingdom, and not threaten it with the designs of her family. Such a woman would not be easily found.

As had become the custom, when the court finished dining, a young woman was brought forward. His chamberlain presented her.

"My King, this is Isabella, daughter of Richard of Zouche."

The young woman was fair indeed. Her dark hair was piled high upon her head, and her simple dress of dark blue revealed a graceful figure. Her eyes were wide, but she did not appear unduly frightened, nor possessed of vulgar overconfidence. The king remembered the name his chamberlain had offered.

"Richard of Zouche fought at my side a decade ago," he said, remembering the skilful knight fondly.

"It is so, my King," Isabella acknowledged, sweeping a low curtsey.

"He gave his life to save my own. I did not know he had a child, why were you not presented here before?"

"My King, it was my father's wish that I should grow up peacefully in the country."

The king nodded, liking her manners.

"And what skills or bounty do you wish to share with us tonight?" the king enquired.

Isabella raised her eyes and looked him squarely in the face.

"I should like to tell you a story."

They had heard stories before, either recounting the king's many triumphs, or dwelling on old myths. This tale proved to be something entirely different.

"There was once a king, who sought a wife," Isabella began, and the court drew in its breath as one, realizing what dangerous ground she could stray upon.

Isabella told of a young man who sought the very best wife the land could offer, and how a magician cast a spell upon a young woman, making her fairer than all others, and blessing her with extraordinary sexual prowess. The tale unfolded, line by line, growing ever more daring and bawdy with each new twist and turn. The king forgot to be shocked and found himself laughing along with the others.

"And what was the fabulous sexual secret this maiden possessed?" he asked.

"My King, I will tell you how the maiden of my story answered that question. She bowed very low and said, 'Your Majesty, I could not possibly tell the whole court, I should die of shame to utter such words. If you would grant me a private audience, I will tell you.'" Isabella remained quiet, allowing her words to sink in.

"Then you had best come with me," the King said.

He took fair Isabella to a little chamber not far from the hall, and closed the door so that they were alone.

"Tell me, then, what is the conclusion to this tale?"

Isabella blushed very prettily.

"My King, in the story, the maiden was very clever, and would not tell the prince until they were married, but he was not disappointed in her."

"And would you keep your virtue in the hopes of making such a bargain?"

Isabella looked long into the king's eyes.

"You are not a man to be toyed with, nor are you a foolish youth to be won by tricks," she said. "I will confess that, though it ruins me to do it, I would rather show you the trick and risk that you do not choose me as a bride."

He could see the desire in her face.

"Like the lady of my story, I am a maiden, but I know certain arts that might please your highness."

"I grant you leave to show me."

At this, Isabella dropped to her knees before him and, without hesitation, she reached into his costly garments and pulled out his already growing cock. The king could not have counted the number of girls who had performed this little trick for him, and he was partial to the warm moisture of a willing mouth. Isabella's lips were firm and eager. Her tongue snaked around his girth, flicking over the tip, and then coiling down his length. The king marvelled in these sensations as he sank deeper in. Then her tongue caressed his balls, without her lips relinquishing him. She licked these two globes of kingly power, sliding over them, reaching back further still to tease at his nether orifice. His cock was deep in her throat by this time, and the king sighed in blissful satisfaction as her impossibly long and dexterous tongue slithered against his backside and pressed against his sack. This was a rare and remarkable gift, he realized.

They were married a month later and, for a time, the king was very happy with his young wife. She proved willing to serve, and with her skilful tongue she bestowed many remarkable favors upon him. With her wit and good humor she soon won many friends in the court. Being the orphaned daughter of a heroic fighter, she attracted good will, but had no family of her own to advance. The court welcomed her and, for the most part, felt that she was less likely to scheme and plot than other girls might have been. For a while, things were indeed very happy for them.

Six months passed, and the Queen showed no signs of pregnancy, despite every effort to conceive. Not a day passed but she had the king's long prick in her but, even so, there was no sign of the all-important heir the kingdom so needed. A year came and went, and still her stomach did not swell. The king began to wonder if one of them might be infertile, and this thought ate into him, making him watchful. She was so beautiful, his

Isabella, so funny and charming and popular. Fear made him jealous and seeded dark paranoia in his heart. He thought perhaps his lady wife had a lover and that she used some art to avoid conception. She would probably outlive him and might rule after he died if there was no child. She could marry again and a strong man might gain the throne through her. These were dangerous thoughts, and slowly they poisoned his heart against his young wife and ruined his marriage.

One day, the king summoned his court magician, a cunning and talented man by the name of Osric. For more than a year, he had worked spells and charms that had failed to help the king father a child. Conscious that he could pay with his life for such a shortcoming, Osric dared not question any command his ruler made.

"How may I serve your majesty?" he asked in an unctuous voice.

"I find I doubt my queen's loyalty. You have tried everything to secure me a child, but it has failed. I have been thinking, and there is something I want you to do for me. I want you to make the queen ugly, so that none will desire her but I."

"Your Majesty, it will be done."

When Isabella woke on the following day, she was fair no longer. Her cheeks had lost their rosy bloom and the light was gone from her eyes. Her nose was longer and crooked, her white teeth grown uneven and yellowed. She stood before her mirror and regarded the hag she had become, and wept for the loss of her beauty. Isabella knew she had duties to perform, so she dressed herself in regal attire, and used make-up to disguise the bags beneath her eyes and the loss of color, but she could not truly hide what had been done to her. As she strolled in the palace, heads turned in her direction and courtiers and servants alike muttered behind their hands. Isabella faced it all with courage and dignity. She smiled as she had before, and made jokes. She tended to the sick, gave money to the poor, and went about her work as though nothing was wrong.

Time passed, and it was not long before the king called upon his magician again.

"Osric, it is not enough that she be ugly of face, for her body is still fair and fine, and men look at her lustfully."

The magician gave Isabella the hunched and sagging body of an old woman. Even this was not enough for the jealous king. He found her singing too alluring, so Osric took that, and then her capacity to speak. Still Isabella hobbled around the palace, carrying out her duties as best she could, hiding her grief with courage, and facing the court gossips and the cruel jokes made at her expense. When they were first wed, the king had come to her every night, but as she grew more hideous, his interest in her waned and she missed his visits. She could not blame him for loathing what she had become, and never thought to blame him for her suffering.

Rumors spread that the king meant to put his ugly, barren wife aside and marry again. Soon young girls were appearing at court, offering their skills and dowries in the hopes of catching the king's eye. Isabella treated them with kindness, although she could not speak and struggled to walk. She could still write, and gave orders that these women be well treated. In truth, she thought the fault her own and was willing to give up her place to any girl who might give the kingdom the heir they so urgently needed.

Isabella was hobbling through one of the courtyards, when she heard a group of her rivals laughing and ordering servants to loose dogs upon some poor peasant man. Kind hearted as she was, Isabella hurried forwards, waving frantically at the soldiers and servants to stop in their barbarous sport. No one would tell her what had happened, but there was a poor man lying on the ground, his hands around his head as though he was trying to protect himself. His clothes were soaked with water. The girls were still laughing, but seeing the queen they hurried away, leaving her with the stranger.

Kneeling down, the cursed queen touched the man lightly, and he started violently. When he realized she meant no harm, he raised his head.

"Thank you, Lady," he said, "I do not know what I did to offend them so."

From his voice she could tell he was a foreigner. Isabella wished she could speak to him. He was filthy and half starved, but she could see things in his eyes that made her think he was a good man. She reached for the pad of paper she always carried at her waist, and wrote a note for her lady in waiting.

"The queen is afflicted and cannot speak," the lady in waiting said, "but you are to have a bath and lodgings and, if you have some petition to make, you can do so. The queen asks me to tell you she is sorry you have been treated so badly."

The stranger was shocked when he heard this, for he had heard of Queen Isabella, but would not have recognized her. He bowed deeply and followed the servant who the lady had summoned to guide him.

Isabella did not know it, but the stranger she had aided was a man of high birth, sent as an envoy by the king of a neighboring country. His ship had been set upon by pirates, and Earl William of Vesey reached land by clinging to the wreckage. All he had were the clothes upon his back, and a leather case containing letters from his ruler. So important were his messages that he had pressed on, ignoring great hardship to reach the palace. He had been turned away at the gate, but Isabella's kindness resulted in a room being found for him, and poor but serviceable clothing being given in place of his rags. He was glad to be able to present himself in a more becoming manner than he had on arrival.

Dressed much like a servant, William found himself at liberty to wander the palace. He thought it wise to look around and learn what he could for his king. It did not take him long to discover how fair Isabella had grown ugly in a few short years, and lost her voice. It seemed mysterious to him, and he felt sorry for the woman, who he felt in his heart was kind and good. His roaming took him up a winding tower, at the top of which was a closed door. William was about to descend, when he heard voices.

"No, it will not do, we must wait until the moon is dark to make this spell."

"Are you sure, Master?"

"Oh yes, magic such as this cannot be made in a new moon, we must wait a month almost."

"I am not sorry to hear it, Master."

"Nor am I. I have done many things for the king, but this goes further than even I can stomach."

"At least this way she will suffer no more pain, Master."

"I am sorry she has suffered at all, and at my hand. I wish he would put her aside, rather than demanding her death."

William ran lightly down the stairs—he had heard enough and could guess the rest. The king wished to have his wife murdered by magic so that he could marry again. William guessed that a terrible curse had been laid upon the queen and he resolved, there and then, to break it. He did not know how such a thing could be done, so he waited at the foot of the tower for the king's magician to emerge. William followed Osric back to his quarters and, before the magician could lock himself into his room, the young earl forced the door open and rushed in. The magician was unprepared, and was about to intone a spell when he was pushed roughly to the ground.

"I know you have been ordered to kill the queen, and I know it weighs heavy on your conscience," William hissed.

The magician made no answer to this.

"I will take her away from here, and you may say that she is dead if you will, but first you must tell me how to lift the curse that is upon her."

"If you will take her far from court, I will give you money and horses to help you," Osric said. "I cannot lift the curses I have placed upon her. Only one of true heart may do that."

A little after dawn, William found the garden where the queen liked to walk in the early hours. He saw a stooped and battered old crone moving slowly between the roses, her face the ugliest he had ever laid eyes upon, but William remembered her kindness and the warmth he had seen in her eyes, and he approached her. There were no ladies in attendance on her: she had been forgotten. He swept a low bow.

"Good morning my Lady," he said.

She smiled at him, and dipped her head to acknowledge his greeting.

"I came to thank you for your kindness in aiding me yesterday."

Isabella was surprised by this, for she did not recognize the man as the same dirty stranger she had helped and could not imagine who he was. He took her hand and raised it to his lips, pressing several kisses against her wrinkled skin. Looking down, he saw that something very strange had happened. Where his mouth had touched her, Isabella's skin was as white as milk, without flaw or blemish. He saw that she too was looking. Knowing he was taking a great liberty, William raised her other hand to his mouth, and the same thing happened—the imprint of his lips wiped away the marks of age and ugliness. William understood then what Osric had said.

Isabella looked at her hands in amazement, wondering what enchantment this could be.

"Lady, you have been cursed," William told her. "I know the secret that will restore you to yourself, if you will let me help you?"

She nodded her consent.

"You must know this, Your Majesty: the curses laid upon you were made by your court magician, on the orders of your husband."

Tears stung Isabella's eyes as she heard the truth. She could not imagine why the king would have done such a thing to her, but she had no voice to ask why.

William took her hand and led her to the tiny room he had

been given. He kissed her forehead and the tip of her nose, watching her features slowly transform into those of a beautiful young woman. The press of his lips brought color into her cheeks, and fullness to her lips. When he fetched the tiny mirror from the wall and showed her how she had changed, Isabella wept for joy. William kissed her face and hands, finding the task all too easy. She was fair indeed beneath her cursed disguise, and fairer still for having a warm and loving heart that had suffered many ills.

When he unlaced her clothing and bared her skin, Isabella made no move to stop him. Her breasts had shrunk and sagged so that they hung down towards her stomach. William caressed them lightly, then kisses followed, and each one left her skin a little firmer. He sucked upon her nipples until they grew rosy and full between his lips, then continued across her stomach and hips, kissing away the curse.

The sun was high in the sky when William finished kissing Isabella. He had covered every part of her body with his mouth. Wrinkles and age marks had vanished at his touch. Before, there had been a broken old woman in his room, but he now saw a fair-faced young creature with soft, pale skin and shining eyes. However, the curse was not yet fully dispelled, for she still had no voice, and her body was still twisted. He had no idea how to cure these ills, but having spent so long in kissing and touching the queen, he was wild with arousal. When her fingers closed around his shaft, he knew he was lost. William tore off his clothing and threw it to the floor.

Isabella opened her arms for him and welcomed him into the small bed. It had been a long time since anyone had shown her affection, much less made love to her. She had no idea how this gorgeous, young man had managed to heal her, but she welcomed it, and meant to give herself to him by way of thanks. He had acted out of kindness alone, while those she had trusted had betrayed her utterly. His thick cock pressed against her, and then found its way in. Isabella held him tightly as he rocked against her, savoring the sweetness of his touch and the pleasure of being held. It did not take her long to realize this was very different from the sex she had known of late. Her king had grown careless with her, using her when it suited him, but doing little to satisfy her needs. This man used his hands and mouth to good effect, augmenting the influence of his shaft. Isabella melted in his arms, until his cock brought her pleasure.

"Oh," she moaned, "oh, yes," and then she was gasping at each thrust, her voice freed from the spell as she cried out, "I'm coming!"

William held her and stroked her face. She gazed up at him, looking deep into his eyes. It was then that she recognized him as the man she had helped on the previous day. She knew that her limbs were as straight as they had ever been. She no longer felt old or weary.

"How did you do that?" she asked. "I think you must have a magic cock."

"You flatter me, Majesty. I was told that a man of true heart could break your curse, that was all."

"Call me Isabella," she said, "and I must know your name."

"I am William. Earl William of Vesey."

"Earl William, you have given me back my life. I am forever in your debt."

"I would take you from this place," he said. "You are not safe here."

"I have been wronged," she said, "and now I have been unfaithful, but I will not run from here like some thief."

"THE QUEEN ISABELLA is dead," the King announced. "It is my intention to take a new wife at once. I must have an heir."

No one argued with him, even though few liked his speech. One by one, girls were brought forward and the king examined each in turn. He had always liked the best of everything and hoped to make a better choice of wife this time. He was just finishing his inspection of a busty little blond who squealed when he pinched her, when a veiled woman entered the room on the arm of a handsome young man. She walked so gracefully it seemed as though she was dancing. Her dress was of a dark blue, and simply cut. The king had a horrible feeling of déjà vu, but could not think who this mysterious woman might be. She curtseyed low, and the man at her side made a deep bow of respect. As she stood, the woman pushed back her veil, revealing her pale skin and dark hair.

The king staggered backwards, shocked by the sight of a woman he thought dead.

"Osric!" he cried out, "there is some foul magic at play here."

Osric was nowhere in sight. He had long since fled from the palace and was never seen again.

"There has indeed been foul magic, my husband. Treacherous magic made a hag of me so that you could put me aside and take a new queen in my place."

"You are not Isabella, Isabella is dead."

Isabella smiled, and extended her tongue until she could lick the tip of her nose. The great hall echoed to sounds of astonishment at this feat and even William's eyes grew wide. The king staggered back, a look of pain etched across his face. He crumpled to the floor, his heart having stopped within him as he realized the truth. His jealousy had killed him at last.

IN THE CHAOS that followed, William and Isabella slipped away. She had money enough to see them safely through the country, and they took a boat back to William's homeland, where they were married and lived happily ever after. Isabella showed her new husband every trick she had for using her unusually long tongue, and he loved her all the more for it. Few things made her happier than to wrap her lips around the cock that had lifted her curse, and show him just how much she appreciated him. She would spend long hours kissing and licking him, her agile tongue working its own magic upon his body. William remained generous in his favors and they grew to love each other very much his passion for her growing stronger as time passed.

As the years went by they had several pretty children. Isabella remained beautiful and, with her charm and wit, she made many friends in her new home. William took joy in her success, and the cold hand of jealousy never closed over his true heart.

VIRGIN EAR ⁓ *Donna George Storey*

NOT SO LONG ago nor particularly far away, there lived a young woman with a very special power. Gina—for that is our heroine's name—did not always possess this power. She was born an ordinary girl, although in an extraordinary time. The ways of the kingdom were changing thanks to a magic pill that, it was promised, would enable the fair sex to perform as well as men in the bedroom and the boardroom. Perhaps even better.

Gina listened, wide-eyed, to the fairies, the pretty golden-haired one with big glasses; and the crone with her wise, rasping voice, who urged her to wake from the age-old enchantment that kept females chained and coy. Their tales stirred her mind with a bright, burning hunger to scale the patriarchy's slippery bastions to earn the title doctor or professor or CEO. Her body burned, too, but with darker longings for pleasures of the flesh, not the tepid tearoom fare of married love, but a groaning board of male bodies spread out for her delectation, to choose or discard as fancy moved her, names strictly optional. Her immediate quest, in short, was to fuck like a man.

But, sadly, in spite of so many nights wrestling naked strangers on waterbeds, too many mornings groping for the name of the man asleep beside her, deep in her heart, she heard no trumpets of triumph for her mastery of this time-honored sport of the male tribe. There was nothing but silence. That is, until one crisp afternoon in the autumn of her nineteenth year.

On this fateful Friday, Gina was sitting at her desk in her dorm room reading *Jane Eyre*. Now and then she paused to gaze through the mullioned window to the stone spires and archways of her college. Here the noble youth of her country were sent to be instilled with the qualities of leadership, though many chose instead to consume a surfeit of intoxicating beverages and couple awkwardly on narrow dormitory beds.

Into the hallway of her suite lurched a young man who, by the smell of him, had already downed a few cocktails. He was her roommate's boyfriend, a fellow named Jim from the balmy southern reaches of the realm, so Gina nodded a greeting and returned to her reading. She was at first only dimly aware of his voice as he chatted with her roommate at the door, a deep, lazy river drifting through the words on the page. But slowly, as if by magic, the feisty exchange between Jane and Mr. Rochester faded into very different words: Jim's drawling joke about a farmer's daughter and her X-rated obsession with an overgrown zucchini, punctuated by her roommate's giggles.

"Hey, watch it out there! You're offending my virgin ears,"

Gina called, a smile in her voice in spite of her words. In truth, bawdy talk amused her.

"We'll have to do something about that," Jim shouted back and before she knew it, he was beside her, jeans unzipped, putting his penis in her ear. She laughed and let it happen. Laughing and letting it happen pretty much described her sex life in college.

It was over almost before it began: a wiggling softness in the hollow of her ear, a glimpse of his baby-pink tube of flesh as he tucked himself in his briefs, zipped his fly, and went back to the hallway, to his girlfriend, to the world where everyone knows exactly what will happen next.

Later that evening, Gina stood before the bathroom mirror looking for some sign that something important had happened to her. She had done the very same thing after she lost—or to be more accurate, foisted onto the first willing taker—the virginity that seemed to matter most to the elders of the kingdom. That time, to her disappointment, she saw no outward change at all. Even inside, there was nothing but a lingering whisper of soreness between her legs. But this night, as she turned her head from side to side to study her ears, the debauched one seemed quite noticeably fuller and rosier in hue. It was hotter to the touch, too, and as she circled the ridges and valleys with her fingertip, the mild tingling sensation began to grow until it was just short of an ache.

As if it wanted more.

Did it—she—want more? Gina shook her head. Her reflection agreed, but her ear gave the lie with its hungry, insistent throbbing. It all came back so easily, the velvet warmth of entry, the friction of his member against the faintly oiled cup of her auricle, the surprisingly perfect mating of her ear with the pliant helmet of a cock in repose.

Gina gazed into her own eyes, her lips curving into a smile. It made her special to have just one virgin ear. She understood that her ear and her life had been transformed—irrevocably opened to something strange and new—but she imagined this change was small, secret, within her control.

That was her first mistake.

A FORTNIGHT LATER, Gina found herself in bed with another young man, one she'd had her eye on for some time. Each step on the path that led her to this place—half-dressed and squirming under the sweat-slick, regatta-toned body of Talbot Worthington Duckworth the Fourth—had been utterly predictable. First came the locked eyes by the keg and some brief banter about a mutual class. Next was the stroll in the moonlight and his slurred confession—I always thought you were really cute. And surely it was no accident that their wanderings led them right to the door of his room.

The rest, too, proceeded to script. Hot melting kisses, fingers tangling as they crept to buttons and flies, the dance of his tongue and her nipples—the boy clearly had thing for breasts— and then Gina's moment in the spotlight. Blowjob time.

How many times had she done that, too, slithering down over her lover's chest and belly, his expectant eyes glowing down at her through the midnight shadows? Gina took pride in her fellatio. The fact she would do it at all delighted most boys, but for her own sense of achievement she kept adding techniques she'd studied in scrolls and parchments now readily available in markets throughout the kingdom. Light, rapid tongue flicks just below the tip. Long ice-cream cone slurps, from the thick root to the quivering head.

Talbot arched back into the pillow and groaned.

Gina paused in her work to smile.

"Hey, there."

It was a male voice, soft and low in her ear.

She blinked, then squinted up at Talbot. The voice was deeper than his, and besides his mouth was set in a tight grimace, lost as he was in the lazy motion of her spit-moistened fist.

"Hey, Beautiful, can I ask you a favor?"

She cocked her head. The sound was definitely coming from his crotch, just inches from her face.

"Excuse me?" she whispered. She'd only had two half-cups of watery beer, not nearly enough to hear voices.

"Could you suck me now? I like a fair amount of pressure, but not too much. Watch the teeth, too, if you don't mind."

Gina frowned, but complied. Even if she were hearing voices, the advice seemed sound enough. Talbot moaned louder. Between strokes, a fainter, but no less appreciative refrain echoed through her palate.

She paused again. "How was that?"

"Fantastic, baby. This is the best blowjob I've ever had."

That voice was definitely Talbot.

"A little more suction, if you don't mind. And faster. But you're doing great. Way better than most of the bimbos he brings over."

That voice was definitely not.

"Who are you?" Gina whispered as softly as she could.

"I'm sorry, I forgot my manners, although in all fairness no one's ever bothered with introductions before. The guy upstairs calls me lots of things. Cock. Pud. Big Fella. I prefer Dick. More human, if you know what I mean. It's very nice to meet you."

Eyes wide, Gina inclined her head politely in return.

"Forgive my candor, but if I know the boss, we don't have too much time. I like you, Beautiful. You're good at this. You should see some of the losers that come down here. First they try to yank it off and then they give me a couple of slobbering gobbles like they're chewing on a Slim Jim. It's clear they only want one thing—to get it over with as fast as possible." The voice cracked. "You know, you're the first one who's ever really talked to me."

In spite of herself, tears sprang to Gina's eyes. She knew well enough what it was like to be unappreciated and alone.

"But you're special. You even act like you're enjoying it." Talbot's dick seemed on the verge of weeping, too.

His plaintive words tugged at her heart. "Tonight I am. I guess I like you, too."

"Ha, are you blind? Or are you just into short, one-eyed bald guys with purple faces and tufts of hair sprouting from their toes?"

Gina tried her best to muffle her laughter.

"What's so funny down there?" Talbot mumbled from the pillow, which suddenly seemed a thousand miles away.

"Sorry, got something caught in my throat." Gina pumped her fist faster.

"So, what's your name, Beautiful?" The tone was mellow now, like a warm, silky robe sliding over her flesh.

"Gina."

"Gina the genie. Magic lips, magic tongue."

The simple sincerity of his compliment touched her. On impulse she bent forward and kissed him right below his moistened eye, where she imagined his lips would be.

She heard a soft sigh . . . followed by the ominous thunder of Talbot himself, clearing his throat.

When the voice spoke again, it was all business. "All right, I'd love to talk more, but the boss is getting restless up there. How do you feel about swallowing, Gina? Be honest with me now."

Gina shrugged. She did swallow, but usually not on the first night with a guy. Still, she appreciated the fact that Talbot's dick was gentleman enough to inquire.

Dick seemed to understand. "I keep trying to get him to eat more cinnamon and celery, but does he ever listen to me? I'll be sure to give you fair warning before I blow my top. It won't be long now. Oh, and he keeps the box of tissues under the bed."

"Thanks," she murmured, drawing a deep breath for the home stretch. "And thanks for the pointers on technique."

"Believe me," Talbot's dick said, "the pleasure was all mine."

GINA HAD PEGGED Talbot as a one-night stand, but to her surprise, he called the very next day. He seemed most anxious to see her again. Gina agreed, less for the prospect of a movie and dinner at the Mexican place on Nassau Street than the chance to curl up under the covers for another talk with Dick.

"He blames me for his troubles with women," Talbot's dick

complained, "but it's totally unfair. I go for the ones who pay attention to me. They're the keepers—generous, thoughtful, curious about the world. He's a sucker for giggly blondes with big boobs. Not that I mind the boobs per se. It's nice to nestle between some lubed up knockers now and then. But for me, it's not what a girl looks like that matters. It's what she does and what she's like inside."

"My sentiments exactly," Gina replied. She'd finally found a male she could connect with on a deeper level, though she'd had to endure hours of Talbot's bragging about his summers on the Italian Riviera and his not-so-subtle leering at her small, but perky tits. She couldn't ignore the sad truth: Talbot's dick was more interesting than he was.

That night, she learned something else rather troubling. She could only hear Dick with her left ear. If she turned her head, he was mute.

Was it all a lecherous spell cast by the sorcery of her own suggestive mind? All-out insanity? Or merely an allergic reaction to half a pitcher of stale beer? These were the voices swirling in her head as she shimmied beneath the blankets a few weeks later with her next conquest, a shy, but sturdy chemistry major named Andy.

"Hi," she whispered to his penis, more than half hoping there would be no response.

"Glad to make your acquaintance," the penis answered with a slight, nodding twitch.

It was at that moment she vowed to give up cheap beer forever.

In the meantime, however, she saw some advantages to this,

be it madness or magic. And so she began a longer relationship with Andy's dick, a more sensitive fellow who preferred the name Willie, and the slow, wet glide of the female astride position to oral calisthenics. In his science geek's gratitude, Andy was more patient than the prickly Talbot. He never once complained when Gina spent hour after hour under the blankets with her cheek on his thigh, murmuring and giggling as she caressed his member or lavished kisses on the tip. In her year with Andy, Gina almost forgot there was anything at all usual about long, cozy chats with your boyfriend's most sensitive appendage.

Alas, her enchanted days in the Ivy bower were bound to pass, and Gina moved to the Big City and the world of Real Men, with their own apartments, paying jobs, and closets jammed with business suits, or on occasion, sculptures made from metal coat hangers that at least one gallery owner claimed showed artistic promise.

Competition was fierce in the citadel for money, good apartments, and attractive males, but Gina's special power proved most useful in keeping her date book filled. Men always called the next day, voices trembling with an eagerness they themselves didn't seem to understand. At first, the variety thrilled her. There was absurdly wealthy young investment banker with a cock as imposing as the foot-long, whale-shaped Steuben paperweight on his desk, yet it spoke with a timid, breathy voice, like Marilyn Monroe on steroids. Her next partner was the lead singer in a moderately successful experimental rock band. He was uncircumcised, and she feared she'd lost her power until she rolled back his foreskin and he serenaded her with a medley of Frank Sinatra tunes all night long. She even dabbled with a man old enough to be her father, charmed by his courtly propriety and their trysts in five star hotels, until his Mr. Miracle spilled out scandalous stories about the whores in Bangkok and Saigon.

Yet, as men came and went until her partners numbered three times three times three again, Gina began to long for an earplug, one she could insert stealthily beforehand, like a diaphragm. Sometimes when she slipped beneath the rumpled quilt of a first-time lover, she purposely turned her deaf ear to his member to get a break from the fleshly chatter, the raw need. But in the end she could never resist the lure of knowing her lover's penis, its hopes and fears and dreams, better than he did himself.

For a while she convinced herself it was research for a book of interviews—talking genitals were hot on the lecture circuit that year—but she didn't really have it in her to suck and tell. How could she betray her new friends, all the Rods, John-Thomases, and Peters, perpetual inmates of jeans and trousers, boxers and briefs, let out only for R&R in the men's room or in bed with snotty females who wouldn't give them the time of day? Besides, whether the fellow was puny or large enough to put a donkey to shame, left-leaning or solidly New Right, all the stories were essentially the same. The poor, talk-starved cocks wanted nothing more than to be respected and loved.

Alas, in time, the power she had once been so proud of seemed more like a curse. Experience made her debauched ear ever more sensitive, so that she could even hear voices calling to her in the street from the crotches of businessmen striding past with briefcases, from the grizzled old man in the mustard-stained apron at the hot dog stand.

Set me free, pretty lady. How about a kiss? Hey, Princess, can we talk, just talk?

Nights on her own gave no respite. In her dreams she'd walk into a party where all the guests were penises, tall as grown men, talking at her, weeping tears of pre-come, demanding her attention. When she awoke, her nightgown soaked and smelling vaguely of newly mown hay, she yearned to be awakened yet again from this enchantment gone wrong. In the old days, liberation was so much simpler—a kiss from the right man and all your troubles were gone. Gina knew the ways of the kingdom didn't work that way anymore, but she had her own reasons for keeping faith in the fantastic. If penises could talk, was it really so far-fetched to believe a knight in shining armor would some day come riding by her window?

Indeed one day he did arrive, borne in a vintage Mustang. His name was Brendan Regal. The Prince.

HIS EYES WERE dark and wary, though Gina liked that, as if he held something inside of him worth protecting. He was careful in his courtship, too. She had to wait through a coffee date, two movies, an afternoon hike, and one fancy dinner before she found herself in his bed, his bare skin warm against hers, his hard-on nestled between them like a promise. There he did something to Gina no man had ever done before at such a time and place.

He talked to her.

It was strange—and wonderful—how words alone could make her whole body glow, her breasts swell and tingle, so the mere touch of the sheets chafed her sensitive nipples in a rather pleasant way. That place between her legs, too, was plumped and slick, almost as if his voice were caressing her there. But then, alas, Brendan uttered those all-too-predictable words: "I think I'm falling in love with you."

In the darkness, Gina rolled her eyes. Still, this declaration usually came after she'd charmed the penis with her special power. To hear it beforehand was an intriguing change.

"You don't even know me," she answered, but kindly.

"I want to know everything about you," he whispered. "Tell me something about yourself you've never told anyone else before."

Taken by surprise—no one had ever asked such a question before—she blurted out the story of Jim and her ravished ear. She said nothing about the special power.

His smile flashed in the dim light. "Which ear was it?"

"The left one."

His gaze shifted to her ear, which began to feel warm, the skin taut and swollen. She had not been conscious of such a feeling for a long time.

"Did you enjoy it?" he asked.

Gina thought for a moment, amazed at how easily it came back to her, the fading light of the autumn dusk, the fragrance of fallen leaves on the breeze, the softness, almost like velvet, pressing into the hollow of her ear.

"Yes, I liked it," she admitted. "And the funny thing is, after that I always had a special feeling for Jim. I guess the first time is always special."

He nodded as he stroked her arm. "Where else are you a virgin? Or not, as the case may be."

"Well, no one ever put a penis there." She laughed as his fingertips brushed the crease of her elbow, a very sensitive place. A weird image flashed into her head: her arm oiled up, bent just so to clasp a cock, not sweet and silky like Jim's, but ruddy, swollen, demanding.

Brendan laughed, too. "I wasn't thinking of that, although it might be interesting to try. I meant the first time you felt pleasure there."

Gina began to wonder if he possessed a magic power of his own to loosen women's tongues. Under the heat of his steady gaze, the tale poured forth from her lips like warmed honey, a story from her girlhood, when she listened to the evening news every night with her parents. She loved the deep voice of the newscaster, and before the first commercial she would find her chance to slip her finger under her sleeve and stroke the smooth skin of her inner arm, tracing circles and loops to the rhythm of that resonant bass crooning on about violence in the Middle East, stagflation, and dead rock stars. By some odd trick, tickling her arm made her tummy feel lusciously tight and prickly. She couldn't stop herself from doing it, though she tried to hide it from her parents, easy enough in the flickering blue shadows of the black and white set.

Gina paused and blushed, well aware she'd just confessed to a relative stranger a habit of self-pleasuring that seemed like one short step away from masturbation—which, as further explorations of other sensitive parts of her body in her bedroom soon after would prove, it was. Her breath quickened. It was only fair then to ask him about a secret story buried in his flesh.

He thought for a moment.

"I guess there's my knee."

"Left or right?"

"Right."

Gina smiled. She could picture it perfectly: Brendan and a faceless beauty at a fine restaurant chatting decorously over their wine, while beneath the linen tablecloth the woman's silk skirt was hiked up to her hips, her legs parted as she rubbed her pussy steadily, shamelessly against his trousered knee, staining it with the secret liqueur of her desire.

"Do tell," she said.

Brendan frowned a bit in concentration. "It was my junior year of college, too, oddly enough. I played trombone in the joke of a marching band at the football games. You know, the kind where the kids run around like drunks, which we were most of the time. I had a terrible crush on one of the clarinet players, and I managed to sit next to her on the bus on a road trip. All we did was talk, but later, when the sun went down she fell asleep. I sat there watching her and dreaming of touching her, stroking her, melting into her. And then suddenly she shifted and her leg brushed against my knee. Just for a moment. I thought my kneecap was going to burst. In a way it did. The explosion licked through my whole body like flames. I didn't exactly come in my pants, thank God." He snorted softly. "Actually, it was better than coming. It's hard to explain."

Hard to explain, yes, but Gina understood. It was time for them to go beyond ordinary words. She burrowed under the covers, pausing, for old time's sake, to nod a greeting to his cock, then sinking deeper to the bony crown of his right kneecap. She held her ear—the deflowered one—against it. She waited.

She heard nothing.

Instead, a faint whiff of drugstore perfume, the kind teenage girls give each other as birthday gifts, seemed to rise from the flesh. Puzzled, she turned and pressed her nose to his knee. Only then did it reach her, the low hum of a bus rolling through an autumn night, sleepy chatter drifting from a few seats away, the catch in his breath. When she touched the tip of her tongue to the outside of it, her whole body was suddenly awash with a hot, helpless feeling she could only call lust.

Brendan sighed.

Gina glided her ear along his thigh and drank in the musk of female pleasure, gossamer layers of spice and seawater, each one a gift from a lover of times past. Her nose took in their moans as they rubbed themselves against him there, the smack of their cunt juices, *Fuck me, Brendan, please fuck me now*. Her lips on his chest felt the softness of their breasts, the points of their nipples pressing into him.

At first she was only dimly aware of his fingers tracing shapes on her forearm, but soon she breathed in a new sound: a gravely murmur drifting up from the skin, "And that's the way it is, July twentieth...." Just the beginning, of course, of the things that voice used to tell her as she lay on her bed, one hand creeping inside her underwear, the other hiking up her night-gown to expose her chest to the cool air and the flickering eyes floating in space above her.

"Play with your breasts for me, honey. That's right. Lick your palms and move them around and around over those stiff pink nipples. I'm watching you through the TV, watching every-thing you're doing. Why don't you pull your panties all the way down and let me see your pussy? I have an idea for us to try tonight. Why don't you take your pillow and push it between your legs? Now rock your hips into it. It feels good, doesn't it? You're going to come. I know that's the way it will be, because I know everything."

Brendan seemed to hear the voice, too, for now his moistened palms were gliding over her nipples in slow circles. His thigh, warmer and harder than her pillow, was wedged between her legs for her to ride. Ride him she did, her wetness flooding over him, laying its claim to his flesh. Whimpering with need, she pulled him on top of her—ah, his cock slid right home—and wrapped her legs around him.

Suddenly another voice rose up to fill the air around them— a female voice. Hers.

Don't thrust yet, let me push up against you. Slow and steady, that's right. Tease my nipples with light kisses, then suck them hard, tug that magic cord that ties them to that secret place deep in my belly.

Her lips weren't moving and yet he seemed to know just what to do as his mouth kissed and tugged, sending pulses of pleasure from her breasts to her cunt. He seemed to understand, too, that he should hold himself still and let her set the pace with the short, jerking thrusts that drove her ever closer to the edge.

Then yet another voice joined the chorus, boyish and shy, whispering forbidden desires. Telling her to rake her fingers over his ass cheeks. Dip down and stroke the delicate, satiny groove. Circle around the hole with her fingertip then touch it right on the puckered lips. Then tap it, as if she were knocking on tiny door. And when it opened, would she nudge her finger gently inside?

The bed was alive with sound, the soft suck of flesh joining, the hiss of nerves aflame, a choir of phantoms chanting tales of bygone pleasures, until it all merged together in her guttural cry of release, his groan as the muscles of his asshole milked her finger in the sweet, familiar rhythm of climax.

They lay quietly in each other's arms for some time before the old ritual overcame her.

"What are you doing?" he called down through the tunnel of the sheets

"Going to have a little get-to-know-you chat with your cock."

"I have a pretty good idea what he's going to say."

"You might be surprised."

She took her usual position and whispered hello, but the only reply was a reedy whistle, like a sleeping man lost in a luscious dream. Surely Brendan's penis had some complaint to unburden, some story to tell? She'd never met a cock that didn't want more of something, or less of another, from the guy upstairs.

Then, with a start, she realized she'd been listening with her virgin ear. Smiling, she turned her head and bent her knowing ear close, but the sound was the same, just as clear as before, a faint snore of satisfaction.

Gina lay back on the pillow and clutched her lover's arm. Something was gone, a weight, like a stone, on the left side of her jaw, and for an instant she feared her body might float away, a child's lost balloon racing for oblivion, but for the anchor of Brendan's body.

"What did you hear down there?" he asked. There was no mockery in his voice. If anything, it held a touch of fear.

"Do you really want to know?"

He murmured assent. The low, rich sound filled her chest. She heard a future in it.

She rose up on her elbow and studied his ear. She liked the slim, elfin shape of it. She took her finger and traced the curved rim, circled lower, to the first ridge that flares out in a C shape. Such an accepting thing, an ear.

She hesitated.

It would be the first time she'd ever done this.

It was not that she would miss the adventures of the quest—she was more than ready to go deep instead of wide.

Yet, what she was about to do would change everything.

Gina brought her lips close to his ear.

She began to tell him.

Everything.

THE PRINCE OF BYZANTIUM *Seneca Mayfair*

I SIT ON my window ledge high above this town of crowded
streets, and scribble over a page on which the sun's golden light
dances. From my window, I can see the busy port where sailing
ships dock, and where the merchants ply their trade with the
East Indies. The breeze from the sea carries the fragrant scent of
wild spices. Gulls scream and swoop over the fishing boats making their way home. Here, I dream of my prince who lives far
away in a land of gold and magic.

When Greta looks up from sweeping the steps before my
father's shop, she will see me. She will drop the broom, and rush
to tell my mother of my transgression. It is unseemly for an
unmarried woman to expose herself as I do. Our servant Greta
does not like to sweep, and is pleased when I disregard custom.

At Greta's news, my mother will complain to my father,

and my father will send his assistant Nicholas to tell me to close the shutters. Since the day the banns for my marriage to Nicholas were published, my mother and he worry about my reputation. It matters little to me. I will never be Nicholas's wife. I belong to the Prince of Byzantium. When I have joined my love and I am no longer here, I believe Greta will be the only one to miss me.

Nicholas sees in me his succession to my father's trade. My sisters, each as beautiful as the wind through the trees, have married prosperous merchants. They have made, as my mother says, good matches. Each of them is younger than I. I am all that is left of father's seed. I am the last to be planted and germinated to start the process of his life again; but it will not come to pass.

My mother would keep out the light to shade her ugly duckling. She does not care that I am unmarried, yet expose myself to the glances of strangers. Propriety does not apply to women of little worth in this town of merchants. Only those women born with the small round faces of my sisters, their lips full and pouty, their skin the softness and the texture of pure cream, are worthy to keep with care. My sisters with their small breasts and slim hips have found husbands. The rough-faced girl with the large breasts and the wide hips of a common servant was hidden. But now, at last, my parents have found a man who will take me—not for me, but for what my father will give to him.

I bend my head over the page. I am again with my prince. He stands straighter and taller than any man in the busy town over which my window looks. His softly curling black hair falls in wild beauty around his angular face. I have run my tongue over his high cheekbones to memorize them. The Prince of Byzantium wears silk robes of purple and gold. He claps his hands, and magic is born. He flies to me, and I to him. He has promised I will be his when the time has come. I feel the time is near.

Until then, I must write. We live in the swirls and the lines of the ink running from my quill to his. Our love has found a way to pass through time and space. I walk with the walk of a woman well loved, a woman whose flesh has felt the hard beauty of a man's desire. I smell of jasmine, roses, and musk, and carry the scent of a man's lust. My mother senses this. Nicholas feels it. They do not understand it. They do not think it is possible.

When my mother sees me walk with the love of my Byzantine prince deep within me, she worries that even Nicholas will not have me. She suspects I have given myself to some rough man. I do not argue with her when she says I am common. Let her believe what she will. She cannot guess where my spirit dwells. She sees my quill scratching across the page, but does not guess I am with my dark prince. She cannot hear my sighs as my lover caresses me.

My prince commanded the winds of the earth to find she whom he had sought for centuries. Finally, the cold and bitter winds of the north found me. I was sitting here in my tiny room on the third floor of my father's house, with the shutters closed against winter. My soft hair was pulled tightly back and tucked beneath a prim linen caul, and my body of love was covered by a rough woolen shift. I was writing.

The strong north winds blasted open my shutters. The inkwell spilled, and I dropped my quill. The winds spiraled around me, and flew beneath my shift. It was as if a million hands were seeking to know me. It was cold at first, and I feared I might freeze. The winds caressed parts of my body I had not known existed. I grew warm from their touch. Laughing, I surrendered to them, and reveled in this new ecstasy.

When the last sigh of pleasure died on my lips, the winds left me as abruptly as they had entered. I ran to the window to watch the winds leave, but was too late. I closed the wooden shutters, and returned to my writing desk.

The desk is the only present of value my father has given to me. It is the concession of a merchant to the necessity of a daughter's literacy. A wife must help tend the books of her husband, and thereby increase his profit.

I love this desk. I spend many hours writing at it. It is a small desk of fine oak, and its secret drawers tend my dreams when I cannot be with them. I returned to it, thinking to record my experience.

The ink spilled by the winds had covered the page on which I had been writing. As I looked at the pattern created by the ink, it moved. It became a dark glass through which I saw a strange garden.

I gazed in wonder at the garden's lush greenery and brilliant flowers. A summer sun played with a gentle breeze among the leaves. The sweet scent of thousands of roses awakened my desire. Without knowing where or what this garden was, something within me knew it was my true home. This was a garden where desire and love were touched and tasted, and where value was found in craving the feel of wild grass beneath one's bare feet, or in delighting in the patterns created by rose petals. These were things that could not be bought and sold. This was experience. This was my heart's dream. How could a woman whose senses were filled with desire be ugly?

I felt the touch of a man's hand as he wiped the tears from my cheek. I looked up and into his dark almond-shaped eyes. I had never seen a man of such beauty. The men of business, who stride over the cobblestone streets of my town, were nothing when compared to he who sat before me. He cupped my rough face between his palms, and gently kissed me. His lips were full and soft, and tasted of sweet spices. For a moment, I forgot who I was, and that I was not valued by men. I gave myself up to this first kiss.

He drew away from me, and smiled. Trying to hide my face from him, I rose from the bench on which we sat beneath a tree covered by deep red flowers, and looked for escape. I could not bear to see his eyes turn from my homeliness.

"Stay, my love," he said. His voice was strong and clear. "I have searched for you long and hard. Do not take from me the hunger and the desire the north winds have brought to me. Stay."

I turned to him, but bowed my head. His strong arms encircled me and drew me close to him. He kissed the top of my head and laughed. I stiffened, still afraid.

"No, no," he said. "It is this thing you wear on your hair. Whatever this hideous thing is, it must come off." He pulled off the caul I wore, and let my braid fall free. His fingers played through my hair. "Yes," he said, "you are as I have dreamed."

His tongue traced the curve of my neck. Shivering, I forgot who I was. I knew only the heat of his body close to mine, and the flames rising between us. His hands drew my woolen shift over my head, and I stood naked and trembling before him. His eyes moved from my breasts to my hips, painting me with his desire. My nipples hardened as his brush touched them, and I felt moisture between my thighs. His silk robes of purple and gold fell from his shoulders as he again drew me to him.

For the first time, I felt the wonder and the beauty of a man's body. I delighted in the feel of my nipples crushed against his hard, flat chest. I do not know how I knew what to do, but I did. I trailed my palms lightly over his shoulders and down his muscled arms. His hairs stood on end at my touch, and I laughed as they tickled me. I wanted to touch him all over, to memorize his narrow hips and his strong thighs. I wanted every part of him.

I slid down before him, and gazed at that which I had never seen, but now wanted. He was erect and hard. I burrowed my nose in the coarse dark hair around his sex. He pressed my head close to him, and I could have stayed there forever inhaling his scent.

After a time, he too fell to his knees, and took my face between his hands. His tongue softly touched mine. His taste was sweeter even than the honey my father sells. He pushed me down until I rested beneath him on the grass. I should blush when I think of how his lips and tongue explored my body. I cannot. I can only long for the gentle bite of his teeth on my nipples, and the touch of his tongue on the folds of the lips between my thighs.

I gladly gave him my maidenhead. It did not hurt: I longed to feel him deep within me. A little blood was shed, a small price for such great pleasure.

He has taught me to crave him. Each day I must write so that I can see, touch, taste, and smell him. He has made me his, though he says it has always been so. He has created me from roses and jasmine and musk. I live within his desire. He is my dark prince. He is the Emperor's own son. He is the Prince of Byzantium.

"Marcella, Marcella," Nicholas calls.

I do not answer but continue to write. Nicholas is nothing to me. He would have me bound to him for the price of my father's shop. My prince wants me, nothing else. He longs to set me free. He despises the garments I must wear to hide my body. Now, when I meet my prince, I boldly untie the ribbon holding my bodice tight. His hand cups my breast, and he sighs. He will clothe me in flowing silk that will open with the merest touch of his desire.

Nicholas pounds on my closed door.

"Marcella," he says in a loud and stern voice he thinks will please my mother. I long to tell him not to worry because he will have my father's trade. He will not need me. In time, all will be his, and he will have it without the rough-faced girl who will not have him.

Nicholas has thrust open my door, and stands glaring at me, his arms crossed.

"Marcella, you must close the shutters. Or else move back from the open window. It is not seemly," he says.

I have memorized this speech. I hear it most days, especially on those days when Greta feels cheated that she, who is lovely like my sisters, is the servant, while I, who am ugly, am the daughter of the house. She punishes me for this. I do not mind. At least Greta sees me.

There are those in this town who have never seen me. At the May fair the men of the town have walked by and have glanced at me, and, then, without a smile, have looked elsewhere. I have watched them take their partners for the dances. They choose only the prettiest, most valued women. It does not matter now. My prince, who is wise, knows I am beautiful.

The great Prince of Byzantium impatiently waits for our marriage. It is the timing of magic that keeps us divided by centuries, and allows only brief visits. When the winds gather to play, as they do every hundred years, at the crossroads of dark and light, and, when day briefly becomes night, then may a rose be joined with a man. I am my lover's rose. The time comes soon. It may be today. I sense it near. I will be avenged, not with violence, but with the possession of a love that will last an eternity and be sung about forever.

I smile at Nicholas, and return to my writing.

"Marcella. Now. You must do this now," Nicholas says with more force. It makes me laugh. The quiet voice of my lover is as a roar compared to the mewling of this boy with the sour face. My laughter sets Nicholas stomping down the stairs. Next it will be my mother who will visit my door.

The time is soon. I feel the winds gathering in the distant place that is to be my home. I hear their laughter. The winds are playing together. It is midday here, and yet it is growing dark outside, as if the night has forgotten its proper time.

I hear my mother's heavy tread as she walks up the stairs to my room. Does she not see that the sun outside has been covered by the dark of midnight? Can she not hear the winds in their play? The time has come to join my love. I am right. It is today. It is now.

"Marcella," my mother shouts from below my room. She shouts when she is angry. She has only ever shouted at me. I am her disappointment. This time, she will not find me. Her ugly duckling will have flown to her own true home.

"Marcella," my mother shouts again. She is much closer to my room.

"My rose," I hear my prince call. "Now, my love. Come to me. It is time."

I drop my quill. There is no further need of it. My mother's footsteps sound closer. I will not miss her, or this world. I stand at the window. The sun is covered. In the dark of day, the playing winds have found me.

"I come, my love," I call.

My dark and beautiful Prince of Byzantium takes my hand. His love has found me across centuries, and we will live forever. We walk across the night of this day, touching the stars, holding hands. He leads me to where the soft clouds wait for us. He will clap his hands, and we will fly to our garden beside his father's golden palace.

As I fly through the night, I hear my mother's scream. It does not matter. I am the Princess of Byzantium. I am loved.

THE UNICORN AND THE STRUMPET
Teresa Noelle Roberts

ONCE UPON A TIME in a town on the edge of a great forest, there lived two sisters, Lillian and Isabella, the daughters of a respectable merchant. They were equally comely of face and graceful of form, but their characters were very different. Lillian was a dutiful daughter. She wished for little more in life than to please her parents and, some day, to marry well so her parents could enjoy a comfortable old age. She excelled at embroidery, at polite small talk, and at managing a household. As such, she was the pearl of her parents' heart and held up as a model of young womanhood to the girls of the town.

Isabella, on the other hand, was held up as a model of what a young woman should not be. She had no patience for the arts suitable to a girl of her station and less patience with suitors who had much to offer her purse, but nothing to offer her heart or her body. She refused several, all well-to-do, respectable older men of the sort a girl of good but not wealthy family should favor. Some seemed dull as yesterday's dishwater, but a few spoke her fair, telling stories of their travels to far lands, or bringing her books containing new tales, and she thought briefly that being married to a kind and learned older man might not be so dreadful. Then she thought of their fat bellies and balding heads, and how their touch was as exciting as her father's, and she shied away.

Instead, she would climb out her window at night to go to low taverns and flirt with stable hands, minstrels, and other riffraff. But that, too, was unsatisfying. They were fine to look upon, with handsome young faces, broad shoulders, long, muscular legs, and other interesting attributes that she could feel through their clothing when they embraced her. She liked the illicit thrill of touching them and being touched. But for the most part they were ignorant lads. While her body would quiver and clench and moisten to tell her that it would be wonderful to run away with this night's flirtation and enjoy the promise behind his kisses, her mind knew that she would be bored within a week.

Thus it was that when she met the baron's third son, she was heart-whole and despite the whispers to the contrary, a maiden.

The baron's son looked like one of the ancients' imaginary but beautiful gods. He had been educated in foreign lands and was sophisticated and well read, or at least he seemed so to a curious but uneducated girl. He wore dashing clothes of the most fashionable sort, and high boots of black leather. In short, he was the sort of young gamester that girls craved and mothers rightly feared.

The baron's third son saw something in the headstrong Isabella. He spoke her fair. He spoke her wild. He spoke to her with clever quips and erotic poetry until one night she climbed out her window and down the trellis and met him in an inn on the waterfront.

There he spoke to her with clever hands and more erotic poetry and a skillful tongue plied on shy nipples and on the still-innocent heat between her legs. Then he offered some hemp rope and suggested she use to immobilize him while she discovered what made a man a man. Before that night ended, Isabella was no longer a maiden, and neither she nor the young man was entirely heart-whole.

Her parents stormed. His parents sneered. Lillian cried, for despite their differences, she loved her sister.

"Why did you do such a thing, Sister?" she asked Isabella over and over again.

At first, Isabella tried to explain the fire, the yearning that his touch caused and only his touch could ease, but she could tell from Lillian's eyes that she was too young and naïve to understand. In the end, the only explanation that made sense was, "I am not you, Lillian. I had to do what my heart prompted."

Of course there could be no wedding, but Isabella, already ruined, figured she might as well enjoy her ruin. Soon she moved into a house on the baron's estate, and the fact that people called her his whore bothered her not a whit, or so she claimed.

And most of the time it did not, for he was educating her senses in a hundred different ways. Isabella had always wanted to learn magic. Now she learned the magic that her lips could work on a man's cock, that a man's cock could work inside, that rope and wax and leather could do to her own body or to his. It wasn't the magic of her girlhood dreams, but at the best moments the colors danced as they had in those daydreams of enchantment and the rest of the time it was still quite wonderful.

At least most of the time it was. Sometimes, he would invite his boisterous companions to visit and then, in truth, she did feel like his whore. When she was being honest with herself, though, she admitted she enjoyed the moments when she found herself on her knees before one friend and then the next, serving each with her mouth, or the time she spanked one fellow, berating him for some imaginary crime, until he spent his seed in her lap to the howling delight of his drunken companions. What she really despised was being ignored the rest of the time during these visits. The baron's son, when they were alone, would speak to her of many things, but among his friends he would ignore her conversation and think only of her lips and breasts and honeypot.

It was during one of those rowdy visits that word came that a unicorn had been spotted in the forest.

No unicorn had been seen in the area for over one hundred years, and instantly the town came alive with excitement. Unicorns were dangerous beasts, but also magical. To kill a unicorn and take its horn was to gain an artifact of great power against poison, disease, and impotence, one that could be sold for a fortune in gold. So said all the old tales, which were dredged out at every tavern and around every table in the town, including the table at the baronial manor house and at the rather less

THE UNICORN AND THE STRUMPET

seemly one where the Baron's youngest and wildest son gathered with his companions and their mistresses, Isabella among them.

Venery is a word with two meanings, and the young noble-men who gathered to the baron's son were ardent in hunting both women and game. On this night, abuzz with excitement over the unicorn, talk turned to venery of the second sort. Would it not be a great coup to kill a beast thought by many to be a mere legend? Better yet, they would capture it, tame it, and present it to the King for his menagerie, which would surely win them acclaim and the love of hitherto unattainable women.

"There's only one problem," said one of the young men, who was either a bit more thoughtful than the others or a bit less drunk. "To catch a unicorn, you need a pure-hearted virgin girl as bait. All the legends say so, and the antique tapestry in your father's hall shows it being done. Where are we going to get a virgin? It's not as though any maiden is going to head off into the woods with the likes of us, not if she wishes to stay a maiden."

Everyone laughed, Isabella included, for it was naught but the truth.

"How about a maid who doesn't much care if she stays one?" said the Baron's son. "When I met my Isabella, she still had her maidenhead, but she was glad enough to be rid of it. We've all met lasses like that, ones who were ripe to fall but hadn't worked up the courage yet. Perhaps one of them would do, and they're easy enough to find if one sniffs around."

Isabella kept her peace and said nothing.

"But then," another man pointed out, "she'd not be pure of heart. Think back to being a green boy! I dreamed of tupping every lass I saw and spent day and night wanking away at myself until a serving wench finally took pity on my madness. I can't imagine that a virgin who needs a man would be any different, even if she didn't rightly know what she craved."

Isabella turned red then, remembering herself not so long ago, but said nothing.

The baron's son caressed her breasts, making it hard for her to think. "Do you not have a sister, my sweet, one who is famously chaste and proper?"

She nodded, trying to fight off the pleasure roiling through her. "And she has been well warned off from men like you." She said it with a smile to soften the blow. In truth she liked her lover and his friends for their wildness and sensuality, but she thought of her sister's naïveté and feared for her. Would Lillian even know if she were being seduced?

"And did you not say that she could not conceive why you might even wish to lie with a man, so great was her innocence?"

"She is a good girl, who listened to our parents and the priest," Isabella said smiling, "unlike me." Her body arched like a cat's, enjoying his hands on her.

"Then she is the one we need!" Seeing dismay replace pleasure on his mistress's face, he added, "I swear no harm shall come to her. Your own father shall be there as witness, and a priest if he likes it. But we need a pure girl for our hunting of this unicorn."

Isabella feared for her sister's safety, not so much from the young noblemen, who would value their word once it was given, but from the unicorn itself and the dangers of hunting even a non-magical wild beast. But her lover pooh-poohed her fears and soothed her with caresses and lovemaking. In the morning the letter went to her parents' home, an order couched as a request.

When the day of the hunt came, Isabella rode forth with the men to pick up her father and sister, whom she had not seen since she had chosen to live with the baron's son. Her father smiled sadly at her but did not speak beyond a polite greeting, as one would give a well-dressed, but dubious-looking stranger. Lillian, though, greeted her with squeals of excitement.

"I knew you would do something to help me!" she exclaimed, clutching her sister's hand.

Isabella thought to say it had been none of her idea, but saw that the girl was honestly grateful and kept her peace.

"Father despaired of making me a good marriage after you ran away, but when the unicorn comes to me, everyone will know I'm..." She flushed and turned away, unable to say the words. "Perhaps with such acclaim, one of the noble huntsmen might even wed me."

"Why would you want to marry someone you despise me for associating with?" Isabella asked. "He would still be wild and wanton and keep wagtails and ladybirds on the side. Such a man doesn't change."

Lillian shrugged her pretty shoulders. "But I would be his wife. Our children would be of noble blood, and Father and Mother would be pleased. Oh, Isabella, I'm so excited!"

Isabella watched the hunting party ride off toward the forest. Then she followed them.

Partly she was worried for her sister, and for the young men, whom she thought foolish for undertaking to hunt a creature of great power so carelessly.

And partly she merely wished to see the unicorn in its glory, laying its head in her sister's beautiful lap like the one on the tapestry in the baron's hall. She had no illusion that she could approach it—if the old tales were true, the beast would flee a wanton woman like her—but perhaps she could see from a distance while it was still proud and free, before the men killed or subjugated it.

The woods were thick in this area, thick and wild, but the large hunting party was noisy enough that she had no difficulty following it undetected. (How they thought to catch their quarry with such racket confirmed her suspicion that their plan was ill-conceived.)

Finally the group reached a clearing, Isabella on their heels. Lillian sat down on a blanket on the grass under a great ancient oak. She toyed with her crewel-work, looking out of place in the forest in her grand gown. The huntsmen faded into the tree line, although to Isabella they seemed quite obvious. Were unicorns not fabled to be wise as well as potently magical? An ordinary stag would spot these boys. Surely nothing would come of this idiocy, and they would all go home and have a good laugh.

Except for her sister. Her sister would be mocked for being unable to catch the unicorn, and between that and Isabella's wantonness, her good name would be ruined.

Isabella felt a surge of anger. Some of it was at herself, for having put her sister in such a fix, but some of it was at the world that would judge a girl so strictly for such a foolish reason.

They waited. Flies buzzed. In the bushes, a horse whinnied. Lillian gave up pretending to embroider and started actually doing it in order to pass the time. Much as she hated such pursuits, Isabella found herself wishing she had embroidery, knitting, something to distract herself from waiting.

And then the unicorn came.

He came into the glade on silver hooves, moving as smoothly as water. He resembled a horse as a hearth cat resembles a panther, which is to say many of the particulars were the same, yet the whole was so different as to defy the comparison. His horn was silver and his mane and tail were silvery white, but his coat was sable. He was the size of a large pony, but more delicately built, and his beauty brought tears to Isabella's eyes.

He was also erect, with a cock smaller than a horse's, but much larger than any man's. It was plain to her sister that Lillian's gaze was irresistibly drawn there as it might be to a frightful accident. Her eyes widened, her face screwed up in horror, she backed up as if trying to flee into the very heart of the tree, yet she could not look away.

Isabella could not look away either. Her lover's instrument always seemed to her to have a homely, foolish appearance, despite the pleasure she took in its actions, but the unicorn's great cock had the same dignity and beauty as its silver horn or elegant hooves. It was a part of the beauty of the whole.

He went to Lillian, sniffed at the shrinking girl, pawed the ground next to her.

Then he proclaimed in a voice as melodic as bells, "You are not the one. Innocent you are and fair to look at, but your heart is sullied and your spirit is cowardly." He turned away, hanging his head in what looked to be grief.

An arrow soared at him.

Something very like a fiery hand materialized out of the air and batted it away.

Then he lowered his great horn and charged the bush whence the arrow came, causing the archer and several of his fellows to flee and one to climb the nearest tree. Regardless, several of the other young men shot.

This time the arrows deflected back at them. From the cries coming from the bushes, all hit non-lethal, but painful marks.

After that, the shooting stopped. The young noblemen were bold and impetuous, but it was plain they had been outmatched.

The unicorn stopped, sniffed at the air. "You are here, though, my beloved. I can smell you. I can taste your wild heart on the wind. Come to me."

There were no other women present, yet the unicorn could not mean Isabella. She was a wagtail, a lustful girl who'd chosen life as a mistress over that of a respectable wife and mother.

Yet who else could the unicorn mean?

She took a trembling step forward, emerging from the bush where she was hiding. The unicorn moved impossibly quickly to join her; one second on the other side of the glade, the next by her side. "Beloved," he said, the rich, wise voice incongruous from the nonhuman mouth. Then he lowered his horn and touched it gently where her legs joined her body, its point caressing the very pearl where she was most sensitive.

Fire shot through Isabella's body. All the pleasure she had ever taken with her lover, all the pleasure she'd found in her own touch, all paled next to the convulsion that overtook her at the mere touch. And along with the orgasm came a wave of under-standing, of love, even, unlike anything she had ever experienced. She cried out, felt herself falling, but the body of the unicorn supported her.

"Come with me," the unicorn said. "You have the heart and spirit to be my mate. But do you have the courage to join me?"

Isabella looked into his eyes. They were an impossible violet, but other than the color they were those of a man, not a horse—a man who looked at her with both respect and passion.

She glanced at her sister, who was still cowering under the tree, weeping.

She glanced toward her lover, who had ventured forth from his hiding place. "You've got the wrong girl!" the baron's son exclaimed. "That one's mine, and a sweet slut she is, no maid."

"She is only yours if she so chooses. Do you so choose, Isabella?"

"I was with him," she said, "and we enjoyed each other. But I do not belong to him. Let us go, Unicorn."

The baron's son raised his crossbow. He lowered it when he saw the look on Isabella's face.

The girl and the unicorn walked out of the glade unmolested, and Isabella was never seen again. Her fate remained unknown, although in the usual way of such things she became a cautionary tale. It was assumed, despite the unicorn's seeming tenderness toward her, that he ended up slaying her for her wicked, wanton ways.

*

THE TRUTH WAS different, as the truth often is.

They walked together deeper in the woods, until they reached a moss-lined pool hung all around with willows. There they stopped.

"I have long sought a companion, one who might become my mate," the unicorn said to her. "But if we male unicorns are creatures of magic as much as flesh, a female unicorn is more so. No female unicorns are born. Each female unicorn begins her life as a human girl with a pure heart and an adventurous spirit and a passion for living. Such a girl I can transform into a unicorn, beautiful and immortal, with my seed and my horn and my magic, but only if she chooses. You are such a girl."

And Isabella turned away. She chuckled bitterly. "You do have the wrong woman, my dear unicorn. Adventurous and passionate I may be, but I am hardly pure. When my lover named me a slut, he spoke me true, for I lay with him unwed rather than marry a suitor of my father's choice, and since then I have lain with more men than there are decades on the rosary." The latter was not true, but a touch of bravado kept her voice from shaking. The unicorn was the sort of marvel she had always dreamed of finding, and he spoke to her like the lover of her dreams, but now he was sure to reject her.

"Human stories say we seek virgins?" The unicorn laughed, and his was a true laugh that sounded like music in the forest. "That would explain the poor, frightened child waiting under the tree. When I say pure, I mean brave and honest enough to follow her own nature, regardless of what others would say—not like the girl at the tree. She was one who lied even to herself, denying that she is even curious about the ways of man and maid. She is a virgin from fear and duty, not her own wish, and she has no dreams that others had not handed to her."

Isabella nodded. "She is my sister, and I love her, but you name her true."

"For a unicorn, an honest strumpet with a brave and merry heart and a lust for life is much more attractive—and you are such a woman. But do you wish to change from what you are to what I am? It means immortality and magic, but also means leaving behind all you have known."

"All I have known, I have already known. I'd rather discover something new. I have always dreamed of finding magic and beauty and love, but until you all I have found is fun and sex and with them trouble of various degrees. I can't complain of what I've had, but I'd be a fool to turn my back on this. On you." Impulsively, she flung her arms around the unicorn's neck and kissed him. It was an odd kiss and a chaste one given his horse-like lips, but it seemed more truly warm and affectionate than the baron's son's most passionate kisses ever had.

"Then take off your clothes, my honest strumpet, for soon you will not need them."

Isabella had taken off her clothes often in her young life, but never with such a high heart as that time. She started to fold them, out of habit, then decided to let them lie in a heap on the grass.

Once again, he bent his head, touched the silver horn between her legs. This time, knowing the pleasure she would feel, she opened them eagerly. He ran the horn over her secret mound, already swollen from his earlier ministrations, and her nether lips, already wet, and she gasped and bucked her hips to give herself more contact. Once again, the pleasure struck her with what she knew must be magical force, ringing her body with tension and release, drawing forth cries that made the forest echo. She felt herself opening, opening as she never had before, opening as if she could take his enormous cock as easily as she would a man's.

"And so you read my thoughts as I do yours," the unicorn said tenderly. "I have chosen well. The spell is beginning to work. Now you must stroke my shaft."

She crouched below him with a combination of excitement and trepidation, her heart and her cunny alike pounding. The great organ was almost too large for Isabella to circle with her two hands, but it jumped at her touch as a man's would. Warm and hard and covered in velvet, it was a delight to stroke. She moved her hands up and down it, circling the head, listening excitedly as the unicorn's breathing quickened. Her cunny flooded, her juices running down her legs.

As if in answer, a drop of fluid formed at the cockhead, just as it would on a man, but in greater volume. Impulsively, Isabella licked it away.

It tasted like honey, like heady wine, like home.

She licked again, her hands working, hoping to call forth more.

"Isabella . . ." the unicorn moaned, and it did not seem odd that he knew her name, for she knew his now: Iaramor.

More of the wondrous fluid oozed onto her waiting tongue.

And both Isabella and Iaramor started to glow.

Her body felt odd, weighted in the pelvis, yet curiously light and fluid. The colors in the glade seemed brilliant, jewel-like, aglow from within and accented with tones she had never before seen. Silver and purple light shimmered off the unicorn, gold and purple light off her. Even the scents were sharper: crushed grass, trees, clean water, and moss.

"It is time," Iaramor intoned. "Climb onto that flat rock and offer yourself to me."

She felt a second of fear, wondering how, even with a body that seemed to be altering by the second, she could possibly take in Iaramor's organ. At the same time, her cunny clenched in anticipation, then opened, opened....

It would work.

She climbed up as directed, got on all fours, raised her buttocks high.

Iaramor positioned himself over her, casting a shadow that, to her new vision, was shaded with violet and rose. He smelled nothing like a horse or a human, more like amber warmed in the sun. The huge head of his cock nudged at her, sending shudders of pleasure through her body. She literally felt her pelvic bones shifting, making way.

"Do you truly wish to become a unicorn and my mate, Isabella?"

What came to her mind was, "Stop talking and swive me!" but she sensed that he must ask the question and must get a truthful answer for the spell to work.

"I truly wish to become a unicorn, Iaramor. I would be your companion and lover, gladly, and mayhap in time your mate, but it seems too soon to make eternal vows when we have just met."

"Honestly answered, and wisely."

The colors changed again, and Isabella realized it was because Iaramor was glowing so.

And then he entered her.

Just the head at first, just an inch or two of his length, stretching her out, opening her as she had never been opened before. Pain and pleasure mingled, but mostly it was pleasure, pleasure and a sense of something changing within her.

He froze, letting her get used to the feeling, until she rocked her hips back, taking in more.

Ah! Almost too much, but not quite. Her body seemed to reshape herself around Iaramor's cock. Perhaps it truly was.

She felt her legs and arms change as well, stretching.

"Now!" he cried, and thrust the rest of the way in.

This time it was certainly pain she felt. Things inside her tore. Yet as soon as they tore, they repaired themselves. She could feel it, feel her flesh knitting into a new form, feel her bones reshaping.

The glade swirled around her. Her womb contracted—an orgasm or a birthing, she was not sure, the pleasure and pain were so mingled. Iaramor's weight was crushing her, but she didn't care.

"I cannot prolong this," Iaramor said, seemingly through clenched teeth. "The spell must be finished with my seed, and soon, or you will be damaged." Iaramor's cock jumped inside her. She felt the rush of hot seed and her body answered. Her voice soared, startling the birds into panicked flight. Her cunny clamped down on the great cock and she bucked against him so hard her tail lashed around to tease at her pearl.

"My tail?" she thought. And then she fainted.

She came to on a soft bed of moss in the glade with Iaramor nestled by her side. His horn was crossed over hers. Hers was golden, and the mane that fell forward over her eyes was the same rich gold as her human hair had been. Her coat was the warm rose-white of a fine pearl.

"I hope that did not hurt you overmuch," Iaramor said, nervousness in his rich voice.

"It was strange," she replied, and found her voice was lovely as a lute now, rich and resonant. "Pain that became pleasure, pleasure so great it felt like pain. I look forward to our lovemaking now that we are better matched." She nuzzled him. "And now that you don't have to rush to complete a spell."

He chuckled. "That is the other reason we do not really seek out virgins, my honest strumpet. Virgins are highly overrated."

FAERY PIX NIXED ❧ *M. Christian*

"You tryin' ta fuck with me, Titty? Is that what yer tryin' ta do ta me? Is that what yer tryin' ta do? Is that it—it must be, bitch, cause that's hat it fuckin' sure feels like," Oberon thundered into the business end of a june bug as he sprawled, apparently sublime, obviously tense, on a curled poppy leaf. "—don't forget who yer dealin', Tit: I'm the fuckin' MAN, baby. You just fuckin' remember that—fuck with me, bitch, and you'll ain't never gonna fly in this town again—"

With a painful shriek, the junebug chirped and was silent— Titania's voice vanishing as she broke the connection.

"BITCH!" Oberon screamed, crushing the innocent insect in his hand. "Well, go on then—but not from this fuckin' grove till I torment you, bitch, for this injury…yeah, that's the ticket!" Then, grabbing a second june bug, he screamed into it's startled, compound eyes, "PEASEBLOSSOM!"

"Yes, oh, kind, noble, worshipful, mighty, Liege of the Other World, Prince of the Supernaturals, His Majesty of the Old Ones, Sovereign of the Little Forces, King of Faery, Lord of Magic ... boss—?" the tiny faery said, riding up to his/her/its chief on, on stiff attention on the back of a particularly diminutive dragonfly.

Oberon, King/CEO/Head "honcho," took a lengthened second (for time, among other things, is quite an elastic material for his kind) to stare storm clouds at the minuscule figure before growling (and thunder, thinking he was speaking its language, echoed an elemental "yeah?" in the distance), "Tell me somethin' good, 'blossom—tell me that somethin's working fer once around here. ..."

Peaseblossom paused (for time, as everyone—faery or other—knows, can be quite elastic during extremes of emotion ... such as terror), swallowed a tiny amount of magical saliva, and said, "Well—"

"Come on 'blossom, gimmie somethin'—anything—good. Come on, make my fuckin' day—"

"Well—"

"Theseus?"

"He—" ahem, ahem "—got caught in that Savings and Loan scandal a year or so back. They got him serving five to ten ... at least. I got a call out to De Niro and Pacino but their agents haven't returned my calls."

(sigh) "Hippolyta?"

"Made it big on the academic lecture circuit after Thes' got sent up—you know, wrote that book *The Amazon as the Ultimate Extension of Rightful Feminine Anger*? Even Paglia's supposed to be scared of her. Mote suggested we try Kathy Bates but she's booked the rest of the year."

"Fuck—Philostrate?"

"Working Vegas. He's definitely willing—but he's supposed to be snorting as much as he's making. Cobweb's negotiating with Iglesias' people but they haven't been able to nail down a figure."

"Crap—Egeus?"

"Retired and living in Florida, part of the golf and gin crowd. Totally not interested—at least not for what we're offering. Heston's put in a bid...but he's not offering us nearly enough for what he's worth. I think Hoffman, but he's too fucking overexposed—"

"Son of a—Hermia?"

"Finally tracked her and Lysander down to a trailer park in Buttonwillow, near Fresno...five kids and a propane cooker. Demi Moore's interested but wants script approval, so we're talking to her about that, and, of course, Keanu Reeves keeps calling—"

"Fuck no. Tell him I'm dead or somethin'. Demetrius?"

"Branaugh got him working with Jim Carrey on *Merry Wives of Windsor*—can't be bothered with us—"

"Fuck him, we can get fucking Michael Keaton. Helena?"

"Split from him two years ago, she's doin' syndicated talk...you know, one of those 'my husband is screwing my cousin' ones? Makes Springer look classy—but she doesn't want to 'associate' with us anymore—"

"Screw her, when she's making cat food spots in Spanish she'll be sorry. What's happening with the mechanicals?"

"Um, er, ah...the *Seinfeld* people said something about...hell freezing over—"

"We can't wait till next year—what about those *Friends* guys?"

"Sent them the script but they said they don't do...well, foreign language productions—"

"Jesus...okay, what about *Baywatch*? You can't tell me Hasselhoff's not perfect for that cocksucker Bottom—"

"We're still working on it—but what with the musical coming out this year they're being real picky about new projects."

"Come on, 'blossom, I'm dyin' here—can't ya give me somethin' that's working right around here? Come on, you faery-fucker, make my fucking day—"

"Well, Mickey Rooney's available—and, well, Sean Young's over in the next field wearing these...um, wings, and won't leave till you let her read for Titania—"

"Christ, that's just what I need."

Peaseblossom ducked his elfin head down as if avoiding the blow before it came, saying, with a softness only a dandelion and thistledown sprite could (which was gentle, indeed): "I take it the call to Titania, didn't go—well?"

"'Didn't go well'? 'blossom you cocksucking moron, does it look like it fucking 'went well'? The bitch still won't sign over the goddamned property unless she gets twenty percent of the gross, full damned control, and with her fucking saggy self in the lead. I'm getting fucked, 'blossom—royally, totally, and without even a goddamned phone call after. . . . How the fuck could I have let that bitch do that to me—Jesus, I was so fucking stupid—"

"Sir—"

"—and don't you fucking agree with me! Crap! So what the fuck is it, 'blossom?" Oberon said, leaning forward on his leaf and rubbing his temples with two very thin, very pale, and severely quaking, fingers.

"It's just that, well, your attorney is here—"

(sigh) "Makes sense, doesn't it? Mention getting fucked and your lawyer shows up—"

HOT MINDING THE hay fever biting at his sinuses, even through the solidly thunking, firmly sealed, doors of his car, Sol waited. It was a good time, even though fear nibbled at the sides of his mind—threatening to become booming, thundering, if he should decide to look directly at it. Instead, he just sat in his car and enjoyed the warm loneliness. Too many of his clients—well, to be honest the few that remained—seemed to like padding their lives with secretaries, receptionists, administrative assistants and the like. People, Sol often thought of, as flesh and blood rental furniture—whose only job seemed to be to make people like the young attorney uncomfortable during his perpetual waits.

Of all his clients, Oberon was one that inspired some of his most overpowering dread—honesty time again: But then all of Sol's clients frightened him in one way or another, as did every other person in the world. But the fear that Oberon called up in him was different—seeing him, or not, depending on the

"Faery King's" mood, that was obvious, and otherworldly. But, even though Sol's dread tapped firmly on panic when he was with him, he had actually begun to look forward to his infrequent visits to see him. Yes, his client could turn him into a tiny jeweled beetle; yes, Oberon, could twist him into an sad oak; yes, His Majesty could make him sleep for a thousand years—but at least his waiting room was quiet, calm, and devoid of obvious "people"...at least those that Sol could see. And even if they were there, in whatever form, at least he could pretend they weren't.

Leaning back in the driver's seat of his ten-year-old—and not because of any particular love of antiques—Lexus, eyes closed, Sol tried not to think about what his client might do on a "bad" day and, instead, relished in the quiet solitude of the badly maintained car sitting on the side of a wild-run field.

For a moment, it was possible to just "be" and not really be a tenth-rate (to be optimistic) attorney, and, in general, a frightened little man. Self-pity? No, just a thinking of too many years being scared of every footfall, every decision, every case, every hour of every day—at least that's how it seemed to appear to him most of the time.

A humble laugh bubbled out, and Sol, opening his eyes, thought about the irony of Sol Rearden, Emperor of the Scared, being the court-appointed attorney to the King of the Faeries: "But if I had wit enough to get out of this wood—"

"Mister Rearden?" a tiny, scratchy voice said from beyond the windshield, matching the bobbing movements of a sparkling dragonfly, "His Majesty, Oberon, will see you now."

*

"**DO I LOOK** like someone who enjoys getting fucked?" the King of the Faeries said.

"N-No, Sir," Sol said, the hammering of his heart making his vision hop with a trembling 2 x 2 beat.

"Then why is it I keep getting fucked, Rearden?"

"I don't know, Sir."

"Maybe it's my cute ass—"

"Well, it is kind of—"

"—don't answer that, Rearden," Oberon said. "Don't you dare. Look, Sol—it's okay if I call you Sol, right? Look, Sol, this project is fuckin' important. I mean, just think of it . . . four hundred years since Shakespeare wrote that damned play about us—it's a fuckin' package just waiting to take off. I've already got fuckin' distributors knockin' at my door. It's too good, man, it's just too fuckin' good."

"Yes, Sir—I agree, Sir," Sol said to Oberon, or at least guessed he said it to him: Sol was in the middle of a field of California wildflowers, his car parked a sneezing, sniffling half-mile behind him, talking to a voice that could have out-rumbled Cecile B. DeMille. Sol thought he might be on a particularly brilliant flower close by but, without stooping and staring, he couldn't quite be sure.

"Damned right, Sol—it's happening! Well, it fucking would if Tit would just play ball. I need ya, Sol—I need ya to get out there and earn your fuckin' gold. It's what I pay you for, right? Get out there and do your own kind of fuckin' courtroom magic and get that damned script outa the bitch. Go on, Sol—make her full of hateful fantasies, I don't give a shit: just get me that fucking script!"

315

*

THE PROBLEM WITH immortality, Robin Goodfellow thought as he calmly, methodically sorted poppy seeds into small, smaller, and smallest, is that it's too damned long.

Small, smaller, and smallest... one after another, as he'd done for four hundred years and, if Oberon kept his word—and there was damned little to suggest he wouldn't—something he'd be doing for at least another four hundred years.

Small, smaller, and smallest... for God's sake, it's not like I did anything really wrong... just some fun, that's all, kept folks on their toes... small, smaller, and smallest... sheesh, it's not like I really fucked with anyone... it was only love... small, smaller, and smallest... love for Christ's sake... small, smaller, and smallest... small, smaller, and smallest...

Robin sorted and thought as he'd done too many times, thoughts ringing through his head—going from fantasies of enamoring Oberon of an ass (a real ugly one, at that), to kissing his same ("I'm sorry"), to a dim pit of self-sorrow ("Christ, I'm fucked!"), to a kind of faery zen at his short ("—what is the sound of small, smaller, and smallest...?"). With each seed, each tiny dot going from unknown to his three overly familiar categories, as stated, Robin's mind tripped through his own usual categories. One day being like the one previous, the one before—

Then....

... small, smaller, and smallest...

..."Puck? Hey, Puck, shake out of it, man—" a tiny voice said, floating distantly down from the silhouetted body of a dragonfly "—the boss wants to see you—"

*

THE WORDS WOULDN'T come—not even one of them. Flying on his ill-used, and rather stiff wings, Robin hovered before Oberon's poppy flower and couldn't speak.

"It's like this, Rob: I'm behind this mega-deal, right? I'm talkin' eight figures here—maybe nine, and the whole shit-hole is hung up because that bitch Titania won't pass over the fucking rights to the fucking play. So here I was, right, getting all royally pissed and all and—bam!—it hits me. The fuckin' play, right, the whole thing... the Athenian crowd, our bunch, those fucking mechanicals, and—yeah, you guessed it—that fucking flower. Bam! I get it—get ol' Robin out of fucking cold storage, get the little bastard to get me some more of that little ol' Love Potion Number 9, zap the bitch with it, show up in all my studly glory and-fuckin' A—the script's as good as mine. So, Robin-my-man, do we have an 'arrangement' around this or what? A little Obsession for the lady, and, say, a reduction in your punishment... say a few thousand years or so?"

Small, smaller, and smallest...

"Robin? You there, Robin? You hearing what I'm saying here—a bit of the old amour for my bitchy ex-wife, and you get to stop counting those damned poppy seeds in just a few hundred years. Do we have a deal?"

Small, smaller, and smallest... ("I'm sorry"), Small, smaller, and smallest... ("Christ, I'm fucked!"), Small, smaller, and smallest... ("—what is the sound of small, smaller, and smallest...?")—

"Come on, Robin, we have a fuckin' deal or what? Or do

317

you really groove on being a seed-counter for the rest of your goddamned life?"

Small, smaller, and smallest...

Small, smaller, and...

"Yeah," Robin finally said, with the feeling of poppy seeds draining between his fingers, "we do—"

TITANIA, THOSE WHO knew her said, wasn't ill met by moonlight anymore. Sadly, she wasn't met by anyone, ever—though that wasn't something she allowed herself to feel: Not that the emotion wasn't present in her, but because the idea of identifying it would have given it power. So Titania went through her days, and her nights, in a kind of slow, lethargic, bittersweet melancholy.

For this story, we join her lounging by the pale blue waters of her swimming pool, lazily enjoying the warm rays of a Beverly Hills afternoon, trying to play a kind of tune with the ice cubes in her gin and tonic, and not to think about her depression. It wasn't a bad life she had made for herself, spinning it out of her magic before disguising herself behind a facade of humanity. She had her friends, she had her house, sparking with materialistic trinkets, she even had a few echoes of her former life, sparkling lights that her human friends had often seen, and that she had innocently explained to them as "fireflies and heat lightning."

One of them, in fact, danced around the glittering condensation of her glass, speaking in the ringing language of faery: "We miss you, Queen."

"Get off it, old girl—ain't no queens around here. Just Ms. Titan of the bridge club and Neiman Marcus."

"The realm is less for your absence."

"Nonsense, I'm sure Obi's ego's more than made up for me not being around."

"Our essences are diminished by the knowledge of your chosen humanity."

"Piddle, you guys are getting along fine—besides, there's something to be said for fallen arches, the monthlies, and body fat."

"You hide your true beauty within a shell of common mankind. This makes us sorrowful."

"Oh, come on—I'm the same person, just minus the wings and a (ahem) few extra pounds."

"You seek to hide your somberness, but we hear it in the tones of your words. Leave this behind and rejoin us in the Other Place."

"Sorry, kid—ain't happening, not while Obi's still around. Besides, *Dr. Quinn*'s on tonight—"

"We will return to make your departure less of an agony. Our love remains with you."

"Whatever—don't knock yourself out, Mustard. Give my best to the rest of the folk—don't let the door hit ya on the ass on your way out."

The sparkle departed, leaving her glass a little less brilliant. Rather than dwell on the dark fact that she was, again, just Ms. Titan of Beverly Hills, Titania, late of the Faery Realm, swirled her drink and took a hefty swig...relishing in the subtle unreality the liquor brought to her human form.

No, she didn't miss the Other Place—the human world had it's benefits after all: Sunday night television, gin and tonics, a really good hand of cards, a sale at Neiman Marcus, and, well, gin and tonics....

Suddenly the sun was too warm, her glass too empty. Getting up, she adjusted her favorite pink one-piece swimsuit and walked around the pool—aiming for the cool insides of her sprawling house and, in particular, the bar. One middle-aged foot in front of another, she concentrated on the feeling of the almost too-warm, sandpapery, texture of the concrete and not on the memories that came unbidden and unwanted...memories of dancing on the moon, of charming young farmhands, of curling up inside a walnut and dreaming dreams...that only faery could dream. Instead she thought about warm, abrasive concrete and the welcoming embrace of a cool house, and her fourth gin and tonic of the day—

Then, she felt something else. She might have recognized the sensation, had she allowed the warm sea of memories from when she was Titania, Queen of the Faeries, but since she was Ms. Titan, of Beverly Hills, she didn't remember it, at least not immediately.

It was a good feeling, a kind of golden bath of hope and excitement. It stirred the body she wore in ways since...well, since she'd watched the pool boy work that one afternoon. Walking, still feeling the sun on her shoulders, the cement underfoot, she also felt her body...the weight of it, the tightness (and looseness) of her skin, the way her largish breasts pulled and swayed, the tightness of the swimsuit between her legs, the slowly heating pool in her belly, the tightness of her nipples, the fullness of her lips.

Slowly, the world of sun and kidney-shaped pools lifted away from her and she found herself walking through another realm—not faery, but rather the steamy domain of the human body. It was a sensation (except for that other afternoon and watching the pool boy work) that she had all but forgotten—so trapped she'd felt by her disguise.

It wasn't a bad sensation—far from it. Walking inside, she relished in the chill shadow descending over her, the way it made her body feel even more alive, even more vibrant. Running a warm hand over her shoulder, she slipped it under the strap of her suit, electrified by the feeling of skin on skin, the way it tightened—even more—the grip of her suit around her.

Slowly, she pulled the strap down, relishing the way her right breast gained weight, feeling, as it became gently unsupported—

Then the doorbell rung. A cold water shock—half shame, half disappointment—and the suit's strap was back on and a more-than-sweaty hand was through her brilliant red hair. "Breathe, breathe—" she murmured to herself, moving towards the door.

"Hang on, be right there—" Ms. Titan, of Beverly Hills said, throwing the bolt and swinging the door wide—

OBERON WAS, AT that moment, stuck in traffic: Screaming words too profane and fiery even for this book at the flock of sparrows that blocked him in, preventing him from proceeding any faster than their wings could carry them.

SHE OPENED THE door to reveal the most gorgeous man she had ever seen.

"Queen Titania? Good morning—I mean good afternoon. My name is Sol, Sol Rearden, I'm your husband's—excuse me, ex-husband's attorney. I-I-I was wondering, if you're not too busy that is, if I could have a very brief moment of your time to discuss—"

"Please, come in!" Titania said, grabbing Sol firmly by the shoulder and jerking him inside.

"—thank you ever so much for allowing me to speak to you, Ms. Titania—" Sol said started to say as the pink-bathing-suited dervish rushed him into the house.

"Oh, get off it, handsome—just call me Ms. Titan, like everyone here does. Though if you're really good—" giggle "—you can call me Titty, though no one's called me that in four hundred years...." she said leaning him in and sitting him down in a large burnt orange sofa. "Drink?"

"Thank you very much," Sol said, sitting cramped and shy, slightly hunched over, "but I wouldn't want to put you out or anything."

"No trouble at all, sweetie—want it sweet or sinful?" The ex-Queen of the Fairies said, turning with a sensual wiggle of her shapely behind to the wetbar.

"Um, just sweet, I guess—" Sol said, ducking his head even lower, as if shading his eyes from her flamboyance.

"Sweet it is, then!" she said, laughing a laugh half her...well, half her apparent age—for half her real age would still be too old to know any kind of merriment. "So you're from Obi? What's that old cocksucker up to now? Still trying to get that property out of me?"

"Well—um, er, ah—I have been retained in that, um, capacity, but I really...um, er, ah...thank you," he said, smiling up at her as a tumbled was...eased, slowly and sensually into his hand, her fingers weaving around his own.

"Now, now; don't go thanking me yet—" sparkling laughter "—we hardly know each other. You know, you really look much too...young, to be an attorney, and far too...nice."

Sol smiled, flickering his eyes up at her beaming smile, and feeling a blush warm his face. "T-thank you, Ms. Titania—I mean Ms. Titan. Now, about the property—"

"Property, smoperty—I don't give a fuck about that damned thing. Tell you the truth...Sol...the only reason I haven't given the damned thing to Obi is just because he's a fucking asshole. I sure as shit don't want anything he has—I just get this you know, thrill, from fucking with him."

Sol smiled and looked up, seeing her too close...and too warm...next to him. "He is...I mean, I can see that...I mean—"

"Just laugh and agree with me, Sol."

He smiled and nodded. He felt lightheaded and confused, unused to having a conversation addressed to Sol, and not his profession. Needing something to do, he sipped at his drink—super sweet cold liquid meeting his parched throat, almost making him cough. After his sip, he lifted the glass gently to her: "Thank you" but it wasn't for the drink—

With an electric spark her lips were on his. The charge was so great...the reflex started, the gentle panic of the unfamiliar, but he resisted and let the kiss last and grow. It was a step, and with it Sol felt much...larger. Yes, there (filthy mind) but also inside him, down deep where Little Sol had been in the dark for so long—

Titania's lips were rose petals and silk, heated in the sun of a lovely afternoon. Her scent was beyond explanation: the aroma of freshly turned earth, a thousand spices from a thousand unknown lands and times, the scent of flowers unseen by man, a hint of Chanel No. 5, and the touching bouquet of excitement.

Her hand, he noticed, was on his leg, kneading the muscles there. His own hand, he also noticed, had gone to her side, and was stroking the material of her swimsuit—and the silken skin beyond.

The kiss was a connection, a discussion beyond words. Hot, certainly, but also a touching: Yes? Yes!

Titania, late of the Faery Realm, was simply a woman in the middle of her life, feeling the burning passion of blood, muscles, and skin... and, by the Forces of the Universe, was she wet! Sol was just a man, but he also felt the flames—putting the torch to hesitation, humility, and shame... and, God, was he hard!

The kiss stretched and their hands roamed. Each was aware—Titania to Sol's thigh, Sol to Titania's breast—but more of the kiss, the exchange of flames. It stopped, so they both could breathe, so they laughed, giggled, and playfully tried to bit (no teeth) and swallow each other's lips as Sol kneaded a firm, full breast topped by a fat, hard nipple (through her suit) and Titania felt a long, hard cock tipped with a silken head (through his suit).

The laugher and the nibbles continued, as did the touching—finally, too hot to resist, Titania smiled and sensually drew down first one, then the other, strap of her suit—allowing her breasts to hang real and firm.

Still kissing, Sol's hand went to their handsomeness, their exciting symmetry: large, silken and firm, topped by nipples rosy and firm. Still kissing, he allowed his hands to trace her form—the thousand different forms of silk, velvet, and satin from her sloping top, her deliciously rounded under, her tight sides . . . exploring the delights of her breasts. Breaking the kiss, he dropped down and, dry and tactile, felt the swollen nubs of her nipples, the thrill of the them crinkling and swelling even more as he licked, then—taking them into his hot mouth—sucked.

Titania inhaled a teeth-clenching hiss of air, feeling the shock of his mouth race up and down her earthly, fleshy spine. All the while her hand didn't stop its firm stroking of his cock through his pants, all the while she didn't stop thinking of what he might taste like (salt? bitter? sweet? sweat?), all the while she didn't stop thinking of how far down her throat she could get his cock, all the time she didn't stop thinking of how he could fill her cunt. . . .

Firmly, she pushed him standing. Quickly, she undid his cheap belt and slid his pants to his ankles. Feverishly, she yanked down his average underwear . . . Big? Yes. Long? Perfectly. Hard? Extremely—freed, it bobbed up fast, striking her gently on the chin and cheek.

Then she wasn't thinking how he would taste, or how far down—his pubic hairs tickling her nose, she swallowed and consumed him till it felt like she'd be feeling the smooth skin of his stomach with her nose.

Ah, the music Sol made—though he was completely unaware of his sighs, moans, hisses and discordant words, ("fuck . . . ohmigod . . . oh, God . . . so good" . . . etc.), being so consumed with Titania's oral attention to his cock. The world, right then, right there, was just Sol's cock and Titania's mouth around Sol's cock.

Time passed—ex-faery and human not knowing exactly how long and absolutely not caring—all of it in fleshy revelry: cock in and out, sliding down a warm and very willing throat. Cock in a flexible and sensual throat.

After a point (time, as said, flexible and indeterminate) Sol wanted nothing more in the universe than to feel his cock in the embrace of a faery cunt—and Titania wanted nothing more than mortal dick in her celestial pussy. So, at once, he said and she said: "I want you."

Laughter, a sparkling enjoyment bubbled between them as Sol rolled back onto his haunches, then his back, and Titania stood and quickly pulled down the rest of her suit.

Sol, seeing—eyes wide with delight—quickly tried to do the same, but pants do not clear still-tied shoes and ties do not come off too quickly if tied too tight. Laughter again, as the game became "Get Sol naked" past the puzzle of human business attire. Finally (too long, but impossible to measure) the shoes were jerked from his feet (still tied), socks were tossed over the back of the sofa, coat was wadded in one corner, shirt (almost buttonless) and tie (frayed completely) following, underwear thrown far, he was as bare as the day he was brought into the world—but much bigger (everywhere).

Hissing further delight, Titania rolled her soft, full body up and down his, relishing (and echoed for Sol) in his skin, his softness and his firmness. Up, his mouth her breasts and, again, her nipples swelled and knotted from the passionate actions of lips, tongue and (gentle) teeth. Down, his cock thumped firm and satin again her cheek and, again, his cock slipped into her mouth and down her throat.

But theses were only part of the laughter, a portion of the fun being shared—a little suck of a nipple, a little suck of a cock—a tease. But, finally, the tease wasn't enough....

On top, body reflective with a glimmer of delightful lust, Titania worked her body back and forth—relishing in the suspense of Sol's hard cock grazing against the slick lips of her cunt, the head parting them just enough to spread her wetness across the head.

Then, Sol of earth—presently in a far better place—had enough. Then, Titania of faery—presently in a far better place—had enough: he moved his hips up, pushing in, as she moved down, also pushing in.

It was a new kind of swallowing, being swallowed. Slowly, again relishing, they pushed themselves together till they were both hissing, both breathing hard, both moaning....

The filling and being filled became the two of them. The world could have ended (but it didn't), the whole of faery could have been watching (none were—maybe), all kinds of things could have happened but the point was that neither of them cared...they were in love, and fucking merrily.

Then, it started. Slowly, it built and built and built some more—a slow-motion explosion of exaltation, of bodily ecstasy. For him, a tightness in the balls, a heavy-liquid pressure up the shaft of his too-hard cock, a lightness around the head, a lifting of the spirit...for her, a tingling within, waves rolling up and through, a lightness around the head, a lifting of the spirit. Till, till, till—

Love makes fools of us all, but at least can sometimes grant simultaneous orgasms—

Bursting, exploding, coming, they shivered and shook, quaked and cried, moaned and clenched, jerked, spurted, and strings cut, bodies loose, they collapsed into a slick puddle of delighted smiles—

—then the doorbell rang.

THE CHAMPAGNE WAS from the hidden cellar of Napoleon, the flowers only something that the King of the Faeries could bring (from the distant mountains, in a distant land that only the Children of the Other knew), the chocolates were Godiva—the best he could do on short notice. At least they weren't See's.

Teeth brushed? Yep, teeth brushed. Shoes polished (damned uncomfortable things)? Yep, shoes polished. Tie straight (damned uncomfortable thing)? Yep, tie straight. Body handsome (damned uncomfortable thing)? Yep, handsome—or at least as much as he could make it on short notice.

"Come on, Titty, goddamnit—where the fuck are ya?" The King of the Faeries said, leaning on the doorbell again.

Struggling with his champagne (getting warm), flowers (starting to wilt), and chocolate (getting soft), he was just about to pound on the door when it clicked and swung wide: "Hey, Obi—what you doin' in this neck of the woods?"

She looked . . . different. Of course it had been four hundred years or so, but Oberon still thought that she looked . . . different: Was that a flush to her cheeks? Was she really wearing that (shudder) body with a sense of . . . pride?

Shaking it off, he pushed forward with a loud, brassy "Baby! Hey, does the King of the Other World really need an excuse to visit his Queen of the Morning?"

"Well, since your 'Queen' walked out on you a long time ago, I'd think she'd deserve at least a call first, Obi."

"Hey, doll, relax, take a chill pill. Just happened to, you know, be in the neighborhood and thought I'd stop by to see how you're doin'. Still hanging with the human motif and all? I do have to say, baby, that on you it does look mighty good," Oberon said, stepping in and putting his booty down on a convenient table. "Come on, doll, doesn't your daddy deserve at least a little kiss? You know, for good time's sake—"

Smiling (burrrr!), Titania stepped towards him and, sharply, ran a finger down the stripe of his tie. "Well, you know, Obi, I do have to say—"

"Yeah, baby—yeah...."

"—that you're just about as...overbearing...rude...and fucking disgusting as you've ever been. And to think, I was enamored of such an...ass."

"What the—" Oberon started to say, anger and confusion fighting across his human mask.

"You gotta admit, Oberon, when the lady's right, the lady's right," Sol said, stepping out of the bathroom, handsomely wearing a yellow bathrobe.

"What the fuck—!" the King of the Faeries said, looking at him, looking at her and looking at him again.

"Come on, Obi, you know Sol—your old attorney and now my new attorney."

"What the fuck is—"

"You know, Obi—I can call you Obi, right? You know, Obi, I was just talking to Titan here about, you know, the property, and we really don't think that we can accept anything less than at least forty percent of the gross...and complete creative control, fifty percent of the merchandising take...."

Oberon—finally—was able to say: "Fuck me."

To which Sol smiled, and Titania said: "As a matter of fact, there is the little matter of just that. Seems the last time we had a little...disagreement, Obi, I was the one who got, well, fucked. This time, baby, it's gonna be a little different—"

Sol smiled wider, playing with the cord of his robe. "Just be thankful, baby, that Sol here's not exactly in poor old Bottom's league—though I think you'll definitely, well, feel it—that is if you really want...what it is I've got...."

SMALL, SMALLER, AND smallest...

Small, smaller, and smallest...

Small, smaller, and smallest...

...one seed after another...small, smaller, and smallest... Robin counted, sorted...but was that a smile, playing on his lips? Small, smaller, and smallest...small, smaller, and smallest....

Sparrows are so easy to trick....

Small, smaller, and smallest...

...almost as easy as Kings....

Small, smaller, and smallest....

THE MAIDEN OF GRAND PROPORTIONS *Sage Vivant*

AT THE DAWN of the age where humans accepted nature as "a good start" and where anything plastic, mechanical, enhanced, or otherwise doctored was viewed as an improvement, Ilsa was born.

She enjoyed the most unfettered and supportive of childhoods, encouraged to explore and question. She achieved good grades and academic awards without having to study very hard because her native intelligence supplemented her book learning so well. And unlike other children, she never became hooked on phonics, which pleased her parents immensely.

By all standards—those of the pre-polyethylene days as well as modern times—Ilsa was pretty. Her lips rivaled those from any collagen treatment and her cheekbones had been placed where any plastic surgeon would have deemed correct. Her pleasant disposition and her competitive spirit combined to make her an enviable athlete. In fact, in her midwestern village, she was much sought after for sporting events ranging from softball to tetherball. By the time she was nine, her tall physique and sportsmanlike attitude became as notable as her good looks.

At the age of nine, however, a strange and bewildering phenomena took place. One day, as she sprinted from home base to first in a rousing game of softball attended by most of her classmates, small, sharp, unfamiliar pains radiated from her chest. Oh my, she thought, whatever could be causing this pain? A group of boys pointed at her, snickering and nudging each other while they pointed at her chest. Why would anyone be amused by her pain, she wondered?

Halfway to first base, she instinctively crossed her arms across her chest in an attempt to confine the pain or at least to give her some comfort. It was at that moment that she felt the disconcerting jiggle of flesh, the telltale bounce of feminine heft that would henceforth become as familiar to her as breathing.

They didn't hurt when she stood still, but when she ran—and especially when she ran fast, as she was known to do—the pain always returned. They slammed up and down like two little pouches but their movement was constrained to the skin that encased them so the pouches, try as they might to break free, never could.

And although she finished the game and brought in a run for her team, she understood that these new growths she sported would make continued athletic pursuits uncomfortable. That same weekend, her mother took her shopping and when they returned with a new dress for Ilsa, her mother made her model it for visiting relatives.

"Look at our young lady," her mother announced proudly as Ilsa stood in her new frock. But then her mother placed her fingers under Ilsa's burgeoning breasts and made them shake like those colorful, vitamin-injected gelatin pops that were the latest rage in health food. The adults uttered appreciative ooohs and ahhhhs but Ilsa was rather mortified at being the center of attention for something she had no control over. So, her mother seemed proud of her breasts and wanted her relatives to be proud, too. Was Ilsa to be proud, as well? The young woman did not know what to make of her prodigious growths.

It didn't take long for her to realize that breasts were desirable but not necessarily for a nine year old and not if they threatened to be bigger than those of the average fashion model.

Ilsa's mother bought her a training bra, thereby leading Ilsa to believe that her breasts would be trained to stay put and perhaps not grow any further if she wore the bra religiously. Such was not the case, however. Rounding the bases was indeed less painful but the boys still gawked, which made her too self-conscious to concentrate on the game.

Ilsa grew somewhat quiet and slightly shy as a barrage of conflicting feelings swept over her that summer. Grown-up ladies wielded breasts with style and grace, she had observed, and breast augmentation was a common Sweet Sixteen birthday gift. Breasts, therefore, were clearly a benefit in life, despite being a liability in sports. Why, she had even heard that they helped a girl find a husband!

Her curse was that hers were both large and natural.

She would sometimes stare at her breasts when she was alone to discern what the fuss was about. Her nipples were pink and perky and the round softness of her breasts fascinated her. She would play with scarves and tie them over, around, and between them to discover the myriad shapes of which they were capable. She didn't understand why it was so exciting to play with her own breast this way, but she knew that she was supposed to keep her excitement to herself. Would they continue to grow? Would running become a completely untenable prospect as they did?

With great regret, she withdrew from her athletic activities and took up more sedentary pastimes such as knitting and origami. She spent more time reading.

Boys were not the only ones who were curious about her breasts. Girls, too, would come to her as if she were a sage of sorts who could answer their questions.

"Does it hurt when they grow?"

"What does it feel like to wear a bra?"

"Do you let boys touch them?"

"How big will you get?

Ilsa didn't always know the answers but she provided information as she could. No, they didn't hurt as they grew, bras without seams were more comfortable than bras with seams, her mother would kill her if she let boys touch them, and she had no idea how big her breasts would get. The girls seemed to be grateful for anything they could glean.

Ilsa's friend Marietta convinced her to let one girl into her garage at a time to let them see her breasts. "It will help them know what to expect," Marietta explained. Ilsa thought that sounded like a noble thing to do, but when she discovered that Marietta was selling tickets and pocketing the profits, she returned to her knitting, reading, and origami and stopped trying to elucidate her life for the curious adolescents of the village.

BY THE TIME Ilsa reached the age of sixteen, her fondness for her breasts equaled her frustration. They made her feel simultaneously desirable and marginalized.

Young men paid great attention to her and offered to take her places and buy her things, but something always went horribly wrong. Frequently, they would forget that they had promised her an elegant dinner or a sparkly ring. Many of them seemed compelled to drive her to the woods, where trees and darkness shielded their rough, inconsiderate attempts to see and touch her breasts.

"Ilsa, your tits are fantastic. I'll die if you don't let me suck them."

Despite her mother's warnings about men being little more than animals, if she liked a boy, sometimes she wouldn't fight when he reached into her blouse to pull out one breast or unhooked her bra to release them both. Once they handled them with their big, fumbling hands or sucked her eager nipples with too-hungry mouths, they would inevitably remark with surprise that her charms were indeed real. Ilsa was then to understand that they'd be sharing this discovery with their friends, and so, when they then assumed they could stuff their very stiff penises into her, she ended the date and demanded to be taken home immediately.

Breasts of the 38DDD variety, such as hers, were highly

valued—if they were purchased. But Ilsa's pair were home-grown and as such, a curiosity. She had been advised by friends as well as her doctor to undergo breast reduction surgery and allow firm, reliably shaped implants to replace the unsightly jiggling masses she now carried.

"You'd be so much sexier if you'd just stop being so natural," Marietta told her, barely able to disguise her disgust. She had received her implants that very year and already had offers not only from a bevy of suitors but a number of Ivy League colleges as well.

Ilsa didn't really know why she refused to submit to the surgeon's knife but no amount of peer pressure could convince her to do it. She was so enamored with her breasts! Every day, she hoped some nice man would also find them appealing but each date brought her a new disappointment. They always asked her out to ferret out for themselves whether the girth and heft of her breasts were real and when they learned they were silicone-free, they ran screaming, as if the absence of manmade materials made her suspect and somehow dangerous.

As she got older, it seemed that many men were drawn to her for other factors quite distinct from the size of her breasts and this always delighted her, for she believed that if a man could accept her for who she was, he might overlook any less-than-stellar physical attributes.

One such man found her smart and funny—which she was, without question—and they enjoyed a few dinners as well as a number of movies. Sometimes he would lie with her on her bed and caress her curvaceous hips and thighs while he kissed her. After several weeks and still no sign of his penis, she confronted him.

"I have noticed your appreciation of my backside, but you never touch my breasts," she said to him. "Don't you like them?" He did not appear interested in finding out, as so many did before him, whether they were real and his lack of interest baffled her.

"Oh, they're fine," he assured her. "But I find them a little intimidating."

Ilsa discontinued the relationship, for she feared that any man intimidated by breasts would not make a suitable life partner for her.

Reader, it must be stated here that Ilsa's proportions were quite balanced. The size of her breasts, albeit voluptuous, were rivaled only by the shapely curves of her derriere. At the age of thirty, her measurements were 44-30-44 (and those are inches, if you please). Although she possessed an hourglass shape, the size of that hourglass gave significant pause to many, thereby making her the...butt...of more unkind jokes. As a result, Ilsa decided to embark upon a program of weight reduction, believing that if she could bring her posterior down to the more widely acceptable 36 inches, her breasts would reduce as well, and perhaps then she'd only have to contend with the men who objected to her natural softness rather than those who were also afraid of her formidable breasts.

A strict regimen of organic greens and herbally enhanced water soon brought Ilsa into the realm of beautiful people. Her dimensions made her more attractive to the masses, who sought to emulate (if they were female) and acquire (if they were male) emaciated and physically enhanced women, who they revered as role models. Job offers were extended to Ilsa, and handsome men who knew the secrets of advanced technology pursued her. She wore clothing that accentuated her smallness, and never left the house without her minimizer bra. Small came to mean innocuous to Ilsa, as it did subliminally to everyone else. And innocuous was safe.

She was careful never to allow interested men to feel her shrunken breasts for they would surely dismiss her upon discovering her naturalist folly. And so, while her life was less fraught with angst and rejection, her bed remained empty and she and her breasts continued their isolated existence.

I can no longer live this way, Ilsa decided with determination of the most motivated sort. Her breasts craved the touch of an amorous, appreciative man yet now that she was closer to getting one, she still could not permit herself to be fondled, caressed, or otherwise touched for fear of discovery. I miss my big, beautiful breasts! I will eat some rich, processed food to get back to my previous size, and when I do, I shall love my breasts with the ardor that they've always deserved!

Ilsa was true to her emphatic statement. She plumped back up, although compromised at 40-28-40 so as not to exclude all of those particularly lucrative job offers. When she reached that goal, she stood before the mirror, naked, and smiled at her reflection. It was true that her breasts did not stare back at her with the inflated confidence of those found on porn stars. It was also true that if she were to lie down, her breasts would tend to loll to her underarms rather than stare at the ceiling.

But as she held one in each hand and began to knead and squeeze, those attributes endeared her more than ever to her breasts. Each meaty handful of delight felt like a precious object, pliant and ready to feel the full scope of her appreciation.

She closed the blinds of her room and ensured that all video surveillance equipment was turned off. On her digital music player, she dialed up her *Sounds of Nature* CD that she'd bought on the black market, and sighed as chirping birds in a water-drenched forest shared their joy. Ilsa adjusted the lighting to its most complimentary intensity, then donned a dress that was too small. The dress forced her breasts upward. Her excess flesh extruded from the low-cut neckline in a deliciously obscene manner.

When she had purchased the dress, her cleavage had been compelling enough but she hadn't the nerve to wear it. Drawing attention to her natural breasts had always been too risky, even though she longed to show the world what she had. Now, though, in the privacy of her bedroom under perfect lighting and with nobody to criticize either the softness or size of her breasts, she let herself cream at the startling image before her. Big, bountiful breasts, straining to break free of the dress, desperate to be sucked and squeezed, grateful to be loved.

"My big titties," she whispered over the ringing in her ears. "Finally, you get the adoration you deserve."

Ilsa did not concern herself with propriety or modesty. She grabbed overflowing handfuls of her tit flesh and stared as it yielded to her rough, demanding touch. She jiggled her great mounds and watched as they moved the way she directed them. Could she suck her own nipples, she wondered? Ilsa soon found that she could and did so for hours while she observed her busy mouth consuming even more than she imagined it could. Mouthfuls of titty swelled her cheeks as she forced more and more of it between her lips. Sometimes she needed two hands to handle it all, so she would just remove one hand from her soaking wet cunt and smear her juices on the breast she sucked. Hours flew by. Her nipples were nearly raw and she had a slight crook in her neck from trying to angle her head just right, but nothing could stop her now that she had given herself permission to enjoy her body as she had always wanted to.

When her knees grew tired and her feet began to ache, she moved to the bed and dispensed with the mirror. On her back, she slapped her tits together endlessly just because she loved the way it sounded when flesh met flesh. There was no limit to the intrigue provided by breasts that wobbled and swayed, swung and jiggled—all at her command.

All of this pent-up desire could not be spent in one night. It took several months of regular masturbation sessions for Ilsa to truly bloom into the sexual animal she had hidden for so many years. Night after night, she engaged in her breast appreciation ritual, squeezing and kneading and licking and sucking and bouncing until sleep could no longer be postponed.

In her daily life, Ilsa was a changed woman. Everyone noticed it. She must be in love, they whispered, wondering who would deign to fuck a naturally big-titted woman and that it was little wonder that his identity was a closely guarded secret.

Having endured a lifetime of unkind conjecture and ridicule, Ilsa was immune to this new round of it. Her eyes now sparkled and she carried her head high with pride. If only she'd given herself permission to worship her own breasts ages ago— how much happier she could have been! How much heartache she could have spared herself! But there was no use in regrets. She was happy now and that was all that really mattered to her.

One day, as she bounced down the street, relishing the way her footsteps on the pavement reverberated through her breasts, a man reached out and tried to grope one of her breasts. She ducked to avoid him but in the process, tripped and fell. Instantly, another man came to her rescue to help her to her feet.

As his strong arms righted her, she heard him chastise the groper.

"How dare you help yourself to a woman this beautiful! Police! Arrest that man! He tried to accost this woman!"

Ilsa got up just in time to see a blue uniform dart down the street in hot pursuit. She turned to the gentleman who helped her and looked directly into his bright green eyes, fringed with dark eyelashes. He was looking at her as if she were a princess.

"Thank you," she said. "I'm glad you were here."

"Oh, I'm here every day," he blurted out.

She stared at him, uncertain about his meaning. "You mean out at lunchtime?"

"Well, yes, but really, I follow you. I've been following you for months. I'm not a stalker, though!" He seemed alarmed that she might garner the wrong impression.

"Okay. Whatever you say," she smiled politely. Her ankle hurt a little but she thought she could probably walk on it.

"I'm serious. I don't even know your name. I just love to watch you walk. You exude something so . . . seductive."

His plaintive manner weakened her defenses. No man had ever looked at her with such sincerity. Ever.

"Well, thank you. I'm flattered." She knew she ought to return to work but she had trouble averting her gaze from his sparkling eyes.

"I'm glad you aren't frightened. I'm actually relieved that that jerk tried to touch you—it gave me an opportunity to introduce myself. I've been too shy to figure out how to do it."

"I'm Ilsa," she said, extending her hand.

"I'm Frank," he replied, taking it eagerly and shaking it warmly. "You seem so content, so at peace with yourself. I'm afraid I'm quite smitten." He smiled and her ankles weren't the only joints whose strength was tested.

She suddenly pictured him lapping at her breasts. The image shocked her not because she didn't desire it but because she'd never pictured a man pleasuring her breasts upon meeting him. She fought the urge to bring his head to her chest and instead just smiled back at him.

He found the courage to ask her out and treated her to a fine and scrumptious dinner. They went to the movies and she didn't protest when he maneuvered his arm to press against her breast. At his apartment, he opened a bottle of wine and as he handed it to her, posed a question.

"I think, Ilsa, that your breasts are the most captivating that this or any other village has ever produced. If you tell me they are also real, I will be beside myself with glee."

She was stunned. "You want them to be real?"

"Yes, but I will adore you either way."

She paused and took a sip of her wine. "They are real."

To say that they lived happily ever after would fail to capture the full extent of their mutual satisfaction. Frank provided Ilsa with pleasures beyond what she had provided to herself, and in turn, Ilsa loved Frank with affection and gratitude only a lifetime of pain can release.

Each night, as his wide, wet tongue brought her nipples to attention and his big, strong hands held her breasts, he would tell her how it was her confidence, as much as her incredible breasts, that drew him to her. Perhaps someday she would tell him how much masturbation it had taken to build up that confidence, but for now, the delectable swirls of his tongue around her aureole were all she wanted to think about.

ABOUT THE AUTHORS

D. ANTONI loves his writing career, as it gives him the chance to indulge in anything that interests him—science, the paranormal, world trade and such. Erotic adventure certainly interests him, hence, "The Satyr."

KATHLEEN BRADEAN's stories can be found in *Amazons: Sexy Tales of Strong Women, Best of Best Women's Erotica, Blood Surrender*, and the Clean Sheets Web site. Visit her blog at: KathleenBradean.blogspot.com.

M. CHRISTIAN is the author of the critically acclaimed and best-selling collections *Dirty Words, Speaking Parts, The Bachelor Machine*, and the upcoming *Filthy*. He is the author of the novels *Running Dry* and the upcoming *The Very Bloody Marys*. He is the editor of *The*

Burning Pen, *The Best S/M Erotica* series, *The Mammoth Book of Future Cops*, *The Mammoth Book of Tales of the Road* (with Maxim Jakubowski) in addition to fifteen other anthologies. He has collaborated with Sage Vivant on four previous books, including *Leather, Lace and Lust; The Best of Both Worlds: Bisexual Erotica; Amazons: Sexy Tales of Strong Women,* and *Confessions: Admissions of Sexual Guilt*. His short fiction has appeared in over two hundred books, magazines, and Web sites, including *Best American Erotica, Best Gay Erotica, Best Lesbian Erotica, Best Transgender Erotica, Best Fetish Erotica, Best Bondage Erotica*, and . . . well, you get the idea. He lives in San Francisco and is only some of what that implies.

BRYN COLVIN is a British author with a passion for all things strange and unusual. Her work has appeared in various anthologies, and she has a paperback novel *The Shifting Heart* published by Magic Carpet. The rest of her work is electronically published by www.extasybooks.com, www.venuspress.com, www.loveyoudivine.com and www.whiskeycreekpress.com . She writes erotica, and high fantasy for the greater part. Anyone interested in her work is welcome to join http://groups.yahoo.com/group/brynsbookgroup. She writes for Custom Erotica Source.

MACKENZIE CROSS has been writing erotica for the last five years. Much of it is based on his own personal experiences as an educator, mentor, and trainer in the area of dominant/submissive relationships. When he is not writing erotica he can be found downhill skiing, reading obscure science fiction and underground comics, or sampling fine single malt whiskies. More information about Mackenzie Cross can be found at his Web site: www.mackneziecross.ca.

KATE DOMINIC is the author of *Any 2 People, Kissing* (Down There Press, 2003), a *Foreword Magazine* Book of the Year Award finalist. Kate has published over three hundred erotic short stories, writing under a variety of pennames in both female and male voices. Her recent work is available in *The Best of Best Women's Erotica, The Many Joys of Sex Toys, Naughty Spanking Stories from A–Z, Dyke the Halls, and Luscious.* Kate's column "The Business End" appears monthly at the *Erotica Readers & Writers Association.* Visit Kate at her Web site: www.katedominic.com.

JJ GILES is a BDSM romance author of *The Mistress and The Mouse, Lady Dragon, She, The Trophy, and Puss in Boots* (www.loveyoudivine.com) For more information, please visit, www.jjgiles.com.

BRYN HANIVER is inclined towards topics that are oceanic, scientific, and sexy, and writes fiction from islands or peninsulas whenever possible. Previous credits include the anthologies *Rode Hard, Put Away Wet, Taboo, Down and Dirty 2*, and *A Taste of Midnight.* For something quick and salty, check out a pair of noteworthy short shorts on Desdmona.com.

HILARY JAYE grew up in Calaveras County, California. Maybe it was the countryside, infused with Mark Twain's rebellious, tongue-in-cheek legacy that made her start writing things she didn't want to show her mother. Now a veteran of the first Gulf War, Hilary has seen enough real-world ugly that she much prefers to highlight pretty. For fun, she keeps a lot of cats, eats chicken-fried steak, and will also be featured in an upcoming issue of *Prometheus*, The Eulenspiegel Society's volunteer publication,

with her story "Ten Strokes." She does not have an obsession with
frogs.

CATHERINE LUNDOFF lives in Minneapolis with her fabulous partner. Her short fiction has appeared in such anthologies *as Stirring Up
a Storm, Amazons, Naughty Spanking Stories from A to Z, Ultimate
Lesbian Erotica 2006, Blood Surrender, The Mammoth Book of Best
New Erotica 4 and Best Lesbian Erotica 2006*. Torquere Press released
a collection of her lesbian erotica, *Night's Kiss*, in 2005 and she has
an erotic writing column called "Nuts and Bolts" at the Erotica
Readers and Writer's Association (www.erotica-readers.com).

SENECA MAYFAIR's story "The Prince of Byzantium" first appeared
at the Ophelia's Muse Web site. Her abiding interest in sex and reli-
gion led to the anthology *Sacred Exchange*, which she coedited with
Lisabet Sarai. Mayfair, a native Angelino, lives in the beautiful
Pacific Northwest with her family and a pack of wild dogs.

This is **MICHAEL MICHELE**'s first appearance in an anthology.
Previous work has appeared in magazines and online. Fascinated by
the way sex and lust shape people's lives, Michael creates edgy,
well-written erotica exploring the many "packages" our sexuality
comes wrapped in. Look for more in the Erotica Readers and
Writers Association Web site archives.

REMITTANCE GIRL lives in a state of wanton depravity in Ho Chi
Minh City, Vietnam, where she worships orchids and writes things
the authorities wouldn't like. Her stories have appeared on the

Erotica Readers and Writers Association website, and she maintains her own at www.remittancegirl.com.

TERESA NOELLE ROBERTS' erotic fiction has appeared in many publications including *Best Women's Erotica 2004 and 2005, The Good Parts: Pure Lesbian Erotica,* and Fishnetmag.com. She also writes as Sophie Mouette (writing with Dayle A. Dermatis.) Sophie Mouette's first erotic novel is *Cat Scratch Fever* from by Black Lace Books (UK). Teresa is a Middle Eastern dancer, an avid cook, and a member of the Society for Creative Anachronism.

JASON RUBIS lives in Washington, DC. His erotic fiction has appeared in *Leg Show, Variations*, and many anthologies, including *Sacred Exchange, Erotic Fantastic, Blood Surrender, The Best Of Both Worlds, Confessions, Amazons,* and *Leather, Lace and Lust.* He is pleased to dedicate "Beauty Thrasher" to Ruth Manning-Sanders, whose fairy-tale collections originally set him on the writer's path. He writes for Custom Erotica Source.

Half a dozen years ago, **LISABET SARAI** experienced a serendipitous fusion of her love of writing and her fascination with sex. Since then she has published three erotic novels including the classic *Raw Silk*, and co-edited the anthology *Sacred Exchange*, a collection of fiction that explores the spiritual aspects of BDSM relationships. Her latest work, a highly praised collection of her short stories entitled *Fire*, was released in June 2005 by Blue Moon Books, and her erotic-noir novel, *Exposure*, will be published by Orion in 2006. Lisabet also reviews erotic books and films for the Erotica Readers and Writers

Association (www.erotica-readers.com) and Sliptongue.com. Lisabet lives in Southeast Asia with her husband and felines. For more information on Lisabet and her writing visit Lisabet Sarai's Fantasy Factory (http://www.lisabetsarai.com).

DONNA GEORGE STOREY is saving her virgin ear—the right one—for a very special occasion. Her fiction has appeared on the Web at Clean Sheets, Scarlet Letters, and in the anthologies *Taboo: Forbidden Fantasies for Couples, Foreign Affairs: Erotic Travel Tales, Mammoth Book of Best New Erotica 4 and 5, Best Women's Erotica 2005 and 2006* and *Best American Erotica 2006*. Read more of her work at www.DonnaGeorgeStorey.com.

SAGE VIVANT operates Custom Erotica Source (www.customeroti-casource.com), which offers tailor-made erotic fiction to individual clients. She is the author of the upcoming novel *Giving the Bride Away* and the guide *29 Ways to Write Great Erotica*. With M. Christian, she has edited *Confessions: Admissions of Sexual Guilt, Amazons: Sexy Tales of Strong Women, Leather, Lace and Lust,* and *The Best of Both Worlds: Bisexual Erotica*. Her stories have been published in dozens of anthologies, including *Best Women's Erotica, Stirring Up a Storm,* and *The Mammoth Book of Best New Erotica*.

SHARON WACHSLER confesses that in her co-op days fifteen years ago, she failed to wash her guests' dishes. Despite this flaw, Sharon has become a widely published writer of fiction, nonfiction, and poetry, even managing to get published in *On Our Backs* and *off our backs* in the same month. Her erotica appears in numerous journals and anthologies, including *Good Vibes* online magazine and consecutive years of *Best American Erotica* (2004 and 2005). She is the founder and editor of Breath & Shadow (www.abilitymaine.org/ breath), the only literary journal written exclusively by people with disabilities. As a humor columnist, Sharon has a small, cultishly devoted following.

CYNTHIA WARD was born in Oklahoma and lived in Maine, Spain, Germany, and the San Francisco Bay Area before settling in Seattle. She has published stories in *Asimov's SF Magazine, Bending the Landscape: Horror*, and other anthologies and magazines. With fellow Seattle writer Nisi Shawl, Cynthia has coauthored the writing manual *Writing the Other: A Practical Guide* (Aqueduct Press, http://www.aqueductpress.com/), the companion book to the Writing the Other fiction workshop (http://www.writingtheother.com). Cynthia is completing her first novel, tentatively titled *The Killing Moon*. Her Web site is http://www.cynthiaward.com.

PERMISSIONS

Copyright Notices